Praise for The Best Horr … olume Eleven:

"Even with the overall high quality of the latest of Datlow's anthology series, there are some remarkable highlights . . . this excellent anthology demonstrates that Datlow's reputation as one of the best editors in the field is more than well-deserved."

—*Booklist* (starred review)

"Datlow has drawn her selections from a wide variety of sources that even the most dedicated fans may have overlooked, and her comprehensive introductory overview of the year in horror will uncover still more venues for great scares. This is an indispensable volume for horror readers."

—*Publishers Weekly* (starred review)

Praise for Ellen Datlow and The Best Horror of the Year Series:

"Edited by the venerable queen of horror anthologies, Ellen Datlow. . . . The stories in this collection feel both classic and innovative, while never losing the primary ingredient of great horror writing: fear."

—*The New York Times*

"A decade of celebrating the darkest gems of the genre as selected by Hugo-winning editor Ellen Datlow, whose name, by this point, is almost synonymous with quality frights . . . [and] contributed by a murderer's row of horror authors. . . . Essential."

—*B&N Sci-Fi and Fantasy Blog*, "Our Favorite Science Fiction & Fantasy Books of 2018"

"With the quality ranging from very good, to fantastic, to sublime, there just isn't the space to discuss them all. . . . If I need to make a pronouncement—based on Datlow's fantastic distillation of the genre—it's that horror is alive, well, and still getting under people's skin. If you have even a vague interest in dark fiction, then pick up this book."

—Ian Mond, *Locus*

"A survey of some of the best horror writing of the last decade . . . highly recommended for anyone interested in contemporary horror and dark fantasy, as well as anyone looking for a collection of some of the best and most horrifying short fiction currently available."

—*Booklist* (starred review), for *The Best of the Best Horror of the Year*

"A stunning and flawless collection that showcases the most terrifyingly beautiful writing of the genre. Datlow's palate for the fearful and the chilling knows no genre constraint, encompassing the undead, the supernatural, and the cruelty perpetrated by ordinary humans. Exciting, literary, and utterly scary, this anthology is nothing short of exceptional."

—*Publishers Weekly* (starred review), for *The Best of the Best Horror of the Year*

"Datlow's survey of the first decade of her Best Horror of the Year series is also an argument about the field's major talents and trends. Its contents make a compelling case for the robustness of the field, a condition Datlow herself has done much to nourish."

—*Locus*, "Horror in 2018" by John Langan

"Award-winning editor Ellen Datlow has assembled a tasty collection of twenty-one terrifying and unsettling treats. In addition to providing excellent fiction to read, this is the perfect book for discovering new authors and enriching your life through short fiction."

—*Kirkus Reviews*

"For more than three decades, Ellen Datlow has been at the center of horror. Bringing you the most frightening and terrifying stories, Datlow always has her finger on the pulse of what horror fans crave . . . and the anthologies just keep getting better and better. She's an icon in the industry."

—*Signal Horizon*

"Datlow's The Best Horror of the Year series is one of the best investments you can make in short fiction. The current volume is no exception."

—*Adventures Fantastic*

"As usual, Datlow delivers what she promises, 'the best horror of the year,' whether it's written by the famous (Neil Gaiman) or the should-be famous (Laird Barron and many others)."

—*Washington Post*

"You just can't have a list of recommended speculative anthologies without including an Ellen Datlow anthology. It's. Not. Possible. The line-up in *The Best Horror of the Year Volume Eight* is absolutely stupendous, featuring the most frighteningly talented authors in horror fiction."

—*Tor.com*

"Once again, [Ellen Datlow supplies] an invaluable book, featuring excellent short fiction and, in addition, providing as always precious information about what happened in the horror field last year."

—Mario Guslandi, British Fantasy Society

Also Edited by Ellen Datlow

A Whisper of Blood
A Wolf at the Door and Other Retold Fairy Tales (with Terri Windling)
After (with Terri Windling)
Alien Sex
Black Feathers: Dark Avian Tales
Black Heart, Ivory Bones (with Terri Windling)
Black Swan, White Raven (with Terri Windling)
Black Thorn, White Rose (with Terri Windling)
Blood Is Not Enough: 17 Stories of Vampirism
Blood and Other Cravings
Children of Lovecraft
Darkness: Two Decades of Modern Horror
Digital Domains: A Decade of Science Fiction & Fantasy
Echoes: The Saga Anthology of Ghost Stories
Edited By
Fearful Symmetries
Final Cuts: New Tales of Hollywood Horror and Other Spectacles
Haunted Legends (with Nick Mamatas)
Haunted Nights (with Lisa Morton)
Hauntings
Inferno: New Tales of Terror and the Supernatural
Lethal Kisses
Little Deaths
Lovecraft Unbound
Lovecraft's Monsters
Mad Hatters and March Hares
Naked City: Tales of Urban Fantasy
Nebula Awards Showcase 2009
Nightmare Carnival
Off Limits: Tales of Alien Sex
Omni Best Science Fiction: Volumes One through *Three*
The Omni Books of Science Fiction: Volumes One through *Seven*
Omni Visions One and *Two*
Poe: 19 New Tales Inspired by Edgar Allan Poe
Queen Victoria's Book of Spells (with Terri Windling)
Ruby Slippers, Golden Tears (with Terri Windling)
Salon Fantastique: Fifteen Original Tales of Fantasy (with Terri Windling)
Silver Birch, Blood Moon (with Terri Windling)
Sirens and Other Daemon Lovers (with Terri Windling)
Snow White, Blood Red (with Terri Windling)
Supernatural Noir
Swan Sister (with Terri Windling)
Tails of Wonder and Imagination: Cat Stories
Teeth: Vampire Tales (with Terri Windling)
Telling Tales: The Clarion West 30th Anniversary Anthology
The Beastly Bride: And Other Tales of the Animal People (with Terri Windling)
The Best Horror of the Year: Volumes One through *Eleven*
The Best of the Best Horror of the Year
The Coyote Road: Trickster Tales (with Terri Windling)
The Cutting Room: Dark Reflections of the Silver Screen
The Dark: New Ghost Stories
The Del Rey Book of Science Fiction and Fantasy
The Devil and the Deep: Horror Stories of the Sea
The Doll Collection
The Faery Reel: Tales from the Twilight Realm
The Green Man: Tales from the Mythic Forest (with Terri Windling)
The Monstrous
Troll's-Eye View: A Book of Villainous Tales (with Terri Windling)
Twists of the Tale
Vanishing Acts
The Year's Best Fantasy and Horror (with Terri Windling, and with Gavin J. Grant and Kelly Link)

THE BEST HORROR OF THE YEAR

VOLUME TWELVE

THE BEST HORROR OF THE YEAR

VOLUME TWELVE

EDITED BY ELLEN DATLOW

NIGHT SHADE BOOKS
NEW YORK

Night Shade books may be purchased in bulk at special discounts for sales promotion, corporate gifts, fund-raising, or educational purposes. Special editions can also be created to specifications. For details, contact the Special Sales Department, Night Shade Books, 307 West 36th Street, 11th Floor, New York, NY 10018 or info@skyhorsepublishing.com.

Visit our website at www.nightshadebooks.com.

10 9 8 7 6 5 4 3 2 1

Library of Congress Cataloging-in-Publication Data is available on file.

Cover art by Reiko Murakami
Cover design by Mona Lin

Print ISBN: 978-1-59780-973-3

Printed in the United States of America

Thanks to Kathe Koja for her recommendation of a writer with whom I was unfamiliar.

Thank you to all the magazine and book publishers who sent me material for review in a timely manner.

Thank you to Ysabeau Wilce and Theresa DeLucci who helped with the reading.

And special thanks to Jason Katzman, my editor at Night Shade.

Table of Contents

SUMMATION 2019

Here are 2019's numbers: there are twenty-two stories and novelettes, and one novella in this volume. The lengths range from 1,400 words to 29,500 words. Twelve stories are by men, nine by women, and one by a nonbinary contributor. The authors hail from the United States, the United Kingdom, and Canada. Eleven of the contributors have never before appeared in any volumes of my *Best Horror of the Year* series.

Awards

The Horror Writers Association announced the 2018 Bram Stoker Awards® winners at StokerCon in Grand Rapids, Michigan, on May 11, 2019, during the banquet at the Amway Plaza Hotel.

Superior Achievement in a Novel: *The Cabin at the End of the World* by Paul Tremblay (William Morrow); Superior Achievement in a First Novel: *The Rust Maidens* by Gwendolyn Kiste (Trepidatio Publishing); Superior Achievement in a Young Adult Novel: *The Dark Descent of Elizabeth Frankenstein* by Kiersten White (Delacorte Press); Superior Achievement in a Graphic Novel: *Victor LaValle's Destroyer* by Victor LaValle (BOOM! Studios); Superior Achievement in Long Fiction: *The Devil's Throat* by Rena Mason (*Hellhole: An Anthology of Subterranean Terror*) (Adrenaline Press); Superior Achievement in Short Fiction: "Mutter" by Jess Landry (*Fantastic Tales of Terror*) (Crystal Lake Publishing); Superior Achievement in a Fiction Collection: *That Which Grows Wild* by Eric J. Guignard (Cemetery Dance

Publications); Superior Achievement in a Screenplay: *The Haunting of Hill House: The Bent-Neck Lady*, Episode 01:05 by Meredith Averill (Amblin Television, FlanaganFilm, Paramount Television); Superior Achievement in an Anthology: *The Devil and the Deep: Horror Stories of the Sea* edited by Ellen Datlow (Night Shade Books); Superior Achievement in Non-Fiction: *It's Alive: Bringing Your Nightmares to Life* by Joe Mynhardt and Eugene Johnston (Crystal Lake Publishing); Superior Achievement in a Poetry Collection: *The Devil's Dreamland* by Sara Tantlinger (Strangehouse Books).

The Lifetime Achievement Award: Graham Masterson

The Silver Hammer Award: Jess Landry

The Mentor of the Year Award: JG Faherty

The Richard Laymon President's Award: Brad Hodson

The Specialty Press Award: Raw Dog Screaming Press—Jennifer Barnes & John Edward Lawson

The 2018 Shirley Jackson Awards were given out at Readercon 30 on Sunday, July 14, 2019, in Quincy, Massachusetts. The jurors were Chikodili Emelumadu, Michael Thomas Ford, Gambino Iglesias, Kate Maruyama, and Lynda E. Rucker.

The winners were: Novel: *Little Eve*, Catriona Ward (Weidenfeld & Nicolson, an imprint of The Orion Publishing Group); Novella: *The Taiga Syndrome*, Cristina Rivera Garza (Dorothy, a Publishing Project); Novelette: "Help the Witch," Tom Cox (Help the Witch); Short Fiction: "The Astronaut," Christina Wood Martinez (*Granta 142: Animalia*); Single Author Collection: *All the Fabulous Beasts* by Priya Sharma (Undertow Publications); Edited Anthology: *Robots vs Fairies*, edited by Navah Wolfe and Dominik Parisien (Saga Press)

The World Fantasy Awards were given out at a banquet in the LAX Marriott Sunday November 3, 2019. The Lifetime Achievement Awards: Hayao Miyazaki and Jack Zipes were announced in advance. The judges were: Nancy Holder, Kathleen Jennings, Stephen Graham Jones, Garry Douglas Kilworth, and Tod McCoy.

Winner of the Best Work 2018: Best Novel: *Witchmark* by C. L. Polk (Tor.com); Novella: *The Privilege of the Happy Ending* by Kij Johnson (Clarkesworld, August 2018); Best Short Fiction: (tie): "Ten Deals with the Indigo Snake" by Mel Kassel (Lightspeed, October 2018) and "Like a River

Loves the Sky" by Emma Törzs (Uncanny Magazine, March-April 2018); Best Anthology: *Worlds Seen in Passing: Ten Years of Tor.com Short Fiction*, edited by Irene Gallo (Tor.com); Best Collection: *The Tangled Lands*, by Paolo Bacigalupi and Tobias S. Buckell (Saga Press/Head of Zeus UK); Best Artist: Rovina Cai; Special Award, Professional: Huw Lewis-Jones for *The Writer's Map: An Atlas of Imaginary Lands* (University of Chicago Press); Special Award, Non-Professional: Scott H. Andrews, for *Beneath Ceaseless Skies: Literary Adventure Fantasy.*

NOTABLE NOVELS OF 2019

Gideon the Ninth by Tamsyn Muir (Tor.com) is a fabulously original dark, dark, dark sword and sorcery/science fiction novel creating a rich world as complex and as fascinating as that of Mervyn Peake's *Gormanghast.* Gideon is an orphan indentured to the Ninth House of an empire and destined to die and be reanimated—whether she likes it or not—but all she wants to do is escape with her sword and her porn magazines—and fight. Instead she's taken by the Necromancer to whom she is assigned as cavalier, to protect and serve during a fierce and deadly competition for elevation to the undead.

Black Mountain by Laird Barron (G.P. Putnam's Sons) is the powerful follow-up to Barron's first crime novel, *Blood Standard.* This one's even better and darker, as former hit man Isaiah Coleridge, having relocated to upstate New York, is "persuaded" by the mob he'd hoped to leave to investigate the brutal deaths of two of their number.

A Cosmology of Monsters by Shaun Hamill (Pantheon) is about a young boy who—along with the rest of his dysfunctional family—sees monsters, and how they deal with this. A weirdly beautiful, disturbing, and heartbreaking first novel imbued with a love of horror.

Inspection by Josh Malerman (Del Rey) is a terrific dystopic novel about a group of twenty-six boys isolated from the outside world in an ambitious psychological and sociological experiment. As they accidentally learn secrets kept from them during their first twelve years, the experiment begins to unravel.

The Wolf and the Watchman by Niklas Natt och Dag (Atria) is a grisly, page-turning crime novel set in eighteenth-century Stockholm, and opens with a night watchman recovering a mutilated body from the city's fetid lake. He and a police investigator join forces to discover the victim's identity and what led to his grotesque death. A remarkable debut translated from the Swedish.

The Pandora Room by Christopher Golden (St. Martin's Press) is an effective thriller about an archaeological team in Northern Iraq that discovers an ancient artifact which may be the supposedly mythical container dubbed Pandora's Box, containing all the ills and curses of the world.

Just One Bite by Jack Heath (Hanover Square Press) is the sequel to the 2018 novel *Hangman*, about an FBI consultant who happens to be a cannibal. In *Just One Bite*, he's currently working in body disposal for a crime lord when he discovers a body that was not the one he was assigned to dispose of. He's pulled back into the consulting gig and is asked to investigate the disappearance of the dead man he found (and partially has eaten). Dark and simultaneously kind of cheery in a gruesome sort of way. It definitely kept me reading.

The Twisted Ones by T. Kingfisher (Saga Press), inspired by Arthur Machen's work, is about a young woman pressed by her father into cleaning out her late, nasty, hoarder-grandmother's house. This terrific piece of folk horror is one of the best horror novels of the year, as it scours the reader with wit, memorable characters, and best of all—deeply unsettling images.

The Bone Weaver's Orchard by Sarah Read (Trepidatio Publishing) is a dark, riveting debut about a boy sent by his widowed, soldier father from Cairo during the 1926 riots to school in Northern England. Over a period of years, boys disappear from the school, and the others have always been told that they've run home. Charley discovers something that makes him doubt that explanation.

A Lush and Seething Hell by John Hornor Jacobs (HarperVoyager) contains a previously published novella and a new, powerful short novel of cosmic horror, the latter titled *My Heart Struck Sorrow.* In it, a grieving librarian discovers a recording that leads him to follow in the footsteps of a government musicologist who during the '30s, traveled throughout the Deep South searching for the elusive later verses of one of the region's most famous tunes.

The Toll by Cherie Priest (Tor) is an absorbing Southern gothic taking place in the Okefenokee Swamp in Georgia. A honeymoon couple on the way to a cabin in the swamp encounter a one-lane bridge. Hours later, one of them awakens in the middle of the road, to find the bridge—and their mate—gone.

Curious Toys by Elizabeth Hand (Mulholland Books) is a terrific dark novel taking place in Chicago during the summer of 1915. Pin, the fourteen-year-old daughter of the Riverview amusement park's resident fortune teller, witnesses what may be a horrific disappearance from the carnival's popular Hell's Gate ride. She encounters a strange, crazy man, Henry Darger, and together they investigate. There are lovely, juicy bits about the Chicago film industry and those who work there—their unsavory vices and their bad habits. Not really horror but a great read.

Starve Acre by Andrew Michael Hurley (John Murray) is the third novel by the author of the award-winning *The Loney*. A British couple leave the city for the moors of Yorkshire, "a bad place"—in horror terms—after their young son dies. Hurley's sense of time (the '70s) and place (rural England) is again pitch perfect, creating a powerful piece of folk horror.

The Possession (The Anomaly Files) by Michael Rutger (Grand Central Publishing) is the energetic and thoroughly enjoyable follow-up to *The Anomaly*. The four creators of the YouTube program *The Anomaly Files* decide to investigate a California town with seemingly randomly built stone walls. They're greeted with suspicion by the locals because of the recent disappearance of a teenage girl. Then she reappears and things get really weird.

ALSO NOTED

Dark Carnival by Joanna Parypinski (Independent Legions Publishing) is about a young man returning home for his father's funeral. In returning, he becomes caught up in the enduring mystery of his mother's disappearance at a traveling carnival fourteen years earlier. *Cari Mori* by Thomas Harris (Grand Central Publishing) is the author's first novel since 2006's *Hannibal Rising* and his first standalone since *Black Sunday*. It's about several groups after a huge haul of cartel money located in a deserted villa. It's a fast read, with an interesting female hero, but she doesn't make up for the thin, predictable plot and the disgusting albeit uninteresting villain. *Before the Devil Fell by* Neil Olson (Hanover Square Press) is a dark fantasy about a man who, because of a family emergency, returns to the village where he grew up outside Boston, and is forced to confront the repercussions of a ritual gone wrong when he was a boy. *Hellrider* by J. G. Faherty (Flame Tree Press) is about the vengeance of a murdered member of a biker gang in a small Florida town on the edge of the Everglades. *Alistair Boone* by Torvi Tacuski (self-published) isn't exactly horror, despite the fact that Death is a major character. A quirky psychologist becomes popular as his reputation for being honest (if nasty) to his patients spreads. *Us* by John Shupeck (Necro Publications) is about a serial killer with multiple personalities. *The Plague Stones* by James Brogden (Titan) is about a traumatized family that moves from the city to an historical town seeking peace, unaware that the standing stone in their cottage garden is a guardian against plague that must be appeased through an annual ritual. *Mistletoe* by Alison Littlewood (Quercus) is about a woman who, mourning her dead husband and child, moves to a dilapidated farmhouse in northern England to escape the forced joy of the Christmas season. *Wanderers* by Chuck Wendig (Del Rey) is a dystopian sf/horror epic about an epidemic of sleepwalkers creating terror and shattering society. *Coyote Heaven* by Owl Goingback (Independent Legions Publishing) is about Coyote, the shape-shifter of native American lore, going on a murderous rampage to overturn human rule of earth, and those who try to stop him. *The Last Astronaut* by David Wellington (Orbit) is an sf/horror novel about a first-contact mission into space in which the alien organism is less than friendly. *Kthulhu Reich* by Asamatsu Ken (Kurodahan Press) is a novel made up of seven stories about post WWII occult imaginings and Lovecraftian monsters. *The Bride Stripped Bare* by Rob Bliss (Necro Publications) is about a guy invited to the wedding of a friend he hadn't seen in several years—the bride is gorgeous and sexy, but things are not as they seem—the story moves into extreme horror territory. *A Sick Gray Laugh* by Nicole Cushing (Word Horde) is about a depressed writer whose new medication seems to be the cure for her problems. *The Reddening* by Adam Nevill (Ritual Limited) is about what happens when evidence of prehistoric cave dwellers is discovered in a remote area of England. *Memento Mori* by Brian Hauser (Word Horde) is about an underground filmmaker of the late '70s who disappears under mysterious circumstances. *The Remaking* by Clay McLeod Chapman (Quirk Books) is about what happens in a rural Virginian town decades after a woman and her daughter are burned as witches in the 1930s. *A Spectral Hue* by Craig

Laurance Gidney (Word Horde) is about a graduate student's investigation into the one haunting color used by generations of artist residents of a town in Maryland. *A Hawk in the Woods* by Carrie Laben (Word Horde), inspired by Lovecraft's "The Thing on the Doorstep," opens with devastating news for the protagonist, spurring her to break her sister out of prison and return to the family cabin in Minnesota. *Remains* by Andrew Cull (IFWC Publishing) is about a woman whose son has been murdered and the efforts she makes to reach out to him in the afterlife. *The Dollmaker* by Nina Allan (Other Press) is an unsettling fairy tale about a dollmaker who searches for the woman who placed a personal ad in his collectors' magazine. *Blood Sugar* by Daniel Kraus (Hard Case Crime) is about an angry outcast who hatches a nefarious plan to use Halloween as a means of revenge. *The Migration* by Helen Marshall (Titan) is an sf/horror novel about a worldwide immune disorder affecting children and teenagers, and what happens when the dead may not actually be dead. *Anno Dracula: Daikiju* by Kim Newman (Titan) is a new entry in the alternate vampiric world that the author has presided over since 1992. *Cardinal Black* by Robert McCammon (CD) is the seventh volume in a dark, historical series taking place at the turn of the eighteenth century about a professional "problem solver." *The Institute* by Stephen King (Scribner) begins with a boy being kidnapped and brought to an "institute" where he and other children are trained to use their innate special talents. *Pursuit* by Joyce Carol Oates (Mysterious Press) is about a newlywed who the day after her marriage steps into traffic and is almost killed. This incident prods her and her husband to delve into a past that plagues her present with nightmares. *The Grand Dark* by Richard Kadrey (HarperVoyager) is a darkly futuristic standalone novel about an ambitious bike messenger living in a fragmented, dystopian world in which one war has ended but another is always possible. *Water Shall Refuse Them* by Lucie McKnight Hardy (Dead Ink) takes place during a heat wave in Wales in 1976. A family that's lost one of their children in an accident retreat to a small village for a month, hoping the change will nudge the grieving mother back into the world. But their teenage daughter creates a form of witchcraft as her own way of coping. *Wakenhyrst* by Michelle Paver (Head of Zeus) is a dark gothic ghost story about a young girl living with her repressive father in a manor house in Edwardian Suffolk, England.

Magazines, Journals, and Webzines

It's important to recognize the work of the talented artists working in the field of fantastic fiction, both dark and light. The following created dark art that I thought especially noteworthy in 2019: William Basso, Joachim Luetke, Wendy Saber Core, Jim Burns, Daniele Serra, Garry Nurrish, Matthew Davis, Cat O'Neil, Horacio Quiroz, David Alvarez, Stephen Mackey, Ben Baldwin, Toni Tošić, Michael Sawecki, Danielle Hark, Adrian Borda, Dave Senecal, Andrea Bonazzi, Allen Koszowski, Harry O. Morris, Sabinaka, Sophie E. Tallis, Michael Bukowski, Mikio Murakami, Kojima Ayami, Colin Nitta, Catrin Welz-Stein, Stephen Mackey, Les Edwards, Paul Lowe, Samuel Araya, Miranda Adria, David McNamara, Kim BoYung, Toru Kamei, Matthew Revert, and Caniglia.

Rue Morgue edited by Andrea Subissati is a Canadian nonfiction magazine for the horror movie aficionado. It's not very deep, but it's entertaining and has up-to-date information on most of the horror films being produced. The magazine includes interviews, articles, and lots of gory photographs, along with regular columns on books, horror music, and graphic novels.

The Green Book: Writings on Irish Gothic, Supernatural, and Fantastic Literature edited by Brian J. Showers is a marvelous resource for discovering underappreciated writers. There was only one issue published in 2019. It contained fourteen articles about writers active between the seventeenth and twentieth centuries.

Lovecraft Annual edited by S. T. Joshi is a must for those interested in Lovecraftian studies. The 2019 volume includes wide-ranging essays about the author's work, life, and philosophies.

Wormwood: Literature of the fantastic, supernatural and decadent edited by Mark Valentine is another excellent journal, somewhat less academic than the *Lovecraft Annual*; more for a general audience.

Dead Reckonings: A Review of Horror and the Weird in the Arts edited by Alex Houstoun and Michael J. Abolafia brought out two worthy issues in 2019, both filled with reviews, commentaries, and essays.

Revenant is a peer-reviewed e-journal dedicated to academic and creative explorations of the Supernatural, the Uncanny, and the Weird. The theme of the 2019 issue was Gothic Feminisms and was guest edited by Frances

Kamm and Tamar Jeffers McDonald. The issue included four articles on cinema and seven reviews.

Weirdbook Annual #2: Cthulhu edited by Douglas Draa features fiction and poetry, with this issue's theme heralded in the title. There's notable fiction by Glynn Owen Barrass, Adrian Cole, Darrell Schweitzer, and Kenneth Bykerk. Regular issue #41 was a good one, with notable stories and poems by Arasibo Campeche, Alistair Rey, Luke Walker, Erica Ruppert, Adrian Cole, Sean McCoy, and R. A. Opperman.

Black Static edited by Andy Cox continues to be the best, most consistent venue for horror fiction. In addition to essays, book and movie reviews, and interviews there was notable fiction by Stephen Volk, Steve J. Dines, Erinn L. Kemper, Tim Lees, Stephen Hargadon, Steve Sheil, Seán Padraic Birnie, Kristi DeMeester, Sarah Read, Tom Johnstone, Natalie Theodoridou, Cody Goodfellow, Eric Schaller, Michelle Ann King, Amanda J. Bermudez, S. Qiouyi Lu, Ralph Robert Moore, Mike O'Driscoll, Jack Westlake, Kay Chronister, David Martin, and Jack Westlake. The Lu, Lees, and Read are reprinted herein.

Nightmare edited by John Joseph Adams is a monthly webzine of horror and dark fantasy. It publishes articles, interviews, book reviews, and an artists' showcase, along with two reprints and two original pieces of fiction per month. During 2019, it published notable horror by Natalie Theodoridou, Adam-Troy Castro, Dennis Staples, Nibedita Sen, Simon Strantzas, Merc Fenn, Gwendolyn Kiste, Cadwell Turnbull, Rich Larson, Senaa Ahmad, Ray Naylor, and Carlie St. George.

The Dark edited by Silvia Moreno-Garcia and Sean Wallace, is a monthly webzine dedicated to dark fantasy and horror. It publishes new stories and reprints. During 2019, there were notable stories by Sara Saab, Angela Fu, Carlie St. George, Ruoxi Chen, Elizabeth Childs, Kay Chronister, Vaishnavi Patel, and Nibidita Sen.

Sirenia Digest has been published by Caitlín R. Kiernan for several years and might be considered an early iteration of Patreon. Sponsors pay a set amount for a monthly digest of excerpts, new stories, vignettes, and other bits springing from the mind of this excellent writer. Subscribe and enjoy.

Cemetery Dance edited by Rich Chizmar published one issue in 2019, containing notable stories by Ralph Robert Moore, J. P. Hutsell, and

Eric Rickstad. The issue also featured the usual columns by Thomas F. Monteleone, Bev Vincent, Michael Marano, Marl Sieber, and me.

Supernatural Tales edited by David Longhorn is as always an excellent source of supernatural fiction, and the two issues published in 2019 were no exception. Good, dark stories by S. P. Miskowski, Steve Duffy, Tracy Fahey, Jane Jakeman, Lynda E. Rucker, Patricia Lillie, Peter Kenny, David Surface, Jeremy Schliewe, Laura Lucas, and an oddly hopeful post-apocalyptic tale by Helen Grant.

Vastarien: A Literary Journal debuted in the spring and published three issues during 2019. Edited by Jon Padgett, it's an ambitious mixture of weird fiction and essays influenced by Thomas Ligotti and his work. There were notable dark stories and poetry during the year by Lisa Swope Mitchell, Matthew M. Bartlett, Gemma Files, Fiona Maeve Geist, Natalie Theodoridou, Jayaprakash Satyamurthy, Lucy A. Snyder, Eden Royce, Robert S. Wilson, Patricia Lillie, Charlotte Begg, David F. Shultz, Dan Stintzi, and Robin Gow. In addition, there were essays about the work of Mark Samuels, Charlotte Perkins Gilman, Roman Polanski, Tom Ligotti, and other purveyors of the weird.

Pseudopod edited by Shawn Garrett and Alex Hofelich is a regular fixture of audio horror podcasts. In 2019, there were notable stories by Donyae Coles, Lora Gray, Kurt Hunt, Vivian Shaw, Rosemary Hays, Kristi DeMeester, Annie Neugebauer, Pierce Skinner, and Rhoads Brazos. The DeMeester is reprinted herein.

Mixed-genre Magazines

BFS Journal edited by Allen Stroud and Sean Wilcock is a twice yearly non-fiction perk of membership in the British Fantasy Society. It includes reviews, scholarly articles, and features about recent conventions. *BFS Horizons* edited by Shona Kinsella, Tim Major, and Ian Hunter is the fiction companion to *BFS Journal*. There were notable dark stories by Andrew Wallace and Seán Padraic Birnie. *On Spec*, Canada's best-known genre magazine, is published quarterly by a revolving committee of volunteers since 1989. They don't often include horror in their mix, but in 2019 they did publish good horror stories by Paul Alex Gray and Lynne M. MacLean. *Aurealis*, edited by Dirk Strasser, Stephen Higgins, and Michael Pryor is one of only a few long-running Australian mixed-genre magazines. It occasionally publishes horror and in 2019 there were notable dark stories by Gordon Grice and Michelle Birkette. *Weird Tales* is back yet again with dark fantasy and horror. Jonathan Maberry has come onboard as editorial director with Marvin Kaye remaining as editor. The issue, the first in full color, promises a bright future, with excellent poetry by Stephanie M. Wytovich and notable horror by Victor LaValle, Josh Malerman, and Lisa Morton. *The Magazine of Fantasy and Science Fiction* edited by C. C. Finlay is one of the longest running sf/f/h magazines in existence. Although it mostly publishes science fiction and fantasy, it often publishes very good horror. During 2019, the strongest horror stories were by R. S. Benedict, Cassandra Khaw, Adam-Troy Castro, Erin Cashier, Rebecca Campbell, Rich Larson, Sam J. Miller, Andy Stewart, G.V. Anderson, Pip Coen, Debbie Urbanski, and Diana Peterfreund. The Peterfreund is reprinted herein. *Bourbon Penn* edited by Erik Secker and published twice a year is a reliable source of interesting, often weird, sometimes dark, and always entertaining short fiction. In 2019, there were notable darker stories by Kali Wallace, Setsu Uzumé, George Edwards Murray, Charles Wilkinson, Hamdy Elgammal, Sam Rebelein, Saul Lemerond, Dona McCormick, Brendan James Murray, T. B. Jeremiah, and Dawn Sperber. The Rebelein is reprinted herein. *Weird Fiction Review* edited by S. T. Joshi is published annually by Centipede Press. The 2019 edition contains over 400 pages of fiction, poetry, essays, interviews, and art, much but not all of it dark. There was notable dark fiction and poetry by Victor LaValle, Laird Barron, Jonathan Thomas, Clint Smith, Ashley Dioses, Stephen Graham Jones, and James Ulmer. *Fireside Quarterly* edited by Julia Rios is an illustrated magazine with fiction, poetry, and essays. Only a few of the stories are horror but, in 2019, the magazine published notable dark fiction by Karolina Fedyk, George Lockett, and Iliana Vargas. *Not One of Us* edited by John Benson is one of the longest-running small press magazines. It's published twice a year and contains weird and dark fiction and poetry. In addition, Benson puts out an annual "one-off" on a specific theme. The theme for 2019 was *Else*, about things and people different in identity. There was notable work by Donna Smiley and Gordon B. White. *Dimension6* edited by Keith Stevenson is a digital sf/f/h magazine published three times a year out of Australia. In 2019, there was interesting horror by Deborah Sheldon, Mark T. Barnes, and Jason Fischer. *Conjunctions* edited by Bradford

Morrow and published by Bard College, is one of the more genre friendly literary magazines in the US. The two 2019 themed issues *Nocturnals* and *Earth Elegies* contained strong dark works by Joyce Carol Oates, Peter Gizzi, Hilary Leichter, and Brian Evenson. *Uncanny* edited by Lynne M. Thomas and Michael Damien Thomas is a webzine publishing fantasy, speculative, and weird fiction, poetry, podcasts, interviews, essays, and art. In 2019 there were good dark stories by Karen Osborne, Sarah Pinsker, Delilah S. Dawson, Vina Jie-Min Prasad, Ellen Klages, and A. C. Wise.

Anthologies

Hex Life edited by Christopher Golden and Rachel Autumn Deering (Titan) contains eighteen original dark fantasy and horror stories by women, involving witches. The strongest are by Sarah Langan, Chesya Burke, Tananarive Due, and Ania Ahlborn. The Langan is reprinted herein.

Tales from the Shadow Booth Volumes 3 and *4* edited by Dan Coxon (The Shadowbooth) considers itself a journal, but in actuality seems more like an anthology. Volume 3 features eleven weird and usually dark stories. The strongest are by Robert Shearman, Verity Holloway, Tim Major, Richard V. Hirst, and Gregory J. Wolos. Volume 4 has fourteen stories, with the best by Giselle Leeb. The Shearman is reprinted herein.

American Gothic Short Stories edited by Gillian Whitaker (Flame Tree Press) brings together fifty-three stories, fourteen new. The classics, which include Ambrose Bierce's "An Occurrence At Owl Creek Bridge" and Charlotte Perkins Gilman's "The Yellow Wallpaper," are mostly familiar to readers, but the book includes some notable contemporary reprints and one good, new story by Mike Robinson.

Ghost Stories: Classic Tales of Horror and Suspense edited by Lisa Morton and Leslie S. Klinger (Pegasus Books) contains seventeen stories and a ballad by Edgar Allan Poe, Edith Wharton, M. R. James, Wilkie Collins, and others. With an overall introduction and introductory bios of each author, placing their stories in historical context.

Stokercon™ 2019 Souvenir Anthology edited by Linda A. Addison was given out to all members of the convention, and contains reprinted fiction and poetry by the Guests of Honor and recipient of the Life Achievement Award, plus interviews with each of them and essays about some of the categories.

Haunted House Ghost Stories: Anthology of New and Classic Tales edited by Gillian Whitaker (Flame Tree Press) is a large, mostly reprint anthology of forty-nine classic reprints, contemporary reprints, and eight new stories. Two notable originals are by Bill Kre'pi and M. Regan.

An Obscurity of Ghosts: Further Tales of the Supernatural by Women, 1859-1903 edited by J. A. Mains (Black Shuck Books) collects sixteen tales that have not been anthologized since their original publications, by writers such as Lucy Hardy, Margaret Barringer, Olive Harper, and others.

Echoes: The Saga Anthology of Ghost Stories edited by Ellen Datlow (Saga Press) is a massive anthology of twenty-nine ghost stories, all but three new. Covering the traditional to the weird. The novelettes by Gemma Files and Paul Tremblay are reprinted herein.

Spirits Unwrapped edited by Daniel Braum (Lethe Press) is an anthology of fourteen stories about mummies, all but two originals. The strongest are by Joanna Parypinski, Lee Thomas, Cassilda Ferrante, John Langan, Michael Cisco, and Rhodi Hawk.

Wicked Weird edited by Amber Fallon, Scott T. Goudsward & David Price (NEHW Press) has twenty-one mostly pulpy stories about monsters, with notable tales by Matthew M. Bartlett, William D. Carl, Paul R. McNamee, Errick A. Nunnally, and K. H. Vaughn.

Terror Tales of Northwest England edited by Paul Finch (Telos) is the twelfth volume in this folk horror anthology series. It contains fifteen stories, all but three new, with interstitial material by the editor. There are notable stories by Cate Gardner, Simon Kurt Unsworth, Simon Bestwick, Christopher Harman, and John Travis. The Bestwick is reprinted herein.

The Seven Deadliest edited by Patrick Beltran and D. Alexander Ward (Cutting Block Books) features seven stories purportedly about each of the seven deadly sins. I say purportedly because not all the stories relate to those sins, even although the contributors attempt to squeeze in a thematic relationship. Even so, all the stories are good. They're by Richard Thomas, Kasey Lansdale, Brian Kirk, Bracken MacLeod, John C. Foster, Rena Mason, and John F.D. Taff.

The Pulp Horror Book of Phobias edited by M. J. Sydney (LVP Publications) is a large, very pulpy anthology of twenty-six stories concerned with phobias (all but two of them real). The best stories are by John Skipp, Tim Waggoner, Sèphera Girón, Hank Schwaeble, and James Chambers.

Nightscript V edited by C. M. Muller (Chthonic Matter) features nineteen unthemed dark, dark tales. Included are notable stories by J. A. W. McCarthy, Simon Strantzas, Brady Golden, Charles Wilkinson, J. C. Raye, Dan Stintzi, M.K. Anderson, M. Lopez Da Silva, and Sam Hicks. The Hicks is reprinted herein.

Fantasmagoriana Volume Two edited by Keith Cadieux (WIWF) is a mini anthology written as part of the Winnipeg International Writers Festival. It consists of four stories written by writers who stayed in the Dalnavert Museum, a supposedly haunted mansion. The authors are Adam Petrash, Jess Landry, J.H Moncrieff, and David Demchuk.

Great British Horror 4: Dark and Stormy Nights edited by Steve J. Shaw (Black Shuck Books) is a fine annual showcase of British horror, with one international guest contributor. The best of the eleven stories were by Priya Sharma, Catriona Ward, Ren Warom, Simon Avery, and G. V. Anderson. The Warom and Ward are reprinted herein.

Welcome to Miskatonic University: Fantastically Weird Tales of Campus Life edited by Scott Gable and C. Dombrowski (Broken Eye Books) is an entertaining anthology of thirteen stories and an imaginary "who's who of Arkham." The best of the stories are by Bennett North, Kristi DeMeester, Nate Southard, Joseph S. Pulver, Sr., and Scott R. Jones.

Polish Extreme edited by Edward Lee and Karolina Kaczkowska (Necro Publications) is an anthology of four new stories by Polish writers plus a new novella by Edward Lee. If you're familiar with Lee's fiction, you'll know what you're getting into.

The Virago Book of Witches edited by Sharukh Husain (Virago) collects more than fifty stories about witches from around the world.

Vampiric: Tales of Blood and Roses From Japan edited by Heather Dubnick (Kurodahan Press) features fifteen stories published in English for the first time. While the cultural variations are interesting, only a few stories do anything different with the idea of the vampire. The best stories were by Asukabe Katsunori and Inoue Masahiko (two by the latter, and one of those not really vampiric and not even horror but quite good).

The Big Book of Blasphemy edited by Regina Garza Mitchell and David G. Barnett (Necro Publications) features thirty stories of "extreme horror." There are notable stories (less than extreme) by Gerard Houarner, Brian

Keene, Robert Allen Lupton, Laura Blackwell, Mark Mills, Charlee Jacob, and Alessandro Manzetti.

Midnight in the Graveyard edited by Kenneth W. Cain (Silver Shamrock Publishing) contains twenty-five ghost stories, all but two new. There are some good ones by Kealan Patrick Burke, Alan Clarke, Chad Lutzke, Elizabeth Massie, and Hunter Shea.

I Am the Abyss edited by Chris Morey (Dark Regions Press) is a beautiful-looking anthology of nine original horror and dark fantasy novellas about the afterlife, with nine original illustrations by Les Edwards. I was most impressed by the works of Greg F. Gifune, Reggie Oliver, and Michael Marshall Smith.

The Twisted Book of Shadows edited by Christopher Golden and James A. Moore (Twisted Publishing/Haverhill House) is an unthemed, crowdfunded, all original anthology of seventeen stories. The strongest stories are by P. D. Cacek, Jeffrey B. Burton, Kristi DeMeester, John Linwood Grant, and Eóin Murphy.

Mannequin: Tales of Wood Made Flesh edited by Justin A. Burnett (Silent Motorist Media) is an anthology of sixteen stories, most of them horror, all but two original. There are notable stories by Jon Padgett, S. P. Dunphey, Justin A. Burnett, and William Tea.

Sharp & Sugar Tooth: Women Up to No Good edited by Octavia Cade (Upper Rubber Boot) is an impressive anthology of twenty-two sf/horror/weird stories (six of them reprints) by women about unsavory appetites. Despite the misleading subtitle (not all the women in the book are "up to no good"), there are notable stories by H. Pueyo, H. R. Henle, Kathryn McMahon, Jasmyne J. Harris, and Katharine Duckett.

The Abyssal Plain: The R'lyeh Cycle edited by William Holloway and Brett J. Talley (JournalStone) is an anthology/novel of four sections written by five writers (one is a collaboration) about events that are precursors to the rising of a Lovecraftian horror.

The New Flesh: A Literary Tribute to David Cronenberg edited by Sam Richard and Brendan Vidito (Weird Punk Books) is an original anthology of eighteen horror stories. The most interesting contributions were by Brian Evenson, Gwendolyn Kiste, and Jack Lothian.

The Porcupine Boy and Other Anthological Oddities edited by Christopher M. Jones (Macabre Ink) is an unthemed, original anthology of fourteen stories. There are especially strong entries by P. D. Cacek, Ray Cluley, David Nickle, Priya Sharma, and Lucy Snyder. The Cluley is reprinted herein.

Shivers 8 edited by Richard Chizmar (Cemetery Dance Publications) has twenty-seven stories, about half of them new. The strongest of the originals are by Stephen King, Michael M. Hughes, Tina Callaghan, Darrell Speegle, Bentley Little, Jack Dann, and Bruce McAllister.

American Monsters Part 2: North America edited by Margrét Helgadottir (Fox Spirit Books) has seventeen stories, six of them reprints. The best of the new ones are by Anne Michaud, Pepe Rojo, and Kelly Sandoval.

Horror for RAICES: A Charitable Anthology edited by Jennifer Wilson and Robert S. Wilson (Nightscape Press) contains thirty-two stories, eighteen of which are new. The strongest of the new stories are by Livia Llewellyn, Max Booth III, Ramsey Campbell, Gwendolyn Kiste, and Jessica McHugh.

The Chromatic Court edited by Peter Rawlik (18thWall Productions) has twelve new Lovecraftian stories related to art. The most interesting story is by Joseph S. Pulver, Sr.

Invocations (no editor listed) (A Black Library Publication) is an anthology of all new horror stories taking place in the brutal Warhammer world.

Re-Haunt: Chilling Stories of Ghosts & Other Haunts edited by Kelly A. Harmon and Vonnie Winslow Crist (Pole to Pole Publishing) has sixteen reprints by writers such as Nancy Springer, Darrell Schweitzer, S. Baring-Gould, and Jody Lynn Nye.

Mountains of Madness Revealed edited by Darrell Schweitzer (PS Publishing) is an all original anthology of nineteen stories and poems inspired by H. P. Lovecraft's novella *At the Mountain of Madness*. There were notable stories by Adrian Cole, Darrell Schweitzer, John Linwood Grant, Frederic S. Durbin, and James Van Pelt.

Best New Horror #29 edited by Stephen Jones (Drugstore Indian Press) features twenty-one horror stories. One story overlaps with Paula Guran's *The Year's Best Dark Fantasy and Horror 2018* and none overlap with my own *The Best Horror of the Year Volume Ten*. Jones has an extensive summary of the year in horror which includes publishing news and an overview of all media. Plus a Necrology.

Dark Mirages edited by Paul Kane (PS Publishing) is an anthology of unmade film and television scripts and treatments by such writers as Stephen Gallagher, Muriel Gray, Peter Crowther, and a collaboration by Stephen Jones and Michel Marshall Smith.

Twice Told: A Collection of Doubles edited by C. M. Muller (Chthonic Matter) contains twenty-two stories about doppelgangers, most of them dark, some of them horror. There are especially notable ones by Tom Johnstone, Gordon B. White, Jack Lothian, Esther Rose, Patricia Lillie, Chris Shearer, Clint Smith, and Steve Rasnic Tem. The Lothian and White are reprinted herein.

Shadmocks and Shivers: New Tales Inspired by R. Chetwynd-Hayes edited by Dave Brzeski (Shadow Publishing) is an anthology of fifteen new stories inspired by the late British writer. The best is by John Llewellyn Probert.

The Mammoth Book of Nightmare Stories: Twisted Tales Not to Be Read at Night edited by Stephen Jones (Skyhorse Publishing) contains sixteen stories that their authors consider their favorites or feel have been overlooked. Some contributors are Michael Marshall Smith, Joe R. Lansdale, Poppy Z. Brite, and Neil Gaiman.

Terrifying Tales to Tell at Night: 10 Scary Stories to Give You Nightmares edited by Stephen Jones (Sky Pony Press) is a young adult anthology of ten stories, some of them new.

MIXED-GENRE ANTHOLOGIES

A *Secret Guide to Fighting Elder Gods* edited by Jennifer Brozek (Pulse) is an all original young adult anthology of thirteen dark fantasy stories about teenage encounters with Cthulhu and other creations of H. P. Lovecraft. No horror, but some notable stories by Jonathan Maberry, Lucy A. Snyder, and Premee Mohamed. *Soot and Steel: Dark Tales of London* edited by Ian Whates (Newcon Press) contains nine original and seven classic reprints of stories about London. Not much horror in here but there are some good, darker stories by Paul StJohn Mackintosh, Terry Grimwood, Susan Boulton, and Reggie Oliver. *Tales for the Camp Fire* edited by Loren Rhoades (Tomes & Coffee Press) was initiated by the San Francisco Bay Area Chapter of the Horror Writers Association, in order to benefit the survivors of the Camp Fire in California. Of the twenty-four stories included, five are appearing for the first time. Of those, Erika Mailman's is the best. *Nowhereville: Weird Is Other People* edited by Scott Gable & C. Dombrowski (Broken Eye Books) has nineteen urban weird stories, nine of them new. There's one notable new story by Stephen Graham Jones. *Pop the Clutch: Thrilling Tales of Rockabilly, Monsters, and Hot Rod Horror* edited by Eric J. Guignard (Dark Moon Books) is good, pulpy fun, but you won't find much horror within the pages. The best of the darker stories are by Kasey Lansdale & Joe R. Lansdale and Seanan McGuire. *Machinations and Mesmerism: Tales Inspired by E.T.A. Hoffman* edited by Farah Rose Smith (Ulthar Press) contains sixteen new stories, all in the weird tradition, several horror. The best horror stories were by LC von Hessen, Jennifer Quail, K. H. Vaughan, and Nidhi Singh. *Cutting Edge: New Stories of Mystery and Crime by Women Writers* edited by Joyce Carol Oates (Akashic) features fourteen new noir stories, a series of six poems by Margaret Atwood, and one reprint. The best and darkest stories are by Livia Llewellyn, Cassandra Khaw, S.J. Rozan, and Valerie Martin. *Pareidolia* edited by James Everington and Dan Howarth (Black Shuck Books) has ten new stories about the phenomenon of the mind perceiving shapes or hearing voices where there are none. The anthology is a mixture of weirdness and horror with the best dark stories by Daniel Braum, Sarah Read, Tim Major, Carly Holmes, and G.V. Anderson. The Braum is reprinted herein. *Gorgon: Stories of Emergence* edited by Sarah Read (Pantheon Magazine) is an unusually intriguing anthology of more than forty short-shorts about myth and transformation. All but six stories are new. The best of the dark original ones are by J. Ashley Smith, Doug Murano, Steve Toase, Richard Thomas, Gwendolyn Kiste, Aimee Ogden, and Carina Bissett. *The Woods* edited by Phil Sloman (Hersham Horror Books) is the sixth in a series of mini-anthologies. The theme of these five very readable stories is the woods. The strongest are by Cate Gardner, James Everington, and Mark West. *The Unquiet Dreamer: A Tribute to Harlan Ellison* edited by Preston Grassmann (PS Publishing) contains thirty-three short stories in several genres, essays, and remembrances. All but two of the stories are new, by writers who admired Harlan Ellison's fiction. There are two very good dark stories by Steve Rasnic Tem and Kaaron Warren. *Straight Outta Deadwood* edited by David Boop (Baen) is an entertaining, all-original anthology of seventeen weird, dark, and horrific western stories. The best are by Jeffrey J. Mariotte, Stephen Graham Jones, Alex Acks, and Cliff Winnig. *Dark Lane 8* edited by Tim Jeffreys (Dark Lane) has twenty-three stories of weird, sometimes dark stories. The strongest are by Bill Davidson, Charles Wilkinson, Michael Packman, Carolyn Stockman, Mark Keane, and Nici West. *Pluto in Furs: Tales of Diseased Desires and Seductive Horrors* edited by Scott Dwyer (Plutonian Press) has fourteen stories of occasionally erotic dark fantasy and horror. There are notable stories by Clint Smith and Jean Claude Smith. *We Shall Be Monsters* edited by Derek Newman-Stille (Renaissance Press) is an anthology of twenty-four stories and poems commemorating the bi-centennial of Mary Shelley's *Frankenstein*. The most interesting stories are by Priya Sridhar, Lisa Carreiro, and Kaitlin Tremblay. *At Home in the Dark* edited by Lawrence Block (Subterranean Press) is an anthology of eighteen crime stories, some exceedingly dark. Those that could be considered horror are by Joyce Carol Oates, Laura Benedict, and Joe R. Lansdale. The Lansdale is reprinted herein. *Their Dark & Secret Alchemy* by Richard Gavin, Colin Insole, and Damien Murphy edited by Robert Morgan (Sarob Press) is an attractive little hardcover consisting of three new dark novellas and novelettes. *The Book of Flowering* edited by Mark Beech (Egaeus Press) is an excellent (and beautifully produced) anthology of seventeen, all-but-one new, weird and decadent stories and one poem, a few of which could be considered horror. The best of the darkest stories are by Thomas Strømsholt, V.H. Leslie, Alison Littlewood, N. A. Jackson, Rebecca Kuder, Timothy J. Jarvis, and Colin Insole. Also edited by Beech and published by his press was *A Miscellany of Death & Folly,* a fascinating mix of poetry, nonfiction, and weird and fantastical and sometimes dark fiction. I was especially impressed with stories by Angela Slatter, Brendan Connell, Kaaron Warren, Cate Gardner, D. P. Watt, and Suzanne J. Willis. *Nox Pareidolia* edited by Robert S. Wilson (Nightscape Press) is an unthemed anthology of thirty-one weird and horror stories, all but one original to the volume. The best of the darker stories are by Gwendolyn Kiste, Kristi DeMeester, Paul Jessup, Greg Sisco, Michael Wehunt, Alvaro Zinos-Amaro, Lynne Jamneck, Dino Parenti, Kurt Fawver, and Carrie Laben. Each story is illustrated in black and white by Luke Spooner. *The Far Tower: Stories for W. B. Yeats* edited by Mark Valentine (The Swan River Press) presents ten original stories of fantasy and dark fantasy (and a wee bit of horror), each inspired by a phrase from Yeats' poems, plays, stories, or essays. There are good, dark pieces by Lynda E. Rucker, D. P. Watt, and Reggie Oliver. *Bending to Earth: Strange Stories By Irish Women* edited by Maria Giakaniki and Brian J. Showers (The Swan River Press) is a reprint anthology of twelve stories. With an extensive introduction to the authors by Giakaniki. *Ten-Word*

Tragedies edited by Christopher Golden and Tim Lebbon (PS Publishing) is an anthology of nineteen stories inspired by lyrics written by a musician named Frank Turner who bought a trove of old postcards at a thrift store. The thematic gimmick would have been more effective if the postcards were included, but despite this many of the stories make good reading. The best of the darker ones are by Dan Chaon, Alison Littlewood, Stephen Volk, Josh Malerman, Scott Smith, and Stuart Neville. *The Pale Illuminations* edited by Robert Morgan (Sarob Press) presents four supernatural novellas and stories by Peter Bell, Reggie Oliver, Derek John, and Mark Valentine in a handsome hardcover edition with jacket art by Paul Lowe. *Scarlet Traces: An Anthology Based on War of the Worlds* edited by Ian Edginton (Abaddon Books) is fun but there's minimal horror in it. The best of the dark tales are by Maura McHugh, Mark Morris, and Emma Beeby.

COLLECTIONS

An Ecstasy of Fear by Wilum Pugmire (Centipede Press) contains twenty-two stories and prose poems by the late writer. This is a beautiful, limited edition with an introduction by S. T. Joshi and interior illustrations by Tom Brown. Hippocampus Press published a smaller, much less pricy Pugmire collection titled *An Imp of Aether*, including twenty-six pieces, some in his Sesqua Valley universe, three in collaboration with Maryanne K. Snyder, one with Jessica Amanda Salmonson. Two of them are new. The two collections do not overlap. Each contains the quirky, poetic, weird work that was the hallmark of Pugmire.

Black Shuck Books continued its excellent Shadows series of mini-collections with volumes nine through fifteen: *Winter Freits* by Andrew David Barker has three powerful new stories. *The Dead* by Paul Kane contains three interconnected reprints. *The Forest of Dead Children* by Andrew Hook consists of five mixed-genre stories, a couple quite dark, all but one new. *At Home in the Shadows* by Gary McMahon has two new horror stories and three reprints. *Flowers of War* by Mark Howard Jones has four stories, three of them new. *Shadowcats* by Anna Taborska contains four stories, one of them new, and a new poem. *Suffer Little Children* by Penny Jones has six stories, five of them new.

Skidding Into Oblivion by Brian Hodge (CZP) is the author's sixth book collection. He's become one of the best contemporary authors of short horror fiction. This volume has eleven stories published since 2011, with one new—a dark, science fiction heart stopper about the end times. Hodge also provides story notes.

Growing Things by Paul Tremblay (William Morrow) is an excellent collection containing nineteen dark, weird, creepy, and supernatural stories, two of them new, one related to Tremblay's terrific novel *A Head Full of Ghosts.*

Sefira and other Betrayals by John Langan (Hippocampus Press) is Langan's powerful third collection and it includes seven stories and novelettes and one short novel. Two, including the short novel, *Sefira*, appear for the first time. There are extensive story notes, and an introduction by Paul Tremblay.

Wounds: Six Stories From the Border of Hell by Nathan Ballingrud (Saga Press) is the author's second collection and is a match for his first. The book includes four stories and two novellas. One, *The Visible Filth* has been adapted into the film *Wounds*. The second, *The Butcher's Table*, published for the first time in the collection, is reprinted herein.

Sing Your Sadness Deep by Laura Mauro (Undertow Publications) is the first collection by this British author. There are thirteen stories, two new. One was the winner of the British Fantasy Award. One of the originals is reprinted herein.

The Companion and Other Phantasmagorical Stories by Ramsey Campbell (PS Publishing) is a sampling of Campbell's prodigious output of short fiction over sixty years. The more than thirty stories were chosen by the author.

Houses of the Unholy by JG Faherty (Cemetery Dance Publications) collects eighteen stories, three new ones plus a new novella sequel to the first story in the collection, "The Lazarus Effect." Several are sf/horror.

And Cannot Come Again by Simon Bestwick (CZP) is an excellent new collection of fifteen stories published since 2003, two of them original. With an introduction by Ramsey Campbell and story notes by the author.

The Man Who Escaped This Story and Other Stories by Cody Goodfellow (Independent Legions Publishing) is the author's fifth collection, and contains sixteen reprints and two impressive new stories. With an introduction by the author.

12 Tales Lie: 1 Tells True by Maria Alexander (Ghede Press) is the multi-award winner's first collection of fiction, and features twelve stories, one of them new—plus a creepy new, true story.

Lady Bits by Kate Jonez (Trepidatio Publishing) is an impressive debut collection, with sixteen stories, published since 2012, six of them new.

On the Night Border by James Chambers (Raw Dog Screaming Press) is the author's third full collection (a collection of four Lovecraftian novellas was published in 2011) and it's a strong one. This volume has fifteen stories, three new. With an introduction by Linda D. Addison.

Suicide Woods by Benjamin Percy (Graywolf Press) is the third fiction collection by an author who writes terrific horror and weird stories. The ten here are all reprints, although the excellent final novella was published in two parts, the conclusion in 2019.

Murmured in Dreams by Stephen Bacon (Luna Press) is the author's second powerful collection with nineteen mostly horror stories, two of them new. Three of the stories were reprinted in earlier volumes of my *Best of the Year*. With an introduction by Priya Sharma.

Monks of a Separate Cloth by Darren Speegle (JournalStone) is the author's ninth collection and has thirteen stories, all but the three new ones reprinted from earlier collections.

World of Hurt: Selected Stories by Thomas Tessier (Macabre Ink) is a compilation of twenty-eight novellas and short stories previously published in earlier collections by the author. John Langan has provided the introduction.

In Dreams We Rot by Betty Rocksteady (Trepidatio Publishing) is the debut of a relatively new writer, with twenty stories, two of them new.

Everything Is Fine Now by Steve Rasnic Tem (Omnium Gatherum) is another strong collection by the award-winning short story writer. It features twenty-five stories, two of them new. A second collection by Tem, *The Night Doctor and Other Tales,* is filled with another twenty-five wonderfully haunting stories and was published late December by Centipede Press. Two of the stories are new.

Legends of Cthulhu & Other Nightmares by Sam Stone (Telos) has fifteen stories, almost half Lovecraftian. A few are published here for the first time.

Song for the Unraveling of the World by Brian Evenson (Coffee House Press) features twenty-two weird, dark, and absorbing stories, three of them originally published or reprinted in earlier volumes of my *Best Horror of the Year.*

Out of Water by Sarah Read (Trepidatio Publishing) is the author's first collection, with eighteen horror stories, four new. One of the reprints was taken for *The Best Horror of the Year Volume Ten.* Gemma Files has written the introduction.

Served Cold by Alan Baxter (Grey Matter Press) is a powerful collection, featuring sixteen stories, three of them new and quite chilling. With an introduction by John F. D. Taff.

The Last Ghost and other Stories by Marie O'Regan (Luna Press) is the third collection by the author. It includes seven ghost stories, one new. With story notes.

Where Shadows Gather by Michael Chislett (Sarob Press) is an excellent collection of thirteen ghostly tales, five of them new (a few with the same characters).

Full Throttle by Joe Hill (William Morrow) has thirteen stories, two of them new. One of them, "Late Returns" is a beaut, but not horror.

Not to Be Taken at Bed-Time & Other Strange Stories by Rosa Mulholland (The Swan River Press) is a beautiful little hardcover of the nineteenth century Irish author's seven best supernatural tales. With an introductory essay by Richard Dalby.

The New Annotated H. P. Lovecraft Beyond Arkham edited by Leslie S. Klinger (Liveright) is a must for anyone interested in Lovecraft's fiction. The introduction by Victor LaValle (author of the award-winning Lovecraftian-inspired novella *The Ballad of Black Tom*) acknowledges LaValle's early love for Lovecraft's work and his mature revulsion at the author's racism and xenophobia—and how he subsequently reconciled the two disparate reactions. Leslie Klinger provides a brief preface. The volume itself is filled with twenty-five stories, numerous illustrations, annotations, plus a complete gazetteer of the places mentioned in Lovecraft's fiction.

Number Ninety & Other Ghost Stories by B. M Croker (The Swan River Press) contains fifteen supernatural stories by a bestselling Irish author of the late nineteenth and early twentieth century. With an introduction by Richard Dalby. The cover design is striking, as are all the press's covers, all designed by Meggan Kehrli.

Gaslight, Ghosts, & Ghouls: A Centenary Celebration by R. Chetwynd-Hayes edited by Stephen Jones (PS Publishing) is a career retrospective of the author, who died in 2001. It contains sixteen stories, an extensive interview with Chetwynd-Hayes, conducted by Jo Fletcher and Jones, a bibliography, a photographic section, and much more.

Mixed-genre Collections

On Dark Wings by Stephen Gregory (Valancourt Books) is the first collection by the author best-known for his short novel *The Cormorant*. This thin volume has fourteen stories, six never before published. I admit to being disappointed, as most of the stories are not horror, or even that dark. But for fans of his work, you might take a chance and take a dip. *You Know You Want This* by Kristen Roupenian (Scout Press) is a debut of twelve stories, several never before published. Some of them are dark. For context, Roupenian is the author of "Cat Person," a story in the *New Yorker* that went viral. *Shout Kill Revel Repeat* by Scott R. Jones (Trepidatio Publishing) is another debut, this one by a Canadian writer of science fiction, dark fantasy, and horror, with several of the seventeen stories imbued with a weird mysticism. Three of the stories are new. With an introduction by Ross E. Lockhart. *The Controllers* by Paul Kane (Luna Press) has six stories (two new), a poem, story notes, and bonus material including reproductions of the author's handwritten and typed edits for several of the stories that were written in the late '90s/early oughts. Also included are sketches by the artists who illustrated some of the stories. *And the House Lights Dim* by Tim Major (Luna Press) contains fourteen stories and a novella. Two of the stories are new. One of his stories was reprinted by me in *The Best Horror of the Year Volume Ten*. *Of One Pure Will* by Farah Rose Smith (Egaeus Press) features eighteen weird, gothic, sometimes dark stories (five of them new). *The Ballet of Dr Caligari and Madder Mysteries* by Reggie Oliver (Tartarus Press) takes six stories previously published in the hard-to-find Ex Occidente Press edition of fiction and nonfiction, *Madder Mysteries*, and adds several stories written by Oliver since *Holidays From Hell*, the author's 2017 collection. One story is new. *The Complete Short Stories of Mike Carey* by Mike Carey (Drugstore Indian Press) covers two decades of mixed-genre stories by the author better known as a novelist (particularly for *The Girl With All the Gifts*). Of the eighteen stories, about half of them are new. *Salt Slow* by Julia Armfield (Flatiron Books) is a very promising debut by a British writer whose best work is off-center, sometimes weird and/or dark. Six of the nine stories are new. *Imperfect Commentaries* by Ruthanna Emrys (Lethe Press) has twenty-seven stories and poems and is more often dark fantasy than horror, but Emrys's wonderful "The Litany of Earth" about a survivor of Innsmouth is only one of several of her excellent contemporary riffs on Lovecraft. *Magpie's Ladder* by Richard A. Kirk (PS Publishing) is an excellent debut collection of five dark fantasies, that occasionally slip into horror. Each story is beautifully illustrated by the author. *In the Garden of Rusting Gods* by Patrick K. Freivald (Barking Deer Press) is the author's first collection, including sixteen dark fantasy, weird, and horror stories published between 2013 and 2019, three of them new. With an introduction by Weston Ochse and spot illustrations by Greg Chapman. *The Boughs Withered When I Told You My Dreams* by Maura McHugh (Newcon Press) is another debut collection, this one by a talented author of Irish weird and dark fiction. The twenty stories were published between 2004 and 2019, with four of them new. With an introduction by Kim Newman. *This House of Wounds* by Georgina Bruce (Undertow Publications) is the author's first collection, bringing together sixteen stories, four new, including her British Fantasy Award-winning story "White Rabbit." *All the Things We Never See* by Michael Kelly (Undertow Publications) is Kelly's third collection of weird, often dark fiction. There are thirty-one stories and haiku sets, three new. *Collision* by J. S. Breukelaar Meerkat Press contains eleven stories (three new) and one new novella, in various genres. With an introduction by Angela Slatter. *Last Stop Wellsbourne* by Tom Johnstone (Omnium Gatherum) is a collection of eighteen interrelated stories about the seaside British town of Wellsbourne, where mysterious, often dark things occur. All but seven are new. *A Flowering Wound* by John Howard (The Swan River Press) collects ten stories about people who feel dislocated from where they live and from society. Two stories are new. The little hardcover book has a beautiful wraparound cover designed by Meggan Kehrli with art by Jason Zerillo. *Petals and Violins: Fifteen Unsettling Tales* by D. P. Watt (Tartarus Press) is the perfect self-descriptor for this new volume of Watt's weird and/or dark stories. Seven of them are new. *Something Other* by Jacob Romines (Petrifying Pages) is an all-original collection of twenty-three very brief tales by a new writer. *To Rouse Leviathan* by Matt Cardin (Hippocampus Press) showcases fifteen reprinted cosmic and weird stories and one new novella co-written with Mark McLaughlin. *Keyhole* by Matthew G. Rees (Three Imposters) is a fascinating debut collection of eighteen stories (three reprints) by a Welsh writer to watch. Not really horror but twisted, on occasion. *Rag* by Maryse Meijer (Farrar, Strauss and Giroux) is an excellent second collection of fourteen stories, five of them new. Nothing uncanny or supernatural here, just an extreme darkness of the heart. *The Very*

Best of Caitlín R. Kiernan (Tachyon) is a retrospective of Kiernan's short work with twenty stories that encompass science fiction, dark fantasy, the uncanny, and horror. Introduction by Richard Kadrey.

Chapbooks/Novellas

Your Favorite Band Can't Save You by Scotto Moore (A Tor.com Book) is a charmingly horrific tale about a music blogger who gets caught up with a mysterious singer and her band. I was surprised at how much I ended up enjoying it because rock 'n' roll novels (in this case novella) are usually not my cup of tea. *The Haunting of Tram Car 015* by P. Djèlí Clark (Tor.com) is a charming, fast-moving, dark fantasy taking place in an alternative Cairo of 1912 where magic and technology merge, and sometimes, as in this case, create a problem-a tram car seems possessed. If not by a ghost, than what—and why? Egypt's Ministry of Alchemy, Enchantments, and Supernatural Entities is assigned to investigate—just as a court decision on giving women the right to vote is being decided. *The Monster of Elendhaven* by Jennifer Giesbrecht (Tor.com) is a pitch-black fantasy about a sorcerer and the murderous monster he takes on as his servant, both of whom reside in the plague-racked city of Elendhaven. Nicholas Royle's Nightjar Press published six chapbooks in 2019: two of them, by M. John Harrison and Nicola Freeman, are not horror, although the Harrison contains a touch of the weird. "Jutland" by Lucie McKnight Hardy is a deftly drawn bad dream of domestic horror. "Broad Moor" by Alison Moore is a creepy little excursion into dangerous territory. "Le détective" by HP Tinker comes across like a postmodern shaggy dog story. *So this is it* by Paul Griffiths is a slight ramble into the strange. *Into Bones Like Oil* by Kaaron Warren (Meerkat Press) is a powerful novella about a grief-and-guilt stricken woman who moves into a rooming house haunted by ghosts that nevertheless promises peace and an escape from reality. *To Be Devoured* by Sara Tantlinger (Unnerving Press) is a harrowing novella about a woman obsessed with both vultures and with her lover. *At the Setting of the Sun* (Enigmatic Press) is a chapbook with two traditional, entertaining ghost stories by British writer MPN Sims. *A Love Like Blood* by Simon Bestwick (Dark Minds Press) is a chapbook with two excellent new works: a novelette and a novella. Borderlands Press continues its "Little Books" series with *A*

Little Red Book of Requests by Josh Malerman, featuring three original stories. *A Little White Book of Screams and Whispers* by Thomas Ligotti has eleven mini-interviews with the author, providing a fascinating peek into the mind of this unique fantasist. *La Belle Fleur Sauvage* by Caitlín R. Kiernan (Dark Regions Press) is a gorgeous, post-apocalyptic horror show of interconnected stories making up a novella that takes place twenty-six years after a "plague of the womb" destroys much of the world. *Anaïs Nin At the Grand Guignol* by Robert Levy (Lethe Press) is a very dark fantasy written as an imagined lost volume of Nin's infamous diaries. She becomes enthralled by a star of the grand Guignol: Paula Maxa, "the most murdered woman of all time," being led into grave danger physically and spiritually. *Legionnaire* by C. E. Ward (Sarob Press) is a sort of homage to the traditional adventure/ghost story, and is about a company of French Foreign Legionnaire's assignment to shut down a fort in North Africa, just as WWI is beginning. *The Half-Freaks* by Nicole Cushing (Grimscribe Press) is a handsome hardcover with jacket and interior graced with full color art by Harry O. Morris. It's a darkly weird novella about a hapless guy forced to take on the funeral arrangements for his mother. *Green Tea* by J.S. Le Fanu (The Swan River Press) is a lovely, collectible hardback produced for the 150th anniversary of the publication of this classic story. It's illustrated by Alisdair Wood, has an extensive introduction by Matthew Holmes, an appendix with a "meditation" on the story by Jim Rockhill and Brian J. Showers, plus a section of contemporary assessments of the story compiled by Rockhill and Showers. Also, it comes with a CD of the audio drama recorded by Reggie Chamberlain-King of Belfast's Wireless Mystery Theatre. Overall, quite a package.

POETRY JOURNALS, WEBZINES, ANTHOLOGIES, AND COLLECTIONS

Dwarf Stars 2019 edited by John C. Mannone (Science Fiction and Fantasy Poetry Association) collects the best very short speculative poems published in 2018. The poems are all ten lines or fewer and the prose poems one hundred words or fewer.

*Star*Line* is the official newsletter of the Science Fiction Poetry Association. During 2019 it was edited by Vince Gotera. The journals regularly publish members' science fiction and fantasy poetry—and the rare horror poem. Three issues came out in 2019 and there was good, dark poetry by Joshua Gage and Michelle Muenzler.

HWA Poetry Showcase Volume VI edited by Stephanie M. Wytovich features about fifty different poets (not seen).

Spectral Realms edited by S. T. Joshi and published by Hippocampus Press, is a showcase for weird and dark poetry. Two issues came out in 2019. In addition to original poems there's a section with classic reprints and a review column. There were notable poems by Carl E. Reed, Frank Coffman, Ross Balcom, Abigail Wildes, Ann K. Schwader, Oliver Smith, Wade German, Darrell Schweitzer, and Curtis M. Lawson.

The Place of Broken Things by Linda D. Addison and Alessandro Manzetti (Crystal Lake Publishing) is a fine collection featuring thirty-five dark poems written solo and in collaboration.

Dragonfly and Other Songs of Mourning by Michelle Scalise (Lycan Valley Press) is dark and moving as it deals with pain and grief.

Choking Back the Devil by Donna Lynch (Raw Dog Screaming Press) features some very tasty bites of horror poetry among the thirty-five plus pieces.

The Coven's Hornbook and Other Poems by Frank Coffman (Bold Venture) experiments (as in his previous work) with many poetic forms, often creating miniature stories. There are fifteen sections to the book, the first ten covering traditional horror subjects such as witches, sorcery, hauntings, werewolves, Halloween, vampires, Lovecraft, weirdness, ghouls, and the gruesome.

Oracles From the Black Pool by D. L. Myers (Hippocampus Press) is the first collection by a poet who has been writing and publishing poetry in the tradition of H. P Lovecraft, Robert E. Howard, and Clark Ashton Smith for the past decade.

The Apocalypse Mannequin by Stephanie M. Wytovich (Raw Dog Screaming Press) is an excellent collection of dark poetry, mostly centered around apocalyptic themes.

The Demeter Diaries by Marge Simon and Bryan D. Dietrich (Independent Legions Publishing) is a luscious prose poem retelling of *Dracula*.

The 2019 Rhysling Anthology: The Best Science Fiction, Fantasy & Horror Poetry of 2018 selected by the Science Fiction Poetry Association edited by David C. Kopaska-Merkel (Science Fiction Poetry Association) is used by members to vote for the best short and long poems of the year. The book is separated into two sections: Short Poems First Published in 2018 (86) and Long Poems First Published in 2018 (54 poems). It's a good resource for checking out the poetic side of speculative and horror fiction.

NONFICTION

The Lady from the Black Lagoon: Hollywood Monsters and the Lost Legacy of Milicent Patrick by Mallory O'Meara (Hanover Square Press) is about how the legacy of Patrick, makeup artist, special effects designer, and one of the first female animators for Disney, was buried by sexism. *Parenting in the Zombie Apocalypse: The Psychology of Raising Children in a Time of Horror* by Steven J. Kirsh (McFarland). Drawing on psychological theory and real-world research on developmental status, grief, trauma, mental illness, and child-rearing in stressful environments, this book critically examines factors influencing parenting, and the likely outcomes of different caregiving techniques in the hypothetical landscape of the living dead. *West of Wherevermore and Other Essays* by Donald Sydney-Fryer (Hippocampus Press) is a collection of travel essays, reviews, two accounts of Lovecraft conventions in Providence, Rhode Island, and a series of poetic experiments. *The Black Pilgrimage & Other Exploration: Essays on Supernatural Fiction* by Rosemary Pardoe (Shadow Publishing) collects all of Pardoe's essays on M. R. James's ghost stories. Also included are essays on the work of Fritz Leiber, E. G. Swain, and Manly Wade Wellman, plus miscellaneous pieces on Phil Rickman, Megan Lindholm, Paul Cornell, and others. Pardoe was a co-founder of what is now known as the British Fantasy Society, and might best be known for her editorship of *Ghosts & Scholars* and *The Ghosts & Scholars M. R. James Newsletter. H. P. Lovecraft, Lord of the Visible World: An Autobiography in Letters* edited by S. T. Joshi and David E. Schultz (Hippocampus Press) is an updated edition of the book originally published by a Ohio University Press in 2000. *Letters of Lovecraft volume XIII: Letters to Wilfred B. Talman and Helen V. and Genevieve Sully* edited David E. Schultz and S. T. Joshi (Hippocampus Press), as with earlier volumes, this tremendously valuable resource contains a bounty of correspondence between Lovecraft and his contemporaries covering philosophy, discussions of various cities and people they visited, writing, etc. *Lovecraftian Proceedings No. 3* edited by Dennis P.

Quinn (Hippocampus Press) is the official organ of the Dr. Henry Armitage Memorial Symposium established in 2013 as part of NecronomiCon, in Providence, Rhode Island. The symposium "fosters exploration of Lovecraft as a rationalist who created and elaborate cosmic mythology, and how this mythology was influenced by, and has come to influence, numerous other authors and artists." This volume has a collection of twelve papers from the 2017 Symposium. *Black Celebration* edited by Sumiko Saulson (self-published) is a collection of articles, essays, and interviews with and by African American horror writers on black representation in horror. *Shapeshifters A History* by John B. Kachuba (Reaktion Books) is a history of the myths and legends and fairy tales that abound in different cultures around the world about such creatures as vampires, werewolves, skinwalkers, demons, etc. *Celebrity Ghosts and other Notorious Hauntings* by Marie D. Jones (Visible Ink) is a fun book to dip into, but actually spends only a bit of its time on purported celebrity hauntings. Instead it covers haunted battlefields, ships, hotels, plantations, prisons, and other venues where ghosts have been spotted, plus urban legends, and personal experiences. *Bela Lugosi and the Monogram 9* by Gary D. Rhodes, and Robert Guffey (BearManor) is a loving study of nine movies made with Bela Lugosi between 1941 and 1944. *Monster, She Wrote: The Women Who Pioneered Horror and Speculative Fiction* Lisa Kröger and Melanie R. Anderson (Quirk Books) is a good introductory survey of women writers from Margaret Cavendish of the seventeenth century to the current crop including Lauren Beukes, Rebecca Roanhorse, and Cassandra Khaw. *H. P. Lovecraft: Letters with Donald and Howard Wandrei and to Emil Petaja* edited by S. T. Joshi and David E. Schultz (Hippocampus Press) is a deep dive into Lovecraft's correspondence with his peers on all sorts of subjects, personal and professional. With extensive notes by the co-editors. *Providence After Dark and Other Wri*tings by T. E. D. Klein (Hippocampus Press) is a mix of essays, book and movie reviews, convention reports, and professional memoir. S. T. Joshi compiled the book. *Weird Tales: Essays on Robert E. Howard and Others* by Bobby Derie (Hippocampus Press) is a collection of twenty-six essays ranging from the correspondence between Howard and H. P. Lovecraft to Howard's mentions of marijuana use in his fiction. *Darkly: Blackness and America's Gothic Soul* by Leila Taylor (Repeater Press) is a rich, fascinating memoir/cultural critique by an African American, former Goth kid examining her experience as an outsider within an outsider culture. *Fear: The Autobiography of Dario Argenti* adapted, illustrated, and annotated by Alan Jones (FAB Press) covers the filmmaker's childhood and his career.

ODDS AND ENDS

Come Join Us By the Fire is the first in what is intended as a series of audio-only anthologies edited by Theresa DeLucci for Tor's new Nightfire horror imprint. The first volume of thirty-five short stories is mostly reprints (two are new—by Stephen Graham Jones and Kat Howard).

The Ghost Box III edited by Patton Oswalt (Hingston + Olsen) is a collectable package of eleven reprinted ghost stories from writers ranging from Richard Matheson, Terence Taylor, Poppy Z. Brite, Livia Llewellyn, and seven others. Each story is an individual chapbook and all are in a black box with a black satin ribbon.

The Twilight Man by Koren Shadmi (Humanoids) is an entertaining (and moving) graphic novel adaptation of the life and career of the great Rod Serling, creator of one of the most iconic television shows in the medium's history.

THE BEST HORROR OF THE YEAR

VOLUME TWELVE

~~ICE COLD LEMONADE 25¢~~
HAUNTED HOUSE TOUR: 1 PER PERSON

PAUL TREMBLAY

I was such a loser when I was a kid. Like a John-Hughes-Hollywood-Eighties-movie-typecast loser. Maybe we all imagine ourselves as being that special kind of ugly duckling with the truth being too scary to contemplate: maybe I was someone's bully or I was the kid who egged on the bullies screaming "Sweep the leg," or maybe I was lower than the Hughes loser, someone who would never be shown in a movie.

When I think of who I was all those years ago, I'm both embarrassed and look-at-what-I've-become proud, as though the distance spanned between those two me's can only be measured in light years. That distance is a lie, of course, though perhaps necessary to justify perceived successes and mollify the disappointments and failures. That thirteen-year-old-me is still there inside: the socially awkward one who wouldn't find a group he belonged to until college; the one who watched way too much TV and listened to records while lying on the floor with the speakers tented over his head; the one who was afraid of the *Jaws* shark appearing in any body of water, Christopher

Lee vampires, the dark in his closet and under the bed, and the blinding flash of a nuclear bomb. That kid is all too frighteningly retrievable at times.

Now he's here in a more tangible form. He's in the contents of a weathered cardboard box sitting like a toadstool on my kitchen counter. Mom inexplicably plopped this time capsule in my lap on her way out the door after an impromptu visit. When I asked for an explanation, she said she thought I should have it. I pressed her for more of the *why* and she said, "Well, because it's yours. It's your stuff," as though she was weary of the burden of having had to keep it for all those years.

Catherine is visiting her parents on the Cape and she took our daughter Izzy with her. I stayed home to finish edits (which remain stubbornly unfinished) on a manuscript that was due last week. Catherine and Izzy would've torn through this box-of-me right away and laughed themselves silly at the old photos of my stick figure body and my map of freckles and crooked teeth, the collection of crayon renderings of dinosaurs with small heads and ludicrously large bodies, and the fourth grade current events project on Ronald Reagan for which I'd earned a disappointing C+ and a demoralizing teacher comment of "too messy." And I would've reveled in their attention, their warm spotlight shinning on who I was and who I've become.

I didn't find it until my second pass through the box, which seems impossible as I took care to peel old pictures apart and handle everything delicately as one might handle ancient parchments. That second pass occurred two hours after the first, and there was a pizza and multiple beers and no edits between.

The drawing that I don't remember saving was there at the bottom of the box, framed by the cardboard and its interior darkness. I thought I'd forgotten it; I know I never had.

The initial discovery was more confounding than dread inducing, but hours have passed and now it's late and it's dark. I have every light on in the house, which only makes the dark outside even darker. I am alone and I am on alert and I feel time creeping forward (time doesn't run out; it continues forward and it continues without you). I do not sit in any one room for longer than five minutes. I pass through the lower level of the house as quietly as I can, like an omniscient, emotionally distant narrator, which I am not. On the TV is a baseball game that I don't care about, blaring at full volume. I consider going to my car and driving to my in-law's on the Cape, which would be ridiculous as I wouldn't arrive until well after midnight and Catherine and Izzy are coming home tomorrow morning.

Would it be so ridiculous?

Tomorrow when my family returns home and the windows are open and the sunlight is as warm as a promise, I will join them in laughing at me. But it is not tomorrow and they are not here.

I am glad they're not here. They would've found the drawing before I did.

I rode my bicycle all over Beverly, Massachusetts the summer of 1984. I didn't have a BMX bike with thick, knobby tires made for ramps and wheelies and chewing up and spitting out dirt and pavement. Mine was a dinged up, used-to-belong-to-my-dad ten-speed and the only things skinnier and balder than the tires were my arms and legs. On my rides I always made sure to rattle by Kelly Bishop's house on the off-off-chance I'd find her in her front yard. Doing what? Who knows. But in those fantasies she waved or nodded at me. She would ask what I was doing and I'd tell her all nonchalant-like that I was heading back to my house, even though she'd have to know her dead end street wasn't exactly on my way home. Pesky details were worked out or inconsequential in fantasies, of course.

One afternoon it seemed part of my fantasy was coming true when Kelly and her little sister were at the end of their long driveway, sitting at a small fold-up table with a pitcher of lemonade. I couldn't bring myself to stop or slow down or even make more than glancing eye contact. I had no money for lemonade therefore I had no reason to stop. Kelly shouted at me as I rolled by. Her greeting wasn't a 'Hey there' or even a 'Hi', but instead, "Buy some lemonade or we'll pop your tires!"

After twenty-four hours of hopeful and fearful *should I or shouldn't I,* I went back the next day with a pocket full of quarters. Kelly was again stationed at the end of her driveway. My breaks squealed as I jerked to an abrupt and uncoordinated stop. My rusted kickstand screamed with *you're really doing this?* embarrassment. The girls didn't say anything and watched my approach with a mix of disinterest and what I imagined to be the look I gave ants before I squashed them.

They sat at the same table setup as the previous day but there was no pitcher of lemonade. Never afraid to state the obvious, I said, "So, um, no lemonade today?" The fifty cents clutched in my sweaty hand might as well have melted.

Kelly said, "Lemonade was yesterday. Can't you read the sign?" She sat slumped in her beach chair, a full body eye-roll, and her long, tanned legs spilled out from under the table and the white poster-board sign taped to the front. She wore a red Coke tee shirt. Her chestnut brown hair was pulled into a side-high ponytail, held up by a black scrunchie. Kelly was clearly well into her pubescent physical transformation whereas I was still a boy, without even a shadow of hair under my armpits.

Kelly's little sister with the bowl-cut mop of dirty blonde hair was going to be in second grade; I didn't know her name and was too nervous to ask. She covered her mouth, fake-laughed and wobbled like a penguin in her unstable chair. That she might topple into the table or to the blacktop didn't seem to bother Kelly.

"You're supposed to be the smart one, Paul," Kelly added.

"Heh, yeah, sorry." I left the quarters in my pocket to hide their shame and adjusted my blue gym shorts; they were too short, even for the who-wears-short-shorts 80s. I tried to fill the chest of my *NBA Champs* Celtics tee shirt with deep breaths, but only managed to stir a weak ripple in the green cloth.

Their updated sign read:

~~Ice Cold Lemonade 25¢~~ Haunted House Tour: 1 Per Person

Seemed straightforward enough but I didn't know what to make of it. I feared it was some kind of a joke or prank. Were Rick or Winston or other jerks hiding close by to jump out and pants me? I thought about hopping back on my bike and getting the hell out before I did something epically cringe-worthy Kelly would later describe in detail to all her friends and by proxy the entire soon-to-be seventh grade class.

Kelly asked, "Do you want a tour of our creepy old house or not?"

I stammered and I sweated. I remember sweating a lot.

Kelly told me the lemonade stand thing was boring and that her new haunted-house-tour idea was genius. I would be their first to go on the tour so I'd be helping them out. She said, "We'll even only charge you half price. Be a pal, Paulie."

Was Kelly Bishop inviting me into her house? Was she making fun of me? The "be a pal" bit sounded like joke and felt like a joke. I looked around the front yard, spying between the tall front hedges, looking for the ambush. I decided I didn't care, and said, "Okay, yeah."

The little sister shouted, "One dollar," and held out an open hand.

Kelly corrected her. "I said 'half-price.'"

"What's half?"

"Fifty cents."

Little sis shouted, "Fifty cents!" her hand still out.

I paid, happy to be giving the sweaty quarters to her and not Kelly.

I asked, "Is it scary, I mean, supposed to be scary?" I tried smiling bravely. I wasn't brave. I still slept with my door open and the hallway light on. My smile was pretend brave, and it wasn't much of a smile as I tried not to show off my mouth of metal braces, the elastics on either side mercifully no longer necessary as of three weeks ago.

Kelly stood and said, "Terrifying. You'll wet yourself and be sucking your thumb for a week." She whacked her sister on the shoulder and commanded, "Go. You have one minute to be ready."

"I don't need a minute." She bounced across the lawn onto the porch and slammed the front door closed behind her.

Kelly flipped through a stack of notecards. She said she hadn't memorized the script yet but she would eventually.

I followed her down the driveway to the house I never thought of as scary or creepy but now that it had the word *haunted* attached to it, even in jest . . .it was kind of creepy. The only three-family home in the neighborhood, it looked impossibly tall from up close. And it was old, worn out, the white paint peeling and flaking away. Its stone and mortar foundation appeared crooked. The windows were tall and thin and impenetrable. The small front porch had two skeletal posts holding up a warped overhang that could come crashing down at any second.

We walked up the stairs to the porch, and the wood felt soft under my feet. Kelly was flipping through her notecards and held the front screen door open for me with a jutted out hip. I scooted by, holding my breath, careful to not accidentally brush against her.

The cramped front hallway/foyer was crowded with bikes and shovels and smelled like wet leaves. A poorly lit staircase curled up to the right. Kelly told me that the tour finishes on the second floor and we weren't allowed all the way upstairs to the third, and that she had written "one per person" on the sign so that no pervs would try for repeat tours since she and her sister were home by themselves.

"Your parents aren't home?" My voice cracked, as if on cue.

If Kelly answered with a nod of the head, I didn't see it. She reached across me, opened the door to my left and said, "Welcome to House Black, the most haunted house on the North Shore."

Kelly put one hand between my shoulder blades and pushed me inside to a darkened kitchen. The linoleum was sandy, gritty, under my shuffling sneakers. The room smelled of dust and pennies. The shapes of the table, chairs, and appliances were sleeping animals. From somewhere on this first floor, her sister gave a witchy laugh. It was muffled and I remember thinking it sounded like she was inside the walls.

Kelly carefully narrated: The house was built in the 1700s by a man named Robert or Reginald Black, a merchant sailor who was gone for months at a time. His wife, Denise would dutifully wait for him in the kitchen. After all the years of his leaving, Denise was driven mad by a lonely heart and she wouldn't go anywhere else in the house but the kitchen until he returned home. She slept sitting in a wooden chair and washed herself in the kitchen sink. Years passed like this. Mr. Black was to take one final trip before retiring but Mrs. Black had had enough. As he ate his farewell breakfast she smashed him over the head with an iron skillet until he was dead. Mrs. Black then stuffed her husband's body into the oven.

The kitchen's overhead light, a dirty yellow fixture, flashed on. I saw a little hand leave the switch and disappear behind a door across the room from me. On top of the oven was a cast iron, black skillet. Little sis flashed her arm back into the room and turned out the light.

Kelly loomed over me (she was at least three inches taller) and said that this was not the same oven, and everyone who ever lived here has tried getting a new one, but you can still sometimes hear Mr. Black clanging around inside.

The oven door dropped open with a metal scream, like when an ironing board's legs were pried opened.

I jumped backward and knocked into the kitchen table.

Kelly hissed, "That's too hard, be careful! You're gonna rip the oven door off!"

Little sis dashed into the room and I could see in her hands a ball of fishing line, which was tethered to the oven door handle.

Kelly asked me what I thought of the tour opener, if I found it satisfactory. I swear that is the phrasing she used.

Mortified that I'd literally jumped and sure that she could hear my heart rabbiting in my chest, I mumbled, "Yeah, that was good."

The tour moved on throughout the darkened first floor. All of the see-through lace curtains were drawn and either Kelly or little sis would turn a room's light on and off during Kelly's readings. Most of the stories featured the hapless descendants of the Blacks. The dining room's story was unremarkable as was the story for the living room, which was the largest room on the first floor. I'd begun to lose focus, and let my mind wander to Kelly and what she was like when her parents were home and then, perhaps oddly, what her parents were like, and if they were like mine. My dad had recently moved from the Parker Brothers factory to managing one of their warehouses and Mom worked part-time as a bank teller. I wondered what Kelly's parents did for work and if they sat in the kitchen and discussed their money problems too. Were her parents kind? Were they too kind? Were they overbearing or unreasonable? Were they perpetually distracted? Did they argue? Were they cold? Were they cruel? I still wonder these things about everyone else's parents.

Kelly did not take me into her parents' bedroom, saying simply, "Under construction," as we passed by the closed door.

I suggested that she make up a story about something or someone terrible kept hidden behind the door.

Kelly to this point had kept her nose in her script cards and jotted down notes with a pencil when not watching for my reaction. Her head snapped up at me and she said, "None of these are made-up stories, Paul."

There was another bedroom, the one directly off the kitchen, and it was being used as an office/sitting room. There was a desk and bookcases tracing the wall's boundaries. The walls were covered in brownish-yellow wallpaper and the circular throw rug was dark too; I don't remember the colors. It's as though color didn't exist there. The room was sepia, like a memory. In the middle of the room was a rolling chair, and on the chair was a form covered by a white sheet.

Kelly had to coax me into the room. I kept a wide berth between me and the sheeted figure, aware of the possibility that there was someone under there waiting to jump out and grab me. Though the closer I got, the shape wasn't uniform and the proportions were all off. It wasn't a single body; the shape was comprised of more shapes.

Kelly said that the ghost of a man named Darcy Dearborn (I remember his alliterative name) haunts this room. A real estate mogul, he purchased the house in 1923. He lost everything but the house in the 1929 stock market crash and was forced to rent the second and third floors out to strangers. He took to sitting in this room and listening to his tenants above walking around, going about their day. Kelly paused here and looked up at the ceiling expectantly. I did too. Eventually we could hear little footsteps running along the second floor above us. The running stopped and became loud thuds. Little sis was jumping up and down in place, mashing her feet into the floor. Kelly said, "She's such a little shit," shook her head, and continued with the story. Darcy, much like Mrs. Black from all those years before, became housebound and wouldn't leave this room. Local family and neighbors bought his groceries for him and took care of collecting his rent checks and doing his banking and everything else for him, until one day they didn't. Darcy stayed in the room and in his chair and he died and no one found him until years later and he'd almost completely decomposed and faded away. His ghost shuts the doors to the office when they are open.

The door to the kitchen behind us opened and shut.

I remember thinking the Darcy story had holes in it. I remember thinking it was too much like the first Mrs. Black story, which muted its impact. But then I became paranoid that Kelly had tailored these stories for me somehow. Was she implying that I was doomed to be a loner, a shut-in because I stayed home by myself too much? I had one new friend I'd met in sixth grade but he lived in North Beverly and spent much of his summer in Maine and I couldn't go see him very often. I wasn't friends with anyone in my neighborhood. That's not an exaggeration. Throughout that summer, particularly if I'd spent the previous day watching TV or shooting hoops in the driveway by myself, Mom would give me an errand (usually sending me down the street to the White Hen Pantry convenience store to buy her a pack of cigarettes—you could do that in the 80s) and then tell me to invite some friends over. She never mentioned any kids by name because there were no kids to mention by name. I told her I would but would then go ride my bike instead. That was good enough for Mom, or maybe it wasn't and she knew I wasn't really going to see or play with anyone. Mom now still reacts with an unbridled joy that comes too close to open shock and surprise when she hears of my many adult friends.

I envisioned myself becoming a sun-starved, Gollum-like adult, cloistered in my sad bedroom at home until Kelly led me out of the first floor living space to the cramped and steep staircase. The stairs were a dark wood with a darker stair tread or runner. The walls were panels or planks of the same dark wood. I was never a sailor like Mr. Black, but it was easy to imagine that we were climbing up from the belly of a ship.

Kelly said that a girl named Kathleen died on the stairwell in 1937. Kathleen used to send croquet balls crashing down the stairs. Her terrible father with arms and hands that were too long for his body got so sick of her doing it, he snuck up behind her and nudged her off the second floor landing. She fell and tumbled and broke her neck and died. There was an inquest and her father was never charged. However, his wife knew her husband was lying about not being responsible for Kathleen's death and the following summer she poisoned him and herself while picnicking at Lynch Park. At night you can hear Kathleen giggling (Kelly's sister obliged from above at that point in the tale) and the rattles and knocks of croquet balls bouncing down the stairs. And if you're not holding the railing, you'll feel those cold, extra-large hands push you or grab your ankles.

I wasn't saying much of anything in response at this point and was content to be there with Kelly, knowing I would likely never spend this much time alone with her again. I was scared but it was the good kind of scared because it was shared if not quite commiserative.

The second floor landing was bright with sunlight pouring through the uncovered four-paned window next to the second floor's front door. It was only then that I realized each floor was constructed as separate apartments or living spaces, and since I hadn't seen their rooms downstairs, that meant Kelly's and her sister's bedrooms must be here upstairs, away from her parents' bedroom. I couldn't imagine sleeping that far away from my parents, and future live-at-home-shut-in or not, I felt bad for her and her sister.

Inside there was a second kitchen that was bright and sparkled with disuse. The linoleum and cabinets were white. I wondered (but didn't ask) if the two of them ate up here alone for breakfast or at night for dinner, and I again thought about Kelly's parents and what kind of people would leave them alone in the summer and essentially in their own apartment.

The tour didn't linger in the kitchen nor did we stop in what she called the playroom, which had the same dimensions as the dining room below on the first floor. Perhaps she didn't want to make their playroom a scary place.

We went into her sister's room next. I only remember the pink wallpaper, an unfortunate shade of Pepto-Bismol, and the army of stuffed animals staged on the floor and all facing me. There were a gaggle of teddy bears and a stuffed Garfield and a Pink Panther and a rat wearing a green fedora and a doe-eyed Brontosaurus and more, and they all had black marble eyes. Kelly said, "Oops," and turned off the overhead light.

The story for this room was by far the most gruesome.

John and Genie Graham bought the house in 1952 and they had a little boy named Will. To make ends meet the family rented the top two floors to strangers. The stranger on the second floor was named Gregg with two g's, and the third floor tenant was named Rolph, not Ralph. Very little is known about the two men. For the two years of the Gregg with two g's and Rolph occupancy, Will would periodically complain he couldn't find one of his many stuffed animal companions and insisted that someone stole it. He had so many stuffed animals that with each individual complaint his parents were sure the missing critter was simply misplaced or kicked under the bed or he'd taken it to the park and left it behind. Then there were locals who complained that Rolph wasn't coming to work anymore and wasn't seen at the grocery store or the bar he liked to go to, and that he too was misplaced. Then there was a smell coming from the second floor and they initially feared an animal had died in the walls, and then those fears became something else. When Mr. and Mrs. Graham entered the second floor apartment with the police, Gregg with two g's was nowhere to be found. But they found Will's missing stuffed animals. They were all sitting in this room like they were now and they were blood stained and tattered and they smelled terribly. Hidden within the plush hides of the stuffed animals were hacked up pieces of Rolph, the former third-floor tenant. There were rumors of Gregg with two g's living in Providence and Fall River and more alarmingly close by in Salem, but no one ever found him. Kelly said that stuffed animals in this house go missing and then reappear in this bedroom by themselves, congregating with each other in the middle of the floor on their own, patiently waiting for their new stuffing.

"That's a really terrible story," I said in a breathless way that meant the opposite.

"Paul! It's not a story," Kelly said but she looked at me and smiled. I'll not describe that look or that smile beyond saying I'll remember both (along with a different look from her, one I got a few months after the tour), for as long as those particular synapses fire within my brain.

Kelly led me to a final room, her bedroom in the back of the house. The room was brightly lit; shades pulled up and white curtains open. Her walls were white and might've been painted over clapboard or paneling and decorated with posters of Michael Jackson, Duran Duran, and other musicians. There was a clothes bureau that seemed to have been jigsawed together using different pieces of wood. Its top was a landfill of crumpled up notes, used candy wrappers, loose change, barrettes, and other teen debris. At the foot of her bed was a large chest covered by a knit afghan. On opposite walls of each other were a small desk and a bookcase that was half-full with books, the rest of space claimed by dolls and knickknacks. The floor was hardwood with a small baby-chick yellow rectangular patch of rug by her bed, which was flush against the wall and under two windows overlooking the back yard.

Kelly didn't say anything right away and I stared at everything but her, more nervous to be in this room than any other. I said, "You have a cool room." I might've said "nice" instead of cool, but god, I hope I didn't.

I don't remember if Kelly said, "Thanks," or not. She pocketed her notecards, walked ahead of me, sat on the rug, and faced her bed. She said, "I dream about it every night. I wish it would stop."

I hadn't noticed it until she said what she said. There was a sketch propped up by a bookend on the middle of her bed. I sat down next to Kelly. I asked, "Did you draw that?"

She nodded and didn't look at me. She didn't even look at me when I was staring at her profile for what felt like the rest of the summer. Then I too stared at the drawing.

The left side of its cartoonish head was misshapen, almost like a bite had been taken out, and the left eye was missing. Its right eye was round and blackened by slashes instead of a pupil. The mouth was a horrible band of triangular teeth spanning the horizontal circumference. Three strips of skin stretched from the top half of the head over the mouth and teeth and wrapped under its chin. What appeared to be a forest of wintered branches stuck out from all over its head. The wraith-like body was all angles and slashes and the arms were elongated triangles reaching out. It had no legs. The jagged bottom of its floating form ended in larger versions of its shark teeth.

There are things I don't remember about that day in Kelly's house and many other things I'm sure I've embellished (though not purposefully so). But I remember when I first saw the drawing and how it made me feel. While this might sound like an adult's perspective, I'm telling you that this was the first time I realized or intellectualized that I would be dead someday. Sitting on the bedroom floor next to the cute girl of my adolescent daydreams, I looked at the drawing and imagined my death, the final closing of my eyes and the total and utter blankness and emptiness of . . .I could only think of the phrase "not-me." The void of not-me. I wondered if the rest of my life would pass like how summer vacations passed—would I be about to die and asking *how did it all go so quickly?* I wondered how long and what part of me would linger in nothingness and if I'd feel pain or cold or anything at all, and I tried to shake it all away by saying to Kelly, "Wow, that's really good."

"Good?"

"The drawing. Yeah. It's good. And creepy."

Kelly didn't respond, but I was back inside her sunny bedroom and sitting on the floor instead of lost inside my own head. I asked and pointed, "What are the things sticking out? They look like branches."

She told me she tried to make up a story for this ghost, like maybe the girl who lived in the house before Kelly was sneaking around peeking into houses and sometimes stealing little things and bits no one would miss (like a thumbtack or an almost used up spool of red thread) and she got caught by someone and was chased and in desperation she ran behind the house and she got stuck or trapped in the woods and she died within sight of her big old ratty house. But that didn't feel like the true story, or the right story. It certainly wasn't the real reason for the ghost.

Kelly told me this ghost appeared in her dreams every night. The dreams varied but the ghost was always the same ghost. Sometimes she was not in her body and she witnessed everything from a remove, like she was a movie camera. Most times Kelly was Kelly and she saw everything through her own eyes. The most common dream featured Kelly alone in a cornfield that had already been cut and harvested. Dark, impenetrable woods surrounded the field on all sides. She heard a low voice laughing, but then it was also a high-pitched, so it was both at the same time. (She said 'both at the same time' twice). Her heart beat loud enough that she thought it was the full moon thumping down at her, giving her a Morse code message to run. Even though she was terrified she ran into the woods because it was the only way to get back to her house. She ran through the forest and night air as thick as paint and she got close to her backyard and she could see her house, but no lights were on so it was all in shadow and looked like a giant tombstone. Then the ghost came streaming for her from the direction of the house and she knew her house was a traitor because it was where the ghost stayed while it patiently waited for this night and for Kelly. It was so dark but she could see the ghost and its horrible smile bigger than that heartbeat moon. And the dream ended the same way every time.

"I hear myself scream but it sounds far away, like I'm below, in the ground, and then I die. I remember what it feels like to die until I wake up, and then it fades away, but not all the way away," Kelly said. She rocked forward and back and rubbed her hands together, staring at the drawing.

The ceiling above us creaked and groaned with someone taking slow, heavy, careful steps. Kelly's little sister wasn't around and I hadn't remembered seeing her since we got up to the second floor. I figured sis was walking above us wearing adult-sized boots. A nice touch for what I assumed was the tour's finale.

I said something commiserative to Kelly about having nightmares too.

She said, "I think it's a real ghost, you know. This is the realest one. It comes every night for me. And I'm afraid maybe it's the ghost of me."

"Like a doppelganger?"

Kelly smirked and rolled her eyes again but it wasn't as dismissive as I'm describing. She playfully hit my non-existent bicep with a backhand, and despite my earlier glimpse at understanding the finality of death I would've been happy to die right then. She said, "You're the smart one, Paul, you have to tell me what that is."

So I did. Or I gave her the best close-enough general definition that the thirteen-year-old me could muster.

There were more footsteps on the floor above us, moving away to other rooms but still loud and creaking.

She said, "Got it. It's kind of like a doppelganger but not really. It's not a future version of me, I don't think. I think it's the ghost of a part of me that I ignore. Or the ghost of some piece of me that I should ignore. We all have those parts, right? What if those other parts trapped inside of us find a way to get out? Where do they go and what do they do? I have a part that gets out in my dreams and I'm afraid that I'm going to hear it outside of me for real. I know I am. I'm going to hear it outside of me in a crash somewhere in the house where there isn't supposed to be, or I'll hear it in a creak in the ceiling, and maybe I'll even hear it walking up behind me. I don't know if that makes any sense and I don't think I'm explaining it well but that's what I think it is."

Little sis burst out of Kelly's closet and crashed dramatically onto the chest at the end of her bed, and shouted, "Boo!"

Kelly and I both were startled and we laughed and if you'd asked me then I would've thought we would've been friends forever after instead of my never speaking to her again after that day.

As our laughter died out and Kelly berated her sister for scaring her, I realized that little sis jumped out of a closet and not from behind a door to another room that had easy access to the rest of the apartment and the stairwell to the third floor.

I said to little sis, "Aren't you upstairs? I mean, that was you upstairs we heard walking around, right?"

She shook her head and giggled, and then there were creaks and footstep tremors in the floor above us again. They were loud enough to shake dust from the walls and blow clouds in front of the sun outside.

I asked, "Who's upstairs?"

Kelly looked at the ceiling and was expressionless. "No one is supposed to up there. The third floor is empty. We're going to rent it out in the fall. We're home alone."

I made 'come on' and 'really?' and 'you're not joking?' noises, and then in my memory—which for this brief period of time is more like a dream than something that actually happened—the continuum skips forward to me following Kelly and her sister out into the hallway and the stairwell to the third floor. Little sis led the way and Kelly was behind me. I kept asking questions (is this a good idea? are you sure you want to end the tour all the way up on the third floor?) and the questions turned to poorly veiled begging, my saying that I should probably get home, we ate dinner early in my house, Mom was a worrier, et cetera. All the while I flowed up the stairs and Kelly shushed me and told me to be quiet. The stairwell thinned and squeezed and curled up into a small landing, or a perch. An eave intruded into the headspace to the left of the third floor apartment's door. The three of us sardined onto that precarious landing that felt like a cliff. There was no more discussion and little sis opened the door, deftly skittered aside, and like she had on the first floor, Kelly two-handed shoved me inside.

This apartment was clearly smaller than the first two with the A-frame roof slanting the ceilings, intruding into the living space. I stepped into a small, gray kitchen that smelled musty from disuse. Directly across the room from me was a long, dark hallway. It was as though the ceilings and their symmetrical slants were constructed with the sole purpose of focusing my stare into this dark tunnel. There wasn't a hallway like this in either of the other apartments; the third-floor layout was totally different and the thought of wandering about with no idea of the floor plan and fearing that I would find whatever it was making the walking noises made me want to swallow my own tongue.

Little sis ran ahead of me, giggling into the hallway and disappearing in the back end of the apartment. I still held out hope that maybe it was her, somehow, who was responsible for walking noises, when I knew it wasn't possible. I stood for a long time only a few steps deep into the kitchen, which grew darker, and watched as the hallway grew darker still, and then a stooped figure emerged from an unseen room and into the gloom of the hallway. The whole apartment creaked and shook with each step. It was the shadowy ghost of a man and he diffused into the hallway, filling it like smoke, and my skin became electric and I think I ran in place like a cartoon character might, sliding my feet back and forth on the linoleum.

An old man emerged into the weak lighting of the kitchen shuffling along with the help of a wooden, swollen-headed shillelagh. He wore a sleeveless tee-shirt and tan pants with a black belt knotted tightly around his waist. An asterisk of thin, white hair dotted the top of his head and the same unruly tuft sprouted out from under the collar of his tee shirt. His eyes were big and rheumy, like a bloodhound's eyes, and he smirked at me, but before he could say anything I screamed and ran through Kelly and out of the apartment.

On the second step I heard him call out (his voice quite friendly and soothing), "Hey, what are all you silly kids up to?" and then I was around a corner, knocking into a wall and clutching onto the handrail, and maybe halfway down when I heard Kelly laughing, and then shout, "Wait, Paul! Come meet my grandfather. Tour's over!"

I just about tumbled onto the second floor landing with everyone else still upstairs calling after me. I was crying almost uncontrollably and I was seething, so angry at Kelly and her sister and myself. I don't know why I was so angry. Sure they set me up, but it was harmless, and part of the whole ghost tour/haunted house idea. I know now they weren't making fun of me, per se, and they weren't being cruel. But back then, *cruel* was my default assumption setting. So I was filled with moral indignation and the kind of irrational anger that leads erstwhile good people to make terrible, petty decisions.

I ran back into the second floor apartment and to Kelly's bedroom. I took the drawing of her ghost off the bed, tucked it inside my tee shirt, ran back out of the apartment and then down the stairs and out of the house and to my bike, and I pedaled home without ever once looking back. I didn't ride my bike by Kelly's house the rest of that summer.

I can't remember planning what I was going to do with her drawing. I might've initially intended to burn it with matches and a can of Mom's hairspray (I was a bit of a firebug back then . . .) or something similarly stupid and juvenile. But I didn't burn it or crumple it up. I didn't even fold it in half. Any creepiness/weirdness attributed to the drawing was swamped by my anger and then my utter embarrassment at my lame response to her grandfather scaring me. I knew I totally blew it; Kelly and I could've been friends if I'd laughed and stayed and met her grandfather and maybe middle school and high school would've gone differently, wouldn't have been as miserable.

While on occasion I had nightmares of climbing all those steps in the Bishop house by myself, I don't remember having any nightmares featuring the ghost in the drawing even though I was (and still am) a card-carrying scaredy cat. I wasn't afraid to keep the drawing in my room. I hid it on the bottom of my bureau's top drawer along with a few of my favorite baseball cards. While I obsessively picked through the play-by-play of that afternoon in Kelly's house and what she must've thought of me after, I never really focused on the drawing and would only ever look it by accident, when the top drawer was all but empty of socks or underwear and I'd find that toothy grin peering up at me. Then one day toward the end of that summer the drawing was gone. It's possible I threw it away without remembering doing so (I mean, I don't remember what happened to the baseball cards I kept in there either). Maybe Mom found it when she was putting away my clean clothes and did something with it, which would explain how it got to be in her box of kid-stuff keepsakes, but Mom taking it and never saying anything to me about taking it seems off. Mom fawned over my grades and artwork.

She would've made it a point to tell me how good the drawing was. Her taking the picture and putting it on the fridge? Yes, that would've happened. But her secreting it away for safe keeping? That wasn't her.

That summer melted away and seventh grade at Memorial Middle school was hell, as seventh grade is hell for everyone. The students were separated into three teams (Black, White, and Red) with four teachers in each team. The teams never mixed classes, so you might never see a friend in Black team if you were in Red team and vice versa. Kelly wasn't in my team and I didn't even pass her in the hallways at school until after a random lunch in early October. She stood with her back against a set of lockers by herself, arms folded. It wasn't her locker as I didn't see her there again the rest of the school year. Normally I walked the halls with my head down, a turtle sunk into his protective shell, but before disappearing into my next class, I looked up to find her staring at me. That look is the second of two looks from her that I'll never forget, though I won't ever be sure if I was reading or interpreting this look correctly. In her look I saw I-can't-believe-you-did-that, and there was a depthless sadness, one that was almost impossible for me to face as it was a direct, honest response to my irrevocable act. Her look said that I'd stolen a piece of her and even if I'd tried to give it back, it would still be gone forever. To my shame I didn't say anything, didn't tell her that I was sorry, and I regret not doing so to this day. There was something else in that look too, and it was unreadable to me at the time, but now, sitting in my empty house with dread filling me like water in a glass, I think some of that sadness was for me, and some of it was pity and maybe even fear, like she knew what was going to happen to me tomorrow and for the rest of my tomorrows, and not that there would necessarily be a singular calamitous event, but a concatenation or summation of small defeats and horrors that would build daily and yearly and eventually overtake me, as it overtakes us all.

I would see her in passing the following year in eighth grade, but she walked past me like I wasn't there (like most the other kids did; I'm sorry if that sounds too woe-is-me, but it's the truth). At the start of ninth grade she returned to school a totally transformed kid. She dressed in all black, dyed her hair black, and wore eye-liner and Dead Kennedys and Circle Jerks and Suicidal Tendencies tee shirts and combat boots, and hung out with upperclassmen and she was abrasive and smelled like cigarettes and weed, and in our suburban town, only a handful of kids were into punk, so to most of us, even us losers who were picked on mercilessly by the jocks and popular kids or, worse, were totally ignored, the punks were scary and to be avoided at all costs. I remember wondering if the Michael Jackson and Duran Duran posters were still hanging in her room and I wondered if she still had that dream about her ghost and if she still thought that ghost was some part of her. Of course, I later became a punk when I went to college and I now irrationally wonder if *punk* was another piece of her that I stole and kept for myself.

The summer after ninth grade Kelly and her family sold the house and moved away. I have no memory of where she moved to, or more accurately, I have no memory of being told (and then forgetting) where she moved. I find it difficult to believe that no one in our grade would've known to what town or state she moved. I must've known where she relocated to at one point, right?

The baseball game is still on and I'm on the couch with my laptop open and searching for Kelly Bishop on every social media platform I can think of, and I can't find her, and I'm desperate to find her, and it's less about knowing what has become of her (or who she became) but to see if she's left behind any other parts of herself—even if only digital avatars.

Next to my laptop is her drawing. That it survived all this time and ended up in my possession again somehow now feels like an inevitability.

Here it is:

I remembered it looking like the product of a young artist and being more creepy and affecting because of it. I remembered some of the branches at the top forming the letter 'K.' I remembered the smile and the skin strips and the triangle arms as is.

I didn't remember the shadow beneath the hovering figure and I don't like looking at that shadow and I wonder why I always peer so intently into those dark spaces? I didn't remember how its head is turned away from its body and turned to face the viewers, as though the ghost was floating along stage left until we looked at it, until we saw it there. And then it sees us.

I know it's not supposed to be a doppelganger but I remember it looking like Kelly in some ineffable way, and now, thirty plus years later I think it looks like me, or that it somehow came from me. Even though it's late and she's in bed, I want to call Mom and ask her if she looked through the cardboard box one last time before leaving it here (I know she must've) and if she saw this drawing and recognized her son from all those years ago in it.

I am glad Catherine and Izzy are not here. I keep saying that I am glad they are not here in my head. I say it aloud too. They would've found the drawing before I did and I don't know if they would've seen me or if they would've seen themselves.

My reverie is shattered by a loud thud upstairs, like something heavy falling to the floor.

There is there applause and excited commentators chattering on my television, but I am still home alone and there is a loud thud upstairs.

Its volume and the suddenness of its presence twitches my body, but then I'm careful to stand up slowly and purposefully from the couch. Worse than the incongruity of noise coming from a presumably vacant space is the emptiness the sound leaves behind, a void that must and will be filled.

I again think of driving to the Cape or just driving, somewhere, anywhere. I shut the television off and I anticipate the sound of footsteps running out of the silence, or a rush of air and those triangle arms reaching out toward me and the shadow on the floor behind it.

Everything in me is shaking. I call out in a voice no one is there to hear. I threaten calling 911. I tell the empty or not-empty house to leave me alone. I try to be rational and envision the noise being made by one of the shampoo bottles sliding off the slippery ledge in our shower but instead I can only see the figure in my drawing, huddled upstairs, waiting. And it is now *my* drawing, even if it's not.

The ceiling above my head creaks ever so slightly. A settling of the wood. A response to subtle pressure.

I imagine going upstairs and finding a menagerie of Kelly's ghosts waiting for me: there is Greg with two g's tearing apart the hapless Rolph, and the desperately lonely Mrs. Black sitting in a chair patiently waiting, and the feckless shut-in Darcy Dearborn. Or will I find the ghost of a part of me that I never let go: a lost and outcast adult I always feared people (myself included) thought I'd become?

Is that another creak in the ceiling I heard?

I listen harder, and maybe if I listen long enough I'll hear a scream or a growl or my own voice, and it is as though the last thirty years of my life have passed like the blink of summer, and everything that has happened in between doesn't matter. Memories and events and all the people in my life have been squeezed out leaving only room for this distilled me on this narrowing staircase, and right now even Catherine and Izzy feel like made up ghost stories. There is only that afternoon in Kelly's place and now the impossibly-older me alone in a house that's become as strange, frightening, and unknowable as my future.

As I slowly walk out of the TV room and up the stairs toward the suddenly-alive-with-sound second floor, I don't know what I'm more afraid of: seeing the ghost I stole grinning in the dark or seeing myself.

(*drawing by Emma Tremblay*)

A SONG FOR WOUNDED MOUTHS

KRISTI DEMEESTER

It was Brandon who found the teeth. He was the one who picked up the small Mason jar, imagining it to be the perfect thing for B roll, the kind of homespun charm we were hoping to emulate for the video we were shooting for "Litany for Those Who Still Live." He palmed the jar and rattled it at Derek.

"A jar of buttons. Jesus. My grandmother had one of these in her house, too. It's perfect. A lingering zoom shot. An establishment of how it used to be. Before everything went to shit," he said. I tried not to watch the fullness of his lower lip, how it curved around the syllables. But I was the same girl I'd always been, and it was too difficult to rip out the infatuation I'd felt for him since I was fifteen.

Derek shrugged. Forever noncommittal. By the time Brandon shrieked, the jar clattering to the peeling linoleum, I'd already looked away, occupied myself with unraveling the knot of cords in our equipment. Anything to keep from seeing the desperation in Brandon's eyes when he looked at Derek. How he stared, his tongue touching the tip of his upper lip in a reminder of what his body could promise for Derek alone. It was not for me. Never for me.

So when Brandon screamed, I thought it was for effect, something to get Derek's attention. The muscles between my shoulders clenched anyway, and I bit down on my tongue. I swiped my index finger across it, but there was no blood. I wished I could be anywhere but stuck in this abandoned house with the band I'd stumbled into and couldn't leave.

"What the fuck?" I turned, ready to pack it all up before the shoot even began. Brandon had retreated to the opposite end of the kitchen where he curled into the soft parts of himself, his hand clamped over his mouth.

"Teeth," he said. "It's fucking *teeth*."

"They're probably fake. Halloween decorations or something," Derek said. He stood and advanced toward the spot where Brandon had dropped the jar.

"No way. I saw them. They're teeth. Nothing else looks like that."

Stooping, Derek peered down at the jar. I didn't move, my knees aching from the hard floor.

"You guys are assholes, you know that?" I said. "It's already messed up enough that we're here. You don't have to make it worse."

Derek was the one who'd suggested we film in an abandoned house. To provide a visual for the fragmentation in the song; how corporations and government buyouts had toppled families, torn everything that should be safe to ribbons and then left the detritus behind to fester and rot.

"We should go over toward Bent Oaks. There's that whole street of houses at the back of the subdivision that either never got finished or that people were evicted from. Do some shots of the overgrown lawns, busted out windows, rusting swing sets. You know. The degradation of it all." He swigged from the bottle of gin we shared. Brandon said nothing as he took his own pull, but he was eye-fucking Derek the entire time, and when Brandon passed the bottle to me, I drank more than my share. Tomorrow morning, a deep pain would bloom like a dark star at the back of my brain, and my body would ache, but it was better to let the memory fade into a gin-soaked haze than remember everything I could not have.

I hadn't wanted to come here. I was not the one who brought us here. It's important to understand that. It was not me.

Derek kicked the jar, and it rattled across the floor. The sound of a child's toy. A sound long bleached from the walls of this house.

"Holy shit. Those are definitely teeth."

Rising, I swiped my palms against my shirt and told myself they were kidding. They did this sometimes. Teased me because it was easy. Because there was nothing better to do.

Brandon's face was a flood of color. Crimson streaks stretched up his neck, and his cheeks had gone splotchy. My body went heavy. I couldn't move. Couldn't bring myself to go and look at what it was he had found, to look and acknowledge and understand that jar filled with what remained of someone else.

But I didn't have to move. Derek did it for me. Crossing the kitchen, he bent and lifted the jar into the light, and it was almost beautiful—the light catching the glass, those ivory-colored pieces tumbling against one another. He tapped a finger on the lid.

"Baby teeth. That's all. My mom kept mine and my sister's, too. In an envelope in her sewing kit. I always thought it was weird, but she said it was sweet. Like keeping a part of who we used to be alive. All of our cells die off. Regenerate. So the adults we would become wouldn't even be made up of the children we once were. She said she wanted a reminder that we were small once. That we had come from her and lived under her care."

"Should there be that many though?"

Derek shrugged. "Maybe she had a bunch of kids. There's like thirty-two teeth in our mouths or something, isn't there?" Derek tossed the jar back to him. Brandon caught it, his mouth stretching into a momentary grimace at the touch of the glass.

"I guess," he said and turned the jar over in his palms, his touch suddenly gentle. Reverent. As if by touching the jar, Derek had created a holy relic. Those long, pale fingers sanctifying the missing portions of someone else's children.

"We should start if we want to finish before it gets dark," I said. Brandon and Derek didn't even bother looking up, and I thought again of how easy, how simple a thing it would be to just quit—tell them to get fucked and go out on my own or find another band and let them come up with their own lyrics—but I knew I wouldn't. There was something too alluring in the torture. I wasn't ready to give up the edge of that blade. Not yet.

"It should be the closing shot. All of this normalcy, and then the teeth. How it ripped out every part of us that was innocent. Our children ground under the heels of the corporation," Derek said, and Brandon squeezed his upper arm. I went back to untangling cords, pretending not to focus on how my fake leather pants squeezed too tightly around my midsection or how already I'd started to sweat, the eyeliner and glitter I'd gooped on not even three hours ago starting its gradual progression down my face. By the time we finally filmed our individual shots, I was going to look like Alice Cooper's microwaved asshole.

We'd not gone further into the house than the living room and kitchen, but even those rooms were haunted. The furniture had been left behind, and dust veiled the leather couches, the dark, heavy wood of the coffee table, the books still artfully stacked. Everything held the appearance of a showroom, as if the rooms had been scrubbed clean of the usual detritus of day-to-day life. The appearance of family without any of the reality of it. It was unnerving. Like falling into a dream; everything tinged a shade darker than it should be.

"I'm going to look at the rest of the house. See if there are other spots we should shoot," I said. Derek and Brandon nodded, their heads tipping ever closer, as Brandon's hands fluttered at his hair, his throat, his belt.

I thought about leaving them here. Taking the keys and leaving them behind to wither in their skins inside that dead house, but there would be the following day, and the day after that, and they would not vanish no matter how much I longed for them to. Instead, I rose and wandered toward the hallway that led to the bedrooms, my boots thudding against the hardwood and leaving prints, a reminder that I had walked in the silence settling over those rooms.

The walls were smooth, no outlines or holes from where photos once hung, and a dampness wormed against my skin. Where the living room and kitchen were still furnished, the first bedroom was starkly empty, the carpet worn in the areas that once held a bed and dresser. An ochre stain bled outward in the corner next to the sliding closet door.

Behind me, Derek and Brandon's voice dipped and rose. The low murmurs of their conversation should have made me feel less alone, but standing there, in the center of that blanked-out room, I shivered. We are not meant to move among death, and that's what this house was. Death. Or at least, the false sense of it. The edges of it that sloped downward.

"Find anything good?" Brandon's voice was light, and I shouted back.

"No. Empty room. Nothing like what's up there."

"What about the other rooms?"

"Haven't looked yet."

Footsteps shuffled down the hallway, and still they whispered together. I dug my fingernails into my palms. It was only Brandon who came into the room, his eyes taking in everything but me. His cheeks were flushed, and I understood that an answer of some kind had passed between him and Derek.

"Boo," he said.

"I guess. No ghosts here though," I said, but of course, I didn't believe that. We carry them tucked inside of our hearts or curled on our tongues. Those past things we wish we could call back into ourselves but cannot. This house was just another form of loss.

"Where's Derek?" I tried to keep my voice light, but it trembled. Another thing to hate myself for.

"Checking the other rooms to see if there's anything worth using. Guess we can cross this one off the list." He knocked against the wall. I expected something to knock back, but nothing is ever that simple. Things that are sleeping don't wake up just because we ask them to.

"I just want to shoot this thing and get out of here. It's creepy, you know?"

"You're wrong. It's beautiful. It's what tragedy does. Creates a kind of holy ground. You couldn't feel it when we came in?"

"It's a house, Brandon. Just a house where people used to live and now they don't because everything went to hell, and we're here to make a video about that, and that's all. Jesus. You sound like Derek."

Brandon lifted his hands—a gesture of surrender—and backed toward the door, toward the darkness that had swallowed Derek. I opened my mouth to call him back, to ask him not to leave me in the way he was always leaving, to tell him that I'd been stupidly in love with him since Ms. Cook partnered us together in Chemistry when we were Juniors and didn't understand the people we would become.

"Brandon—" He glanced back, and I remembered how he'd carried me into my house after graduation when we'd gone to a party where I'd gotten drunk for the first time in my life, the flutter of his lips against my forehead as he tucked me in. "Let's just pack up and go. Film somewhere else. Or not at all. It's not like we need a video. We're not exactly booking anything spectacular. Ed's is cool and all, but it's a shitty gig, and you know it. Go get a sandwich and out of this creepy house."

"It's gonna be great. You'll see. A fucking transcendent *experience.* People will eat it up and talk about it to everyone, and we're going to blow the fuck *up.* Derek says this is the thing that's going to elevate us. Make everyone see what it is we're trying to say. And he says this is the perfect place to do it. That this place is special. I felt it the second we got out of the car. Like it was singing to my blood."

"Yeah. Derek says. Derek always fucking says," I muttered, but Brandon had already retreated, scuttling back to Derek, his desperation heavy as a coat on his shoulders. I didn't follow him.

Turning to the window, I stared into the side yard where a large rosemary plant grew wild and leggy. Once, there would have been someone to prune it. I closed my eyes, forced myself to think of how the rosemary must smell, the fragrant, almost medicinal sharpness of it, but whispers floated through the walls, and it was worse that they were not breathed out by ghosts. Far worse to be invisible to the living.

Dipping low, the sun cast twisted shadows against the uncut grass, and I remembered a line from some poetry class I'd taken before I dropped out of college to be a failed rock star for a shitty local band. Something about the hair of uncut graves. In the other room, someone sighed, and it was like hearing the walls draw breath, the dampened recesses of lungs pulling air in and out. When I left the room, I listened for the sound of the latch. I did not want the door to that empty space to open again. It felt obscene to think that anything could enter without an invitation. Including us.

The hallway had grown darker, and I reached out my hands and waited for my eyes to adjust.

"Where are you guys?" I called. A low susurrus rose and fell, but Brandon and Derek didn't answer, and I took one shuffling step forward, shifting my gaze over the floor as I tried to determine which of the other doors they'd disappeared behind. This was no funhouse, no labyrinth with a monster hidden in its heart, so there was no reason for the sweat working its way down my chest. No reason at all for my breath to hitch as I took another step, breathing deep as I stared down at the carpet where something shimmered.

The teeth. Either Brandon or Derek or both had laid them out in a line, leading me down the hallway before stopping at the final door. I wrinkled my nose and kicked at one of the teeth with my boot—a perfectly tiny molar—and it went skittering off into the shadows. Another piece of this house lost to the dark.

"This isn't fucking Hansel and Gretel, you enormous twats," I shouted, and my voice echoed back to me as if the hallway went further than I could see.

"We're in the last room. You have to see this, Camryn. It's insane," Brandon said, and I pushed my body against the wall, carefully sidestepping the teeth.

I did not want to touch them again, even if it was through the faux leather of my shit stompers.

Inside, Derek and Brandon crouched at the entrance of the closet; their heads leaned together so that they were touching. Clandestine and innocent as two boys bent over a frog or a bug they find interesting. Around them, the walls were covered in floral wallpaper—all delicate, faded pastels and winding vine—and gilded frames holding watercolors depicting still-life scenes. An ancient wood dresser moldered in one corner and on it sat crocheted doilies and several porcelain bowls with potpourri that filled the room with an unpleasant funeral smell. A grandmother's room. A room that had been lived in, the items carefully chosen and arranged. If the other rooms breathed, this one whispered.

"Look at this." Brandon turned as if it pained him to put even the smallest amount of distance between them, and held out his hand.

"Pictures. Tons of them," Derek said, and Brandon fanned them out. A few of them fluttered to the floor, the faces turning away and then up again.

"So? Plenty of people have pictures," I said. Brandon lifted the stack up to me, but I couldn't move, couldn't bring myself to take the photos because I had seen them and my skin had gone cold.

"Kids. A shit ton of them, too. School pictures, you know? The kind that are in the yearbook," Derek said. The faces reflected back at me, awkward smiles with pigtails and cowlicks and miniature faces. Elementary school. Young. Children.

"Those teeth," I said, and Derek shook his head. Brandon mimicked him, parroted back his movement, and I scratched at my palms to keep myself from slapping him.

"She was probably a school teacher. Kept photos of her students," Derek said, and I looked away from those staring, lifeless eyes, those grins with missing teeth.

"Still weird. I wouldn't want my kid's teacher keeping a picture. I mean think about it. Someone being so obsessed with her students she keeps pictures?" I said. Derek shrugged. Brandon shrugged.

"She was probably just a lonely old woman. Kept them taped up by her desk and then took them down every year and threw 'em in a box. Not a big deal. It'll be great for the video. Show them all piled up. The ruin brought on by a corporation. So many children. Maybe do a shot of them burning, the edges curling up, the flames licking at all of those faces," Derek said.

I shuddered, opened my mouth to tell him absolutely not, but Brandon was already gathering them up, chattering nonsensically about how brilliant it all was, how brilliant Derek was, how brilliant it would all be because Derek was with us. A headache shattered dark and bright deep within my brain. I closed my eyes. Opened them. Still, Brandon was talking, those pictures bending beneath his touch.

"We can't do that," I whispered, my mouth dry, but they ignored me, and I cleared my throat. "We can't do that. Those are someone's children. Those are kids. We can't fucking *do that*."

The last words came out in a growl, and Derek and Brandon looked up at me, blinking as if they had only just realized I was still in the room.

"We need to get started. We're losing the light," Derek said, and together, they stood and stepped past me, Brandon still carrying the pictures. My chest burned, my arms, my cheeks. Everything on fire as if I could self-immolate and become something new. Something better than a shitty lyricist and even shittier bass player in a failed local rock band. This room was obscene. This house. A gutted abomination. The teeth. The photos. Derek could be right; the woman who lived here had been a mother, a grandmother, a teacher, but it felt that if I tore at the wallpaper, there would be rot hidden behind the walls, the potpourri an intentional mask for something more insidious. There were too many teeth. Too many pictures. This was a place to run from. If they couldn't see it, that was their problem. Fuck Derek and Brandon. They could shoot their video without me.

I told myself to move. It was suddenly important not to turn my back on the closet, suddenly important to count backward from twenty, to stare at each corner of the room, to be sure there was nothing lingering there. All of these things I had not done since I was small when my mother had imagined the leather belt my father wore was the instrument that would erase my compulsions. Violence can only be a form of deliverance in death. There was no simplicity or absolution in the exorcism my mother was trying to enact.

On hands and knees, I crept backward out of the room, my lips forming wordless sounds that could have been prayers or incantations to some darker god, and whatever entity lived in that room allowed me to leave but not without harm. I dragged myself over the carpet and my palm pressed down against one of the teeth, a jagged, broken edge meant only for me. I didn't feel when the point entered my skin, when my blood smeared against the floor. Only when I moved again, folding myself to stand, did I see how the tooth stuck to my skin like some weak imitation of stigmata.

I could not keep the thin whine from building in my throat, the awareness of the wrongness of this place, the heaviness it carried, a sudden, blinding awareness falling over my back. The earth should have been salted, but the house still stood, those photos and teeth tucked safely inside like ritualistic totems.

Back in the living room, Derek and Brandon laughed, high and tinny, and called my name again and again. My identity becoming a litany for the dead.

"What the fuck is it this time?" I called, and my voice trembled, and I willed my voice, my hands to go still.

"Come out here," Derek said, but there was something in his voice, some deeper register, that didn't sound like him, and I stayed where I was.

"What is it?"

"You have to see it. Just come out here, Camryn." Brandon's voice deepened to mimic Derek's, and fuck them and fuck this house, and I was done with the both of them, the band, with Brandon and being in love with him while he knew it and strung me along with just enough affection to keep me as his back up emotional support when Derek wouldn't give in to his deeper needs.

"The only place I'm going is out of this goddamned house," I said, and something that was not Brandon, was not Derek, laughed.

I froze and listened again to the tinny shrill of it, how it trailed down and down until Brandon and Derek joined in, all three of them laughing as if the sound could take the world apart.

They'd invited someone else. Some other girl. That was the only explanation for that third voice. They'd invited her to be in the video, to be the fuckable eye candy in place of me because I was too thin, too pinched in the face and always angry, and they'd not told me because they knew it would piss me off, knew I would have told them no immediately, but they did it anyway, and I was definitely out of there.

I took a step forward, another tooth crushed into the carpet beneath my boot, and I kicked at it in disgust. Again, that laughter rose and fell, and I forced myself to keep moving. Another step. Pause. Listen. Breathe. Envision myself far from this place.

In the distance, Brandon and Derek dropped their voices to whispers, the cadence of their speech identical, and I stopped, willed my heart to be silent so I could hear. I couldn't make out the syllables, but it was prayer, it was chanting, and a cold sweat broke out across my back.

"Are you guys practicing or something?" I called, but they didn't respond. I swayed on my feet, unable to go forward or back.

"It's here," they said together. "Look. It knew how to take what was needed. Those small, dying parts. How to wrench them out of squirming mouths. How to keep them quiet even when their bodies needed to scream."

Still, still, still. Important not to move. Important not to make any sound. Important to close my eyes and count. Twenty. Back down. Not to listen. Not to see.

But there was no amount of pretending that could erase that dark form standing at the entrance to the hallway as dying light streamed behind it, casting the features in shadow. It could have been Brandon. It could have been Derek. It could have been something else.

"Look at it, Camryn. How could we have known what we would find here? But we did. It was always here. Among us. Watching and waiting and taking what it needed. How lovely everything was when it was surrounded by life, by small ones shouting to one another in glee and then in fear, and we can bring it all of that again. It can show us."

"What the absolute *fuck* are you talking about?" I said, and behind me, a door opened. Behind me, the closet gaped open as a chasm.

"A god," Brandon said. That dark form had no mouth, but Brandon's voice came from it even as Derek also spoke from it and that third voice rose along with them, and there was nowhere for me to go.

"No. Not that. It was never that. Suffer the little children. No one ever imagined what it could actually mean. What it needed to take to live."

"Cut it out. It's not funny," I said, and the form shifted, bent unnaturally at the neck, and I saw then that it did have a mouth, and it was opening. Too many teeth. All of those it had collected. I thought of the pictures. So many children. And it smiled. It smiled, and there was nowhere for me to go but back into that room, the door closing gently without my having to touch it.

Whatever had lived in this house had never left. It had saved teeth. It had saved pictures. Its stain lingered. Derek and Brandon called it a god, but I'd learned long ago that gods and devils share faces. In evil, in goodness, there is subjectivity. Prayer as poison. Poison as prayer. What infected Derek and Brandon was all of those things, and it had been biding its time. Waiting for supplicants. And if it could not have children, it would take what came to it, what intruded on its quiet.

Outside, Brandon and Derek scratched at the door. Gently. Soft as a whisper. They did not want to frighten me. It never wanted to frighten anyone. But there were *requirements*. There were *things they must do*. They had to *satisfy it*. It had spoken, and they had listened. They didn't think they could ever stop listening.

"It can be simple if you let it," they said.

"They were *children*," I said. Because I could not unsee those pictures. Those faces and how they didn't understand, *couldn't* understand what would happen to them. How they had come into this house and stumbled into an open, foul mouth.

Still, Brandon and Derek whispered at the door until they weren't speaking any language at all, but offering up sounds like warm water, like vanilla, like the sharp tang of blood, and I crammed my fist into my mouth to keep myself from screaming. Eventually, they would find their way into the room, and they would bring *it* with them. Would they hold me down together? Would they pry open my mouth with dirty hands, their fingers pushing past my tongue until I choked?

There was the window, it's glass darkening as the afternoon bled into twilight, and I could go through it, could open it and squeeze myself out, away from the stale air, away from whatever faceless god had made its home here, and I rushed for it, my fingers scrabbling against the lock, and it opened, the metal turning, and I could have cried from the beauty of that sound, but it couldn't be so simple. To be allowed to run. There was a lifetime of stories, of films, that had taught me otherwise, but the window opened easily, and the door behind me stayed closed.

Inside the closet, voices whispered—children speaking in those same syllables Derek and Brandon had uttered—and I hurled myself out the window, the wood frame splintering and catching at my shirt and hair as if it could hold me within, but then I was dropping to the earth, my stomach lurching against the sudden weightlessness and then the heavy pain of my own body crushed into the dirt.

But I was out, and the air around me pressed close, and I drew it into my lungs, and I ran. I did not stumble. Did not fall. Only once, did I look back like Lot's wife among that crumbling suburbia, the fallen, twisted idols of the backyard playgrounds looming up from the earth. Derek and Brandon stood at the window, their mouths against the glass, their tongues lolling behind as they gnashed their teeth and grasped at the emptiness I'd left behind. Their hands would not find my skin. They would not draw me back inside and teach me how to swallow my pain as they took pieces of me apart.

Whatever moved behind Derek and Brandon belonged only to them, to that house, and I was a moving, beating heart. Breath and bone and blood. Teeth. A photograph. I was all of those things, and I ran so I could continue to be all of those things until I grew old.

I hoped the others had run, too. The children. When my chest and legs began to burn, I told myself they had. Again and again until I believed it. Until I could see their shining faces, the way their bodies grew and changed, their teeth glittering in the dark.

BIRDS OF PASSAGE

GORDON B. WHITE

If I didn't inherit my father's natural instinct for adventure, it was drummed into me steadily enough by the time I was a young man that you wouldn't have been able to tell the difference. If you don't go looking for adventure, he would say, adventure will come looking for you. Over the years, I got so used to the counter-programming against my inborn tendency towards the comfort of safety that I wonder—if left to my own natural limits—would I have turned out differently? Are there other dimensions with less driven, but perhaps more content, versions of me? I've thought about that a lot since my father died.

My father and I had plenty of what he would call "adventures," even though we sometimes disagreed on what qualified. Road trip to the mountains and across state lines? Sure, that counted. Pushing his broken car to the dealership and walking home? Not in my book. Nowadays, although I would not trade any of them for the world, the years have smudged away most of our individual adventures. However, I will never forget Cotner's Creek.

I was ten years old and it was Labor Day weekend. I remember that clearly because there are only two real sections of my life: before that trip and after. If I ever were to return, I wonder if there would be a third fork, or if this is it? My father would have known, of course, but he's not likely to tell me now. It's not impossible—nothing truly is—but it's very unlikely.

We'd spent the week before preparing for the trip. In retrospect, I realize now how much of it had been planned in advance, but the way that my father involved me made it seem as much my trip as his; it was as if we were equal partners stocking up for the expedition. From the way he consulted me about which canoe to rent, to the excursions up and down the supermarket aisles shopping for two days of river rations to fill the cooler that would sit between us, I seemed to have a say in every part. Finally, I thought, I was a man and my opinion mattered.

We excavated my mother's garage until we rediscovered the musty relics of sleeping bags, poncho liners, and other accouterments for camping. These were leftover things that had been squirreled away after he'd gotten married and stayed buried after he'd gotten divorced, but even their stale smells were akin to the yellowed pages of an old atlas—a reminder of adventures past and the empty spaces where still more hid. Although we had a tent, too, we agreed that we wouldn't bring it because the forecast was clear and we wanted to sleep beneath the stars. What was the point of two men heading out into the wild only to hide from it all? We wanted to experience everything.

Because I was an equal partner in name and spirit, if not in stakes and logistics, a brackish current of trepidation and excitement swept me along. What if we got lost? What if we capsized? Where would we go to the bathroom? Were there wild animals? Would it be cold? My father laughed at all of these questions but gave me straight answers, although most of those scenarios never came to pass. What did happen, though, was something that I could never have understood how to ask. Even after we went down Cotner's Creek, I'm still not sure I can.

⟜

My mother drove us down to the bridge over Cotner's Creek, out off the interstate between Statesville and Wallace, which is near where my father grew up. The highway crosses through long fields of cash crops slit by the occasional meandering river and further hemmed in by fingers of undeveloped forests. In the summer those fields are heavy and green, swaying under fleshy tobacco leaves or tight-lipped bolls of cotton. By the fall, however, they're in the process of being stripped bare and harrowed through for the next year's planting. It was Saturday, and she planned to pick us up further down the river the next afternoon.

She watched as my father and I off-loaded the rental canoe, our camping gear, and the Igloo chest filled with provisions. It was only years later, when she was moving in with her next husband that I came across a snapshot she had taken that day when I wasn't looking. There I was in a bright red cap and bright orange life preserver, a figurehead on the bow of the canoe like a little ornamental torchbearer. Behind me, my father is caught in just the slightest profile, forever frozen in the act of pushing off along the winding path of water and toward the veil of trees beyond. I've looked at it many times, but I still can't read in that sliver of his face if he knew what was going to happen.

As we set out, though, in the full of morning's light, it was a grand adventure. Paddling with the river gave the sensation not so much of leaving the world behind, but as if we were pushing further inside it. Our surroundings changed along each bend of the river, as if the banks were contorting themselves to show off every aspect as we moved deeper into its coils. Open fields gave way to trees, but then a broken-ankle turn would reveal a fenced-in yard. At times, the creek thinned out to barely a stream, but then another turn opened up to cataracts of near-whitewater rapids. No matter how many stories I'd heard from my father, watching the world switch from inhabited to primeval, from narrow and cultivated to wide and bursting with wild energy, it was seeing the shift with my own eyes that brought an understanding no story ever could. As we moved through these unfolding aspects, all united by the almost arbitrary cut of the creek through their disparate dimensions, it was as if I was moving backwards past my father's stories and into a deeper, stranger imagination.

There is one part, in particular, that sticks out to me more than any other. We had just come through a peculiarly narrow pinch of the creek and opened up into a wide, glassy pool. The water was brown but transparent for about a foot down before it clouded over, resisting the sun that punched through the grasping branches and into the shallows. Beneath us, as if the shade of our canoe was obfuscation from a higher plane, long-bodied gar swam up from the clouded depths and followed beneath us. In our shadow a new layer of their world was presented and so they rose up, their needle-noses and armored flanks primitive and unintelligible in this thin layer. I wondered if they knew that my father and I could have held gig hooks to spear them or nets to ensnare them, but that to us, in particular, they were curiosities. They had lived for decades in this river and their ancestors had for millennia been kings of this simple cut of water through the deep red banks, but even though they knew nothing of us, we could have—had we wanted—been a danger. Still, they swam and basked. They dove back deep into the blackness, and if they saw us—if our canoe and our unused armaments registered to them at all—it only gave them more freedom, allowing them to rise higher in our shadow before descending back into their depths, unable to ever properly describe to their fish wives and fish children what marvels they'd seen.

Is it any wonder, then, that as the whole world of the creek grew so gradually stranger and stranger the further we travelled—as new creatures swam up and the banks bleached from red to gray, as the trees grew crooked and vines hung like witch's hair—that I failed to appreciate the full extent of how different things truly had become?

As the day ended and the palimpsest of sunset colors and evening sounds settled around us, we found a bend in the river with a wide open field next to it. Because it was so vast and clearly unused by other people, we set up camp further off the bank, up on a little rise. The canoe stayed below, wedged into the grey clay at the waterline and lashed to a few saplings. We spread our tarps and bedding over the dead leaves and gnarled roots, but the ground's chill still permeated up through the layers.

The night was cool and a thin film of clouds swept back and forth across the wide, hungry sky. We were just at the point where the ground opened up into the field and the trees overhead still clung to the modesty of a few leaves, but beyond them the silver teeth of stars were starting to nibble through the bruise of the evening. Looking up, the night felt cooler to be that bright with distant fire.

We made our own fire of the thick branches already littering the ground. Although it hadn't rained in days, those long arms of wood had soaked up the moisture from the cool ground and the water below. Their bark hung like damp skin, hissing and whistling before taking the flame. Still, once we had the fire going, the cocoon of light it wove was enough to make me feel safe within its embrace.

After a day of paddling, our provisions of box juice, peel-top soup cans, and King's Hawaiian rolls were practically a feast. As usual, we talked about small things—my school, our plans for a tree house once he found a new place—but all of it took on a grave importance there by the river. It was as if we were discussing ancient things, as if our lives outside the woods had become myths that occurred centuries ago or perhaps that wouldn't occur for centuries yet. Maybe it was that dislocation that unmoored my father, which sent him back down that silver thread of memory outside the firelight. Whatever the reason, he then told me a story I'd never heard before.

"When I was a boy," he began, "I grew up about fifteen miles from the bridge where we set off. You know how I've told you before about my best friend Gary? Well, he and I did this same trip that you and I are doing. Gary and I put in at the same spot—although it was a different bridge back then, an old one made of bricks that they tore down when the highway came through."

The thing about his stories, I've come to realize, is that I never could quite tell when they were true and when they just felt that way. They all felt real enough then and, in time, all of the past takes on that same grain that blurs true and untrue, so the only thing I guess that really matters is who remembers it and how it felt to hear it.

He went on: "When Gary and I made this trip, though, it was summer. It was so humid that year, so damp in the air, that do you remember that little waterfall in the rapids we took after lunch? Well, he and I did the same thing, but we got a good foot further past the edge before we tipped over because the canoe was paddling through that steamy air."

"Was it the same as it is now, though?" I asked. "Because it feels, maybe, strange?"

I couldn't quite put what I felt into words, but from the slight drip of a frown that escaped him, I could tell he knew what I meant, but that he hadn't been planning on taking his story down this path. At least, not yet.

"Yes." He swallowed hard and looked at me with the steel glint that meant that this was man talk. No anger, no fear, but still deathly serious. "I think that's why I brought you here."

"This place is . . ." he fluttered his hand for a moment, trying to conjure the right word out of the fire. "It's a soft place, I think. It isn't quite here, and isn't quite there. There aren't people and there aren't roads, but you can feel that something more surrounds us."

It took me a moment to respond. I held a paper towel napkin in my hands, which I balled and unrolled to an unheard rhythm. He was right, or at least it felt like he was right. Because there I could also feel something under that black dome of sky and all the million fly specks of distant light above us that peered through and then were swept away in the current of clouds. Some enormousness that seemed to both pull me up and press me down at the same time. Out in the distance, the soft yellow bruise of light pollution over far-off cities seemed like dapples of light on the river bottom, obscured by layers of some other medium that my father and I were now suspended in, just like gar in the river.

"I feel it," I said, although the description of it wouldn't come to me for years. But the way I said it, my dad knew. He nodded.

"I don't know what you'd call it," he finally said. With a slender stick, he prodded the embers on our low fire and sent the shadows skipping like water bugs. "Maybe the bigness of nature, or a great spirituality. Something, though, you don't feel at home."

He looked out for a moment at the darkness, at the stars above. "Sometimes," he said, "I think about all the possible worlds we could have lived in, but that we're in the one that makes you my son and me your father and brings us here. It sounds stupid," he paused, "but sometimes I look at you and I think, 'Are you real?'"

"Yeah," I said. He laughed and I smiled, even though I don't know if he saw me do it, there in the shadow just beyond the fire's light. For a while, we just sat and listened to the world.

"Do you feel it everywhere?" I eventually asked, meaning the thing he had talked about and meaning everywhere outdoors, but even though I didn't clarify, my father knew. He and I shared a wavelength like that.

"Maybe if you try real hard, but I've never felt it quite like I feel it here." He leaned back, caught between the orange light below and the silver light above. "Just think," he went on, "that outside of our fire light, it's miles to the nearest town. Straight up and out above us, for millions of miles is nothing but empty space. Beneath our skin, hidden from sight, run rivers of blood and cells and atoms and, deeper still, the empty space between them. You and I and everything else are just thin layers between space and distances, just skins between mysteries we could never know."

He stopped, probably wondering if he'd gone too far or said too much. Then he looked and me and asked, "Are you scared?"

"No," I said, "but it is a little scary."

"Yeah," he nodded as he spoke, "but it's also kind of awesome."

As if to underscore the end of that thread, I threw my crumpled napkin into the fire. I watched, however, as the edges caught the ember, glowing and curling up at the tips like wings. It must have been shaped just right by the chaotic worrying—a broken bird accidentally birthed through dirty origami—because the folds caught the warm air beneath them and it was buoyed up, burning, into flight. Up over the fire, we watched it rise, catching feathers of flame as it rose, shrinking and consuming itself from the outside in as it drafted up towards the stars. All told, it couldn't have taken more than a few seconds, but in my mind there is a forever-playing slow motion shot of the paper phoenix, rising up into the blackness and fading from view—too far, too small, too burned—until it seemed to be swallowed into the night beyond us.

We sat in silence for a moment after it vanished, listening to the wood whisper in its combustion and the crickets sing along. Behind us, the water chuckled softly and, on the other side, the great open field lay quiet in the starlight. Everything just beyond the fire was bluer than the deepest water and, beyond that, only black.

As my eyes grew accustomed to the gloaming, however, a single point of light emerged in the distance. Seeing it, too, my father stood up and pointed across the field. Despite the stars above, the darkness was like a curtain of black wool pulled from the ground to the trees, but across from us, near where I remembered the opposite tree line being, there was a glow. It was faint, but pushing through the cover like a hot vein beneath night's scales.

"Is that a fire?" I asked, but I knew it was. Immediately, I recalled the rising flame from our fire and had visions of a soft coal falling across the field, catching hold there on the ground. "Did we do that?"

"I don't think so," my father replied. "It looks too big, and it's too damp for anything to catch from that little spark."

"Is it other people?" My imagination again went to the other side, now peering around at the possible figures surrounding that distant beacon. I had thought that we were far from town and it seemed unlikely that anyone else would find the same adventure here that we did. I didn't have the capacity then to conjure up a full parade of horribles, but dim shapes around a greasy fire were enough to set my hairs on end.

As we watched, though, across the field a single flake of fire rose up into the air. From our distant vantage, it was just a speck, like a star falling upwards in bad gravity, but I knew what it was. The fragile paper wings of a crumpled bird, rising and vanishing in the air. I knew that ours had looked the same at this distance.

My father moved from the fire's edge to the border of the darkness. Eyes ahead, he leaned down to probe the shadows, returning with a long, broken branch. The branch's tips were still clotted with leaves, which my father then dipped into our dwindling fire. They smoked, but the flame caught hold and soon gripped the branch in full. My father stood, holding the fiery flag before him like a bright red wing. Then, turning to face our far-off friends, my father began to wave the burning branch—back and forth, back and forth, then pause. Then again.

It felt like hours, but must have only been minutes, because my father's makeshift torch had only just burned itself out when we received a response. There it was, across the field as if in the black mirror of a river light years away. The response, or the perfect mimicry, in flaming semaphore—back and forth, back and forth. Then again. Then nothing.

My father was many things over the course of his life, but what he was that night was calm. While images of monsters crowded my head, haunting visions of dark-eyed reflections of a black-eyed father and son waving their flaming lure across the no-man's land between us, my father remained sanguine.

"Okay," he finally said. "Well, it must be people like us. Probably just passing through." I wanted to believe him, but what gave him away was the stoic deadness to his voice. He was a man of large passions and bold humors, so to hear him modulated was even worse than silence.

Still, through his strength and my own dogged impersonation, we managed to ignore our sister camp for the rest of the evening. We let our fire dwindle and die, and then waited as the one across the field similarly faded from sight. As the night wore on, though, if I borrowed my father's strength to set up camp and eventually crawl into the sleeping bag, then actually falling into sleep was my own weakness. I'm fairly certain that even though he lay down, too, my father never truly slept because otherwise he wouldn't have been awake when it happened.

"Are you awake," he asked, but loud enough that it was a question that contained its own answer. It was still thin night, not yet tipping towards morning, and if the sky was a war between black and silver, black was still the clear victor. In fact, as he shook me gently and I first opened my eyes, I wasn't sure it wasn't a dream.

"Are you awake," he asked again, but he saw that I was because he put his rough palm over my eyes. "Just stay like that," he said, "but you remember where the boat is." It wasn't a question. "If I say so, you go and push off and don't stop, understand?" I nodded by instinct more than awareness, but he must have known, because he said again: "Even if I'm not there, you go alone to the bridge. Do you understand?"

There, beneath the clasp of his hand, I knew that he was serious. I took a moment to let it sink in and visualize myself running from whatever unknown horror lay in the space beyond my father's protection. I could do that, I thought. It would be an adventure.

I nodded.

"Okay," he whispered, and drew his hand away. I rose up, though whether on my own or under his power, I can't quite say. I looked out into the distance across the field, expecting to see the neighboring fire rekindled, but instead of illumination all I saw was the roiling dark.

The night itself moved, and the earth itself unrolled.

What at first I had thought to be distant trees moved and swayed, revealing themselves as great long appendages slick with the faint starlight. They towered above us, falling and rising in time to a rhythm that we could not hear. Neither my father nor I could speak to interrupt that moment.

High above, the clouds parted and the bright yellow moon, now full, gazed down on us. Then it rolled its pupil around and the sheer gravity of the thing's attention pinned me to the ground, then slid off me like a wave.

"Does it see us?" I meant to ask, although I don't know if I did or if the way I gripped my father's hand asked for me. But he just shook his head as the giant eye looked away. He hugged me close.

What we saw was awesome, in the truest sense. It was gorgeous and grand and terrible all at once.

It was like the Northern Lights, but of darkest black on a layer of black. It writhed like the coils of giant snakes in the hands of boundless night.

In the distance behind, a mountain shrugged its shoulders and began to move.

And then it was dark again, as if a veil woven of a new kind of darkness had fallen. One that wasn't the absence of things, but rather the richest depths of possibility. A darkness from which anything could emerge.

In the years that followed, I've theorized but abandoned all theories on what we saw. Something ancient from beneath the earth that sunk away again without a trace? An echo of a form on a different dimension, cast like a shadow onto our world? A god? A demon? In the end, I don't know what to call it, but seeing it made me—joyful? In a flash, I had been gifted indisputable proof that there is strangeness in the world that we may never know, but that this universe is an amazing and infinite place. Even if our roles are smaller than we could have ever imagined, to be a part of such a grand machine made me ecstatic.

But even in the twists and turns as my mind reshaped to accommodate the possibilities of what could be born from the fertile dark, something more tangible emerged. Across the field, two globes of light rose up from the ground. Steadily, they began to move, bobbing and undulating like nodding Cyclopes across the field. My father and I both looked down at our hands to make sure we weren't doing anything that these lights were now mirroring, but no. They were moving on their own.

"Shit," my father said. It was a rare curse that slipped past his lips, at least when I was around. What he did when I wasn't around, however, is something that no one but the dead can answer.

At some point, I suppose, he must have planned what he did next, but I don't know when he could have. Maybe, as you get older, you have a store of actual or imagined experiences to draw from as needed, some stock built up in worries or dreams. Maybe when he thought his son was in danger there was suddenly a bloom of possibilities that he had seen all at once as if in a giant knot and, from that, he picked the thread that ran out our cord for the rest of our days. All I truly know is that he moved without hesitation.

He picked up a stick and shoved our remaining roll of toilet paper on it. He handed it to me and grabbed another stick, repeating the process with the roll of paper towels. Two sprays of lighter fluid and a light-anywhere match stuck against a rock, and suddenly we both held torches. Although the burst of light blinded me, washing out the rest of the world beyond that blast of illumination, in the distance I could make out giant shadows crawling across the empty fields toward us. The bulbs of their illumination still gleamed even in my swollen eyes, but I wonder what possible horrors or beauties the glare had spared me.

"Wave your torch up and down with me," my father said. We did, like the beating of a bird's broken wings out of unison. Out across the field, although still drawing closer, the iridescent spheres held aloft by the long, dark things did the same.

"Run out ten steps, wave it, then run back to me."

I ran, every step away from my father pushing deeper into the viscous night. I waved my flaming beacon and saw him do the same with his.

Across the field, the appendages—for what else could they have been other than some intelligent part of that great mass?—mimicked our motion. I ran back to my father, the torch swaying up and down as my distant double did the same.

Reunited by the ashes of our dead fire, in our makeshift torchlight, I saw a look in my father's eyes that I had never seen before. I knew love and I knew dedication, but until that moment, I did not know sacrifice.

He grabbed my torch from me and swung them both up and down, up and down. Across the field and drawing closer, the two lights did the same.

"Stay here," Dad whispered. "Close your eyes and count to one hundred. If I'm not back by then," he nodded towards the river, "you take the canoe. Got it?"

"Yeah," I managed to say.

He smiled. "It's an adventure, isn't it?"

Then he ran, out into the empty field and away from me, swinging the branches of fire like a bird flapping its wings, drawing a path across the dark sky. Across the field, the two lights did the same. They followed him out into the void, towards the wall of the woods on the far side of the field.

I closed my eyes and started counting. Surrounded by the silence, every number in my head was an explosion. At ten I was brave, by twenty I was frightened, I was sucking back tears by thirty. But the night seemed to swallow my sobbing and by sixty I had stopped. I made it to one hundred, because that's what my father would have done. In part, though, I think I wanted to give it as long as I could, to see what might happen.

Most of what occurred next, I can remember, but all the details are so wound together that even now I lack the perseverance to fully untangle them, so I instead decisively cut through it with only a glance at the pieces. How I opened my eyes in darkness and stumbled over roots back to the banks. How I shoved the canoe out into the black road of the river. How blobs of light seemed to follow me along the shore even as the current pulled me away, fading in the growing dawn until I realized that I was starting at patches of the rising sun coming through branches over the smoking silver ribbon of water.

Hours passed. When I finally got to the bridge, I leapt from the canoe. Feet sucking into the red clay bank, I wrestled the boat up into the switch-thin reeds to wait beneath the very literal and mundane crossroads. Over the hours from gray dawn to robin's egg blue morning and on to golden noon, my terror ebbed. In its wake, however, I could feel there was a new high water mark drawn onto my soul—a place where the fantastic had reached up to and left its thin, but indelible line. I didn't know then that I might always be searching for that level again, but in the bright light of day—and later, too, even in the darkest night—I knew that there was nothing in this world, or any other, for me to truly fear.

As a result, when the forest wall down beyond the bend began to creak, I again felt that equal mixture of excitement and trepidation. As the skin of the woods trembled, as the knots of branches began to spread, as something emerged, I was open to the full possibility of what might be emerging.

But, still, I was surprised to see my father stumble out of the brambles.

My father, his face ash gray and his beard much longer than it should have been. My father, staggering beneath some unseen weight, looking gaunt and haunted and as if he was surprised to find himself in the space that he now occupied. He must have seen the canoe or the movement of the weeds, though, because even before I could call out to him, he broke into the closest thing he could manage to a run, bending and tripping through the deep mud and the high grass.

"Gary?" he called out as he approached.

"No," I managed to say. At the sound of my voice, even though every movement was already falling over the top of every other, he moved even faster. He crashed through the last few feet, almost collapsing on top of me, but then wrapping me up in arms that felt thinner than I'd remembered from the night before.

"Is it you?" he asked, pulling me close. "Are you real?"

"Yeah," was all I could say.

He hugged me then, hard, and I'm not ashamed to say I cried. With my face buried in his chest, I could smell the river, but also his sweat and the fire's smoke and something that tingled like if magnets had a smell and you spun them north to south beneath your nose. I never loved anyone more.

"Let's not tell your mom, okay?" he said.

At the time, I thought it was the standard seal of the adventure—that we keep it to ourselves. It was only much later that I realized we wouldn't have been able to adequately describe it. It was better, I now understand, to hold the knowledge of an unlimited world in silence than to make it smaller by trying to explain it.

⊸

We only spoke of it once afterward, years later, when he was in the hospital for the last time. His wife and my sisters were outside talking to a doctor and the whole coterie of aunts and cousins were waiting in the lounge like a conspiracy of ravens, so I was the only one by his bedside when he opened his eyes. I leaned in close, because his throat was parched and his voice was breaking.

"I'm not afraid," he said. He hadn't said what about, but there was really only the one thing—the big Other that hovers over most of us.

"That's good," I said. "Because I might be." I was used to his trailing off by then and was glad of the silence that bubbled up, but then he spoke again. His eyes got suddenly clear and his voice was strong, like we were back on the river and talking serious man talk again.

"Do you remember Cotner's Creek?"

I nodded.

"I'm glad we were together to see it," he said. "Now, though, there's something else."

"I know."

"I'm not afraid," he said again. The way he looked at me but beyond me, I don't know what he was seeing or if he was fully with me, but it's the only thing that I would give anything not to truly know. Then he said it: "It's an adventure, isn't it?"

He squeezed my hand, his taut sinews closing in like a bird's talons or the long mouths of a school of gar. Then he closed his eyes and fell back into something like sleep. Beneath his thin covering, deep blue rivers of veins pumped slowly along and I could hear his breath rattling beneath the paper of his skin and in the great empty space behind his ribs.

I never spoke with him again.

As I myself grow older, I often think back to that night on the river. About how there's a world around us, but beyond us, too. A world that takes things, changes them, but sometimes gives them back. All of it—all of it is ripples.

I think back to the flaming wings of paper, rising up and vanishing into the darkness before the thing came to us. Even though my father has since passed on and I, too, am getting old, I have no fear, because I know that in the sky above, in the water below, past that thin thread of night, there are mysteries that we can never know. There is more to it all than you or I could ever fully comprehend and, while that terrifies me, it also brings me comfort.

I know that even if the universe has no thought or regard for our existence, we can give it meaning through our own actions and our love for one another. Instead of hiding in the darkness, we take to wings of flame that bear us on like birds of passage, beating bravely out into the great unknown.

THE PUPPET MOTEL

GEMMA FILES

Sometimes, if we don't watch out, we might slip inside a crack between moments and see that there's an ebb and flow under everything we've been told is real, a current that moves the world—the invisible strings which pull us, spun from some source we'll never trace. Sometimes we can be forced by circumstance to see that there's a hand in the darkness, just visible if we squint, outstretched towards us: upside-down and angled, palm and fingers curved to flutter enticingly, waving us on. The universal sign for *come closer, my darling, come closer*.

And sometimes, when things get particularly bad, we may suddenly find ourselves able to hear the steady hum under the world's noise, an electrically charged tone far too light to be static, yet too faint to be a crackle; a thin bone whistle reaching through the walls, almost too faint to register. Rising and falling like the breath behind words you can almost make out, if we only try.

That outflung hand, beckoning us on; that unseen mouth, smiling. All the while telling us, without words, its voice the merest whisper in our singing blood: *come here, love—my sweet one, my other, come. Don't be afraid. Come here to me, to my call.*

That tone—that beckoning—is one I've heard far more often than I'd like to admit, mainly because I just keep *on* hearing it, even though I don't want to. It's louder than you'd think, especially once you're no longer able *not* to concentrate on it . . . so much so it makes it hard to sleep, or work, or dream. Sometimes, it gets so loud I'm afraid I might actually start wanting to answer.

If you ever hear that sound, or even suspect you're about to, then my advice to you is simple.

Just. Fucking. Run.

⊸

Everything you can think of is true, somewhere, for someone; is now, or has been, or will be. And proof, for all our demands, has never been more than the very least of it.

For example—my father sometimes talked about this thing that happened to him when he was a kid, but only because I wouldn't stop bothering him about it. How he took the wrong path at the campsite by the lake, walked straight off a cliff, a sharp downward slope. How he fell and fell, mainly through mud, 'til he hit the bottom and cracked his forearm on a rock, buried a hand's-breadth deep. How he stayed down there for what seemed like hours, calling out weakly, hoping his family would hear. But it was Dominion Day, night already falling, fireworks going off. The campsite was a zoo. He couldn't even tell if they'd noticed he was gone.

He lay there, staring up at the cliff's rim, willing somebody to look over. Until, eventually . . . someone did.

So he started to yell, louder than ever before: *Down here, here I am,* please! Waved his good arm, pounded on the ground, tried to pivot himself 'round one-handed, to get the watcher's attention. But the watcher just stood there, bent over slightly, as though it didn't quite know what it was looking at. After which, slowly—very slowly—it stepped over the ridge and began a careful descent. And Dad was happy, ecstatic, up 'til the very moment the person finally got close enough for him to see it wasn't really a *person* at all.

What was it, then? I'd ask; *I don't know,* he'd reply, every time as baffled as the first. *I don't . . . I just don't know.*

(Its head was too long, too wide, and it moved—backward, he said. Too careful, like its feet were all wrong, like it had to think extra-hard about where to step in order to avoid falling. Like it didn't have toes.)

When it was close enough they could have touched, it leaned down. And when he saw its face he started to scream again, *hard*, scrabbling back like a crab and falling straight on his bad arm, the awful, gutting pain of it so sudden he blacked out.

He woke up in the hospital two days after, broken bones encased in plaster, mouth dry from painkillers and sedatives. The nurses said he had no other wounds, though when they gave him back his clothes, his underpants weren't there. Had to be burned, they told him.

Why? I always asked; *Because*, was all he'd say. Except for one time, when he looked down and added, softly—

They told me they were full of blood.

⊸

Everyone has a story like my Dad's, I've since come to realize. The only surprising part, in hindsight, is that it took so comparatively long for mine to find me.

The summer I first heard what I later came to call the tone, I'd stupidly agreed to manage two Airbnb sites for a friend of my then-boyfriend, Gavin—let's call him Greg, a guy I barely knew in real life, though I was already more than familiar with the fact that if you ever made any sort of statement on Facebook which disagreed with popular nerd culture wisdom, he'd suddenly show up out of nowhere to "debate" it into the ground, whether you were actually prepared to argue the point with him or not. But I needed a job for a certain amount of time (June through August, just in time to go back to school), and he was offering one, so how bad could it possibly be? Never ask, that's my policy . . . or always had been, previously.

Not any more, in case you wondered.

Both sites were fairly close to where I lived back then, give or take. One was at 20 George Street, ten minutes' walk away, the same condo this Greg and his wife Kim planned on moving into once his current contract managing I. T. for a South Korean insurance company ran out; the other was a twenty-minute streetcar ride down to King Street East and Bathurst, a brand-new apartment in a building that had just gone up the previous year. Of course, that was twenty minutes at *best*, when nothing went wrong, but how often does that happen? Re-routing, accidents, construction, shitty weather—everything and anything.

One time Greg booked check-ins at both sites within a half-hour of each other, and I had to tell the guests at King to go wait in a nearby coffee shop until I could get there to let them in; while I was en route, a thunderstorm blew up so badly that the neighbourhood transformer was struck by lightning and all the power went off, forcing the coffee shop to shut down early. By the time I got there, I had a family of five from Buffalo, New York standing angrily on the corner by a streetcar stop with no roof, soaked through. "Why didn't you take a damn cab, moron?" the father demanded, to which I could only smile and shrug, trying to look as inoffensively apologetic/Canadian as possible.

In principle I knew I'd be reimbursed for any expenses incurred on the job, up to and including sudden taxi rides, but that assumed I *had* the cash on hand to lay out for said expenses in the first place, and much of the time I just didn't. I was already living hand to mouth, bank account overdraft withdrawal to unexpected credit card charge—that was why I'd needed the job in the first place, for Christ's sake.

I called the place on George Street the House of Flowered Sheets; I suspected Kim had picked out all the linens, which were universally covered in patterns made from peonies, roses, tulips, or geraniums. It was small but airy, the floors panelled in fake blonde wood, with large windows facing Front Street that let in as much light as possible and fixtures of chrome and white porcelain. It got hot sometimes, but the overall air was functional, welcoming; big closets, a high-plumped double bed, cosily archaic furniture, free Wi-Fi. The guard on the front desk nodded back when I nodded to him every time I used the electronic fob-key to get in, and there were plenty of fake-friendly, nosy neighbours. This last part eventually turned out to be a bit of a drawback—but we'll get to that later.

The unit on King Street East, on the other hand, I called the Puppet Motel, because it was creepy, like a Laurie Anderson song. Because it was different, squared. Because it made me feel . . . not myself. And honestly, after only a couple of visits, I couldn't imagine how anybody could possibly want to *live* there after they'd seen it. Not even for a day, much less two or three.

Like I said, the building was new, a boxy modernist monstrosity arranged around what had to be the world's saddest concrete-and-stone park, complete with fake Zen garden sand-lot, which doubled as ineffective camouflage for the parking garage's entrances. In a way, since the property had two addresses (the other was on Bathurst Street, allegedly more convenient for guests driving in from Toronto's Pearson International Airport), each with its own front door/mailroom/security desk/elevator access set-up, you could say the place really functioned as two separate buildings somehow shoehorned one inside the other. Greg's apartment was on the mezzanine level, only accessible from either one specific elevator (off King) or one specific set of stairs (off Bathurst), and there was nothing else on that level except a garbage chute, a gym, and a mirroring apartment, seemingly unoccupied.

The Puppet Motel's windows looked inward, down onto the courtyard, so light was limited at best, a situation not helped by the fact that the entire place had been decorated in vaguely differing shades of black and grey. The bathroom fixtures were all black marble, even the tub, while the bathroom itself was tiled with granite—grey shot with black, like they couldn't decide what would pick up less light. It didn't matter much, anyway, because the main fixture in there didn't even work; the place was lit by vanity mirror fluorescents alone. Some sort of electrical short. Greg kept promising he'd get it fixed, but he never did, not even when guests routinely complained about it on Yelp. The ceilings, meanwhile, were so high that I had to climb on a teetering stool to replace the track-lighting bulbs whenever they blew, which was often. They'd go grey, then pop quietly—an implosion, as if the sound itself was being swallowed whole by that creeping pool of darkness lurking in every corner, poised to rush into any space the light no longer touched. I could feel it waiting at my back as I moved around, raising my neck-hairs, shortening my breath.

After the first day there, I realized just how easy it was to lose all track of time, hypnotized by the vacuum's drone or the dryer's atonal metallic hum; I'd gotten there at noon, done what I thought was a few loads, then glanced up to suddenly see the central shaft engulfed in shadow, with nothing outside the windows but oncoming night. From then on, I set my phone's alarm for twenty minutes a pop, trusting its old-school rising beacon trill to snap me out of . . . well, whatever it was. Oddness, at best, a fugue of disconnection; at worst, a physical queasiness, like I'd stepped through some unseen mirror into a weird, dim world, a cracked reflection of normalcy. On some very basic level, it just seemed *off*.

One day, on impulse, I took a marble out of the big glass vase full of them that decorated the breakfast island and set it down near the far wall, then watched it roll in a slow, meandering zig-zag across the apparently level linoleum to gently *pock* against the inside of the front door. Can you say non-Euclidean, boys and girls?

And there was a tone in there, too. It crept up on you, underneath everything. Sometimes it seemed to be coming out of the fixtures, shivering inside the lamps like an ill-set fuse, a light bulb's tungsten filament burning itself out from white heat into stillness like some glowing metal pistil. Sometimes I felt it coming through the floor, vibrating in my soles, making my toenails clutch and the bottoms of my feet crawl. It set my teeth on edge.

The longer I was in that place, the more I wanted—with increasing desperation—to be anywhere but.

Not that I cared enough to ask, but by the end I was convinced the only reason Greg had bought this unit, in this building, in the first place—the only way he *could* have—was that he'd never actually been here himself; that the entire exercise, from review to mortgage to signing, had been conducted online through virtual tours, remote bank branches and faxed paperwork.

That was the twenty-first century for you, though, bounded in the proverbial bad-dream nutshell. So supposedly interconnected on a global level that you could buy a place to live in a completely different country, without ever having to see for yourself—in person—just exactly what made it so . . . utterly unliveable.

When people ask me what I do for fun, for a hobby, here's what I often want to say: that there's a tone that moves around the world, and I follow it. That it's always been there, buried under everything else, all that static and noise and mess we call ordinary life—blowing high and dim, a wind no one else around me ever seems to hear.

Except, of course, that every once in a while, somebody does.

So I do my research, find the clues, the names and dates and places; I seek those people out, ask my questions and listen carefully, note it all down. Just the facts, if "fact" is ever the right word for something like this—rumour become anecdata, an utterly subjective record of experience, impossible to doubt or verify. Then I input what I learn, reformat it slightly and post it on my webpage, throwing comments open underneath. Leave each story hanging there, an open question, after which I retreat and watch to see who might turn up, who responds with reactions that read like answers.

Every story starts and ends the same way, no matter who tells it. *Remember that strange thing that happened, that one time? How it went on, 'til it stopped? How we never knew why?*

I cycle through these instances, rubbing each one in turn, telling them like the beads of a black bone rosary. They're tiny doors I leave open, so others who've heard the same bleak call can peep through. And it's like I'm mapping the edges of something invisible, something which exists on a completely different wavelength, an inhuman frequency; I'd never catch a glimpse of it otherwise, except through compilation, running the numbers. Just trying to figure out what it's not by grasping at whatever I can, however briefly—a blind woman theorizing, modelling the world's most nebulous elephant, and not even by touch. More by rumour.

It lives in the dark, alongside us, not with us. Impinges on us occasionally—or is it the other way around, maybe? We want to believe we're the point of any exercise, after all, but maybe we're not. Maybe we never are.

Collateral damage, spindrift, spume: we're what's left behind, the wake made flesh. Its tendrils blunder by us and scrape us raw, like shark's skin. And I'm just trying to build a community, I guess, to pare the loneliness down before it cores us clear through—cores *me*. Not as though anything actually gets solved in the process, but at least by the time it's over, we no longer assume we're all crazy.

"I just didn't know who else to talk to," they (almost) always say, and I nod, understandingly.

"Me either," I reply.

◄○►

Back in April, when my original plans for moving out of Dad's place for the summer had fallen through (rooming with school chums, who suddenly decided to tour the world over the summer instead), Gavin had impulsively offered to let me share his apartment until fall; wouldn't even have to chip in on the rent so long as I got a job and paid for my food, he said. In hindsight, this was one of Gavin's bad habits—he was a chronic over-promiser, always on one manic deadline or another—but I was too overjoyed to put two and two together, though we'd never even talked about sharing a place before then. That this pissed Dad off even more than the previous plan just struck me as an extra bonus, at the time.

In practice, Gavin's no-bedroom unit turned out to be way too small for two people, especially when the host was a neat freak and the guest tended to overreact to anything that felt like nagging. Didn't help I already felt indebted, resentful about it, and guilty about that resentment, all of which only played into Gavin's increasingly passive-aggressive attitude. Distracting ourselves in bed worked for a while, but not long. Greg's job seemed like a lifeline, as much for the excuse just to get out of the apartment as for the money, and I can't really make myself believe Gavin didn't sense that.

The general routine went like this: Greg booked residents online, then emailed me with the details of when they were supposed to arrive, at which point I went over and cleaned the selected apartment as sparingly as possible, trying to make it look "welcoming" for his guests. This involved garbage and recycling removal, cleaning all sinks and surfaces, running the dishwasher and washer-dryer, putting fresh sheets on every bed, opening windows and spraying Spring Fresh scent everywhere, plus light dusting. I charged fifty dollars an hour for housekeeping, clocked it, then sent Greg the receipts for any household supplies along with the rest of my weekly invoice.

Eighty dollars to check people in, eighty to check them out; I handed the guests a set of keys the first time 'round, took it back the next. Sometimes they were late, but I didn't get paid for waiting around, so I'd ring that up as part of the housekeeping. Sometimes *I* was late, and they just left the keys on a table by the door, closing the apartment door behind them--I worried about it initially, but it was never a genuine problem. People don't really tend to try other people's door-handles, not even when they're neighbours.

The money was welcome and arrived fairly regularly, but the job itself ate up far more of my time than I'd thought it would, especially when you factored in what Greg liked to call "floating duties." As the only person the guests ever dealt with face to face, I was essentially playing concierge at a non-existent hotel, often getting texts in the middle of the night from people who thought that paying to squat semi-illegally in someone else's apartment entitled them to treat me like their maid. One woman demanded I come over and re-clean the Flowered Sheets bathroom at 2:00 am, because it was so "unforgivably filthy" it was keeping her awake; another demanded I babysit her children for free, because I'd "misrepresented" how kid-friendly the area really was. I remember a father and two brothers who booked the Motel over a long weekend, at the beginning of July, apparently for the express purpose of getting solidly drunk together for three days straight; when I came in on Monday, I found they'd already been gone for hours, leaving behind three teetering pyramids made from beer bottles and a stench that didn't disperse until I propped the front door open and set fans in front of all the windows.

Like any public washroom, people do things in hotels they'd never do at home. They specifically come there to do them, because they expect someone else to clean up after them.

Naturally enough, this soon led to a constant series of Variations on a Collapsing Relationship, repeated riffs on *You're never around anymore, Loren* and *I'm* working, *Gavin*—because what else could I do except trust him to understand? After all, we were rowing the exact same leaky financial boat, essentially: him with his unpaid internship, his under-the-counter graphic design contracts, versus me with my two equally illegal jobs, killing time, and racking up the dough 'til I could go back to Brock University and live on campus. The both of us robbed and left twisting like the rest of our generation, unable to rely on anything but the post-Too Big To Fail world's inherent unreliability. With nobody else to take out our stress on, our arguments grew bitterer and bitterer, repetitious, discordant as bad jazz:

If the job's giving you that much grief, why don't you just quit?

You know I can't.

I know you won't.

You were the one who said I had to pay for my own food.

Fine, but can you at least stop talking *about it all the time?*

What the fuck does that mean?

It means that if you won't do anything to fix a problem, then there's not much point in complaining about it, Loren. So I'm sorry, but shit or get off the pot. Please.

Didn't help that Gavin was a skeptic by nature—I'd tell him about all the weirdness at the Motel, only to listen to him break it all down, carefully, 'til it barely convinced *me* anymore. *It's badly laid floor tile, poor design choices, horrible ventilation,* he told me. *Sick-building syndrome, that's all. And hotel guests behave badly everywhere, nothing needs to be "wrong" for that.* All of it only more infuriating for not being anything I could really argue with.

One evening in mid-July, I finally came home with what I thought might be direct evidence, shoving my phone at him the minute I got through the door. "I've got something you need to hear," I told him, "but first, I have to tell you what happened with these last two guests."

"The women you checked in on Monday?" Gavin asked. I had to give him this—even if he never took anything I said seriously, he did at least listen, and remember. "From Barrie, kept calling it their 'Big-City-cation'—you said you thought they might be a couple."

"Yeah, exactly. Well, I go by today to do checkout and the shorter one's sitting in the kitchen with her head down, looks like she's been crying. Tells me she and her friend had this horrible fight, but she can't remember about what; anyhow, she stormed out, then came back to find her friend was gone. Hasn't been able to reach her since."

Gavin scoffed. "They wouldn't be the first people to fight on vacation, Loren. Probably just turned her cellphone off and went back by herself."

"Yeah, that's what I told her." I sat down on the couch. "But after she left, when I was cleaning, I found an empty vodka bottle in the trash, and the place was also a lot cleaner than usual, like somebody'd gone over it already. Plus there was a smear of something that looked like blood, on the edge of the bedroom door."

Gavin put his hand over his face. "*Jesus,* Loren. I mean, how are you even sure it *was* blood, exactly? You packing Luminol in that kit of yours?"

"Oh please, fuck the fuck off with that CSI bullshit, okay? 'Cause while I may not have airquotes-worthy 'formal forensic training,' I *have* had a period every month of my life since I was eleven . . . so yeah, Gav, I do think I know a bloodstain when I see it, thank you very much."

Hadn't meant my voice to be quite so acid, but I was pissed, and it showed; Gavin flushed, like he'd been slapped. "Fine, then—say it *was* blood. So what? Could just have been from one of 'em whacking her head on the door by accident, especially if she was drunk. 'Cause if you've got *any* sort of firm evidence it was anything else, you should be telling the cops, not me."

I wanted to punch him, but settled for gritting my teeth. "Just listen to the damn file, all right? Tell me if that room tone sounds *normal* to you."

It had taken nearly an hour of creeping around the Motel, holding my phone at wrist-straining angles with its volume jacked to absolute max, but finally I'd found a place where the noise that constantly harassed me seemed both louder and steadier, as if it might be the actual spot it was emanating from directly (today, anyhow). The result was twenty-three solid seconds of ululation, near-inaudible without ear-buds, which I offered.

Gavin sighed, screwed them in, activated the .mp3; I held my breath, watching as he listened, but his expression didn't change, except for the faintest frown. 'Till he closed his eyes, at last, took the buds out, shook his head. Telling me, as he did: "Loren, that's nothing, literally. It doesn't sound like anything."

I tried not to blink as the wave crashed up over me, sheer disappointment turning my voice harsh again. "So . . . I'm just crazy, I guess."

"Did I say that?"

"You didn't have to."

We stared at each other for a moment, before Gavin finally turned away. "I'm going to make some dinner," he said. "You sound like you need a break." He went into the kitchen.

The moment he was gone I grabbed the phone back, shoved the buds in my own ears and hit "play." And there it was—that same note, wavering just underneath the hiss of empty air, making my jaw thrum, my fists clench, scowl sliding to wince. How could he *not* hear it? Were his ears just that *bad,* or . . . ?

(Or. Or, or, or.)

That night I dreamed I was pulling hair out of the drain in the Motel's all-black bathtub, whole sodden clumps of it melted together by decay, reduced to their ropy, keratinous components. It wasn't mine, and it smelled bad, worse than bad—terrible, terrifying, sharp enough to make the back of my throat burn. Like glue on fire. Like mustard gas.

With that *tone* there too, obviously, behind everything—behind, beneath, whatever. That same unseen filament twisting, sizzling, burning itself out; a call from far off, filtering down through great darkness. That shadow, mounting, yet barely visible: five fingers separating on the Motel's master bedroom wall, angled outwards, sketched charcoal grey on grey.

That open, beckoning hand.

⟜

The next morning I kissed Gavin goodbye as he set off for work, putting a little more energy into it than usual, hoping that would revitalize things, agreeing to vague evening plans for dinner and a movie. Then I came back after cleaning the House of Flowered Sheets and checking somebody in only to find my packed suitcases outside "our" apartment door, a note taped to the handle of my laptop case: SORRY, THIS ISN'T WORKING. TRIED TO TELL YOU BUT COULDN'T. LOCKSMITH CAME WHILE YOU WERE OUT, PLEASE THROW KEYS AWAY. I'M GONE FOR TWO WEEKS, NO POINT CALLING. DON'T HATE ME.

"Fuck *you*," I told the wall, hoping he was actually lurking behind it, his coward's ear pressed up close to hear my reaction. And left.

Gaslighting, my friends would have called it—he was making me question my own reactions, my own perceptions. But I was doing that anyways; the fucking Puppet Motel was gaslighting me, not Gavin. Gavin didn't matter enough to gaslight me, and maybe he knew it. Maybe that's why he dumped me. Maybe I would've dumped me too, if I'd been him.

(But I wouldn't have, I know that already. Not when I already knew where I'd inevitably have to end up, after.)

"What are you going to do?" my mother asked me, when we met in our local Starbucks.

"Your place is out of the question, I guess."

To her credit, she looked genuinely unhappy. "You know I *would*, sweetheart, but there just isn't enough room." She knit her hands around her cup, as if for warmth, despite how muggy it was. "And I won't even ask about moving back in with your father, given he's just as stubborn as you are."

"Thanks for that."

"Honesty costs nothing. Seriously, though—you don't have *any* other friends to stay with?"

"They're his friends, mostly," I admitted, "so not crazy about asking. Not that I know who'd have the space, anyway. . . ." I trailed off, realizing the obvious answer.

After Mom left me, I pulled out my phone and checked the time-conversion app I'd downloaded a month and a half before, back when I first took this stupid job; it was just coming up on seven a.m. tomorrow morning in Seoul—Greg might still be at home, hopefully already awake. A quick text later, I had my answer: **George Street unit's free for 2 wks—yrs if u need it**.

I slumped, so relieved that I didn't even realize until later that it was as much for *which* unit he'd offered as that he'd offered one at all.

-<>-

I was so out of practice at dealing with real people, the friendliness of my new neighbours at George Street caught me by surprise. One middle-aged housewife a floor up from me made a point of dropping by to "welcome me to the building," acting so amiable I found myself talking to her when I didn't have to. And, ultimately, telling her a little about my situation—before learning she was actually head of the condo committee.

The very next day, that security guard I usually nodded to handed me a thick manila envelope, telling me the building's by-laws explicitly forbade sub-letting without the proper paperwork—none of which, of course, Greg had ever bothered to fill out. The envelope contained a cease-and-desist letter I was instructed to forward on to Greg as soon as possible, and I was told to be out by eight a.m. next morning, or they'd call the cops. Panicked, I used Greg's own land-line to call his Seoul office directly.

"Oh, that," he said, maddeningly unimpressed. "Yeah, go ahead and send the paperwork, but don't worry; the corporation never bothers following up, it's not worth the legal expense. Just lay low whenever you come in to clean and don't talk to anyone, it'll blow over in a week."

"Does that mean I can stay?"

"Uh . . . ." The cheerfulness faded. "No, better not push it that much. King unit's empty tonight, though; I've got a booking in there day after next, but I can switch them over to George, so you'll be good for a week."

"Dude, are you even hearing me? They know what you're doing now, they're just going to throw out these next guests too—"

"No they're not. Look, Loren, I hate to say this, but this only happened because you gave yourself away to that nosey-parker upstairs; management doesn't really care about this stuff unless somebody on the committee forces them to. You'll still get your money." Then he softened, seeing my face. "Don't worry, Loren. We'll figure it out."

The stifled beat of my own rage got me across town, into the Puppet Motel and halfway through unpacking my first suitcase before the place's eerie quiet started to sink in. I looked around, throat suddenly gone tight. It still reeked of old beer, somehow, with even less pleasant things lurking beneath—a filthy alley stink, antithetical to the cleanser I'd personally coated every inch in. Probably seeping in from the garbage chute outside, I told myself, through the windows I left constantly open; this place wasn't old enough to have accumulated its own funk of decay yet, and Toronto's summer streets were nobody's idea of perfume. But it was either deal with the smell or live in a sweatbox.

I paused in the middle of the living room, listening hard—straining, almost—but heard nothing aside from my own breath, the pulse and rush of blood in my ears. No tone, for once. That was a mercy.

That night, I did something I don't usually do: slept naked atop the bed sheets with a fan on high at my feet, carefully calibrated brown noise playing through my phone's ear-buds, trying to tilt myself into what little breeze the windows let in. It was like I was deliberately breaking my own rules because I wasn't used to being alone anymore, making everything strange, so the underlying weirdness wouldn't stand out so much. And it even seemed to work, at first—I fell asleep quick and hard, then slept deeply, without dreaming.

Waking, however, was a different story.

⊸

"I don't understand the question. Can you try again?"

It was my phone's voice-activated A. I.—familiar even though I never used it, that skin-crawlingly pleasant Uncanny Valley monotone—speaking out of nowhere into my earbuds, jolting me awake. I groaned and rolled upright, the tone back and ringing in both my ears, and yanked the earbuds out. After a beat, its voice went off again, probably repeating the question, words inaudible but the intonation unmistakable. I could see "her" readout twang across the screen, back and forth, an electrified rubber band.

I fumbled my way to the settings screen and turned the A. I. off, then checked the time: half an hour before my set alarm. I lay back, eyes rolling up, a palm clapped over each eyelid; maybe I could get at least a little more sleep, if that fucking amorphous, ever-present *tone* eased up . . . .

"*I don't understand*," the A. I. repeated, so loud I actually yelped. *"Please try again. Please—specify."*

Everything in me locked stiff for an instant, like tensing against a punch. I'd never heard that too-calm no-voice pause before, as if *thinking*; the very implication burnt my throat, froze me all over. I stared down at the inert plastic rectangle, muscles tensed for fight or flight, my whole scalp crawling—but fight what, flee where? What was—

"*Okay*," the A. I. said. *"When can we expect you?"*

The Motel's tone was almost inaudible now, but that didn't help; I felt it in my jaw, my teeth, my tongue, realizing for the first time how it wavered up and down when it hit this particular pitch, arrhythmic yet random. A mouthful of ants, itching against my palate.

"Oh, I see. That's very soon."

Abruptly, the tone seemed to steady once more, pausing; waiting. For what? An—

(answer?)

"*Her name is Loren*," the A. I. told whatever it was responding to, helpfully—and that was *it*, motherfucker: enough, no more, gone gone *gone*. When the phone buzzed next I was already in motion, jackknifed to standing, thighs and stomach twisting painfully as I grabbed my shit and ran butt-naked out into the hall. Somebody (me, I guess) was making a noise like an injured dog, all terrified whimper. I slammed the door shut behind me, fumbled the key in and jerked it 'round, hearing the bolt squeal; had my shirt up over my head with no time for a bra, one arm already inside and the other sleeve dangling empty, hauling my leggings up like I was trying to lift myself high, crotch-first. Not quite fast enough, though, to prevent the A. I.'s voice from telling me I had a *new message* from *unknown caller* even as I scrabbled backwards, hit the stairwell door and wrenched it open, then half-fell headlong downwards, towards the open air.

I erupted out onto Bathurst, shoeless and panting, only to spend the rest of the day riding streetcars from coffee shop to coffee shop, denuding myself of change in pursuit of company, Wi-Fi, noise. Didn't even find the nerve to turn my phone back on 'til the end of the day, at which point I immediately retrieved five messages: three from the George Street renters, demanding help with various chores, plus two from Greg, urging me to call. Nothing else in the file, A. I.'s promises aside—not even a hang-up.

But the tone stayed with me, all day, with no respite. It rang through me tip to toe under any music I put on, no matter what the volume. And always deep enough to hurt.

⟜

"What in the hell's wrong with King Street, exactly, Loren?" Greg demanded, when I finally FaceTimed him back; the barista who was the only other person left in the Second Cup had already told me they were closing in fifteen minutes, which I figured gave an excuse to bail if things got too acrimonious.

How long you got? I felt like asking, but chose to play it dumb/diplomatic. "'Scuse me?"

"Check out the listing, on AirBnB.com. No, I'm serious, do it now. I'll wait."

Once I did, I could see why he was pissed. All but two of the votes were down, and not a single posted review was positive. A few were just the normal stupid shit—"they told me there was a crib but there wasn't" (there was, in the guest bedroom closet, the person just hadn't looked hard enough) or "kitchen electrical plug doesn't work" (which was why there was a label over the wall switch saying DO NOT TOUCH, which people routinely ignored). The rest, however, were . . . odder.

Most've the weekend went okay, but the bathroom light doesn't work and the door kept blowing shut when I was showering, so I'm standing there naked in the dark. I complained and they said they'd fix it (I'd said I'd pass it on to the owner, and had)*, which was total B.S., they never did.*

I always felt like somebody was watching me.

My alarm clock stopped working, so I missed half the stuff I had scheduled.

It was really hard to get to sleep, and REALLY hard waking up.

All we wanted was to just get drunk and watch some sports, but the TV kept crapping out and my Dad and my brothers wouldn't stop arguing.

I heard somebody crying, it sounded like it was inside the wall. It went on all night.

I had a big fight with my girlfriend, left to cool down, and when I came back she was gone. I thought maybe she just went home, but I've been back for three weeks and nobody knows where she is.

It smells funny and looking at the walls gave me a headache. Second night it got so bad I got a nosebleed and had to go to Emergency.

Went to bed and woke up with my best friend having sex with me, and neither of us can explain why it happened. It was like he was sleepwalking. Now he won't talk to me.

My ears haven't stopped ringing since I stayed there. My doctor can't figure out what's wrong with me. DO NOT book this place.

"See what I mean?" Greg demanded, soon as I picked my phone back up.

I was still staring at the laptop screen, surprised by how much it disturbed rather than validated me to be finally confronted with proof I wasn't nuts—that I definitely hadn't been the only one who found the Motel's atmosphere toxic. Up 'till then, the only real mystery I'd encountered directly (aside from my own reactions) had been the Case of the Missing Barrie-ite—and there she was, right in the middle, six complaints down. Yet much as I hated the Puppet Motel itself, the idea that so many customers had apparently left the place I was "responsible" for feeling equally unsatisfied and creeped out was strangely insulting.

"Yeah," I finally said, "that's all pretty weird. Not really sure how they can blame *us* for stuff like the accidental gay experimentation, though—"

"Well, sure, obviously. But what about the rest? If I didn't know any better, I'd think they were talking about sick building syndrome, or whatever—bad wiring, transformers, gas leaks. Some kind of contamination." As I hesitated: "I mean, *you* haven't felt any of this, have you?"

Only every fucking time I've been there, I thought, but didn't say. "It . . . can be a little off-putting, yes," I agreed, at last. "Might be the colour scheme."

Greg hissed. "Well, that's not *my* fault. The place came like that."

"Uh huh, that's what I assumed. Could be an idea to re-paint, though, at least."

That seemed to calm him, or at least make him think twice about whatever rant he had brewing. "Okay, all right, I'm sorry. I just—this place is supposed to pay for itself, you know? At the bare minimum. Optimally, it's supposed to provide a second stream of income for Kim and me, a nest egg to build on for when we come home . . . but it *isn't,* and I guess now we know why. I mean, I get that that's not your problem—but it means I *can't* re-decorate right now, because I don't have the funds."

"I understand."

"I mean, it's not like they built the place over a damn cemetery and only moved the headstones, or anything; the company walked me through full disclosure, right before we signed. Nothing's *ever* happened there, Loren. Not in that unit, not in the building."

"Not 'til I started moving people in, huh?" I ventured.

He snorted. "I'm not blaming *you,* if that's what you think. This is nobody's fault."

I nodded, not sure how to answer. "So," I said, at last. "What do you want me to do?"

"Nothing *to* do, I guess." The early morning sunlight behind him made it hard to read his expression. "Ride it out. I'm back in two weeks and you're back at school, so I'll take over then—Kim'll be joining me once her contract's up. And then . . . we'll just have to see, I guess."

"Okay," was all I said, and hung up on him.

I knew at the time I was being passive, if not passive-aggressive. And in hindsight maybe I *should* have told him everything, begged him to let me go back to the House of Flowered Sheets, pressured him into putting me up in a hotel: *Yes, I have all these exact same symptoms; yes, your awful condo gave them to me; yes, it damn well* is *somebody's fault, and you'll do for lack of anybody else. I've lost time too, felt the dislocation, heard the same ringing. I'm hearing it right now.* But—

—I think the whole thing with Gavin had kind of slapped that particular impulse out of me, at least for the moment. Like Greg said, however bad things got, there was a set time limit to all this, a clock ticking down: I could deal with that. I was an adult. I could take it.

These are the sort of stories we tell ourselves when things get bad, of course, hoping they'll stop them from getting worse. Even though, as we all well know, they so very seldom do. Still, I did the socially acceptable thing, for whatever the fuck *that's* worth: kept it to myself, all of it—then, and for years afterward. Not anymore, though.

Obviously.

Greg was right about the building's history, or complete lack thereof. So far as I could find out, there'd never even been a medical emergency here—like most downtown condos, it was full of young singles and couples, some with babies, more with pets. I couldn't tell if any of the babies or pets started crying outside the Motel's door, because I simply didn't get any traffic. It occurred to me that since I must have personally met every single person who'd ever slept under this roof, I knew damn well none of them had died here, mysteriously or otherwise.

Although one *had* disappeared, at least according to her friend. Or "friend." Or . . . whatever.

It wasn't until I'd finished my cleaning chores over at Flowered Sheets, hours after hanging up on Greg, that I realized the Motel's lingering tone was finally gone—as if the automatic, repetitious, thoughtless movements from appliance to appliance, vacuum and kitchen and washer and dryer, had ritually cleansed me as well. And it stayed gone, didn't reappear even when I went back into the Motel itself after midnight, turning the key the weird way you always had to: widdershins, then opposite, reversing your own natural instincts every time.

The light in the place was still bad, but the air was quiet, and the smell was mostly gone. I swept the floors, had a cool bath, changed into a sleep shirt and lay down, only to realize that despite my exhaustion, I was still buzzing far too much to doze off. So I booted up my laptop instead, and surfed around. On a whim, I googled environmental tinnitus causes, vaguely hoping to find a nice, simple explanation. Made an interesting sidebar into the realm of low-frequency or infra-sound—the kind that's lower in frequency than 20 Hertz or cycles per second, placing it beyond the perceptible/"normal" limit of human hearing, found to produce sleep disorders and vestibular stimulation even in people who couldn't consciously perceive it. In various experiments, listeners exposed to infrasound complained of feeling seasick and emotionally disturbed, prone to nervous bursts of revulsion and fear—they even experienced optical illusions, brought on because 18.5 Hertz is the eye's basic resonating frequency. Because these symptoms presented themselves without any apparent cause, scientists believed that infrasound might be present at allegedly haunted sites, giving rise to odd sensations people might attribute to supernatural interference.

See, Loren? Gavin's voice chimed in, smugly, inside my head. *No ghosts, no goblins—there's your 'something wrong,' probably. Just something resonating around 20 Hertz or less, creeping you out, making you think you hear things, feel things, see things. Making you afraid you* might *see things, at the very least.*

Which did make sense, of a sort. And yet.

So further down the Google click-hole I plunged, until forty minutes later I was wide awake and hunched over my keyboard, speed-reading my way through a website belonging to some guy named Ross Puget who specialized in "esoteric networking," jam-packed with hosted articles about shit like "psychic reconfiguration" and "bioenergetic pollution." The latter, all filed under "*Hauntings Without a Ghost?*" were about locations featuring the usual array of paranormal crap—orbs, cold spots, time fugues, visual and auditory hallucinations—but lacking one key ingredient for a classic paranormal experience: an actual human story, death or what-have-you, to set it all off.

Three months ago, it would have been good for a few laughs or an enthusiastic discussion with Gavin, before falling into bed together. Now, all I could think was *god, oh* god, because almost everything I'd experienced at the Puppet Motel, everything the guests had *implied* they might have experienced—it was all right there, in front of me. In cursor-blinking, eyestrain-saving black on white.

The site linked to Puget's Facebook page as well, and the guy had a startling number of friends—maybe "esoteric networking" was bigger business than I'd thought. Since he was online right now. I opened the site's messenger app, typing: **re hauntings w/out ghosts – questions ok?**

Sure, go ahead. I should tell you up front, though, I don't provide services myself. I just put you in touch with people who do.

Fine, I typed back, **just need info, rn.** I gave him my name, then described the Motel situation, as quickly as I could. Finishing up, I typed: **wwyd?**

What?

What. Would. You. Do.

Define "do." What's your goal here?

Make place ok 2 live in.

Situations like this are difficult to resolve cleanly, or safely. My advice would be to leave and not go back, but I'm assuming that's not an option.

N. Nt really.

All right. In that case, what I'd try to do is get a recording of any phenomena you can, audio or visual, and send it to me. I can review it, and maybe put you in touch with someone.

Omg, thank you. Thank you sm. Can send smthng rn.

Great, go ahead. Hope it all works out.

Me 2, I typed, and signed off.

~

I sent him the .mp3, waited, got no reply. And then . . . I must've fallen asleep somehow, because the next time I surfaced I was out of bed entirely, standing and staring at the primary guest bedroom wall, swaying slightly back and forth with my hand—the left, even though I'm very much right-handed—uplifted, raised halfway, like I'd caught myself in the act of deciding whether or not to touch that dim, dark grey surface. To find out exactly what it'd feel like under my naked fingers, dry and cool and only slightly rough, paint over plaster over baseboard over steel, concrete, the naked dollhouse pillars from which this hell-box of a condo'd been conjured . . . .

Without thinking, I snatched my hand back as if from an open burner, stomach roiling. Then, for the second time in two days, I hauled my shaky ass out of there—more slowly than my first retreat, managing to finish dressing this time, but heart hammering and my throat dust-dry all the same, eyes skittering around like I expected the walls themselves to start clutching at me. And with a lot more dignity, though that deserted me pretty much the second the stairwell door almost hit me in the ass.

Halfway down, my phone's A. I. shook awake and spoke, voice echoing in the concrete stairwell, loud enough I almost screamed. "*Someone wants to talk to you, Loren. Don't be rude.*"

Another bitter lesson, learned that very second: doesn't matter how hip, self-aware or trope-conscious you think you are—when shit gets weird, your instincts take over, fight or flight and nothing but, all pure shivering prey reflex. They can't not.

"*Who?*" I shrieked at the phone in my hand, as if the *really* upsetting thing here was having been called rude by a hunk of sleek plastic for not being willing to speak with a ghost. "*Who* fucking wants to talk? *Who?!*"

Must've come out far louder than I'd thought it would, because my throat hurt, by the time I was done. The text message alert chimed. Hands shaking, I swiped the messaging app, saw UNKNOWN at the top and had just enough time to think *of fucking course* before the message itself appeared, halfway down a blank white screen:

help me

I stared at it, panting. After a few seconds, the three rippling dots of an incoming message followed, and then the same two words again, stark and bleak: **help me**

Sheer reflex took over. I typed back, "keys" clicking: **Who R U?**, then, **Where R U?** Hit send, then waited. The seconds stretched out, my rough breath the only sound in the stairwell under a faint buzz of neon. Finally, the "incoming" dots rippled once more.

inside

Inside where? Name? An even longer pause, this time, and my patience snapped. **NAME**, I typed. **Or fuck off.** Breathing even harsher now, as much with anger as fear.

The reply appeared without warning, as if the "incoming" signal had been turned off. **Inside**, it repeated. **U NO WHERE.**

Then, dropping back into lower-case, as if exhausted: **help me**

I'm nowhere? I thought, before realizing what that space between O and W meant: *You know where.* Which was bullshit, of course; how was I supposed to know anything? Except—

—I did.

No, I thought, mouthing it, unable to find the breath even to whisper it. *No, I'm sorry, no. Not me; not this. Not my job.*

please, appeared on the screen, in its rounded grey box. Then after a longer pause: **please**. And once more: **please**. My screen gradually dimming even as that beat between each word kept on lengthening, exponentially, like each new message was burning through my phantom correspondent's own store of energy and draining my battery at the same time: iPhone as Ouija board, a process impossible to explain, or sustain. Until one last word appeared, grey sketched on ever-darker grey, simply reading—

loren

Behind me, I heard the door to the stairwell rattle once: firm, distinct, imperative. And—

—that was it. The tipping point. Where I instantly knew, in every cell, that I was done.

I leapt to my feet and power-walked to the King Street TTC stop, hands completely steady, deleting the entire message chain as I did. I no longer cared about proving anything, to anyone. Then I called my mother.

It took quite a few tries to wake her up. Ten years ago she'd have been answering a land line, and I had no doubt she would've been supremely pissed. But technology smoothes stuff like that over, these days: she already knew it was me, so a mere glance at the clock was enough to tell her something must be wrong—family doesn't call after two a.m. for anything but an emergency. "Loren?" she asked, half muzzy, half frightened.

I opened my mouth, and burst into tears.

If you're looking for closure here, you won't find much. These stories I collect now are only alike in their consistent lack of completion or explanation, their sheer refusal to grow a clear and satisfying ending—is any story ever "finished," really? Not until we're dead, and maybe not even then.

That's why telling the story, or being willing to listen to someone else's version—this story, or ones just like it—can sometimes feel like enough, though mainly because it has to be; because there's simply no other option. Because what I've learned is that our world is far more porous than it seems . . . full of dark places, thin places, weak places, bad places. Places where things peer in from whatever far larger, deeper darkness surrounds us, whatever macroverse whose awful touch we may feel on occasion yet simply can't perceive otherwise, not with our sadly limited human senses.

Because this is the basic trap of empirical knowledge—just one of a million million traps we're all born into, pressed like a fly between two sheets of this impossible cosmic amber we call time: the "fact" that if all data is essentially, inherently unreliable however it's gathered, just as we ourselves can never be more than imperfect and impermanent, our ideas of the world must always be taken on faith. Even if we have no template for even pretending to view what we come across through faith's lens, because "faith" is just a word to us . . .

. . . not just faith in God, mind you. But faith in *anything.*

⸺

I slept on my Mom's fold-out couch for close to ten hours, not waking until after noon. Several messages from Greg were waiting on my phone. Again, I deleted them all, then wrote him an email that said simply, *I quit*, which I sent without even signing. I half-considered adding *Sorry,* but couldn't bring myself to type the word. So maybe not so much better than Gavin was to me, in the end, but at least I had way more excuse for being brusque, in context; that's what I told myself, anyway.

Mom made me some soup and toast, watched me eat, then cleared her throat. "Honey," she began, "forget what I said before—you can *absolutely* stay with me 'till you go back to school. I don't want you to worry about that, okay? But we should probably at least go get the rest of your stuff."

I shook my head, trying to will my voice calm. "No, that's okay, no point to that—like, at all. It's not a big deal. I . . . don't need it."

"*Any* of it?" I shrugged; she sighed. "Well . . . even so, you do need to leave Greg's keys there, right? For whoever he hires next. That's only fair."

There wasn't anything to say to that except yes, much though I didn't want to.

So back we went to Bathurst and King, in a cab, with Mom visibly struggling all the while to *not* ask exactly what had convinced me I was no longer able to physically occupy that particular space anymore, in the first place. I ran the prospective conversation in my head as I sat there, trying it out, but there was no version of it where I didn't end up sounding frankly insane. *But does it matter?* the memory-Mom in my head replied, logically enough. *Whoever sent you those messages clearly knows who you are, where you live*—one *of the places you live. Might have followed you to the other. That's reason enough to quit right there, without all the rest.*

(I'd left my phone behind, at Mom's, just to be safe—no messages from beyond to interrupt as we blew in there, got my crap, got back out. I'd drop the keys on the breakfast table and be done with it. Just fifteen minutes more, maybe ten, and I'd never have to see that fucking place again.)

Then the *tone* came back, right outside the door, worse than ever—like a punch, or a skewer through the ear. It seemed to happen just as I slipped the key into the lock and cranked it widdershins, in the very second before making the decision to turn it and actually doing so; loud enough I felt the click instead of hearing it, so bad I barely kept myself from losing balance. I hugged the door-jamb as it opened in order to keep myself from doubling over, free hand slapping up to shield my eyes, and cursed like a sailor.

"Are you okay, Loren?" Mom asked, from behind me, as I made myself nod, somehow. "Fine," I replied, skull abruptly on fire, unable to stop my words from slurring—fresh silver agony everywhere on top of the usual pulse in my bones, my jaw, my eye-sockets, a chewed tinfoil drone. "Less juss . . . do this quick, 'kay? Don' wanna be 'n here . . . longer'n I have to."

I know Mom could hear the tone too, if only a little; I could tell from the way she suddenly stopped and stared, almost on the Motel's threshold, as though reluctant to move any further inside—hell, I sure didn't blame her. Once upon a time, simply being able to demonstrate the Motel's awfulness to someone who hadn't already paid to stay there would've been unspeakably satisfying, but I was way beyond that now. From the corner of my eye, I saw Mom knuckle her ears like she was trying to get them to pop after a long flight. "Jesus," she said, voice caught somewhere between disgust and amazement. "This is . . . ugh. Has Greg ever *been* here, in person?"

"Dunno," I replied, staggering forward to wrench the guest bedroom closet's sliding doors open. "Colour's not his fault, though. Came this way."

"*Ugh*," she repeated. "So this was *deliberate*?"

She helped me pull out my suitcases and toted the first one out into the hall while I flipped the other open, stuffing everything haphazardly back inside without any sort of regard as to whether mixing used toiletries with lingerie was a good idea. Some lingering sense of professionalism drove me to check that the fridge was empty and the trash cleaned out, but that didn't take long; Mom was already coming back in as I zipped the second case shut. "Done," I called, voice wobbly, my whole head twinging like a wound. I remember feeling as though if I opened my mouth too wide, my teeth might fall out.

"Great," she called back. "Mind if I just use the toilet?"

". . . 'course not," I lied.

And here is where my memory always starts to bend, the way things do, under pressure—where it speeds up and slows down at once, stuttering and swerving. I remember putting the case near the door and turning 'round, hearing Mom call through the washroom door, sounding slightly ill: "No *wonder* they complained about the lights." I think I actually might have laughed at that. And then there's a weird skip, a time-lapse, some sort of missing piece, an absence: a hole in my mind, a scar or flaw, something either too bright or dark to look on directly. The pain dims; the tone dims. I can't hear my Mom anymore. I can't hear anything but my own breath, my own heart.

I'm back in the guest bedroom, standing in front of the wall. Bright sunlight outside, falling through the concrete shaft like rain. Floating motes of dust lit up like sparks against a grey-black wall.

Loren, a voice says, inside my head. *You came back.*

My knees give out. That's never happened to me before, not even when I'm drunk, and I'd always thought the idea of your knees "giving out" was just a turn of phrase, an exaggeration. But no, apparently it can happen, because it does: boom and down, my ass hits the floor as my teeth clack together, so hard it hurts. And the tone comes back up, so high it's all fuzz, a horrible blur through every part of me at once, yet the voice, that voice—it cuts through. It's barely a whisper, but I hear it, so clear the words seem to form themselves against my eardrums. So clear it's like I'm *thinking* them.

Help me.

You have *to help me.*

I'm a guest.

The *tone*, louder than it's ever been, raw and primordial, wobbling like mercury. Each word vibrating as if a thousand different voices are saying it, at a thousand slightly different pitches. As if the *world* is saying it.

Some gigantic clamp vises my head, forcing it to look upwards once more, at the wall. Too far away to touch, now, but my hand—my *left* hand—reaches for it anyways, pulled as if on a string, a fishing line hooked where that blue "Y" of a vein humps across its back. My vision de-rezzed out to the point that the wall looks like nothing but a swirling cloud, a roiling cumulonimbus storm-head; it's crumbling, disintegrating, just like me. The wall pixilating like static then beginning to clear, its atoms getting further apart, becoming intangible. And at the heart of all that roiling grey I see something else, something new, forming: pale, surrounded by darkness, a monochrome infected wound coming up through colourless skin. It stretches its arms out to me.

But no, not it. Her.

Poor little missing Miss Barrie, come for her now-endless Big-City-cation. Staring out at me from the solid wall, from whatever lies on the other side of all solid walls, with blind, milky eyes and her flesh bleached like cotton, wavering in and out, an illusion of solidity. Her hair floating upwards, mouth stretching horribly wide as some abyssal fish's—a bad parody of a smile made by something that's never known how to, the very opposite of welcoming.

And that voice again, inside me, deeper yet. I feel my lips move as it speaks, pleading.

Caught hold of me, it won't let go, I can't

Are you there?

Help me, please, just reach in

Reach in and pull me out, I'll help

Just help me, please

That fetid, acrid smell back too, so thick, my lungs rigid with it. And then I'm up on my feet again, far too close, unable to remember moving; if only I reach out a little further, I'll plunge effortlessly through solid matter, like grey and filthy water. With Miss Barrie reaching back for me, her fingers almost touching mine, their too-pale tips already emerging from the wall's miasma, making my neck ruff with some sort of itchy, awful, sick-making anticipation—

That's when I see them, all around her: tendrils, trailing. Black strings in blackness, grey-shadowed. These weird strings at the corners of her mouth going up and back into the darkness, pulling and tweaking, twitching her lips, opening and closing her jaws. Plucking at her mouth's corners, hauling her limbs into place, raising her slack, soft, drained hand. Her tongue is working the wrong way for the words she's "saying," and it looks dry. Like she's being played long-distance, like a Theremin. Like a spider's web-filaments, tugged on from afar, tempting in a fly. Like some invisible puppeteer's strings.

Time started working the right way again, then: I wrenched back, just in time to see the blackness just above—behind her—move. There was a sort of stain on her left shoulder I'd thought was just my eyes failing, trying to translate something nobody should ever see into visual signals a human retina could read. But no: as I watched, it rippled, mimicking some much larger wave. A matching mass of utter lightless black reaching out for me, one single finger longer than any of Miss Barrie's limbs first pointing, then wagging slightly—*Oh, you! Always so difficult*—before turning over, crooking, in clear invitation. Curling up and back, then down, then up and back again.

Beckoning.

Come closer, my darling, come closer. Let me touch you, the way I'm touching her. Let me know you. Let us be . . . together.

Loren, come.

At which point I did exactly what I told *you* to do, if you ever see something similar. Threw down Greg's keys, so hard they bounced, and just.

Fucking.

Ran.

⊸

Mom found me back down on the street, eventually, shaking, cases in hand—looked like she wanted to rip into me at first, for leaving her along in that hell-hole, 'til she saw I was crying again. Days later, I got an email back from Ross Puget with an attachment that proved, in the end, not much more informative than any of his site's articles. He talked a lot about liminal spaces, about ownership and possession, the idea that when a space is left empty for too long—especially intentionally—it might tend to drift towards the "wrong sort of frequency," one that renders it easy to . . . penetrate. The Motel's tone, he said, was likely be a sonic side-effect of this collision between existential frequencies, the same sort of tension vibration seismographs pick up from continental plates grinding against one another; people theorized the same kind of fraying might explain what he called "apports," objects mysteriously disappearing and reappearing at particular locations, side-slipping through space from weak point to weak point. Some of these psychic fault lines, he added, seemed to predate human habitation altogether, and could be incredibly localized; a one-story house on the same lot as the Motel might've never have had any problems. If I was still interested in trying to do something about it, he could recommend a few names.

I never answered, which I feel more than a little bad about. I did, however, forward the email on to Greg, with a brusque postscript: *If you can't sell the place, burn it out and collect the insurance. I'm serious.* Then I blocked his number.

Sometimes I dream of my time in the Puppet Motel and wake up heart-sick, breathless, hoping against hope I'm not still there. Sometimes I get texts from an unknown number, and delete them unread. Sometimes my phone's A. I. tries to talk to me, and I turn it the fuck off.

I do still hear it call to me, sometimes, though—it, or her. Because that's the only real question, isn't it, when all's said and done? Was Miss Barrie only ever what she seemed, a drained shell run long-distance, a mask over something far worse? Or is she still hanging there in darkness even now, two or three plaster-layers down, waiting in vain for a rescue that never comes?

Does something have to be human—to have *been* human—to be a ghost? Ross's articles could never quite agree. And that thing I saw, that barest fingertip: malign, or just lonely?

The woman inside the wall, she's a ghost, now. I'm almost sure.

Still. I hear that thin, terrible voice, forever pleading with the empty air: *Loren, Loren, help me.* And see myself forever backing away, hands waving, like I'm trying to scrub all trace of my occupancy from the Puppet Motel's polluted atmosphere. Thinking back, as I do: *Stop saying my name, I don't know you, I can't. I* can't. *I don't* know *you.*

That's a choice, though, to believe that. It always was.

Like everything else.

So I track these stories on my own time instead, and whenever I think I've identified those who might be able to tell me about what happened, I arrange to make myself available. It doesn't always pay off, of course—some are jokes, or pranks; some are mistakes, honest or otherwise. Sometimes, I've found, people try their best to persuade themselves of supernatural influence in order to re-frame their own errors, to cast their own (entirely human) demons as things whose actions they couldn't possibly bear any responsibility for.

But for myself, I know when a tale is true because when I hear it, that *tone* will start to resonate inside me once more, piercing me through from ear to jaw to bowels, ringing at my marrow like a struck bell. I can't stop it, can't help it. I just . . . can't.

So I do the next best thing, and listen. Record, maintain. So that future seekers—people caught in the grip of something they struggle to understand, just like I once was—will have a place to go, to learn. To understand.

This world is full of weak places, after all, where dark things peer through, Beckoning. One of which knows my name, now. And I just have to live with that.

I always will.

THE SENIOR GIRLS BAYONET DRILL TEAM

JOE R. LANSDALE

The bus ride can be all right, if everyone talks and cuts up, sings the school fight song, and keeps a positive attitude. It keeps your mind off what's to come. Oh, you don't want to not think about it at all, or you won't be ready, you won't have your grit built up. You need that, but you can't think about it all the time, or you start to worry too much.

You got to believe all the training and team preparation will carry you through, even if sometimes it doesn't. I started in Junior High, so I'm an old pro now. This is my last year on the team, and my last event, and if I'm careful, and maybe a little lucky, I'll graduate and move on. It's all about the survivors.

I was thinking about Ronnie. She was full of life and energy and as good as any of us, but she's not with us anymore. She got replaced by a new girl that isn't fit to tie Ronnie's war shoes, which her parents bronzed and keep in their living room on a table next to the ashes of Ronnie's pet shih tzu. I saw the shoes there during the memorial. The dog had been there for at least three years before Ronnie died. It bit me once. Maybe that's why it died. Poisoned. I remembered too that it slept a lot and snored in little stutters, like an old lawn mower starting.

Ronnie has a gold plaque on the wall back at the gym, alongside some others, and if you were to break that plaque apart, behind it you'd find a little slot, and in that slot is her bayonet and her ashes in an urn. I guess that's something. Her name is on the plaque, of course. Her years on the team, and her death year is listed too.

There have been a lot of plaques put in the gym over the years, but it still feels special and sacred to see them. You kind of want to end up there when you're feeling the passion, and the rest of the time that's just what you don't want.

Ronnie also has a nice photo of her in her uniform, holding her bayonet, over in Cumshaw Hall, which is named after the girl they think was the greatest player of all, Margret Cumshaw. Cumshaw Hall is also known as the Hall of Fame.

To be in both spots is unique, so I guess Ronnie has that going for her, though it occurs to me more than now and again, that she hasn't any idea that this is so. I'm not one that believes in the big stadium in the sky. I figure dead is dead, but because of that, I guess you got to look at the honor of it all and know it matters. Without that plaque, photo, ten years from now, who's to know she existed at all?

Sometimes, though, the bus ride can be a pain in the ass, and not just because you might get your mind on what's to come and not be able to lose your thoughts in talk and such, but as of late, we got to put up with Clarisse.

Clarisse thinks she's something swell, but she's not the only one with scars, and she's not the only one who's killed someone. And though she sometimes acts like it, she's not the team captain. Not legitimately, anyway.

It's gotten so it's a chore to ride with her on the bus to a game. She never shuts up, and all she talks about is herself. She acts like we need a blow by blow of her achievements, like the rest of us weren't there to perform as well. Like we didn't see what she did.

She remembers her own deeds perfectly, but the rest of us, well, she finds it hard to remember where we were and what we did, and how there have been a few of us that haven't come back. She scoots over the detail about how our teammates' bodies, as is the rule of the game, become the property of the other team if we aren't able to rescue them before the buzzer. You'd think she saved everyone, to hear her rattle on. She hasn't. We haven't.

We managed a save with Ronnie's body, but we've lost a few. That's tough to think about. The whole ritual when you lose a team member to the other side. The ceremony of the body being hooked up to a harness that the other team takes hold of so they can drag the body around the playing field three or four times, like it's Hector being pulled about the walls of Troy by Achilles in his chariot. And then there's the whole thing of the other team hacking up the body with bayonets when the dragging is done, having to stand there and watch and salute those bastards. That happens, the dead teammate still gets a plaque, but there's nothing behind it but bricks.

When we end up dragging one of theirs and hacking on it, well, I enjoy that part immensely. I put my all into it and think of teammates we've lost. We yell their names as we pull and then hack.

Thing was, Clarisse's bullshit wasn't boosting me up, it was bringing me down, cause all I could think about were the dead comrades and how it could be me, and here it was my last game, and all I had to do was make it through this one and I was graduating and home free.

A number of us were in that position, on the edge of graduation. I think it made half the team solemn. Some of the girls don't want it to end. Me, I can't wait to get out. There's a saying in the squad. First game. Last game. They're the ones that are most likely to get you killed.

First time out you're too full of piss and vinegar to be as cautious as you should be, last time out you're overly cautious, and that could end up just as bad.

Clarisse thinks she's immortal and can do no wrong, but sometimes you go left when you should go right, or the girl on the other team is stronger or swifter than you. Things can change in a heartbeat.

Clarisse, for all her skill, hasn't learned that. For her, every day is Clarisse Day, even though that was just one special day of recognition she got some six months back. It was on account of her having a wonderful moment on the field, so wonderful she was honored with a parade and flowers and one of the boys from the bus repair pool; the usual ritual. Me, I have always played well, and I'm what they call dependable. But I've never had my own day, a parade, flowers, and a boy toy. I've never had that honor. That's okay. I used to think about it, but now the only honor I want is to graduate and not embarrass my team in the process, try to make sure no one gets killed on my side of the field. Especially me.

We may be the state champions, but the position can change in one game. More experienced players you lose on the team, through graduation or death, less likely you'll make State Championship. You can train new girls, bring up the bench team. But it's not the same. They haven't been working together with us the same way. They don't move as one, the way the rest of us do. They're lumps in the gravy. They would need to survive several games before they were like a part of us.

Of course, listening to Clarisse you'd think she was the team all by herself. I've heard of some teams who would leave one of their members to the blades, for whatever reason. Maybe haughty teammates not unlike Clarisse. But no matter how annoying she is, that's not the way we play. That's not team work. We stick with her, like her or not. She's a hell of a player, but she's not the official team captain. But with Janey in the hospital they've given her the team for a while, so I guess, like it or not, she does have that position, but I just can't quite see her that way, as a true leader.

Our coach is around, of course, but she rides in a separate car when we go on a trip to a game. She says us having to deal with one another forces comradery. But I think the coach just likes to ride in a car and not hear our bullshit.

She's had a lot of winning teams, but this year, I figure she's done. She knows we know our stuff, and there's not much she can do. Just have us run our drills and give us a pep talk now and again. She was a great champion before she was a famous coach. She has fifty kills to her credit. Only Margret Cumshaw and Ronnie have more than that. But for all practical purposes, she's out of the picture.

"Thing you got to remember," Clarisse said, turning in the bus seat, looking back at us, "is you can't hesitate. Can't do like Millicent last time out. You have the moment, you take it."

Hearing my name mentioned made my ears burn. I hadn't hesitated. Things went a little wrong is all, and in the end, no one died and we won easily.

"Yeah. We know how it works," Bundy says.

Clarisse gave Bundy a glance, but it wasn't a strong one. We all knew Bundy was vital to our success. Clarisse was too, but nobody liked her the way they liked Bundy, though Bundy can connive a little herself, always wanted to be a team captain, end up a coach.

Bundy was one of our corners. She made things look easy. She wasn't fast like me or some of the other girls, but she was strong and taller than the rest.

She had taken on two at a time more than once, and won, leaving them dead in her wake. She had her own parade day, twice, and she also had the scars across her cheeks and chin to prove her moments under the lights. Everyone said it made her look like a warrior, and that's true, but they were still scars. Bundy had been pretty once.

Me, I've done okay in that department. I have a scar on my left side, just below the rib cage, some small ones here and there, but I've come out all right, so far. At least I got both eyes. Bundy has a black pirate patch over her left one.

"I'm merely doing my job," Clarisse says.

"Sounds to me, like you're trying to do all our jobs," I say, and that sets her off a little, but not in words. She just gives me the look.

That burning look she usually saves for when we're on the field, the one she has for the girls on the other team. It's the look she wanted to give Bundy but didn't, so I'm getting it double-time.

"As Team Captain," Clarisse says, "I—"

"Temporary Team Captain," I say.

Now that look from her was stronger. Me and her, we've always rubbed each other the wrong way, even back when we were in grade school, when we first started training with wooden bayonets and swatting dummies full of candy at each other's birthday parties.

The dummies were always dressed up in drill team colors from other schools. It was a way of starting to think right about what we wanted to grow up and become. Me and her, we made the team, way we dreamed we would, and though we were a bit at each other all through school, we mostly got along. Guess you could say more than that. That we were close, like competitive sisters. Lately it was nothing but snide remarks and go to hell stares, grins like sharks. Only thing that held us together was the team.

"Just think," says the new girl, Remington, sitting beside me, fidgety, "tonight, all over the country, stadiums will light up, and teams will go inside, and the crowds will grow, and we'll play beneath the lights."

I turn to look at her. "The lights will go up and the teams will march out and look up into the crowd, and you'll be sitting on the bench, maybe getting us some water when we change out."

"Yeah, I guess so," Remington says, turning red, making me feel a bit like an asshole.

Remington was a little thing, just barely made the team, but the roster was thin for new troops this year, so she was the best of the worst. "But I'm on the team. That means something, doesn't it?"

"Sure," I say. "We all start that way, asses on the bench. But eventually you'll get your shot. You'll be all right."

I didn't really think that. I figured first time she was on the field, after she got through the performance, the ritual, she'd hit the turf running and end up with a bayonet through her throat. I'd seen it happen more than once. The real Rah-rahs, as I called them, often didn't make it out of their first game without being badly wounded or dead, sometimes carried away by the other team for that drag and hack business.

I told myself, she got in the game, she went down, I'd do my best to save her body from the other side, but I'd only go so far. I didn't know her like I knew the others. The loss wouldn't be the same. I kind of felt the same way about Clarisse, and we were long time teammates, but at some point, you draw the line on risk. And tonight, I had drawn that line.

If I lived to get on the bus to go home, I would have had all I ever wanted of red, wet grass and cheering crowds. I could probably get an endorsement deal or two if I played my cards right.

But when I, if I, stepped off that field tonight, from that point on I was a happily bored civilian.

"All I ever wanted to be," says Remington, "is on the team, to wear the white and purple."

"You haven't made it yet," I say. "You have on the colors, and you can say you're on the team, but until you're on the field facing those who want to stab you, and you need to stab them, and you've played through, then you can truly say you're one of us. Not before."

She practically glowed there in the thin inner lights of the bus. "I'll get there."

Maybe.

"It's about our school," she says. "It's about our tribe, isn't it? Nothing really matters but our group, right or wrong."

I thought the problem was just that. The way the tribe takes over logic. The way other girls on other teams are the same. Them against us, us against them. But I say what I was expected to say, what I had to say, "Yeah, sure, girl. That's it."

The bus slowed at a light, adjusted with a whining sound which meant it might need some overhaul or something, and then it moved forward again without dying or going to pieces. It just might get us there.

I thought of something my mother said, that they used to have an actual driver up there, in the seat, and it was always a cranky old fart. She said she missed cars and buses that you drove, but me, I can't imagine such a thing. I was cranky enough tonight without having a cranky bus driver. I looked at Clarisse sitting up front, and I'm thinking there was a time when we gave our dolls swords, and each held one and made them fight one another. We got our fingers banged a lot. Lot of girls that wanted to make the team did that, but I didn't know any started as early as we did. We would sleep over at my house, or me at hers, and we'd talk. I couldn't figure it sometimes. How we went from what we were then to what we were now. It's like someone had cast a spell on us. We had a whole new set of friends outside the Team, and now me and her only talked when we had to, when we needed to for the games.

Sometimes it hurt me to think about what had been.

I looked out the window as we passed a field full of corn. There were lights in the field, and you could see the corn standing high, and beyond the field it was as dark as the space between the stars. I remembered once my mother, who had been quite a team champion herself, told me that when people came here, that was the part that was terraformed first. That very spot.

"Once, it was barren, and there was a dome," she said. "Right there is the heart of our beginning."

That was hard to imagine.

"Remington." It was Clarisse's voice cutting through my moment of silence, and I had so been enjoying it. "I think we might pull you off the bench tonight, you know, let you play first, be up front to feel things out."

"What the hell," I say. "She doesn't know her ass from her elbow."

"She's got about three seconds after they blow the whistle," Bundy says. "Then her dead ass will be taking a tour around the arena."

"Two seconds," I say.

"She's been trained," Clarisse says.

"That's right," Remington says. "I'm on the team. I'm honored to have the chance, Captain."

"Temporary Captain," I say.

"Temporary or not," Remington says, "that's the same thing, though. Right?"

Remington's saying that made my face flush. I hoped that didn't show in the poor light. It took me a long moment to say it, but I did. "Right."

I made a point then of deciding not to get to know Remington at all, because tonight would be her last night. I knew what Clarisse was doing. She was going to use someone we weren't close to for probing the team, seeing how good they were, how long it took them to put Remington down. It was a mean sort of gesture, to put her at the front, like she was important to the team, but what she was, was expendable.

I could practically feel Remington vibrate beside me. In a few hours there wouldn't be any more vibrating. It would be over for her, and we might learn something from her death about the other team, which admittedly was a team that changed up their game plans. They had a lot of solid, long term members, and they were without a doubt the toughest we had ever faced. I had seen some of the film made of their games, and it was chilling. They had an amazing defense and an even more amazing offense. When they left the field, it was always wet with the blood of the other team.

"I'm going to make all of you proud," Remington says.

"Of course you are," Bundy says, and all the other girls said something like that out loud. They were supposed to. I didn't say a damn thing. It might cost me some extra laps at the gym, Clarisse wanted to push it, tell the coach, but the thing was, I was done after tonight. I got home I only had one more week on the team, and that was all ceremonial until the graduation honors. I could run a few laps. I could do extra sit-ups or any other exercise that was asked of me. But tonight, I wasn't going to give Clarisse the satisfaction of agreeing with Remington's sacrifice. Poor Remington. She thought she was going to be a hero, not a corpse.

"Should I attack right off?" Remington says.

I didn't answer her. I didn't say anything. She said a few more things out loud, but I wasn't paying any attention any more. I was sitting there looking out at the landscape, flooded white by the moonlight.

When we got to the café where we always stopped, Clarisse stood by the door of the bus, and as the team came out she reminded us not to eat heavy, the way Jane always did, like we needed to be reminded.

As I started past her, she called my name, says, "I need to speak to you privately."

I took a deep breath and let it out and stood off to the side and let the others pass as they headed into the café.

When it was just me and her, I say, "What?"

"You're supposed to be an example. Keep the new girl up, not try and bring her down."

"She'll go down all right," I say. "She's got about as much chance as a rabbit in a dog's cage."

"She has her training. We were all newbies once, and we all took our chances."

"We were better than her."

"That's how we remember it."

"That's how it was. And why aren't you talking to Bundy? Why didn't you pull her aside?"

"Because you're a Point, like me, like Jane. There has to be a third point, and with Jane out, she's the only one with the jets to play that position."

"Remington's no Jane. She's no anybody. And besides, you don't start the new ones off on Point first game out. Pull Bundy up."

"She's not fast enough. She's better where she is. Remington is fast, I've noticed that at workouts."

"Yeah. All right."

I knew it was a done deal. Clarisse was, much as I hated to admit it, the team captain. Unless the coach decided to override her, Remington would have her two seconds. And then she'd eat dirt.

"You protect the ones who have experience," Clarisse says. "That's how we win, with the regulars."

I quit talking to her then, went inside the café.

There was music playing and I could smell food cooking. I ordered a hamburger, one of the small ones and a side salad. Remington came over and slid into the seat across from me.

"I'm so excited," she says.

"Save some of that," I say. "Tame it, use it."

I don't know why I even bothered. She was a goner.

She chattered on about this and that, about the team, and finally our food came, and still she chattered. I ate slowly, way you need to, and when Remington wasn't chattering, she ate quickly, the way you're not supposed to.

"I know you don't think I'm ready, but I am."

"I know you're not ready."

"I believe in the team."

"That's nice."

"Don't you?"

"Sure," I say, but I wasn't certain. Did I?

Clarisse had already eaten, something small and mostly vegetables, I figured. She always looked great, played great. She came down the aisle of the café, walking between the rows of tables, saying, "Everyone. This is the championship game. This one counts more than any of the others counted. We have to—"

"They all counted," I say, the words jumping out of my mouth. "Ronnie's game counted, didn't it?"

"Of course. That's not what I meant."

"I am so tired of your yacking and trying to act like you're some kind of hot stuff. Why don't you shut up and sit down and just do your part later?"

"You're jealous, aren't you," she says, glaring at me. "You wanted to have a day dedicated to you, and you didn't. Didn't earn one. And you thought you might actually take Jane's place while she was out. Be team captain instead of me."

"You don't know anything," I say, but I was thinking, yep, that's about it. That and the fact that I was tired of the whole thing, tired of dreaming about the final dark, the possible pain. I have nightmares about being dragged around the inner stadium with my dress hiked up and my ass hanging out, flapping along like Clarisse's tongue.

"I'm the team captain," Clarisse says, "like it or not."

"I don't like it much," I say.

Everyone looked from my face to Clarisse's, except Bundy. She says, "This can be settled."

"It can," I say. "The old way it used to be settled."

"We don't do that anymore," Clarisse says.

"You mean you don't want to do it that way," I say.

"You and me, we been friends a long time."

"No, we were friends a long time ago. This whole team captain thing, it can be solved, way Bundy says. It's in the rule book."

Bundy eyed Clarisse, says, "Think she's got you there, Captain."

"Very well," Clarisse says. "This is a bad time for it. Game night. But yeah, I'll give you your satisfaction."

She touched the bayonet strapped to her hip.

That's when Lady Red, owner of the café, her hair dyed red as a beet, drags all three hundred pounds of herself out from behind the counter, wags a finger at us. "You know the rules for any squabbles, fist or bayonets, or just bad language. Take it outside. One of you gets killed, you'll bleed in the parking lot, not on my floor."

"There's no need for this," Remington says. "One for one, and one for all."

"Shut up, Remington," I say.

⟜

The lot was lit with lights and moonlight. It wasn't as bright as the stadium would be, but it was pretty good. We could see how to kill one another, that was for sure.

We spaced off, ten feet between us, our bayonets drawn, the edges of them winking light. Clarisse stood with her legs a little wider than shoulder width, standing to the side, the bayonet in her forward hand, not the back one, way you should hold it if you knew something. We both knew something, but I got to thinking there might be a reason she was team captain, not me, because earlier she had hit it on the head. I wanted that place, thought I deserved it, and Clarisse had always won out over me, in everything. She got the best body and face to begin with, born that way, and she had better clothes and they fit her the way the same clothes would never have fit me, even if my parents had the money to buy them, and she got all the boys, and twice she got my boyfriends, and all she had to do was walk by and smile, and it was a done deal.

I had dreams where she died, and I never knew how I felt about them. Was I happy or sad? I awoke with tears on my face but a happy heart.

"You've always been jealous of me," Clarisse says, like she's been reading my mind.

"You don't know everything," I say, but right then I'm thinking, yeah, well, she knows a lot, and she probably was a pretty good team captain, and she just might kill me tonight, or wound me bad. I didn't have the team to work with against her. I had me and she had her, and that was it.

Thing was, to save face, I had to do it now, and I thought, maybe I'll wound her good enough, or maybe she'll wound me good enough I won't have to go in with the team tonight. I'll be through.

I swallowed and eased forward and she eased toward me.

"Touch off," she says, and though this isn't a game, just a fight, I do it, reach out and tip my blade against hers. They make a clinking sound, and then we both move back one step, like we would in a game, and start to circle one another.

"This isn't team work," Remington says, stepping out of the circle of girls around us, saying that like it might not occur to us that it wasn't.

It's then, that just beyond Clarisse, as we're circling, I see Bundy's scarred face there in the light, her one eye and her black patch on the other, and she's lit up like she's just had an orgasm, first communion, and a ticket to heaven.

Oh yeah, I'm thinking. We do this, I kill Clarisse, or she kills me, or we just get injured bad, neither of us may be able to be team captain, and next in line is Bundy. Wouldn't be a lot of discussion on that, not tonight, when it's the last game and there's no time to rethink things. Bundy ends up captain tonight, and we win the game, she goes out a hero, gets another parade. Me and Clarisse get some hospital time, and maybe the game's lost because we're not there.

Was that why Bundy was so eager to have us fight?

Was I trying to find excuses to dodge out?

Now Clarisse was easing closer, using the fake step, where you drop your back leg behind you, but your front stays where it was, gives the impression she's moving away, might make you think you can get her on the retreat, but it's just a trick.

I knew all her tricks, and she knew mine.

"We're a team," Remington said. It sounded like her voice had been sent to her via wounded carrier pigeon, like it didn't really want to be there.

"Hush," Bundy says to Remington.

But that's when Remington began to sing our fight song, and damn, her voice was good. It rose up and filled the air and it almost seemed as if the lights got brighter, and if that wasn't enough, some of the other girls started to sing. They tightened the circle around us, and the singing got louder. I could feel tears in my eyes, and then one of those tears escaped and streamed down my face, and the other tears, like lemmings, followed.

"And they called to the crowd, and the crowd called death, and the bayonets came down," they sang, and then the chorus, "Came down, came down, like a mountain, came down."

For whatever reason, that chorus always got me, and it had me then, and I think to myself, get it together, lose the emotion, or Clarisse has got you.

But that's when I see Clarisse's face in the light, and it looks like she's just sucked a lemon. The war paint she wears was running over her cheeks, her face was wet. Her bottom lip was trembling.

All of a sudden, she lowers the bayonet to her side and starts to sing, and then I lower my bayonet, and I start to sing, and coming in late, but clear and strong, Bundy begins to sing.

Everyone of the girls is singing now, and just as loud as they can.

Me and Clarisse spin our bayonets into our sheaths in unison, like one of our drills, and we smile at each other, and we keep singing, and when we come to the end of the song we embrace.

Remington says then, "We got time for a cup of coffee. One cup is good for you in a game, coach told me that, but two, that's too many."

I went over and put my arm around Remington, and then Clarisse did the same thing from the other side, and we walked Remington back into the café, the team following.

On the bus, me and Clarisse sat together, up front of everyone else, and were mostly silent in the dark, but when we were maybe like, five miles out, she says, "Do you remember when we were little, how we used to make our dolls fight?"

"Sure," I say. "I remember," not telling her I was thinking just that thing earlier tonight.

"We were close then," she says, "and I always have felt close to you, even when we weren't getting along."

"Me too, I guess."

"I was always jealous of you, Millicent."

"Say you were?"

"You were smart, and could see things quick, and I got to tell you, I maybe overdo a bit when I'm around you, cause I'm thinking whatever I'm doing, you could do as well or better. I don't like to admit that, but I'm admitting it now."

"Yeah, well, you got your stuff too. I never had your looks, your style."

"You say. I mean, you know, you could push your hair back a little more, show your face. You got a good profile, girl."

"Yeah?"

"But mostly you're smart. You're smart, and you'll probably stay smart. No one stays pretty, not in the way they think. My mama told me that."

"She's damn pretty."

"Yeah, but you should see pictures of her when she was younger. She was beyond pretty."

I let that soak in, her compliments, and then I say, "Remington, I don't know. Front lines. I mean, it's your call. She is quick, damn quick, and eager, but I'm thinking maybe you put her in at the back, first round, then move her to the front later, second or third round, third would be best, and by then she's got a feel, isn't quite so eager she's rushing into something she doesn't understand."

Clarisse nodded. "Coach told me, said, you're the Captain, but someone has a suggestion, listen to it, and you like it, do it, you don't, don't do it, but whatever happens it's on your head."

"That's a heavy responsibility."

"Listen here, girl. Let me be completely honest. I wanted Remington up front, because I didn't want you up front. You're great. You can play the spot, you know you can, and you do, but, I figured tonight, we might both go home, and then, we might can, you know, be friends again."

"I'd like that, but I don't want Remington to die for it. And besides, you need me up front with you. Like always."

Well, then we could see the stadium lights, they were pointed out from the stadium toward the sky. A moment later we could see the big open gate that led inside. The bus went in, and then it stopped and we got out.

Clarisse tries to get everyone's attention, but there's too much excitement. Championship game, you know.

"Hey, listen up," I say, and I say it like I mean it. "Captain has something to say."

Everyone goes silent and we huddle around, and Clarisse says, "Remington, you'll play at the back first round, maybe through the second. Then, everything looks good, we'll move you up."

"Yes, Captain," Remington says, and if she looked disappointed, I couldn't tell it.

Clarisse gave us a few more instructions, stuff we already knew, but it's all right to hear it again, to keep sharp.

Then we marched in formation toward the big opening that led onto the field. It was dark in the tunnel and we stopped right at the opening that led onto the field, and looked out. There was some light on the field, but only at the far end, where the other team stood waiting. Being that they were the challenging team, they got to come out first, get hit with their lights.

Clarisse says what we always say before we step onto the field. "We know not what comes."

We chant the same words once, softly, and then Clarisse says, "Remington, lead off with it."

Remington starts to sing our fight song, and then we all start to sing. Bundy slaps Clarisse on the back, and out we go, marching onto the field.

Hearing our voices, our school band starts to play up in the stands, a little heavy on the drums, but good on the horns, and then everyone from our school, parents, students, teachers and so on, they start to sing too, and then the stadium lights flare on us.

We look up and see our supporters standing up, singing, smiling down at us, and we march confidently onto the field, still singing.

THE NIGHT NURSE

SARAH LANGAN

Before

When the night nurse first told Esme that she was a witch, Esme did not believe it. Or at least, she hadn't envisioned the dark arts. She'd pictured a group of Waldorf School mothers sitting in a circle, knitting boiled wool dolls and talking about their menstrual cycles. They had trust funds, smelled like patchouli, and they were gentle as pillows.

Esme first met the night nurse at the Brooklyn Children's Museum. She'd been seven months pregnant with baby number three. *Baby one too many,* in other words.

It had been one of those school holidays that wasn't really a holiday: *White Hegemony Day* or *Teachers Hate Their Jobs and Need Four-Day-Work-Weeks Day.* The museum had been a mob scene of kids with no place else to go, their moms and babysitters punch-drunk with anxiety. She'd lost five-year-old Lucy as soon as they got there. The kid ran straight past the ticket line and into a black-hole-dense crowd of humans. Ten minutes later, Esme assumed the worst: a sex-crazed pervert had stolen her child. Right now, he was speeding across the Lincoln Tunnel, her lovely daughter hogtied in the back of a van.

"LUCY!" she'd screamed while carrying Spencer, who'd been too heavy to carry but had walked too slowly to keep up. Two-year-olds, constitutionally, are passive-aggressive. It's literally a hallmark of their personalities.

She found Lucy in the *Tots* section, dressed in Native American garb and reading *Babar Goes to Paris* to a rapt three-year-old, the picture of maternal sweetness. At this, Esme cried with relief while trying not to cry, because when moms cry it's very upsetting for their children. To an outsider it had looked like hiccoughs, or else those shivers you get when you suddenly have to pee.

The trip ended at the gift shop, where both children conspired against her, begging for an ant farm colony because it was educational. They promised that they would name and love these ants like pets. She'd been blanking out, adrift in a mental vacation along the Amalfi Coast, when the old lady at the register had taken her by the elbow with a plump, callused hand.

Wendy, her nametag read, and Esme had been reminded of the last scene of *Peter Pan*, Wendy all grown-up and shriveled.

"You're goina need some help," Wendy had said in a thick, southern accent. She was about six feet tall and strong looking, her face wrinkled and her eyes bright blue. Her hair was shocking white, like someone had scared the hell out of her thirty years ago, and she was still getting over it.

"Help?"

Wendy'd reached lower, and pressed her hand flat against Esme's belly. It felt awkward and inappropriate, the hand radiating a damp ick. But Esme didn't mind. It's nice, sometimes, just to be noticed. "I can help. I'm a night nurse. Trained and licensed."

"Oh, I'm sorry. I'm broke," Esme had answered.

Wendy'd reached into the pocket of her green corduroy dress and produced a soft and wrinkled business card that smelled like lilacs. "We can work somethin' out. I'll bill your insurance for ya." Then Wendy waved and smiled wide at the kids. Her too-cheerful manner reminded Esme of all her still-single friends who liked kids only in theory. In reality, they preferred something that stuck to a script. A Japanese hug robot, for instance. Or a boyfriend that didn't live with you.

The kids, sensing Wendy's phoniness, had looked away.

"I should warn you. I'm a witch," Wendy had said. "Some mothers don't like that."

"Like, a feminist?"

"No. A real witch." She had this glimmer in her eyes. Delight or something deeper, an emotion that hewed to her bones.

Creepy!

Esme bought the stupid ant colony, then put Spencer in the stroller and Lucy on the kickboard and they took the handicap ramp heading out. "Thanks, anyway!" she called behind her shoulder.

⊸

She got a text from Mike that night, saying he had to work late. After she put the kids to bed, she discovered the lilac-scented card in her back pocket and Googled *Wendy Broadchurch, Night Nurse.* The website showed pictures of the woman from the museum, tall and strong, holding tiny babies with loving skill. Under these were testimonials about how she'd saved families by allowing frazzled parents to sleep, helped babies bond and latch, worked miracles.

WENDY BROADCHURCH, NIGHT NURSE
SHE'S MAGIC!

Literally, every testimonial said she was magic. Her fee was on a sliding scale. New moms, and she dealt only with new birth mothers, could pay whatever price they were able to afford.

Weeks passed. Esme thought about Wendy when she woke early to do her exercises, which included labor-prep squatting and shoving her legs up a wall to drain the swelling from her sad, sick kankles. She thought about her while getting the kids ready for school. She thought about her while cooking dinner, and she thought about her when collapsing into the couch at night, too tired to make it to the bed. The woman had smelled rich as a pine forest, and the touch of her hand had been so soothing. She hadn't really been creepy. It's a special skill to be good with infants, and that skill doesn't often translate to being good with kids or even adults. The woman's words haunted her: *You're goina need help* . . . Even a stranger could see it: this third child was going to sink her.

Esme rubbed her thumb along the wrinkled card as she dialed the number. "Just let me know when you're home from the hospital," Wendy told her. "I'll be right there."

"I'm worried my husband won't be happy about the money. Can he meet you?" Esme asked, and partly this was true, but she also wanted to interview this woman who'd be holding her infant half the night, alert in her home full of sleeping loved ones. But she didn't know how to come out and say that. She was out of practice negotiating with adults.

"I don't deal with husbands," Wendy said, then hung up.

MONTH ONE

Esme felt a cool hand on her forehead. Callused yet strong. She rolled to her side and pulled down her soft, cotton nightshirt. A suckle. It hurt the way it always hurts when newborns first start nursing. The way no one ever tells you, just like they don't tell you that delivering a baby feels like smashing a basketball through a buttonhole.

The baby bit too hard, latching more with skin than nipple. Esme's eyes popped open, and there was Wendy, the white-haired night nurse, her head bent low, holding baby Nicky in place. When she saw Esme's pain smirk, she slipped her thick index finger inside the baby's mouth, un-suctioning the latch and then refitting it.

Before kids, Esme would have been appalled by such intimacies between strangers. But your body's less precious once someone else has lived inside it. A man on the subway might squeeze your ass while you're too busy wheeling the stroller to fight back. Everybody you ever meet might feel obliged to comment on the size of your boobs, your baby weight, how much of it you've lost. You feel you belong to the world, and so it's especially wonderful when someone notices you in particular.

"Thanks," Esme whispered, her voice all gratitude as she drifted back to sleep, and the baby suckled. And along the blue sheet, milk and blood.

Wendy was gone when Esme woke. Her shift lasted from eight at night until five in the morning. At five-thirty, Nicky started mewing and Esme nursed him, then occupied Spenser in the den of their parlor floor apartment, trying to keep them all quiet so Lucy and Mike could get a full rest. Around seven, she put Nicky on the kitchen floor in his boppy, held Spenser to her hip, made toast breakfast, then packed Spencer's snack and Lucy's lunch.

Mike left for work at seven-thirty, which gave her forty-five minutes to brush Lucy's hair and get everybody ready for the day. This involved a lot of running around and then running back to get the thing that had been forgotten, and then socks, always socks! No one could ever find, match, or put on their own socks! And then securing the double stroller, and Lucy would have to walk even though she didn't want to, and somehow, even though Esme had promised she wouldn't yell she was literally screaming and the children became frightened and cried, and then baby Nicky was crying, and they all sat on the couch and wept while Esme explained that *mommy's very sorry,* and then it was off to school.

Getting the kids to school was probably the worst part of Esme's day, in part because she was still tired from the night before, and, having drunk three coffees to make up for it, was now irritable and likely to pee her pants, which happened from time to time.

Also frustrating for Esme were the group of perfectly coiffed moms who materialized at drop off before heading out to jobs like television producer and advertising copy writer and office manager. These occupations, which had once seemed mundane, were now like the tips of sailboats floating away from the horizon, Esme standing on the shore.

The other group at drop-off were the home-maker wives, who wore Lulu Lemon and complained about money, but spent the time their kids were at school in group yoga classes, training for half marathons, or having Friday lunches with unlimited mimosas. They tended to have nice figures and their children tended to be the smartest and best adjusted. They supported each other, too, doling hugs and laughs when this child-rearing gig got *just too darn hard*! Some of them even watched each others' kids and shared cooking obligations. Esme had tried to befriend these women, but they happened to be the same kinds of women who read *Eat, Pray, Love,* and considered *Love, Actually,* the best movie of all time. They were lovely women who would raise lovely children and Esme had nothing in common with them.

Also, now that she had three children she'd broken an unwritten rule of Brooklyn parenting. Everybody kept saying, "I don't know how you do it! Are you moving to the suburbs?" Unspoken and more to the point, it's hard to arrange playdates with a mom who has three kids. Nobody wants that many people in their tiny apartments.

So, drop off. First at PS 11, then the preschool, and then home with baby Nicky, a two-mile walk round trip. By the time it was done, the cold had taken its bite. Though the baby was well wrapped, Esme's hands were frozen too much to flex. But you can't drive in Brooklyn, particularly not with three kids (you can double park, sure, but if you leave anybody in the car some asshole calls child services), so walking it had to be. This was also the problem with alternate-side-parking-street-cleaning days. Don't even ask!

Drinking more coffee, she tried to type while the baby slept. She was working on a story she thought was good, about the prison system in Riker's Island. She thought maybe someone would publish it, like they used to publish her work back when she'd been able to make deadlines. As a favor, her old friend who now worked at the Huffington Post asked for a first look when she finished. But she didn't finish that day, because Nicky started crying. And she knew she was supposed to go help him. All the baby books demanded this. If you did not help a baby when he cried, he didn't properly attach, which led to personality disorders like narcissism and borderline and even psychosis. Yes, you had to answer babies when they cried or you were a BAD MOTHER.

So she got up and held the baby. Offered her breast, which the baby bit, tearing up the scab that had just healed. "I don't want you," she cooed sweetly, because babies don't know English.

Pick-up happened two hours later. Nicky was napping so she had to wake him, because Spencer threw fits when she was late, which it turns out is normal for a two-year-old, but somehow unacceptable at a preschool for two year-olds.

She was in such a rush that she forgot her gloves, or maybe there just wasn't time, but at least she'd remembered that tenth cup of coffee. Off they went, carrier and empty stroller, walking fast as waddling ducks.

The preschool on Prospect Avenue had this cheesy awning of happy stick-figure kids. A bunch of moms were waiting outside—the happy moms who'd all gone out for coffee and talked about their feelings during the last two hours. They smiled when they saw Esme and she tried to smile back but she was sweating at her core and ice-cold on the outside. Like a cherry pie a la mode.

The doors opened and Esme felt the familiar thrill. Her beloved, returned. Toddlers ran out from a large playroom with its indoor slide and bounce animals. They rushed for their mothers and that one overwhelmed, lonely dad. Playdates were arranged for the post nap dead zone. The room emptied.

Esme felt a hand on her shoulder. It was the director. A sixty-year-old woman named Meredith who taught the children about hatching chicken eggs and self-esteem. "He's in the office," she explained. The lagging behind mothers heard this, and offered looks of schadenfreude wrapped in sympathy. She followed Meredith into the office where Spencer sat on one of the small training potties instead of an adult chair, which would have been too big. His put-upon teacher Natalie stood beside him, seeming concerned.

It was always concern. Never anger, frustration, or annoyance. Just concern.

"He ran out of the classroom. We have a stop sign so that doesn't happen. We teach them to read that sign on day one. For safety. But he ran out into the big playroom anyway."

"Oh," Esme said. Spencer came to her. Leaned in. Nicky yawned with closed eyes.

"We planned a field trip for next week. Spencer will have to stay home with you. It's not safe."

Esme felt all kinds of ashamed, which she always felt when this kind of thing happened, but also all kinds of confused. Because Spencer surely knew the difference between a classroom and a busy street full of cars.

"Well, if that's what you think," she said.

"It is. We're so sorry. Maybe you could work with him at home."

She felt she should defend her kid, but she was so tired that she was afraid she'd start crying. "Okay. We'll work on following rules more. Except it's hard because he's two years old."

"That might be the problem.

"Hm?"

Meredith, the big gun, stepped in. "Have you been spending enough time with him? I think it might have to do with the new baby. He's acting out." She said this in front of Spencer, like he wasn't just willful, but retarded.

"Oh. Should I cram this baby I'm holding back into my vagina?" she asked.

Everybody got all quiet and uncomfortable. Even Esme, who was not the kind of person to use the word *vagina* out loud. "Okay! Sorry about the stop sign," she said, took Spencer's hand, and walked out.

⊸⊙⊷

They got home with two hours to spare before kindergarten pick up. Her fingers weren't numb this time, just really cold. She fed everybody and then napped everybody and then they had a half hour. She drank another coffee and somehow peed her panties and jeans, and promised herself to stop having coffee, because she was a grown woman capable of impulse control. Right?

Then she remembered the thing she kept forgetting, which was the ointment Wendy had brought to heal her sun damage. So kind! Because Esme was black, almost nobody ever noticed her sun damage (Her rich, drunk mom used to send her outside all summer long back in East Hampton. She'd felt this was good for Esme, as it had afforded them both more freedom. Esme was less sure.). But now Esme's face had all kinds of weird freckles and parts of her nose were scarred—little spider web calluses from blisters over blisters over blisters, summer upon summer.

She couldn't remember where she'd put the ointment, and then she remembered Wendy saying to her really slowly, "I'll put it in your med'cin cabinet 'cause it's strong magic. I don't want the children messing with it."

So, in her bathroom. She rubbed it on her face. It was a small jar, its contents reeking of frankincense and bergamot. The secret ingredient, Wendy had told her, was the blood and milk she'd collected from Esme's nipples, which may or may not have been a joke.

Her skin tingled in a good way. The ointment pressed through her pores and went deep. She could even feel her bones. She worried briefly that Esme had actually given her a whitener, since hillbillies from Kentucky probably thought blackness was a thing that needed curing. But then she looked into the mirror, and yeah, she could even see it. Her spots softened, the pigment turning uniformly dark. The scars on her nose looked smaller. She glowed.

"I'm still pretty," she whispered with total surprise.

It felt so good she put it on her hands. The cracks merged together to heal. Heat sank deep, into her bones. The chapped red softened into muted brown. She was about to put it on her raw nipples when she looked at the clock. Time to go!

They went out again, this time straight to PS 11. Lucy and her best friend Ritah came whizzing out the side, kindergarten exit. Ritah's mom was this angry twenty-something from Massachusetts who was training to be a doula.

She was always asking Esme to look after Ritah, which was actually pretty easy because Ritah was an easy kid, but it also kind of sucked. Today both moms took all the kids to the park. Lucy and Ritah played on monkey bars and sang their best-friend song and practiced their best-friend handshake. Ritah's mom complained about how hard her life was because her ex-husband had a trashy girlfriend, and then something about how she wished she had some Oxycontin. As Esme surveyed the situation, nodding politely at this woman's litany of mistreatment, Nicky and Spencer stuck to her like extra appendages, Esme decided that private school would have been a better bet. They'd have met a higher class of family, whose kids used more normal cuss words. For example: what the heck is a douche-slut? Does she cheat on one douche with another? Do they even make douches anymore?

Esme, Lucy, Spencer, and Nicky got home at four in the afternoon. Everybody collapsed on the couch. Lucy cried because she would miss Ritah and Spencer cried because two year-olds cry in the afternoons, sometimes for as long as an hour, and Nicky cried because he heard other humans crying and wanted to be in on the fun, so then Esme cried, and then the kids all got really upset because mom was crying, so Esme turned the television to *Animaniacs*, which they streamed for an hour while she ordered groceries from Amazon, thank god for earth-scorching, minimum-wage slavery Amazon, because no way she was getting these kids out of the house one more fucking time, just for Hamburger Helper.

She got the text from Mike that he'd be coming home late. He had this pattern since they'd started having kids. He stayed away until they were sleep-trained. Over the years, she had vocally protested and threatened and at last begged for his help, but her pleas had fallen on deaf ears.

She was not a moron—she'd done the math. But divorced people had to do stupid things, like splitting the kids between apartments three days a week. This sounded fantastic (three nights on her own, her husband stuck taking the kids! A fantasia! She'd brush her teeth and take baths and get real writing done!), but then you consider the practicalities. The kids were attached to their home, which they'd have to leave for something cheaper. Mike would certainly not take care of the kids. He'd have his mom do it. His mom was competent and loving but also a bully, which explained Mike, who never met a confrontation he didn't avoid by either working the longest hours possible or just drinking his feelings into itches. You know how people with hammers are always looking for nails? His mom was an iron, always looking for something to flatten.

The stuff you have to manage—playdates and emotional well-being and simply asking the kids about their lives—this would not happen unless they were with Esme, nor would the doctor appointments and sick days. While she'd not been able to work for years, Mike was finally earning real coin. If she put a wrench in those gears, then they'd all be struggling. And while this situation wasn't working for her—this was, in fact terrible—she indeed loved these people. Even Mike.

She'd planned to revisit the notion of divorce, or at least couples' therapy, once Spencer started kindergarten. Two kids in school full time, she'd have been able to work and make decisions with a clear head. But then she got pregnant again. The pill that was supposed to solve the problem didn't take. And then the second pill didn't take, either. She never got around to making an appointment for an abortion. She'd known it was specious thinking, but with the kid having survived so much, she'd gotten the idea that he'd had more of a right to her body than she did.

When Wendy arrived that night, she wore this red cloak with a black underside and she hugged Esme, hard, like she could guess just by looking how tough the day had been. Esme cried. She wished her mom, or even her husband's mom, had done this after any one of the babies had been born. Just once. She would have cherished it.

Spencer and Nicky were already sleeping. Lucy wasn't keen on Wendy. She thought she smelled bad and was weird, which Esme couldn't actually refute. So it was Esme who put her to bed, this time with three chapters of *Junie B Jones* and a back scratch. When she came back out to say good-night to Wendy, the woman was waiting at the kitchen table.

"Sit," Wendy said.

It felt weird, another woman at her kitchen table, telling her what to do. Even if the woman in question happened to be her savior. "Why?"

"Trust me."

Esme sat. Wendy put Nicky in the bassinet, then pulled a boar bristle brush and a spray bottle from her mammoth, old lady sack of a purse.

"My hair's tricky," Esme said.

"No, it's not." She sprayed something oil-based along Esme's scalp. It smelled like a field of spearmint, and it felt much better that that. Her scalp tingled, drinking thirstily. She felt this wave of freshness wash over her, all the way inside her ears and sinuses and even her bones. Then came Wendy's hands, sure through every snarl. She didn't braid. She let it loose.

Wendy showed her what she looked like in a mirror. Her skin was dewy. Her hair soft and full. She'd never pulled this look off before, always afraid it would appear like a failed afro. But this was something different. Something just her own.

"My mom could never get this right," she whispered.

Wendy handed her the oil. A blue bottle, small. She opened and saw that the contents were clotted white marbled with red. She was too grateful to ask the obvious question: *is this my blood*?

Wendy leaned in, her breath like bergamot, and kissed her on the cheek. This wasn't the first time this had happened. More like the third.

Mike walked in, mid-cheek kiss. He stopped where he was standing, like he'd just caught them fucking a double-ended dildo while smoking crystal meth. "Who's got the baby?" he asked.

Esme looked away, ashamed.

"Is he lost? We thought you had him," Wendy answered. Then she said to Esme, "Go to bed. You're exhausted. And put that ointment on your nipples and vagina. It'll help."

Blushing at the words *nipples* and *vagina*, Esme got up fast and went to her room. From there, she turned on the monitor, where she heard Wendy and Mike talking low so as not to wake the kids. This was new. He didn't usually talk to Wendy. Just came in super late and walked past her, collapsing next to Esme on the bed.

"Did we ever get a resume or references from you?"

Esme died a little bit. Not literally. Or maybe literally. The part of her that loved her husband died a little bit.

"Do you need them?" Wendy asked.

"You know, now that you bring it up, that'd be great!" Mike said.

"I'll give them to your wife," Wendy answered, just as cheerful.

"I can take them," he said, and he said this curtly, like it meant nothing. He was doing her a favor. She recognized the tone. But she heard it with new ears, now that he was employing it on someone else. It occurred to her that Mike, so cowed by conflict, so meek toward the outside world, might also, like his mother, be a bully.

"Actually, I'm so sorry!" Wendy said, with the same tone a person might use when explaining that all the gum in the pack is gone. *There's no more Doublemint! I'm so sorry!* "You can't have my references because you're not my employer."

"You can bet I'll be the one paying you," he said, and now he'd switched from charming to paternal, like he was clearing something up for poor, confused Wendy the sixty-five-year-old hillbilly whose day job was selling ant colonies at the Children's Museum. Which, you know, they'd never ordered the ants for. The ants had involved an online code from the inside of the box. So all they had was an empty ant house in the middle of the living room.

"I'll waive my fee, maybe," she answered.

Nicky started crying, which stopped the conversation. Esme heard shuffling, and then, "Oh, don't be such a piggy," Wendy whispered. "Let your momma relax." Then a beer can cracked open, which would be Mike.

In the dark, Esme rubbed the ointment on her nipples and then her vagina. These, too, went deep. She felt the ointment all through her, vibrant and healing and startlingly alive. The healing felt like a window opening. A mountain moving, just slightly, proving that such things were possible.

It wasn't so surprising, then, when Mike came in an hour later, and kissed her neck and felt between her legs, that she went along with it, and even came, her sore body throbbing with confused joy.

Around midnight, Esme was woken by a callused caress. She rolled halfway. Fed Nicky. He made suckling, animal sounds but her nipples didn't mind as much and there wasn't any blood.

Wendy smiled at the baby and she smiled more at Esme, like she mattered. Like she was a person who could be seen. "Cunt's all cleaned up now, isn't it, lucky girl?" she whispered. "It's like you never had them at all."

⟜

MONTH TWO

The next day Mike slept in because it was Saturday and he was tired. She and the kids padded around the creaky, two-bedroom, brownstone floor-through until nine and then went for a walk in Brower Park and then to the Children's Museum. She was hoping to see Wendy, whom she wanted to talk to about the whole *cunt* thing. She didn't exactly know how to articulate it. She thought she'd say something like, *chill out on the language*. Or, *can we not talk about sex while I'm nursing a four-week-old*? But maybe she'd say nothing. Just smile and pretend everything was fine. Just reassure herself that Wendy was a functional person with a day job and a place in the world and friends. But none of this happened, because they were told she didn't work there anymore. In fact, no one there could remember her *ever* having worked there.

Back home, she put both Nicky and Spencer down for a nap and played Uno with Lucy, but kind of fell asleep during a discard, at which point Lucy climbed on top of her and started humping her face, which—little known fact—most children do until you say, "Get the hell off! Stop humping my face!" and then they stop.

That night, Marlene the date night sitter showed up. She was from Trinidad and the kids loved her rice and beans. They greeted her with utter joy, unlike the way they greeted Wendy, whom they viewed as some kind of smelly penny that kept turning up at their door. Wendy would not return until Monday. She had weekends off.

While Nicky cried in his boppy, Esme took a shower and then used the new spray on her hair so that it shone pretty. Her bones felt different now, from regular ointment use. Stronger and reknit somehow, into a slightly different configuration from the woman she'd once been.

She let her hair hang loose, the best it had ever looked. Her dress was this blue tiger print number that she'd gotten online and she looked great. Mike wore jeans and a suit jacket. They took Nicky with them and headed for the restaurant, where they were meeting the rest of Mike's team along with their spouses.

The restaurant was on Vanderbilt Avenue. Mike walked ahead of her and Nicky that last block because they were late. The table had two spaces left, far away from each other. She was happy for this, which felt a little like betrayal. But only a little.

The food got served family style. She had a glass of wine and fed the baby from milk she'd pumped, so she felt dizzy and cheerful a half hour in. The man next to her was from Scotland. He told her he liked black people. "I do, too!" she said. He thought she was funny. "Mike, your wife's funny!" he said.

Mike nodded, kept talking to the guy next to him, the big boss, with whom he wanted to start a new division. She turned to the woman on her left, who was married to the man on her right. The woman on her left was from a town outside Chicago called Berwyn. She said she loved babies and could not wait to have some. She got tears in her eyes when she said this, like babies were something that came from a bank, and there was a run on them. "Have my baby!" Esme said.

Then she heard Mike say a crazy word. A word she'd never have guessed he knew, let alone repeat. It sounded like *Wigger*.

"What?" she called across the long table. Mike kept talking. The four people around him were laughing hard. "What did you just say?" Esme shouted, loud now and a little angry. They stopped laughing.

"I was just telling them about our hillbilly night nurse," Mike said. Mike was from Florida. The state where people smoked bath salts, then ate each other's faces. Esme was a Presbyterian from Westchester who'd gone to boarding school until college, and who'd have inherited a ton if not for some jerk hedge fund manager's Ponzi scheme. Her people had been professionals for generations, long before the civil war. His people had come over during the potato famine. This is for background. For the establishment of who gets to call whom a low class.

"What about her?"

Mike grinned. It was his phony work grin because sometime between meeting her and the first baby, he'd lost his real grin. "All those potions," he laughed. "She thinks she's a witch or something. The two of you smell like potheads."

"Did you say *wigger*?" she asked. The men and women around him averted their eyes, sheepish. He looked at her like she was crazy. "Of course not."

Nicky and his fucking timing. He started crying.

"I think Dan's on board," Mike said on the walk home. "This is really big."

She broke pace and walked in front of him on the way back to the apartment. "Did you say wigger? Be honest," she called behind.

Mike looked at her blankly.

"When you were telling some mean story about Wendy. Did you call her a wigger?"

"Honey, I'm so drunk. I don't even remember talking about her," he said.

Inside the house, she paid Marlene, and then Marlene asked to speak to her privately, outside the apartment. "Are you using voodoo?" Marlene asked as they shivered on the cold front stoop. She looked upset. Shaking and close to tears.

"Oh! You mean the night nurse?" Esme answered. "She's into organic. She makes all these great ointments. They're really helping me."

"It's voodoo," Marlene whispered. "I can smell it on the children. You're marked."

This sank inside Esme, sidling across her bones. "I don't believe in magic."

Marlene shook her head. "Please."

"Please, what?" Esme answered.

Marlene started down the steps. From the cramped, dim vestibule, Esme watched her turn around the corner, lost to the sideways horizon.

⟜⟞

She put sleeping Nicky down in his bassinet. He'd sleep until his next scheduled feeding at two in the morning. "Can you feed him? I left a bottle," she asked Mike.

Mike popped a last beer, and answered like he'd only vaguely heard. "Sure."

She'd been through this before. *Sure* meant *absolutely not*, but she decided to let it play out.

Like clockwork, Nicky's insistent hunger cries started at exactly two in the morning. She shoved Mike but couldn't wake him, and she knew that if she let Nicky keep going, he'd wake Spenser and Lucy in the next bedroom, and then everybody would be crying messes all day long. Plus, there's that whole attachment parenting thing, about how if you don't hold them when they cry they become psychopaths. Plus, the milk was practically exploding from her nipples. She got up and warmed the bottle and then figured that one glass of wine six hours before wouldn't kill him, and went ahead and nursed.

He looked up at her with soft, small eyes, and she loved him like you might love the first sight of a new and beautiful planet populated by Muppets. "I'm so unhappy," she told him.

She couldn't sleep after that. Too angry. Her first thought was to open Mike's whiskey and get soused. But then she saw how Wendy had cleaned up the tiny corner of her kitchen that was her workspace, arranging pencils next to the laptop. When had that happened? Yesterday? A week ago? When was the last time she'd tried to write?

She sat down there, and saw the note Wendy had written, "You go, girl!" It made her smile, and then chuckle (*You go, Girl?*), and then start typing.

The problem with Riker's Island was that there wasn't enough room for the inmates, so they floated around on barges. If they refused to plea bargain, they had to wait for at least a year, trapped, before they could stand trial. They're stuck there, all these women. On fucking barges.

She finished a draft two-and-a-half hours later, then made herself an exhaustion snack of torn crust from sliced bread smeared directly into a bar of butter—her favorite, secret late-night snack, which maybe explained the stubbornness of the baby weight. But God, it was good. Especially if you sprinkled a little salt on the top.

⊸⊙⊷

Nicky woke up. She took him out of the bassinet and brought him into the bedroom with the bottle. Held him next to Mike until he opened his eyes. "Your turn," she said. He stayed like that for a ten count, then took the baby and the bottle and got out of bed. By the time Esme woke again in was after ten in the morning. Lucy had turned on the television and was watching it with Spencer. Nicky was just starting to coo. Mike had stuck a note to the fridge:

> Putting in a few extra hours at the office. Have a great day!

⊸⊙⊷

MONTH THREE

The next few weeks were uneventful, but also very eventful. Esme kept yelling; Nicky kept eating and sleeping; the weather stayed cold; Spencer kept getting in trouble; and Lucy kept playing with the kid who shouted weird cuss-words at PS 11. Esme's sun damage totally reversed. Her skin could have been mistaken for belonging to a twenty-five-year-old. True to Wendy's word, so could her cunt.

It happened one Friday, that Esme woke to find Wendy still in the house. She'd made pancakes. These were thicker and more cake-like than normal pancakes, and they smelled like lavender. Everybody except Esme took three bites to be polite. Esme drowned them in syrup and butter and then they were fine.

"Thought I'd stick around, help out," Wendy explained.

The kids stayed especially quiet because Wendy freaked them out. No panic attacks about mean teachers or bullying friends. No shouting about how she loved one of them more than the others, or that everything was totally unfair. It gave Esme's nervous system time to breathe.

Wendy waited inside the car with the remaining kids when they stopped at PS 11 and then the preschool, too. They were done quickly, and with significantly less physical tax. Nicky wasn't upset because his nose wasn't cold, and Esme didn't pee her panties even a little.

"Turn left," Wendy commanded, so Esme did. Instead of going home, she directed her to the old Armory in East New York, about two miles down Atlantic Avenue. Wendy told her to pull over. She did. *Do you work here, now?* Esme wanted to ask. *I heard you're not at the Children's Museum. You gave that up . . .. Why couldn't they remember you?*

Wendy smiled at Esme with real warmth, or what passed for it. Her eyes squinted into a grin and her voice got soft, like she was reminding herself that gentle people whisper. "It happens in a blink," she whispered. "And there's so much power in it."

"I know what you mean," Esme said. "It's so nice to have you, Wendy. I can't tell you how grateful I am, to have someone in our house who cares. These first months are so hard. I'm counting down the seconds, wishing they'd pass faster, but I know it'll be over in a snap. It all happens so fast and I love them so much . . .. Saints and poets."

Wendy looked at her with confusion. "Oh. Right." Then she got out of the car.

Always before this, Esme had seen mammoth Wendy behind a register, or crouched by the side of a bed, or sitting at her kitchen table. But now Wendy stood tall. The outdoor expanse was finally wide enough to showcase her girth. She loped up the walk, her body in graceless disjoint, then pushed through an ornate wooden door and disappeared inside.

Esme watched the closed door, the giant turrets above, the pretty red brick faded to the color of city-soot and rust. She had questions. So many.

"What do you think?" she asked Nicky. Nicky cooed, because he liked Esme's voice. All her kids were like that: they loved her more than anybody else in the world. It's a kind of love so momentous that you can't let yourself think about it or you'll be like that guy, Narcissus, drowning in his own reflection.

She took Nicky out of his car seat and headed for the armory, which she realized looked a lot like a church. She climbed the steps. A funny feeling ate at the pit of her stomach.

A piece of red poster paper that looked like it had come from her house read:

No Men Allowed!

She opened the heavy door, and then another heavy door. She entered a giant atrium with an altar at the center. The room was empty. Dust motes filled the air. It stank of patchouli. She headed for the altar, where she found a pile of ashes and amidst this, a knot of black, human hair.

She turned and started out. The door squeaked loudly. She pressed her lips to the top of Nicky's head and, panting, ran out. Up in the window, a top turret, a white-haired face peered down.

⊸⊷

She meant to confront Wendy after that. To say: *Uh, what was that place? Who are you?* But when she got home there were tasks to accomplish, and she was afraid to tell Mike, because once she did that it would be out of her hands. He'd fire Wendy and she'd be alone in this apartment. So she decided to soothe her nerves with the ointment. It calmed her. Ran through her, placid and healing. After that, she ate the kids' and Mike's leftover pancakes, too.

She'd been paranoid. Wendy was a helpful person. She'd taken the morning just to give Esme a hand. She already knew from neighborhood meetings that the armory was a homeless shelter. Wendy surely volunteered. How could Esme possibly respond to her night nurse's kindness with ungracious questions?

Besides, Wendy's work was coming to a close. Nicky would be sleeping through the night any day now. A week at the most. Why end the relationship on a sour note?

⊸⊷

On a Monday, Wendy ran Esme a bath full of clay while chanting softly. Tuesday, she caressed Esme's cheek until she started crying and couldn't stop. While Nicky fed, Wendy held her. Strong, callused hands. At one point, she wiped away a tear and ate it.

"What do you want?" Wendy asked. "If you imagine it, then the spirits give it to you. They divine it."

Wendy thought about her Riker's Island article, and about her friend from the Huffington Post whom she'd sent it to weeks ago, but who still hadn't read it. She thought about this cramped apartment, and the shitty preschool which she wished they could afford full-time, and she thought about the person she shared her bed with, who made her feel so invisible, and mostly she thought about sleep, and how much she missed it.

"I want my mom," Esme said.

Wendy climbed into the bed. Spooned her like her mom had never done, but she'd always wished for. It felt awkward, and then weird, and finally bad. Esme got up, pretending to need to use the bathroom, and didn't come out again until Nicky started crying.

⊸o⊷

Wednesday, at exactly twelve weeks, Nicky slept through the night.

Esme's breasts woke her up. They were too full. It was nine AM. The kids would be late for school! "Lucy! Spencer!" she called. Nobody answered, and she had this irrational fear that Wendy had stolen them. That was the price. And now the loves of her life were gone forever.

She raced into the kitchen, where the dishes were washed and the counters cleaned and Wendy was standing at sweet attention.

"I dropped them off," she said.

"You did? How? What about their lunch sacks? It's such a walk!"

"I took the car. I made their lunches. It was fine."

"Oh."

Esme tried to smile, but she was afraid. Something had changed. Something was wrong. Also, not cool to take a car without permission. "I guess we should talk about your fee. I think you should stop coming."

"See you tonight," Wendy said.

⊸o⊷

Wendy didn't show up Thursday night. So Esme put the kids to bed, finishing up another *Junie B Jones*, and snuggling Nicky until his breath got deep. It felt like the end of something momentous, the beginning of another chapter, too.

Around midnight, she jackknifed awake, sneaked out of the bedroom where Mike was sleeping, and found Wendy sitting at her kitchen table. The apartment felt different. Everything rearranged and of different hue. Was this what happened at night? Did the house switch loyalties, locating a new master?

"Sorry I'm late," Wendy said.

"Oh, it's fine," Esme answered. "But I should pay you. I think we're not in the market for night nurses anymore."

Wendy opened her giant old lady purse and pulled out a deck of Tarot cards—the cheap, Wal-Mart kind. "I made dandelion tea," she said, sipping from and then passing the full mug in Esme's direction. "It'll help dry you out. I'll leave the bottle."

"So, the fee?"

Wendy laid down the cards. The light was low. She was too big for the chair. Twice Mike's size. Probably twice as powerful, Esme suddenly realized.

"Can I read for you?"

"I'm so tired. Can it wait?"

Wendy shook her head. "I've already started." She flipped a bunch of cards. To be polite, to get her on her way, Esme sat and listened. Something about cusps. Something about choices and rebirth and gobble-de-gook that you nod and smile at, because this person had held her defenseless infant all night for three months, and given her love and affection when she'd needed it most, and maybe she was crazy but who else would do such a thing? And then she nodded off, because when she woke up, Wendy was looking at her with this obscene smile on her face; gaudy, wild, and insane.

"Yeah?" Esme asked.

"So you're about to make a big decision," she said. "This is the turning point of your entire life."

Esme stared at the card, which was marked death. She looked back at smiling Wendy. And the cup, she looked inside. Was it really dandelion tea? Because it had curdled to thick, custardy pink.

"You need to think the name. While you sleep, you'll think the name, and in the morning they'll be gone," Wendy said.

"I don't understand," Esme answered.

"Of course you do," Wendy answered. "It's my fee."

"Why don't I just pay you in money from a bank?"

Still with that disquieting, bone-deep psychotic grin, she packed her Tarot cards into her giant canvas purse and left.

⊸

Esme did not go back to sleep. She stayed up all night and drank a lot of coffee and fed Nicky and got the kids ready for school. Before heading out the door, Mike hugged her hard and told her he loved her, which made her wonder if maybe she'd turned psychotic, and none of this life she was living was reality.

Then she dropped Lucy off. Lucy kissed her hand like they were in love, then waved this sweet, adorable wave before disappearing into mammoth PS 11. "I'd love you even if you were a stranger," Esme called out, to her own surprise.

Meredith and Natalie were waiting at the preschool. They ushered Esme and Spencer into the office for another talk, Spencer sitting on the training-toilet.

"Could you get my kid a real chair, please?" Esme asked. Meredith immediately complied, unhooking it from the stack in a closet just behind her desk. Then Natalie suggested a psychological interview, as she was worried Spencer might have oppositional defiant disorder, a rare condition that demanded immediate attention. It came from poor infant attachment and physical abuse. To this, Esme replied, "How much am I paying you? Just . . . Fucking keep him alive for two hours. Can you do that?"

Nicky strapped to her chest in a bright orange Moby Wrap, she left without Spencer (she forgot him!), then returned and took his hand. "I trust you'll give me my money back. A false accusation of child abuse is a big deal. I can't imagine you'll keep your accreditation if I sue."

Back at home, they watched television. Not even *Sesame Street*. *Ozark*, followed by *BoJack Horseman*. It was unclear to her whether she was repudiating or following in her shitty mother's footsteps.

Five hours later, they picked up Lucy. Ritah's mom asked Esme to babysit. "You realize I'm drowning and you've never once offered to watch Lucy, right?" she asked, and then she kept walking, her face red with shocked blush.

Once home, she got an e-mail from the Huffington Post that her story had been accepted and would run front page. This was her first real publication since Lucy, and she was delighted. To celebrate, she brought out her mom's baccarat and everybody drank orange juice out of $200 crystal. The bedtime routine lasted two hours. Mike caught the tail end. He held Nicky, who shared his small ears with joined earlobes. Soon, even Mike was snoring but Esme wasn't, because what had Wendy meant about a fee? About thinking a name before sleep, and when she woke, the person with that name would be gone?

She Googled *Wendy Broadchurch* again, but the website about the night nurse was gone. What she found instead, not even buried, but on the first page, was a newspaper article from the *Washington Post*, about a woman in Whitesburg, Kentucky, who'd stabbed her husband and three children to death. A self-declared witch, she'd then engaged in ritual sacrifice, peeling the skin from their bodies and hanging it on the backyard trees.

Wrong woman, had to be. Except, there was the photo of a young Wendy, her crazy eyes just the same. She used her account at LexisNexis that the *New York Times* had never revoked when they'd fired her for getting pregnant, but had pretended it wasn't because she was pregnant. A down-size upon a downsize upon a downsize of a collapsing industry.

After murdering her family, Wendy served twenty years in a psychiatric hospital in Lexington. She didn't seem to have a handle in chat sites, but her name showed up a lot. Mothers talked about her like she was a ghost. They called her a savior. They called her a monster. They said she'd been their night nurse. They'd met her in dime stores and coffee shops and libraries. She'd earned their trust. And then she'd stolen their children. But no one believed. No one remembered the children, at all.

Esme was shaking when she finished. She still hadn't slept. She didn't sleep. Two nights in a row. That morning, Mike hugged her hard, and kissed her good-bye, because husbands always know when they've pushed you too far. They always come back, because the last thing they want is for you to break.

She got Lucy, Spencer, and Nicky dressed and cleaned for the day, but at the last minute turned back from the front door and had everyone take off their coats. Because it was Saturday. No school day, after all.

While the kids watched television, she went on another Wendy Broadchurch deep dive. There were three mentions of Wendy Broadchurch in the Park Slope Parents Listserve, dating back to 2004, when Wendy first moved to New York. All named her as the nanny they'd employed when their families fell apart.

Esme called one of these women, having located her name in an online directory, and paying the five dollars to get her cell phone number. The woman answered on the first ring. "Hi, my name's Esme Hunter, and I'm writing an article about the Park Slope Parents. I was wondering if I could speak with you?"

Esme explained that her article was about the usefulness of web groups for women over the last twenty years. "Did you find your nanny on a website?"

The woman's voice got soft. "Yeah."

"Right. And she was named Wendy Broadchurch?"

A long pause. Can you feel rage through a phone?

"Is it you?" the woman asked.

"I . . . what do you mean? My name's Esme Hunter?"

"Give me back my fucking baby!" the woman screamed. "Give her back. Give her back. Give her back, you sick fucking cunt. When I find you I—"

Esme hung up. The phone starting ringing from that same number. She silenced it, her heart beating so fast it felt like all the vessels had burst, and blood was everywhere inside, drowning her.

She went to the children and held them one by one, and then altogether. They smelled like patchouli and bergamot and frankincense. The whole apartment reeked of it. She found the dandelion tea, which stank of blood and milk. She found the hair oil and the skin salve. She put them in a Ziploc bag and threw them in the garbage outside the house.

Late afternoon, Esme called Wendy on the phone. "I'd like to pay you your fee. I can sell my family's Baccarat Crystal or I can give it to you. It's worth about five thousand dollars."

Wendy's voice was cold. The deep down voice. The bone voice. "Sleep, honey. Stop avoiding it."

"This is crazy. You're crazy. I know about you. I changed the locks," Esme answered.

Esme heard far away laughter on the other line. She had to strain her ears. Then Wendy hung up.

After that, she really did have the locks changed, and then she texted Mike and asked him to come home. Something was wrong. She needed to explain. He called back right away and she told him everything. "I'm afraid to fall asleep. What if everything changes? Do you believe me?" she asked.

"I believe that you believe," he answered. He said he'd be home as soon as his new department finished its meeting.

At last, she joined the kids on the couch. Her eyes kept closing. *Mister Rogers* played. The soft light of the setting winter sun pushed through the parlor window. Her mind skipped stones.

Wendy. How had they met?

The Children's Museum, where no one remembered her.

Had Mike ever met her? She'd heard them talking through the baby monitor, but what if she'd imagined all that? What if half the interactions she'd had with Wendy were imagined? A wish fulfillment, because it's hard to be a mom when you've never had one. It's hard to run a family when your job commands no respect.

. . .Was Wendy real?

This calmed her down a little. Actually, a lot. She was post-partum nuts. Nobody was trying to take away her kids. It was just a weird, sleep-deprived, hormone-induced psychosis. Baby blues to the power of fifty.

She put Nicky down for his afternoon nap, and then went to her bedroom to get some rest while Lucy and Spencer started a *Teen Titans* marathon. As she dozed, she wondered which child she might have picked. Nicky, of course. Because she loved him, but he'd been a setback. She could do without Nicky, and all the better, if no one had to know.

But she'd never do that.

Lucy and Spencer? No. They were a part of her, sewn in tighter than her stomach.

Mike? In magical fairy land, she could do without Mike, but not in the real world, where cash was exchanged for goods and services. Then again, he did have a life insurance policy.

No, not Mike. He was the father of her children. Not Mike.

In her dream, her skin tingled. Her bones broke and reknit with the architecture of briar patch vines. These vines filled the room and the apartment. They covered the children and then broke the children apart. Everything stank of blood and sour milk.

Not anyone. Of course, not anyone. She chose no one.

And then she thought: *Esme. Esme would love to disappear.*

"Dad!" Esme heard as she awoke in her bed. "There's a lady!"

She stood, and it was Lucy, dressed in a fancy frock adorned with purple hydrangeas, her hair a ragged mess like it had been combed by white people. Then Spencer was toddling beside her, wearing a polo pullover instead of a t-shirt, shorts belted. When he saw Esme, he screamed.

Esme came to them, but they started running. She followed them into the kitchen. Which was different. Her office was gone. It was refinished like she'd always wanted, in sparkling marble. Mike's mom was cooking supper. She wore this frown on her face even before she saw Esme. The frown was the same one the kids wore. A light had gone out inside of them.

Mike's mom lifted the cast iron frying pan as a weapon, but it was hot and burned her hand. She yelped as she dropped it. Esme turned out to the living room. There was Mike, holding baby Nicky. He was about forty pounds heavier, his light gone, too.

"It's a lady!" Lucy screamed again.

"Get out of this house," Mike's mom said, because underneath all that bullying, she'd always been a nervous wreck.

Esme was at the door. Somehow her shoes were on her feet, and her coat on her back. The furniture, she now saw, was different. Crate and Barrel instead of the stuff she'd inherited from her mom. No Baccarat for Lucy to inherit, either.

She was in the doorway, and she wanted to explain, but they were all so upset. And then Mike came closer, baby Nicky in his arms. Nicky wailed at her like he couldn't stand her stench, but something in Mike showed recognition. Something deep remembered. Because he looked at her with the most perfect expression of hatred.

Then he shut the door.

THEY ARE US (1964): AN ORAL HISTORY

JACK LOTHIAN

Isaac Peterson (Producer)

At the time I was working out of an office on the Paramount lot. This would've been a few years before Gulf & Western bought them out in '66. Everyone was feeling the pinch; we'd been strongly advised to look for films that could slide in with lower budgets.

My secretary Sheila would type up reports on books she'd dug up, quick one-paragraph summaries, and she'd highlight any that she particularly recommended.

Sheila Welsh (Secretary)

I'd probably have a proper title now—development assistant or something. But back then I was just "a secretary," no matter what my actual role was. It really was a different time. I was young, and I suppose relatively naive, thought nothing of spending my weekends on the porch with a stack of dime-store novels, trying to hunt down the next big thing. It felt glamorous just to be connected to the industry.

I still remember the first time I read *They Are Us.* It was a relatively simple story—a couple move to the city, and their marriage disintegrates as they renovate a crumbling townhouse. Partway through they start to suspect each other of all manner of affairs and infidelities, and there's a suggestion that maybe they aren't themselves all the time.

It was a little hard to follow, but the basic concept—a couple, a townhouse, a marriage in crisis—felt like the kind of thing Isaac was looking for.

Carl Monkton (Author)

It was the only novel I ever finished, and the only one I ever had published. I wish I'd never written a word.

Isaac Peterson (Producer)

It felt like an easy sell. Small cast. It had potential to be one of those "prestige projects"—get a renowned director on, a couple of stars who don't mind slumming.

I didn't read the book though. That's what I have staff for.

Sheila Welsh (Secretary)

Isaac tried to read it. He stopped halfway through. He said it disturbed him, but wouldn't elaborate. At the time I thought he was just being lazy, spinning an excuse not to finish it, but looking back I'm not so sure.

The book left me feeling oddly unclean. Do you know what I mean? When you read something, and it feels like it's sunk into your pores. There was a cruelty to it like the author enjoyed tearing this couple apart, and by extension, I suppose the reader becomes an accessory to that. We're watching their lives unravel, and we could choose to stop reading, we could close the book, but we read on, and so their pain and misery continues.

It was me who suggested Laurent Loubet as director, although Isaac took credit for that at the time. He doesn't take credit for it now, obviously. I was in love with Loubet's movies, I was pretty much crazy for any French cinema I could see back then. I never thought Isaac would go for it, but apparently Loubet was looking to break into Hollywood, so he was willing to work for scale.

LAURENT LOUBET [DIRECTOR]

I'd never made a movie outside of France. To me, American film was mostly popcorn and soda, but that was a canvas I felt I could work on. I knew that it was unlikely that Mr. Peterson would give me the kind of control I wanted, so I insisted on writing the script as well, at a reduced rate. I understood fairly quickly that his real interest was profit and loss, and that I should lean into that.

CARL MONKTON [AUTHOR]

I sent them a letter, politely asking them not to make the movie. They didn't respond. I had no control over the rights, I foolishly signed them away to the publishing company in the first contract. It's a strange feeling, to hope that your words and sentences aren't popular, that your novel doesn't sell, that it won't do the very thing that stories exist for—to be read.

ISAAC PETERSON [PRODUCER]

Monkton was a bit of a kook, truth be told. Letters, phone calls, even showed up at my office. The guy had no idea of how the business worked, he didn't seem to understand that the publisher had sold us the rights. It got so that I told studio security not to let the guy onto the lot.

Then it escalated.

Arthur Kay (Head of Studio Security, 1962 - 65)

I got a call, around 1am, from Mr. Peterson. He was saying Monkton was outside his house, hammering on the windows. I got there as fast as I could. It was quite the sight. Monkton had cracked the glass with his fists, which were all cut and bloodied. He turned as I approached, and he just bolted straight at me.

I served in Korea, even saw some action. He wasn't easy to drop though. First punch should have taken him off his feet, but he kept coming.

I don't want to speculate about the guy, whether he had personal problems, or whether he was involved in narcotics. He was lucky—Mr. Peterson decided not to press charges, concerned about bad publicity.

I'll always remember though, grabbing him by the collar, trying to force him to the ground. He was laughing like I was doing exactly what he wanted me to, like it was all some sort of game.

You meet all kinds in this job.

Carl Monkton (Author)

I did show up at the studio, yes. But I never went to Isaac Peterson's house. Never.

Laurent Loubet (Director)

I don't think any of them really understood the book. The characters at the start aren't always the characters you're reading about later on. It's about a fractured reality. Can any of us truly know ourselves? If memory is a construct, how can we believe anything that has happened? What if you had to see yourself as you really are, not what you pretend to be, stripped bare of your delusions and self-justifications? To me, that was a terrifying concept.

Isaac Peterson (Producer)

I hated Loubet's screenplay. It made less sense than the book, and that apparently made no sense either. I gave him my usual notes though—*find someone we can root for, keep the romantic sub-plot on the boil, remember this has to play in Poughkeepsie.*

I've had a pretty decent career. Most of my pictures stack up, maybe not always with the critics, but at least at the box office. I understand the business is all about entertainment. We're getting people out of their houses, to hand over their hard-earned cash. That doesn't mean every movie has to be empty and vapid. It's just gotta be worth the trip.

I signed up Bruce Mountford for the lead, and Jayne Southern to play his wife. People forget now, but they were big stars. Maybe not all-time hall-of-famers, but they were on the magazine covers, and they both had some decent hits under their belts. Bruce wasn't the world's greatest actor, but he had charisma, and sometimes that's better.

And Jayne? She was beautiful. She was like a more homely Ava Gardner or Veronica Lake, and I mean that in the best way possible.

I'm still angry with Loubet for what he did. But maybe he was right.

All I know is that *They Are Us* is my biggest regret. Not just in the business. Biggest regret period.

Terry Moretti (1st Assistant Director)

The first few weeks were as smooth as any I've had on set. We'd maybe slipped two or three days behind schedule—there were a lot of hold-ups with the lighting; Loubet wanted it to look like the projector bulb was faulty, so that the audience would really have to peer and squint for some of the scenes. It was very French, and I don't think Mel (Mel Rayner, director of photography) was really getting what Loubet wanted.

There was one day, about a week in, when Loubet went around the set and just started removing bulbs from Mel's lights. I thought Mel was gonna go for him. I had to step in and explain to Mr. Loubet that we didn't really do that sort of thing here. There were unions and what not.

This was all pretty standard fare though. It was around the third week though that things started to go wrong.

SHEILA WELSH (SECRETARY)

I was friends with some of the people on the crew—make-up, costume. We'd meet for drinks, swap stories. I had an inside line to Isaac and his various shenanigans, so that made me popular, especially after a few cocktails.

I heard there were problems with Jayne Southern on set, that she was becoming increasingly erratic. They were having issues with her in the mornings—she'd be partway through getting her face done, and she'd suddenly get up and walk away. Diva-like behavior, I guess, or that's what we thought.

I remember Karen (Karen Chanter, make-up artist) saying that she thought it was the mirror. "She can't stand to look at herself."

KAREN CHANTER (MAKE-UP ARTIST)

I have no recollection of saying that, but that doesn't mean it didn't happen.

There is one thing I've never told anyone. I got to work one morning, and the makeup trailer was trashed. There was powder and blusher everywhere. There was all this writing scrawled across the mirror in lipstick and eyeliner, but the words were all jagged and backward. I didn't know what to do, so I just dug in, cleaned the place up.

I'm pretty sure Jayne had done it, but there's no way I could confront her. I asked security if they'd seen anyone, but they said I was the only person who'd been to the trailer that morning, although they seem to think I'd arrived an hour before I did.

It didn't really matter who was responsible—it was a hell of a mess, and I was worried I'd lose my job, that they'd blame me for not locking up properly the night before.

LAURENT LOUBET (DIRECTOR)

Bruce and Jayne were romantically involved off set, even though they both had other partners. You could see it at rehearsals—they had a spark like there was no one else in the room. It was destined to go wrong, as all affairs of the heart do, but back then I shot chronologically, so I was not worried. If they grew to hate each other, it would help the verisimilitude of the piece. And it did go wrong, but maybe not for the reasons we all thought at the time.

TERRY MORETTI (1ST ASSISTANT DIRECTOR)

It was a simple kitchen scene, about two-thirds of the way through, where the wife becomes convinced that she's not talking to her husband, that he's somehow become someone else. Not physically, I guess, emotionally. They argue, and she throws the pot of water at him.

LAURENT LOUBET (DIRECTOR)

Jayne struggled on the first few takes. I told her to play it naturally, to let the words do the talking, but she kept "acting"—raising her voice, throwing her arms out, all very melodramatic and American.

Something switched on take five though.

KAREN CHANTER (MAKE-UP ARTIST)

I remember sensing something was wrong. Even before Laurent called "action," she seemed stricken. I was trying to do my final checks, and I could see the panic in her eyes. She was like a trapped animal, looking for a way out.

Isaac Peterson (Producer)

She just went for Bruce. Physically attacking him, clawing at his face. Then she suddenly stopped, staring beyond him, through the windows of the kitchen set. She staggered back, and let loose the kind of scream I hope to never hear again. I swear the set walls were vibrating with the sheer force of it.

Of course, you wouldn't have to take our word for it, you could view the footage yourself, if Loubet hadn't lost his mind later on.

Laurent Loubet (Director)

I stand by everything I did.

Bruce Mountford (Actor)

I've never spoken about *They Are Us* and I never will. I'm sorry. I'm just not comfortable discussing it.

Isaac Peterson (Producer)

Bruce had his agent and manager on my back constantly after that "kitchen incident." Things just got worse between him and Jayne—and it wasn't just her. There was one take where Bruce just stood there, staring right down the camera lens. We had two weeks left of the shoot, so it was my job to rally the troops, keep them going, get us over the finish line. I think Loubet enjoyed the chaos, but none of the crew did. Even the set we'd built, a replica of an old townhouse, started to fall apart. They'd come in for work in the morning and find a door hanging off the hinges, or the windows smashed.

We made it to the end though. Almost.

We had enough in the can to complete the movie if we had to. It didn't matter, though, not after what happened.

Sheila Welsh (Secretary)

I still remember getting the call, like it was yesterday. Jayne had driven her car into a brick wall, just off Hancock Park. She died instantly. We were in shock. Utter shock.

Laurent Loubet (Director)

My last conversation with her weighs heavy on me, even now. She told me that she wished she could be who she was before she was her. I assumed she meant stardom, the pressures that came with being in the public eye. Later on, when I viewed the rushes of that day on the kitchen set, went through them inch by inch, I understood what she really meant.

Brenda Southern (Jayne's younger sister)

They said she was on drugs, but for Chrissakes, everyone in the movies was on something. The studios would hand them out like candy. Uppers, downers, whatever it took to get you to work.

Do you know how it feels, to stand there at the funeral, for the person you love more than anything in the world and have those vultures outside with their cameras like she's still part of their damn sideshow?

I tried to get the police to re-open their investigation, but they wouldn't. There was an eyewitness to the crash, though, who said he saw two people in the car, just before it struck that wall. He said he wasn't sure which one was my sister because they both looked the same.

Isaac Peterson (Producer)

One eyewitness out of three or four. My heart goes out to Brenda, but she was looking for answers to a question that didn't exist.

I thought the best thing would be to release the picture, after a respectful period of time, as a tribute to Jayne's wonderful career. There's precedence—Jimmy Dean, Monroe, Jean Harlow. It never happened though. Loubet stole the negative and destroyed everything—all the footage, all the work. The whole damn lot.

LAURENT LOUBET (DIRECTOR)

Jayne is standing in the kitchen, and she attacks Bruce. Then she steps back, and she stares off. The camera was on her, but there's a moment where it shifts to the side, an almost imperceptible move before it racks into a close-up on her face. I'd encouraged Mel to do that—to give an uneasy, dreamlike feel to the proceedings.

I sat there in the editing room, staring at the frame. You could just make someone out, beyond the kitchen window. It looked just like Jayne, staring back at herself, only this other Jayne has her mouth wide open, and it's like the jaws have unhinged, so there's this impossibly dark fissure spreading across the face. Move forward one frame, and it's grown even wider as if it's going to keep going, obliterate the features. In the next frame, the camera has already moved away, centering on Jayne as she prepares to unleash that horrifying scream.

I replayed it over and over and over. Then I loaded all the negatives into my car, drove out to the desert, poured gasoline over them and lit the match.

CARL MONKTON (AUTHOR)

I wrote the book while I was holidaying in Prague. I was staying at a hotel on the edge of the city, and I'd contracted some kind of nasty fever, the sort where you wake up, drenched in your own sweat, shivering hot and cold at the same time.

I don't remember much about the actual writing process. I'd wake and find myself hunched over the desk, my pencil scribbling away on the paper. I was surprised that the whole thing was coherent as it was. Three or four days, and it was done. It wasn't a long book. It wasn't particularly good, but I felt I'd unwittingly captured that sense of affliction, where you're not quite sure what is real or isn't, where it feels like reality is bending around you.

The night before I returned home, I woke up some time past three, aware of someone else in the room. I could see their silhouette, by the window frame. I remember being unsure if I was still dreaming or not, even more so when I realized I recognized the figure; I knew I was looking at myself, but that it also wasn't me. I reached for the light, but understood, on some level, that if I turned it on, I would never recover from what I saw.

So I lay there in the bed, staring at that window in the half-light, at this figure who may or may not have been there, at the way the dark outline of their mouth seemed to stretch and fall forever. I was paralyzed by the fear, by the waiting, sure that something terrible was about to happen, and then I blinked and the sun had risen, and the room was empty. My fever was broken.

I wish I could say I have never experienced anything like that since, but even now there are times when I wake in the dead of night and have to force myself to keep my eyes closed, so that I will not see that figure by the window, the one who is watching and waiting.

I couldn't help feel that I brought something back, hidden between the lines of that manuscript.

I'm not even sure now that it was me who wrote it.

Sheila Welsh [Secretary]

She was such a sweet girl—even though she was older than me at the time, she'll stay the same age forever now. There will always be a Jayne Southern, caught in an eternal celluloid world, never growing old, never changing. She's still smiling somewhere, eyes bright on the silver screen, unaware of what lies ahead, of the end that waits for her.

I still stop by and put flowers by her grave every so often. It's been years, of course, but it feels like the right thing to do. I saw Isaac there once, hunched over, staring at the inscription on her stone. I didn't approach. I suppose her death must have stayed with him as well. I ran into him, a few years later, over on Melrose as he was exiting a restaurant, and I asked him about it, but he denied ever having been there.

The worst thing is I believed him. I don't know why, but I did.

I believed him.

AS DARK AS HUNGER

S. QIOUYI LU

The sun bears down hot and twisted against the nape of Ellen's neck. She wades into the muddy waters, slick yellow-brown silt clinging to her worn rubber boots. The rotten scent of fish hangs heavy in the air, which is loud with the buzz of iridescent flies and the shrieks of cicadas.

Summer here is an oppressive season, sick with humidity. The river floods, then washes back sewage and garbage. As the water recedes, the muddy pools evaporate. Any fish able to survive the reek of dank, infested waters die by suffocation on dry land. Then the gulls, the crows, the carrion-feeders pick at the corpses until they're nothing but bones bleaching in the sun.

The fans Ellen keep running in her house-on-stilts do nothing to calm the heat or drive out the stink. The most they do is add a low, humming drone that keeps the whine and buzz of insects at bay. Still, Ellen never begrudges the flood season. She knows where the cleaner waters are, where, with her hands covered by thick gloves and holding a pail full of bait and a net, she can seed the shallow waters and catch fish without even needing a line. The fish are enough to keep her fed. The work leaves a sheen of sweat on her that traps every sour, marshy scent of the river to her skin.

Ellen drops a catfish into her bucket, where it thrashes for a few moments before going still and playing dead, the only movement the whisper of its gills opening and closing like butterfly wings. Before she can turn and trudge back to the shore, something catches Ellen's eye.

There, beyond the leaves, half-hidden by the thickets of mangroves rooting the path of the river, lies a shining, smooth fish tail—a massive fish, larger even than the sharks sold at the wet market. And, as she watches, the tail twitches once, twice, before beating against the muddy bank, a wet *slop-slop* sound, the earth doing nothing but slither and squelch.

Something must have gotten caught in the mangrove roots during the flood. Ellen sets her bucket on the banks beside her, tugs her boots higher, and wades out toward the thing, her movements steady and her expression calm despite the ever-quickening beating of her heart and the sensation of her throat closing.

Another thrash. The silvery fish scales give way to flashes of skin not white enough to be the belly of a fish. Instead, it's the rich yellow-brown of her own skin. She's never seen mermaids in her time living here, but her grandmother had told her the stories, and Ellen recognizes the form as it emerges.

With every step Ellen takes, her body drags through the water, leaving chevrons in her wake. The surface dimples as water skippers skim away from her, and little bubbles break the surface as fish dart up to eat the algae and insects floating on the surface like gasoline.

When she comes around the last bend, Ellen stops. The tail of a fish flows seamlessly into the torso of a young woman, her arms threaded through mangrove roots. Her long, black hair, slimy with algae and the waste of birds that had roosted above her, is tangled in the branches.

"Hello?" Ellen says, her voice hoarse. When she reaches out, her fingers tremble. "Do you need help?"

The stench of the river mixes with the iron of blood as Ellen takes another step. The mermaid's back is to her. She's caught in the mangrove roots as if they were stocks, her face locked face-down as she struggles. Up close, what Ellen thought was a shadow turns out to be dark smears of blood slicking the silt on the banks.

Another thrash of the mermaid's tail reveals the source of the blood: a gash runs along her abdomen, piercing where a navel would be on a human. The wound is deep enough to reveal the glisten of her intestines. It's a wonder she survived, never mind that she still has the energy to struggle as she does.

"It's okay. You're safe now," Ellen says. She unsheathes her machete and hacks away at the roots, getting one arm loose, and then another, always conscious of where the blade is so she doesn't add to the mermaid's injury. She works more carefully around the mermaid's head, aware of the way the mermaid is breathing too quickly and the way her shoulders are stiff with tension.

When Ellen whittles away the last of the roots shackling the mermaid, the mermaid whips free, riled up with adrenaline and panic, and tries to take off back into the water. But as she twists toward the water, she cries out and clutches her abdomen, her palms slick with blood.

"You'll die if you go back in there," Ellen says. She's speaking in the most widely spoken tongue, but the mermaid isn't responding. Whether she doesn't know the language or is simply too shocked to speak is unclear. Ellen steps toward the mermaid, her boots squelching in the mud, and pushes aside dripping locks of matted hair to take a better look at the mermaid's face.

She freezes. Her mouth goes dry. The furious eyes that glare back at her are eerily familiar.

The mermaid has her face.

⟜

Ellen splashes back to the shore and returns with her boat, her chest heaving with her labored breaths. She ties a few knots with old hemp rope around the mermaid, who yells at her, her teeth bared, the gills under her jaw flaring open and closed. The language sounds familiar and strums through her heart, but Ellen doesn't understand what the mermaid's saying.

"Hush. You'll feel better soon."

Ellen drags the mermaid onto the boat, the knots binding her tail neat and practiced, restraining but not cruel. Her muscles burn with the effort. The mermaid flops onto the boat with a *thud* rather than the slippery *thwack* Ellen expects. Her tail quivers in its readiness to thrash. The engine of Ellen's boat sputters and throws clouds of black smoke into the air as she sets off for her house again.

As the boat skips over the waves, Ellen glances over at the mermaid again, who's glaring at her with the fury of both suns. The edges of the wound are clean, too deliberate to have been a propeller accident or an animal attack, and the way the mermaid's skin sags reminds Ellen of the stray cats who've given birth to litters and litters of kittens, their stomachs now hanging low and empty. A couple specks of bright orange linger against the red of the mermaid's flesh.

As soon as she's docked the boat, Ellen hauls the mermaid hand-over-fist into her home, leaving a slick trail of blood, grime, and slimy algae-water leading from the back sliding door to her only bathroom, where she dumps the mermaid into her bathtub and runs the water. She undoes the knots and sponges away at the mermaid.

She goes into the closet and pulls out a spool of her heavier thread and her sharpest needle. With an experienced hand, she stitches the edges of the mermaid's flesh together, closing the wound. The point where her body transitions from human to fish is strange, firm in a way that feels uncanny on the fingers. Ellen's hand hovers over the scales of the mermaid's tale, her fingers quivering with longing and the desire to touch. But her heart holds her back, telling her that this isn't an animal to examine, but a person to treat with at least the most basic of dignity.

"Can you speak Common?" she says after she ties off the last stitch, carefully avoiding eye contact with the mermaid. With her hair washed, detangled, and combed back, Ellen gets an even clearer look at the mermaid's face. There's no doubt about it—the face is decades younger, but unmistakably her own. Even though the water running over her hands is warm, goosebumps speckle Ellen's arms as revulsion and fear run through her.

"Hui shuo Putonghua ma?" Ellen says, switching to her second tongue. When there's no response, she switches to her third. "Ĉu vi parolas Komuna?"

Still no response, not even a grunt or a gesture that suggests she understands. Hesitantly, Ellen tries a phrase in another language:

"Si gisurembi Gisun?"

The creature takes a deep, rattling breath, then exhales. If Ellen hadn't known what to listen for, she would have missed the mermaid's reply.

"Inu."

The mermaid breathes out a few more words, but they're beyond Ellen's knowledge of Gisun, which she knows only through a few battered children's books and the long-gone creaky voice of her grandmother. She does, however, know how to ask one more question.

"Sini gebu ai sembi?"

The mermaid relaxes a bit, as if finally sure Ellen is on her side. When her eyes meet Ellen's again, the fight has gone out of them, leaving her looking tired and defeated.

"Kiru," she says.

"Kiru," Ellen says, tasting the name, and Kiru watches her wordlessly. Then, Ellen puts a hand over her heart and says, "Mini gebu Ellen sembi."

Kiru offers her a small smile.

"Hojo na, Ellen."

⊸

Ellen awakens the next day to the sound of propellers—a ship is making its way up the river toward her. But this one doesn't sound like it's from around here. Here, Ellen normally hears sputtering, dilapidated boats like her own, red-rusted and sun-faded.

She dons a shirt and a loose pair of pants before stepping outside. There are no government symbols on the ship, just neatly stenciled names. Ellen makes no move to greet the sailors, even after they dock. People don't usually come to the wastetides on good terms.

A tall, slender woman leads the entourage off the ship. She's the kind of lean that comes with years of practical experience, her bearing more tigress than human, her clothing pragmatic and efficient. Her belt holds a few sheathed knives of different sizes, and Ellen knows there are more knives hidden elsewhere on her person. The woman's eyes shine golden-amber in the hazy morning light. As she steps off the boat, she toes aside seaweed clinging to the walkway and wrinkles her nose. The gesture is almost imperceptible, as if she's trying to hide her disgust, but Ellen knows that face too well to miss the gesture.

"Can I help you?" Ellen says, her voice steely and cold. She's a good head shorter than the woman.

"Ellen," the woman replies. Her voice is husky, lower than what her features might suggest.

"Stella," Ellen says, acknowledging her only that much before moving on despite her body's memory: trembling, warm, sweat-drenched. Her eyes flick to Stella's blades, then flick back to Stella's face to find Stella watching her intently.

Ellen says again, "Can I help you?"

Stella sighs. "I suppose I shouldn't have expected anything different."

Ellen lets the remark pass. Stella gauges her reaction. Then, she continues. "Mermaids are returning to spawn," she says. Ellen keeps her expression neutral. She'd closed the door behind her, blocking all lines of sight to the bathroom, and the house is quiet, but Ellen still has the uneasy feeling that Stella knows, somehow, about Kiru.

"Why should I be concerned?" Ellen says. She places her hands on her hips, taking a more open, offensive stance, but it's a bluff—her heart pounds furiously against her chest, and her palms are slick with sweat. The briny green scent of algae growing on the river's surface rises along with the wet stink of the whole place. Somewhere deep in the mangrove thickets, a bird cries out. Stella tilts her head and gives Ellen a simpering smile.

"I would have thought that you of all people would take an interest," Stella says. Ellen flushes, heat rising to her cheeks and churning in her gut, indignation and shame together as one.

"Don't play coy," Ellen says. "It has to be something big for you to show your face again."

Stella's smile doesn't falter, but her eyes narrow, giving her smile an edge of malice.

"They're paying good money for mermaids caught alive," Stella says. Ellen's skin prickles, her stomach dropping in anticipation of what Stella might say next.

"Why?"

Stella considers Ellen for a moment, then buffs her nails and glances at them. Ellen doesn't have to see them to know that they aren't yellowed like her own, with dirt perpetually wedged under them. The lines of power return to Stella's face and posture as she masks her familiarity with Ellen and resumes the stance of a merchant.

"Despite how you may feel, much of the rest of the world sees mermaids as a delicacy, and they fetch spectacular prices on the open market," Stella says. She raises a hand to cut off Ellen's protests. "The reality is that the demand is there, regardless of your personal sentiments. And my crew and I would like to try more humane ways to meet the demand. But we need more mermaids to start with. They only come back to spawn every twelve years, and then only for a few weeks at a time."

"So let them be and leave me alone," Ellen says, turning to go.

"A hundred thousand yi," Stella says, stopping Ellen in her tracks.

"Excuse me?"

"That's how much a live one fetches at the market. More for certain qualities—brindled mermaids are said to be particularly delicious." Stella smiles, and the opacity of the smile has Ellen uneasy with how she can't be sure what emotions it represents. "But even if the pay is generous, I know your interest in them too, Ellen. We have the equipment you don't have to get close enough to a school of mermaids and take them in alive and unharmed. The most you can do alone is get close enough to see a flash of scales before the mermaids scatter and disappear."

Ellen thinks of Kiru and is about to retort that she doesn't need Stella for that, but she catches herself in time. She doesn't want Stella to know about Kiru—the very idea makes her tremble with a serpent's nest of emotion, all knotted together into a twisted ball.

"They're not killed," Stella says, eyeing Ellen's balled fists before meeting her eyes again. "That much has been outlawed. Their tails are just cropped, not unlike a dog's, and they can adapt to that. The process has become quick and preserves as much of the mermaid's range of motion as possible. They say the tail doesn't feel pain anyway, like fish. And a hundred thousand yi is payment for just one mermaid. Hundreds come during a spawning season, and you know this river and their ways better than anyone else here, I'm sure of that."

It's an attractive offer. It wouldn't be much to assist Stella, and she could think of a number of uses for such a salary. She could escape the stinking river once and for all, for instance. Really make something of her life and herself. All she'd have to do is something the rest of the world does anyway.

But then she thinks of Kiru and imagines the horror of having part of her body severed away. The mermaids may survive the whole thing, but, Ellen thinks, living things survive all kinds of pain and cruelty.

"I'm not interested," Ellen says. Stella's expression doesn't change, but she looks Ellen in the eye longer than Ellen feels comfortable with.

"Well, it's your loss," Stella says at last. "If you do change your mind, though, we'll be docking at Ermei Village. Come find me."

With that, she turns on her heel and boards the ship again. Ellen crosses her arms and glares as the ship sails back to the fork in the river, then disappears.

Still, when Ellen goes inside and opens the bathroom door, watching as Kiru stares at the ceiling, gills only barely flaring open and closed, she can't get Stella's last words out of her mind.

Come find me.

She and Stella had had their time together. Their relationship had been explosive and passionate, barbed and toxic. Even after they'd gone their separate ways, she still thought of Stella at times. Healthy or not, happy or not, Stella had been a lot of Ellen's firsts, and one of those that Ellen would never admit is her first love.

Ellen had taken in every detail of Stella. She looked youthful, her face hiding her age, even if her hands showed them. And her hands had been bare. No rings or bands. Just the familiar calluses where the handles of her blades have kissed skin so often it's turned to stone.

Ellen closes her eyes and touches her forehead to a doorframe, grounding herself as she lets out a small sigh. They're different people now. It would be foolish to expect something Stella's never willing to give.

Kiru's shallow, labored breaths punctuate the silence. A disquiet settles over Ellen as she takes in features that are indisputably hers—the uneven dip of the lips, the mole under one eyebrow, the upturned nose—yet completely foreign. She can't help the uneasy fascination, like the first time she'd locked herself in a room with a mirror and truly taken a look at every part of her body. Strange topographies lie before her, uncharted to her own.

Even if Kiru didn't have her face, Ellen would still have done all she could to save her. Her grandmother's stories of their mermaid ancestors cultivated an allegiance in Ellen's heart. Even though she may be only human, to take Stella's offer feels like a betrayal.

Ermei Village.

Ellen leaves the bathroom door ajar behind her. Kiru's breaths whisper through the night.

⟜

It takes three days for Ellen to gather the will and resolve to go to Ermei Village. She'd fought with herself for those three days: True, she's the best to navigate the mangroves, but that only affords her more of a chance to actually find and catch mermaids. Could she mutilate one to satisfy such an unnecessary craving? It happens though, she knows that well enough, even with the very people around her—those who'd spent longer in the wastetides tend to respect the mermaids' spawning season, but newcomers are more unscrupulous and had not only sold mermaid tail at the market, but had also begun to clear the mangroves for other profitable ventures.

Ellen doesn't know if she can treat living beings as strictly business like that. But, at the same time, the stifling stagnation of the wastetides is slowly choking the life out of her. This could be her one chance, and Stella *had* mentioned being humane to the mermaids. Visions of a house in a city thick with the smells of rain and street food, or a cottage in the countryside where she could wake to clean dew and the sweet perfumes of flowers outside her window, grow stronger as they become more of a possibility.

She heads to the main part of town: the hawker center, where dozens and dozens of food stalls serve people late into the night. Even though there are still many people around at this hour, it's far less crowded than usual. Ellen spots Stella finishing the last of a bowl of steaming noodles at a table.

"Changed your mind?" Stella says as soon as Ellen sits across from her. That had been one of the things she couldn't stand about Stella: the way she held herself over you, as if she always knew more, or knew better.

Ellen doesn't fall for Stella's bait. First, she goes over to a stall and returns to the table with a cold drink, sweet and tangy, biding her time as she lets the steam over Stella's tone vent from her. Then, she leans her elbows on the table. "I suppose," she says.

Stella smiles.

"I've thought about you a lot," Stella says. "I know we argued. But we always found a way to make up for it."

Ellen flushes. She remembers the raised voices, the charged emotions, the way she would retreat and sulk for days, nursing her wounds. The way she'd go back into the room, ready to share a bed with Stella again, and how Stella knew as much as she did that that was the most of an apology either of them would get. And then Stella would touch a kiss to her neck, and that would be enough to mend her heart; and then Ellen would ask for Stella's hand, *one, two, three,* and that would be enough to mend her soul.

Ellen is a hard woman, stoic and straightforward; the emotions she shows are earned. Stella is the opposite: The tracest emotion manifests itself in her expression, and she polishes that into brilliance with her charisma. But when it had been just the two of them, they could cross each other's walls, reversing roles, reversing personas. Whether either was "the real Ellen" or "the real Stella" had often crossed Ellen's mind, until she eventually settled that both parts of her were real, and neither part of her was real.

"I need strict boundaries if I'm going to work with you," Ellen says as she sips her drink. Moths flutter against the lanterns hung throughout the hawker center, and the sound of sizzling starts and stops like a round. "One:

You tell me up front if you want something out of me. Two: You tell me the entire truth."

Stella looks taken aback for a moment. There's a second when Ellen isn't sure if it's the flicker of the lights or if anger truly flashes over Stella's face. But when she blinks again, Stella's face is soft, and she nods.

"I understand."

She places a hand on Ellen's. Ellen's skin tingles, pinpricks of sensation blooming, and her breath catches.

All these years, and her body still reacts the same way to Stella's faintest touch.

"We leave at first dawn. The mermaids usually spawn during forthlight, so we'll need to be at a good fishing spot before then. I'll see you tomorrow."

She gives Ellen's hand a squeeze, then pushes her chair back and stands. She downs the rest of her drink and sets the glass on the table.

"I'll need to get some rest tonight. I'm glad you came to me, Ellen."

It only hits Ellen when she's back home on the porch smoking that Stella had been the one to come to her.

"The whole truth," she mutters, then pinches out the rest of her joint. Cicada screeches cut through the muggy air. She toes off her slippers at the back door and steps inside. Her bare feet pad down the hall to her bathroom, where she kneels beside the bathtub.

Kiru's scales have lost some sheen, and her skin looks waxy. Ellen reaches around her tail and, with effort, pulls the plug. The hollow, whirling sound of the water draining away reverberates off the bathroom tile. The water that swirls away is yellow-brown, blood mixed with dust and silt mixed with the grime of the river.

Ellen fishes out the clumps of hair that slow the drain, tossing the wet, soap-globby tangles into the trash can. She rinses Kiru off. The edges of Kiru's wounds have begun to stitch together, but it's too early to see if she has any signs of infection, and Kiru is still too weak to help Ellen bathe her and tend to her wounds. She winces in pain sometimes, crying out words in Gisun that Ellen doesn't know. She takes care to be as gentle with Kiru as possible while Kiru clenches her teeth.

Better than death, Ellen tells herself.

She puts the plug back in and draws another bath. Steam suffocates the room. As the water runs, Ellen goes to the pantry and rummages through the shelves. She returns to the bathroom with a few packets of dried herbs and powders. She places them under the faucet and also throws in a couple of handfuls of salt. She could choke on the smell of the bathroom: blood and waste and medicine.

She doesn't open a window, though. With the steam trapped in the bathroom, Kiru does seem to regain some shine and vigor.

Kiru speaks again, her voice wetter this time, but Ellen still doesn't understand a word other than a couple of the most basic ones.

A part of her gives way as tears come to her eyes. She reaches out and holds Kiru's hand. She'd expected her palm to be clammy, but it's warm like hers. Kiru's fingers twitch as if to try to squeeze Ellen's hand, but her breaths are still shallow, and her body is limp.

"I'm sorry," Ellen says. "I don't understand."

Ellen's grandmother had told her about mermaids. The harpies and the nagas are natural opposites: one has dominion over the sky, while the other has the earth. But the fox spirits and the mermaids are opposites, too. The fox spirit is a shapeshifter and can choose to never settle on one form, while the mermaid can change form in only one way, and only once: She can tear her tail in two to form legs, but in doing so, she gives up her home in the water, and her children are born without tails.

Ellen's grandmother had told her, too, about the last time she'd seen her own father. Her mother had sat on a boulder by the shore, furious tears streaming down her face, as Ellen's grandmother watched from the pebbly shore closer to her father. She had been too young to understand the details, but she knew that it had to do with the fear that smothered their home, the way they and the others around them had pared down their possessions to only what truly couldn't be replaced and always had plans for how to leave somewhere quickly.

"I won't stay here without you," Ellen's great-grandmother had said.

And Ellen's great-grandfather had murmured a few words about the rest of their family and their friends needing his support—that he'd be there to join her once this passed, once this was safe. But for her to have a tail now, for her daughter to have a tail now, was certain death.

Others had hidden. She wouldn't be the first.

Ellen's grandmother never knew what made her mother change her mind in the end. But she could always recall what happened next: Her mother had gripped one side of her tail fin in either hand and, with her teeth clenched, she had ripped apart the silken membranes, hissing as they tore from each other. Blood had dripped down her fingers, fat red beads that clung to the boulder, forming rivulets.

Her father had done the rest of the bifurcation with a hunting knife, cutting away the tailbone, slashing away the thin sinew binding the two sides of muscle together. The fish skin would wither in a few days, and fresh skin would cover the rest of the wounds. Her mother had lain half-catatonic, and raw resentment had flashed across her face as she'd made eye contact with her daughter. Ellen's grandmother had stared and stared into her mother's cold glare, until her father came into her field of vision wearing the saddest smile that soon became all she remembered of him.

"I'm sorry," he'd said.

And then he'd cut her tail in two.

Ellen's grandmother had shown her the scars. They were slight, she'd said, because she'd been young. Her father never returned, and the other mermaids went into hiding. What knowledge of Common they had had dwindled as they isolated themselves more and more from the world. And when they did encounter other peoples, like when it came time to spawn, their Gisun words were unintelligible to them, leading many to believe that mermaids didn't even have a real language.

And here Ellen is now. She'd been exiled from home because of events she'd had no say in. And, as Kiru lies before her—perhaps a sister or a cousin or a niece, or even some other version of herself—she finds herself unable to put together the words to ask about home. To gain the merest entry, a gate left ajar.

Ellen turns off the tap as soon as Kiru is submerged. She squeezes Kiru's hand, then stands—but as she does, Kiru closes her fingers around Ellen's wrist, startling her.

"Baniha," she says.

Ellen lowers her head and blinks a few times before she decides not to hold back her emotions. She looks back up, a smile on her face, and lets the tears fall.

"You're welcome," she says, closing the door behind her as she leaves.

⁓

The suns haven't had a chance to heat up the day by the time Stella and her crew set out on the river. The last of the night insects' chirps die down, to be replaced by the birdsong of early morning. With the horizon going gold against the dark silhouettes of mangroves and cat tails, Ellen could almost call the river beautiful.

She takes Stella south-southeast. They don't find any mermaids there—their nets come up empty or tangled with algae and trash. By the third day of this, Stella starts to get frustrated and impatient, pacing the decks after they've docked and the rest of the crew has gone. Against the darkness of night, she questions Ellen.

"I know these aren't the best waters you're taking me to," Stella says, her lip curling back in a sneer. "You've been wasting my time."

"It's hard to spot anything in the river," Ellen replies, her voice level. "And they've learned to be stealthy. I'm doing my best."

But the response isn't enough for Stella. She's worked up now, energy flashing through her. She sheathes and unsheathes one of her blades, making Ellen sweat. Stella notices and flashes Ellen a smirk. She comes close to Ellen, backing her up against the rails.

"I missed you," she says, pulling Ellen into an embrace, their bodies fitting together in a way that could make Ellen weep. Stella leans her cheek against Ellen's neck, then turns so that her lips almost touch Ellen's skin.

Ellen lets out the tiniest of noises.

"Did you miss me?" Stella whispers. She trails one hand up Ellen's chest to clutch at her throat, her thumb on one artery and two fingers against the vein, pressing like the point of a knife dimpling skin.

Ellen's breath hitches.

"Yes," she chokes out.

Stella plants a kiss against the crook between Ellen's neck and shoulder, making Ellen's knees go weak. Her breath is hot against the shell of Ellen's ear when she speaks.

"Let me take you home."

Stella hitches Ellen's smaller boat to her own. Ellen can't help but watch as Stella's calloused fingers rough over the hemp rope, tying sturdy, neat knots. There's a moment when the boats are hitched together and they've both straightened up when Ellen thinks, *I could say no. I could tell her to stop. She respects that much.*

But the rest of her says *want* and *need*, says *give* and *crave*.

Stella doesn't do anything on the waters down to Ellen's home except fiddle with her blades, glancing at Ellen every now and then and smiling when she sees Ellen shiver.

"I've never met anyone else like you," Stella says. The river is clear as they sail downstream, nothing but mangroves and insects around them as Stella's boat chops through the water.

"Nor have I," Ellen says, quietly. Her skin feels electric, primed to respond. It's been so long since she's been caught breathless like this, thrown into a submissive head space where she can let power fall into someone else's hands. It's intoxicating and fills her with sensation and flighty impulses, makes her head spin with the richness of Stella's scent and the brightness of her touch, tunnels her vision so that only things like *feel* and *taste* and *breathe* remain.

They dock the boats together when they reach Ellen's home. Ellen unlocks her door and fumbles for the light, but Stella knocks her hand away, laughing.

"You think I don't remember everything about this place?" she says. Even in the dark, she can manhandle Ellen around her own home to her bedroom. Ellen goes soft in her hands, her words slipping from her, replaced by sensation and docility. It shocks Ellen, how quickly the change comes over her, how quickly she remembers and responds to it, even though it's been decades since she'd last been with Stella. How much her whole being electrifies now, craving and remembering.

"Let me see them," Stella says, her breath hot against Ellen's skin. Ellen sits on the edge of the bed while Stella kneels, arms propped up beside her. Ellen hesitates, but only for a moment. She unzips her boots and sets them aside, then pulls down her pants and tosses those aside, too.

"They're almost gone," Stella says, coming closer to Ellen's bare thighs. Her skin isn't as youthful now, and the scars have mostly turned white, but a few browner marks remain: scales etched and woven by a blade, each as wide as a thumb, the whole lacework spanning the fronts of her thighs.

"I . . ." Ellen says, then takes a breath. "I miss them."

I miss you, she wants to add, but doesn't. Stella gives her a knowing look all the same, as if she hears the words anyway. She unsheathes her knife and presses the blade against Ellen's skin. Ellen shudders—the blade is fine and cold, but Stella holds it so that it doesn't break skin.

"They don't have to be gone," Stella says. She runs the point of the blade up Ellen's thigh, spiraling to nip at the inner thigh. Ellen hisses, but her skin is only red with a pinch.

Ellen had never shared her wishes with anyone until she met Stella. She'd hardly been able to express them to herself, the way her body didn't feel real, the way parts of her always felt alien and wrong. How she'd never managed to bring the blade to herself, but she knew that having the blade put against her, dragged against her skin, leaving smears of blood—that it would help, somehow, to see the scales carved into herself; that the pain of having her blood revealed to herself would bring her exhilaration and make her body quake and her heart race in ways that nothing else would.

And there had been all the times when, filled with fury and rage, her mind overwhelmed with voices, Ellen would stare into the distance, seeing only her internal vision: her skin flayed from her body, ribbon after ribbon pulled back to reveal what she was inside. She would stand still, unobservable to the outside world, her skin prickling and crawling with the need to be ripped off, with the base desire for destruction.

Only Stella had understood. She was criss-crossed with scarred sigils and seals herself, her skin readable in the dark. By whose blade, Ellen was never sure. She'd never asked.

It became ritual and release, inversions and subversions of power, a place where Ellen could be truly inside her own body with all its pain and pleasure and blood. She'd never seen it as mutilation, but sacrifice.

But the two of them were like fire and wind, each goading each other on, passion and fury, heat and explosions.

Twenty years and Ellen had tried her best to come to peace with herself, to learn her own topography and begin to see her own body as a home instead of a collection of unfitting parts, as true in itself, as a skin to inhabit and not to shed. To grieve for the places she could never go to, the doors shut long before she'd arrived.

Impulse pounds through Ellen. In the end, she's still in the same place: facing a door and unable to read the sign. Familiar fire salts her skin, makes her want to tear everything away in her overwhelming, unarticulated grief and fury.

"Six," Ellen says.

Stella smiles.

The blade runs quick over her. Ellen gasps as her skin pinches apart in the knife's wake. Blood beads up big and wet. Stella's hand is deliberate around the curves of the six scales. Ellen is alight with sensation, her body throbbing with it, exhilarated with the high. Tears well in her eyes, cathartic and hot, her body aglow in the ritual and feeling.

Stella strokes Ellen's skin, her hair, the unbroken skin of her other thigh, and waits for Ellen's breathing to steady.

"Let me clean you up," Stella says. She stands and leaves the bedroom. Too late, Ellen snaps back to her senses, her head rushing with whiplash.

"Stella, wait—"

But Stella's opened the bathroom door. The bed creaks as Ellen gets up, blood trickling down her skin as she dashes over, her stomach dropping as she sees Stella staring straight at Kiru.

"Well," Stella says, her eyebrows raised as she turns back to look at Ellen. "I thought we were telling each other the whole truth."

Ellen mumbles, trying to string together a sentence, but Stella waves her hand as she turns back to observe Kiru.

"Whatever. I don't care about the how or the why. I care that this one got away. But, thankfully, it's still alive."

Words come back to Ellen as her throat opens up again.

"You can't take her."

Stella laughs. She squats down and looks at Kiru. Kiru sneers and spits in Stella's face. Ellen's eyes widen as she braces herself for a fight, but Stella calmly wipes the spit off her cheek. Kiru's chest heaves and her nostrils flare as she stares down Stella, who turns back to Ellen and gestures at Kiru.

"And what will you do? Keep it here or in some miserable pen until it dies anyway? Might as well make the last of its days comfortable."

Stella stands. She hooks her elbows under Kiru's shoulders. Kiru thrashes, protesting Stella's handling, but she runs out of energy quickly, her ribs heaving as she pants, her gills a bruised purple-red. Stella lugs Kiru out of the tub. Kiru slips and lands with a wet *thud* and a shout. She slides herself back, but Stella starts dragging her again by the arms and hair.

It's uncanny, seeing Stella handle Kiru with such force. The rage on Kiru's face is palpable as she claws back at Stella, who doesn't flinch, and Ellen wonders if that's what she looks like when she, too, is filled with rage. She wonders if Stella sees the resemblance, and whether it thrills or horrifies her if she does.

Ellen can't tug Kiru back; she'd probably injure her further. She tries reasoning with Stella, then prying her grip off Kiru, but Stella is stronger than Ellen, her hands like stones. Stella drags Kiru across the dock and the foot bridge into her ship, where she unlocks a large door to the hold and throws Kiru in, doing nothing as Kiru tumbles and screams.

Stella takes the three steps down the hold. Bluish light casts up from the level below, mixing with the indigo-black of night. Ellen descends the three stairs in pursuit, but, just as she readies herself to confront Stella, she stops in her tracks.

A tank with a few lifeless mermaids, their expressions distant and listless, takes up most of the hold. But although her heart leaps to her throat upon seeing them, her gaze lingers longest on a smaller tank filled with orange masses. She flashes to Kiru's wound and the orange dots that she saw before and pieces the memories together.

"You're breeding them? Like animals?" Ellen says as she stares at the thousands and thousands of eggs, however many generations held in captivity.

Stella breaks her stride over to Kiru. She shakes a lock of hair out of her eyes and gives Ellen a cold smile.

"What, you want us to smoke them out of their own homes?" she says. "More reliable and humane this way, in the end."

Kiru thrashes on the floor, the stitches along her abdomen glistening in the light. Stella heaves Kiru's tail over her shoulder and starts dragging her toward the tank. Kiru scrabbles her nails against the floorboards as she resists. The jagged, raised edge of a loose plank catches on her and pries her open, tearing out several of her stitches. Kiru screams as her wound splits open and her blood smears across the wet floorboards.

Stella drops her grip on Kiru's tail. Ellen's hands ball into shaking fists as fury seizes her from head to toe. She runs over to Kiru and kneels, holding her as Kiru sobs.

"You don't care about being 'humane.' You don't care about anyone other than yourself," she spits at Stella. She turns back to Kiru and wipes the grime, sweat, and blood from her face, doing all she can to at least give Kiru dignity if she can't give her life. But when Kiru looks up, her eyes are dazed and unfocused, and she grimaces with pain.

"Mimbe wa," Kiru says. Ellen's mouth goes dry.

"What did it say?" Stella says, already squatting down and heaving up Kiru's tail again. Her nonchalance, her continued brutal manhandling of

Kiru, leads Ellen to believe that Stella asks not because she wants to know, but as a curiosity, like seeing a bird do a trick.

"*She* said," Ellen says, "'Kill me.'"

Ellen darts forward and grabs one of Stella's knives from its sheath. She steps back before Stella can react, her arms still full with Kiru's tail. Ellen doesn't parse the words Stella's shouting. She kneels by Kiru, mouths an apology to Kiru's nod, then, in a swift movement, she cuts Kiru's throat over Stella's shouts. As Kiru sputters, blood flowing thick and hot, Ellen reaches a hand into the slick, gory insides of Kiru's abdomen and finds a greenish, membrane-covered sac.

"Don't you *dare*," Stella says. She drops Kiru's tail. But Ellen's grip on the gallbladder is firm. She yanks it out with a slippery tear of sinew, then slashes it open with the knife and lets the bile spill over the gash in Kiru's abdomen.

"You can't take her," Ellen hisses. She's always careful to remove a fish's gallbladder intact when she prepares a fish so that the bile won't spoil the flesh, but, now, she counts on the bile to seep into Kiru and render her bitter and inedible.

Stella storms up to Ellen and throws her against the wall, a hand around her throat. Ellen gasps as she scrabbles against Stella, the back of her head aching from the slam.

"Useless," Stella spits, watching as Ellen struggles for a few moments longer. She releases Ellen, who collapses, gasping, and heaves the lifeless body of the mermaid out of the hold, rolling it back into the muddy river. The mermaid floats face-up, eyes open. The river carries the body only as far as the next thicket of mangrove roots, where the body comes to a rest.

Stella takes Ellen by the wrist and hurls her down the gangway to the dock. She unhitches Ellen's boat and tosses the line unceremoniously to Ellen, then makes her way back up to her boat. She pauses to look back at Ellen.

"You owe them no allegiance," Stella says. "Get over your fantasies."

She starts her boat and chokes the sky with smoke as she roars away up the river. Ellen gets in her boat, rides across the choppy wake, and propels herself over to Kiru. She pulls Kiru's body up to the banks, where she kneels beside her and closes her eyelids.

"Mujilen be sindaki," Ellen murmurs.

Put your heart at rest.

Ellen lets a hand fall onto Kiru's tail. She lets her fingertips trace over the scales, lets herself observe their rapidly leaving iridescence, lets herself touch what never was. As Stella's ship disappears over the horizon, Ellen takes the last of the gallbladder bile, and drips it into her six still-bleeding scales.

I SAY (I SAY, I SAY)

ROBERT SHEARMAN

So, there was this Englishman, and an Irishman, and a Scotsman. And they were all fighting in some war. And they got captured by the enemy. And the enemy accused them all of being spies, and said they were going to execute them by firing squad. So, the Englishman went up first. They stood him before a wall, they offered him a chance to speak to the padre, a final cigarette. When he was done, the soldiers all raised their rifles, and pointed them at him, and the captain began to give the orders for them to shoot. "Look out! Earthquake!" shouted the Englishman, and the soldiers all turned around in alarm, and in the confusion the Englishman ran away.

That's a good idea, thought the Scotsman. He was taken to the wall. He was offered a padre, a cigarette. Now it was his turn to get shot. The firing squad aimed their guns. "Tornado!" shouted out the Scotsman. The soldiers all whirled around, they didn't want a tornado creeping up behind them, and the Scotsman managed to get away.

This is easy, said the Irishman to himself. And if those two eejits can escape, then sure and begorrah I can too. He was calm as they led him to the wall. He had a casual chat with the padre, really savoured that final cigarette. He allowed himself a smile of anticipated triumph as the firing squad raised their guns. "Ready, aim—" began the captain. The Irishman shouted, "Fire!"

When they were off duty, the Englishman, the Irishman and the Scotsman didn't have much to say to each other.

It wasn't a big room, but over time they'd learned ways of keeping themselves to themselves. The Scotsman liked to sit at the table and play cards. He made no sound at all, save the soft *flip-flip-flip* as he turned them over and sorted them by suit. The Irishman lay on his bunk. There he might doze, or smoke, or drink, however the fancy took him. The Englishman often just sat on the floor and stared off into the middle distance. He called it meditation. The Scotsman and the Irishman both thought he looked ridiculous, but they never let on. They didn't want to provoke an argument. They had enough of that in the act.

Sometimes entire days would pass and they wouldn't say a word. But it was perfectly genial, and they might exchange glances every now and then, and smile.

The Englishman once told them he'd been with another troupe beforehand, and they'd wanted to spend all their free time rehearsing. Over and over again, this other Scotsman and this other Irishman, practising their patter, honing their routine. 'I couldn't stand it,' said the Englishman. "Comedy's got to have a certain spontaneity to it, right?" His Scotsman and his Irishman agreed. Neither could remember a time when they'd performed with another Englishman, as far as they were concerned it had been the three of them in this tiny room forever. It annoyed them to think the Englishman had a bit of history they didn't. But though they were fond of the Englishman, they knew the English were famous liars. He was probably just making it up.

In the evening they took turns to cook. Roast beef and Yorkshire pudding. Haggis with tatties. Irish stew. They didn't necessarily cook what you might expect them to cook; the Scotsman, for example, had a way with Irish stew, and the Englishman's tatties were second to none. Their kitchen skills were quite varied, and in their private lives they sought to avoid cultural stereotyping as much as possible.

The Irishman didn't much mind being the butt of all the jokes. What he resented was the unending predictability of them. The Englishman and the Scotsman might sometimes vary the routine; if they were doing the firing squad sketch, they might instead choose to shout out "Avalanche!" or "Tsunami!" Just to see how it sounded, they said, just to keep things fresh. The Irishman had no such freedom. You can fuck about with the setup, but a punchline is sacrosanct. Sometimes he would envy the Englishman and the Scotsman and their freewheeling improvisational ways, whilst he so laboriously had to stick to the script. Sometimes he would rather hate them.

That said, he was always the one who got the laughs.

⊸⊷

They were never given much notice. There'd be a knock at the door, just the one. It could be day or night. The Englishman, the Irishman and the Scotsman would stop whatever they were doing. The closest to the door would open it, and outside there'd be a box with their costumes in. The Englishman had a bowler hat, the Scotsman a tartan kilt, the Irishman was always dressed in muddy overalls and looked like a tramp.

They wouldn't know which joke they were doing until they got out there. If they were in a desert, it'd be the car door sketch. If it were a construction site, the ham sandwich. Any sort of battlefield, really, if there were soldiers running about and shooting at each other and blowing themselves up, it'd probably turn into the firing squad sketch sooner or later. The firing squad always seemed very popular.

Once in a while they'd get a jungle, and then it would be the canoe sketch. They all enjoyed the canoe sketch, the weather was so nice and warm.

There was this Englishman, an Irishman and a Scotsman. And they were in the jungle. And they got caught by this jungle tribe. Real darkie savages, with bones through their noses, and the chief told them they were all going to die. But this wouldn't be some pointless execution by firing squad, their deaths would be of valuable service to the tribe.

The chief examined the Englishman, felt his skin. He said it was good skin, very tight, very strong. It would make heap good canoe. And he told the Englishman that the next morning he would be killed, and that his skin would be flayed from his dead body and turned into a canoe, but on his last night alive he could have whatever he desired. So the Englishman asked for a bottle of whisky, and a squaw he could have sex with. He was given the bottle, and a beautiful squaw led him to a teepee, and all night he drank and made wild love. And at sunrise he was taken out, his throat was slit, his skin cut off, and he was turned into a canoe.

Pretty soon, though, the canoe went over a waterfall and was lost. So the chief went to the Scotsman and inspected him. He felt his skin, and said that it was very firm, very hairy, and just right to make heap good canoe. The Scotsman was allowed to have whatever he wanted. He chose five bottles of whisky, and hand-picked the five most beautiful squaws in the tribe. He went to the teepee. By sunrise he was already dead, but there was a big smile on his face. And his skin was cut off, and he was turned into a canoe.

Pretty soon the canoe was lost, it went over a waterfall. So the chief went to the Irishman. He liked his skin. He said he could do great things with that skin. Coarse like hemp, when the Irishman's skin was sliced from his body, when every little fleck of it was cut off the bone, and dried, and left to bake in the heat, it would make the heap finest canoe they had ever seen. The Irishman would be killed in the morning. But before he died, for his last night alive, he could have whatever he desired. The tribal barmen got the bottles of whisky ready, and all the squaws lined up in preparation. The Irishman asked for a fork. Nothing else—just a fork. The chief was puzzled, but agreed to grant his wish. They brought him a fork, and it was the best fork the tribe had, it was a golden fork and its tines gleamed in the sun. The Irishman took the fork. He held the fork up high, just for a moment, as if in reverence. And then, suddenly, he brought it down hard, and sank it into his leg. And faster, in a frenzy, stabbing hard all over his body, his arms, his bare chest, his face. And crying out, "Try to get me afloat now, you bastards!"

Actually, the Irishman didn't enjoy the canoe sketch as much as his friends did.

Was it Heaven or Hell? They didn't know. It was just where the dead would finish up. As something the living could laugh at.

On Sundays—they liked to call it Sundays—the Englishman, the Irishman and the Scotsman were let out of their room, and could explore the courtyard, and meet the rest of the comedians. All the other Englishmen, Irishmen and Scotsmen—and Belgians too, and Polacks, and Canadians, and blacks, and cripples, and Jews. All the fat mother-in-laws, the doctors and patients, men walking into bars, and chickens in endless droves crossing roadways and never quite being sure what their intentions were in doing so. It was good to get out, there was always something to tickle the funny bone.

⊸

It had been an especially good gig. Or an especially bad one—either way, there was a present waiting for them on their doorstep the next morning. They couldn't tell how old she was, they had no experience of little girls. She seemed frightened, she didn't want to come in, and all three men had to back off until she dared put a foot over the threshold. She blinked at them, ready to run. Around her neck was a sign that said, '*Your Daughter*.'

But whose daughter? There was no clue. She was beautiful. She hadn't the sallow eyes of the Englishman, the red beard of the Scotsman, the Irishman's skin as craggy as a cliff face. Oh, those eyes. Oh, that hair. "Maybe if she spoke to us," said the Englishman; "We'll tell from the accent," said the Scotsman; "What's your name, little darlin'?" said the Irishman. And the girl opened her mouth, and she couldn't answer them, her tongue had been ripped from her head.

They didn't know how to be fathers. They tried their very best. The Englishman taught the girl how to be prim and repressed. The Scotsman taught her how to be mean and angry. The Irishman taught her to be stupid. And they'd be on their best behaviour around her, they wouldn't swear or fart or scratch at their balls. They'd play games with her, they'd make toys for her out of their few possessions. And in the evening, if she were a good girl, and she was always a good girl, they'd perform for her. They'd do their jokes, but with an eagerness that they'd never showed to the general public, their comedy was pure and true and so touching it even made them cry in spite of themselves. The girl wouldn't cry. She'd giggle and clap her hands and each night when the jokes were over she'd give each of her three daddies a great big hug.

⊸

Comedy is, of course, subjective. What makes one person laughs leaves another stone cold. And the Englishman, the Irishman and the Scotsman all had different tastes. What the Englishman really liked was dry wit, and he had a particular liking for the aphorisms of Wilde and Shaw, and he would have happily entertained his colleagues with examples had they wanted him to do so. They didn't. The Scotsman loved puns. He thought there was something inherently clever about a pun—the way that things had double meanings and were more complex than they first looked, because wasn't that what life was like, really, wasn't that just like life? From what he could remember—and sometimes in the night if it were dark or it were cold, he would reassure himself by counting in his head all the puns he had ever known, and there were fourteen. The Irishman liked pratfalls. So he liked to take the top bunk, and if he woke in the morning suddenly and forgot where he was, he might roll out of bed and tumble all the way to the ground. It gave him something of a thrill.

They would have friendly arguments about the nature of comedy. The Englishman sided with the theories of Freud, and talked about the power of words set into a specific repeated system in order to elicit a response. The Scotsman sided with Kant, and said that comedy was all about dissonance, about the reversal of expectation even to the point of absurdism. The Irishman thought it was all about pointing at people and laughing when they got hurt.

None of them thought the jokes they took part in were especially good. There was no class to them, no wordplay, not enough custard pie fights or falling down stairs. But they were still proud of the services they offered, they'd seen other Englishmen, Irishmen and Scotsmen out there, and they were up there with the best.

And their daughter liked what they did. Even when she was no longer a toddler. Even when she became a teenager, and she was as tall as they were, and had grown breasts and curves. Even when she became a young woman, and was the most beautiful young woman any of them had ever seen. She still giggled, and clapped her hands, and hugged them—and she was there each time they came home from work, and it made everything worthwhile.

There was this Englishman, an Irishman and a Scotsman, and they shared a daughter that they loved with all their hearts. But they knew they couldn't keep her forever, that one day she would leave. She'd have to go out into the world, and find a joke of her very own. She'd have to get married, and fast—women weren't allowed to be in jokes unless they had a husband to nag. The Englishman, Irishman and the Scotsman all took turns to make their recommendations. The Englishman went first. He had a list of suitable English candidates as long as his arm. But when the time came, he couldn't do it—he knew exactly what Englishmen were like, and he went pale at the thought that his beloved daughter would be saddled with a single one of them. Next was the Scotsman. The Scotsman opened his mouth to speak—but out came a sob, he couldn't bear to lose his girl, no one Scottish was good enough to deserve her! Finally came the Irishman. The girl liked the Irishman, he always made her laugh the most of all, and she smiled because she knew he wouldn't let her down. The Irishman said he had considered all the men in the world—not just the English, Scots and the Irish, but the Welsh too, and the Spanish, and the Greeks—he'd been around the courtyard looking for prospective suitors, and there wasn't a man amongst them who was worthy. So he did the only thing he could, and married her to one of the chickens.

After their daughter had left, they couldn't stop thinking of her. It threw them quite off their stride. And the next time there was that one knock at the door, and they were summoned to do their act, they were in tatters. Their comic timing was off. The Englishman and the Scotsman went in the wrong order. The Irishman forgot what he was meant to say, and the firing squad was obliged to shoot him without a punchline. There was no laughter from the void. They went back home quiet, thoughtful, afraid. They'd all heard tales of what happened to jokes that stopped being funny.

"We can't talk about her," said the Englishman; "Never again," agreed the Scotsman; "For our own good," said the Irishman. They fell silent. The Scotsman sat at the table and played cards. The Irishman lay in bed and smoked. The Englishman squatted upon the ground and stared off into the middle distance, he didn't stop staring for three whole days.

⊸○⊷

The Englishman would sometimes try to hang himself. So they'd all push the bunk beds away from the wall, so they could reach the light fittings—the Irishman would usually go up, he was the best with knots, and he'd tie the rope and let down a noose large enough to hold the Englishman's fat head. The Englishman would ask the Scotsman and the Irishman to pull down on his legs to make his death cleaner; he'd get on the chair, and he'd say goodbye to them, and he'd kick the chair away. And the Scotsman would grab one leg, and the Irishman the other, and they'd pull with all their might, but no matter how hard they tried the Englishman's neck would never break. And at last the Englishman would give up trying to choke, and he'd sigh, and sulk, and just stay up there twisting slowly from side to side. If he were particularly disappointed, he might stay in the noose for hours. The Scotsman and the Irishman hated it when he did that, it looked just as stupid as when he was meditating.

So it was no surprise that the Englishman was the first to break ranks. "I've got another job," he told them one day. It turned out he'd been going to auditions secretly behind their backs. He'd got the part of the knock knock man. "You know the knock knock jokes, they're huge," said the Englishman—"Chances are next time you tell one of those, you'll be talking about me!" He wouldn't need his bowler hat any longer, he wasn't an Englishman, he was an Everyman, he was to be the personification of everyone who has ever tried to gain admission through a door, regardless of age, creed or gender.

On his last night in the room they had a farewell party. They drank wine and ate cake and they reminisced about the good old days when they were a team. All the old anecdotes came out—all of them, except the ones featuring their daughter. The Englishman got quite tearful: "I don't want to leave you dear chaps, I've changed my mind, I want to stay here with you!" But no one thought he really meant it. "I'll invite you to my first night," he promised them, "I'll get you in for free!" The knock knock gig was one of the hottest tickets in town. They thanked him, they told him not to bother.

The Scotsman and the Irishman continued their act alone. It still basically worked. They realised the Englishman had been a dead weight, all he'd done was to delay the pay-off. They told themselves the show was just as good as it had always been, and a bit quicker to boot. But they both knew that without the Englishman something was lost in the rhythm. And some nights out would come the whisky and the Guinness. "I miss the stuck-up bastard," the Scotsman would say. "Sure, b'jasus, I miss him too," the Irishman would reply.

They received a postcard from the Englishman one day. It said, '*Wish you were here*.' And on the reverse side, no picture at all, nothing, no, not a thing.

One day the Scotsman admitted, "I'm not even really Scottish. I was born in Huddersfield."

He remembered it all, he said. Where he was brought up. Where he went to school. What his parents looked like, his mother, his beautiful mam. He remembered the party he was thrown for his seventh birthday. His first job, why he was sacked from his first job, his second job. Meeting Annabelle. Marrying Annabelle. Her face, her lips, her eyes, her tongue. Annabelle. The Irishman asked if he remembered his own name as well. The Scotsman said, "No. No. No." He kept trying, but still the name wouldn't come. "No. No. No. I don't know who I am. I don't know who I am."

The Scotsman remembered how he'd died. He told the Irishman all about it.

There was this Englishman, an Irishman, and a Scotsman. And they were captured by the enemy. And the enemy thought they were spies, and decided they would execute them. But they wouldn't shoot them by firing squad, nor would they make canoes from their flayed skin. They would give them a chance. "Go into the forest," they said. "And each of you must return with ten pieces of fruit." And the men did so. "Now, if you can perform this task, we shall set you free. You must insert all of your fruit up your back passage in total silence. If you fail to insert every last piece of fruit, death. If you make a sound whilst doing so, death. If you hesitate, death. Begin." The Englishman had found ten apples. He was able to squeeze two Granny Smiths up between his cheeks, and though his eyes watered he held his tongue. But it was the Golden Delicious that did for him, no matter how hard he poked it in it just kept rolling back out again, and the effort made him wince with pain. "Your life is forfeit," they said, and they took him aside, and strangled him. Then it was the Scotsman's turn. The Scotsman had picked ten blackberries. He bent over, spread his legs wide to give his anus the optimum width, and he began stuffing the blackberries up there one by one. He was doing so well. And then, on the eighth blackberry, the Scotsman could no longer help it, he burst out laughing. "Your life is forfeit," he was told, and, still gigging, he was taken aside and strangled. The Scotsman went up to Heaven. There the Englishman was waiting on a cloud. "What happened?" asked the Englishman. "You seemed to be home and dry!" "I know," said the Scotsman, "but I couldn't stop thinking of that Irishman coming next with his pineapples."

"And that's how you died? For real?" The Irishman thought this was all very spurious, but the Scotsman was sick now, he'd had to pause three times telling the story in order to cough up blood, and the Irishman didn't think it was right to criticise.

"Do you think it's possible to die twice?" croaked the Scotsman. He looked suddenly so small and frightened, because really, who knows what happens to us when our time is up?

The Scotsman died, and the Irishman wept, and held him a wake, and drank all night in his honour. And before he went to bed he put outside all the empty bottles of whisky and the empty bottles of Guinness and the Scotsman's corpse, ready for collection in the morning.

The Irishman was alone, and he felt alone too. If there was any part of his now forgotten life when he had ever experienced such loneliness, he was glad it was gone from his head, he didn't want it back. He lay on his bunk, and dozed, and smoked and drank. But there was no fun in ignoring people when there was no one there to ignore.

One day there was a knock at the door. The Irishman hadn't thought he'd have been wanted ever again. There was a costume waiting for him, his familiar dirty tramp outfit. He put it on, warily. No doubt he was to be teamed with another Englishman and another Scotsman, but they'd be strangers to him. He just hoped there'd be some natural chemistry between them. Comedy was no good without the chemistry.

He went out on to the battlefield. He had been wrong. He had no new partners. He was now a solo act.

There was this Irishman, and he was fighting in some war. Probably. And he got captured by the enemy. And the enemy thought he was a spy, and sentenced him to death by firing squad. And so that's what they did—they shot him.

There wasn't much humour to be gleaned from that, the Irishman felt afterward. The audience hadn't even wanted him to say anything. There he'd been, all prepared to shout out the punchline, he'd got his cheesy grin all ready and had opened his mouth, but it was too late, the bullets tore him to pieces.

He thought it'd be different the next time. It wasn't.

This was the new comedy. It didn't want to waste time on setup, on delay, on delivery. It didn't care about pace, charm or timing. Without the Englishman and the Scotsman to layer the gag, the joke could cut to the chase. The Irishman could come on, and they'd shoot him, or they'd flay his skin to make a canoe, or they'd stick pineapples up his arse.

And the unseen crowds would laugh and stomp their feet and holler for more—and the Irishman couldn't quite see what it was that so entertained them. He was just dying, where was the skill in that? He didn't even have time to pull a funny face.

Back in his room he'd rehearse. Try to adjust to the new act. He concentrated on the pratfalls he so loved, because he could at least be sure at some point there'd be a spot of falling over to be done. He devised amusing ways he could collapse in death. He tried his best. But the truth of it was, for all his hard work and preparation, in performance it never went the way he planned. The impact of the bullets burst his body open, and if it burst at an amusing angle it had really very little to do with him.

Still, the Irishman was very popular. He got lots of bookings.

There was this Irishman, and they shot him. There was a simplicity to that he supposed he should be proud of. As he stood before the firing squad, he knew he was dying for his country. It made him feel better somehow. It gave him an identity. Some days he went out to work with something of a swagger in his step.

There was this Irishman, and he was captured, and put before the firing squad. They denied him the padre, they denied him the solace of a final cigarette. The soldiers all pointed their rifles at him, and the captain began to give the orders to shoot him, as he'd done so many countless times before.

The Irishman looked out amongst his killers, and saw there a face he recognised.

He stepped forward.

"It's all right," he said.

Because she was so frightened. Maybe it was her first time. He didn't know if she remembered him. He saw in her face all the primness the Englishman had taught her, all the meanness the Scotsman had made her practise hard. And he saw what he'd given her, that she was as thick as shit in the neck of a bottle.

And, oh, she was beautiful, she'd been miscast, surely? She shouldn't have been a killer. Those eyes, that hair.

Her rifle trembled as he approached. She tried to say something, her tongueless mouth opened and closed and opened again.

"It's all right," he said once more. "You're doing fine, darlin'." He took hold of the rifle barrel, moved it so it pressed lightly against his throat. "I'm proud of you, and all the folks out there are proud of you. You're going to be a star." He gave her a smile, and she managed a smile back, and he knew that it was all worth it, and there was not a laugh out there in the whole wide world that could spoil it.

"Pull the trigger," he whispered. She did.

THE PAIN-EATER'S DAUGHTER

LAURA MAURO

Sara's dad travels with a brown leather bag. She doesn't know what's inside. Before it was her dad's, it belonged to Grandad and it bears the marks of a long life on the road, criss-crossed with scuffmarks like ancient scars. Sara is not allowed to touch the bag, or to ask what her dad keeps in there. She asked once, when she was younger, and her curiosity could not be quelled, not even by her dad's dark blue stare, the tacit disapproval of his downturned mouth. It's mochadi, he'd said. She understands that mochadi means *dirty*, but not in the way that muddy shoes are dirty, or a used teacup; it means dirty in your soul, the kind of unclean you can't wash away with soap and water. She had wanted to ask him why *he* was allowed to touch it if it was such a mochadi thing, but his eyes were hard frost, and she'd thought better of it.

The brown leather bag rattles when he picks it up; the bright clink of glass against glass, melodious as birdsong. She knows it's heavy because her dad is as strong as a horse and still his arm sags when he holds it. Always in the left hand; black-tipped fingers like frostbite, bruise-blue palm. When she asks if it hurts he just smiles, thin-lipped, and says it's fine. It's because of his work, he says, though she isn't allowed to ask about that either. All she knows about her dad's work is that he might leave at any time and be gone for hours, or days, and the brown leather bag always goes with him.

Her dad might leave at one in the morning and still her grandad will wake her up so that they can both stand bleary-eyed at the front door, in the yellow-lit dark, and wave after the van as it departs, like he's a hero going off to war. As though someday, he might not come back.

⊸

Sara is fourteen when her dad finally relents and takes her out on the road for the first time. Grandad has grown too sick to care for her, and Dad won't leave her at home with him, even though Grandad's sickness is not the kind that other people can catch. Her fingertips tingle with anticipation as she pulls on her hat and jacket, ties her laces with fumbling hands, a child again in her excitement. Her shoes are too small, and they pinch at the toe, but she doesn't complain; they keep the rain out, which is better than the last pair she had.

She slips into Grandad's room. The door is barely ajar, and there is only darkness inside. Dad has covered the windows in cardboard and thick black tape to keep the sun out. The light hurts Grandad's eyes, and so he must exist now in permanent twilight, like the night-animals Sara once saw at the zoo. It is a hoarder's room, a cave of wonders filled floor to ceiling with oddities: horseshoes and sun-bleached model trains, empty biscuit tins, the deflated lungs of a broken old accordion. A mountain range of warped and yellowing paperbacks against the far wall. She enters on light feet, though the soles of her shoes tap-click against the floorboards.

"There she is." His voice, like water gurgling down the drain. "My little Ginger Rogers." His head is propped up on a stack of pillows; eggshell skull, sparse hair like spider silk. "Where're you off to, petal?"

"Dad's taking me to work with him." Up close, she can see the grey lines webbing the whites of his eyes, a roadmap of blue-black veins winding beneath thin skin. Her excitement at the prospect of going on the road feels obscene, suddenly. She has always loved the days spent with her grandad. Those bright days where they would walk down to the park and sit in the sun, and he would teach her about the First World War, or how to do sums. He'd been born under a blue sky, he told her once; he'd been born on the grass and slept under the stars. This was before, he said, when you could live on the road and stop where you pleased. Sara can't imagine a life beyond the bricks and mortar of their flat. Beyond central heating and the gas hob and the warm sanctuary of her bed.

"Ah." It's cold in the room, but her grandad radiates a dry heat; his touch burns, as though he is smouldering beneath the skin. There is a part of Sara—tucked quietly away beneath the obstinate optimism of her adoration—that knows that her grandad is dying. That there is something sinister in the charcoal tint of his lips, the ink-dark whorls of his veins, and that perhaps this too is mochadi. "When I was your age, I was already on the road. It's important work, what we do. It's good to help people. But it's hard work, chavi. Dirty work." He smiles. His loose jowls pull tight, revealing saw-sharp jawbone. Pale, sad eyes. "I always hoped you'd get to be a child longer than I did."

"It's okay, Grandad." Bold jut of the chin, the self-assurance of youth. "I want to be an adult so I can help you and Dad."

"When your dai first brought you home . . ." He sighs, and his eyelids slip shut for a moment. "Ah, but you were so small I couldn't stand to pick you up for fear I might break you. I couldn't understand it. We'd always had big babies in our family, and there you were. Tiny little thing, like a bird. You'll always be a baby to me, Sara."

He is quiet then. His expression is so fond, so distant that Sara thinks he must be somewhere else in his mind. Somewhere where the sunshine heals instead of hurts, and the whole world is home, and she is a china-doll infant nestled in warm grass, beneath the wide blue sky.

⟜⟝

"Where do you work, Dad?"

Sara is small in the passenger seat, puddled in her dad's old jumper. The footwell engulfs her feet, her scuffed shoes. The thrum and rattle of the ancient engine is a mechanical lullaby. She fights to stay awake as they coast down tree-choked country lanes, onto the motorway, which seems to stretch out forever; a monotony of fields growing ghostly in the gathering dark. They have been driving for hours, and the van smells of loose tobacco and diesel and the faint charred-metal scent of the heater. Strange smells, not at all like home.

Her dad hasn't shaved in days, and his chin is dark with black whiskers, hedgehog-sharp. Grandad told her that they used to eat hedgehogs out on the road. Hotchi-witchi, he called them, and said they were God's beasts.

"I work where I'm needed," her dad says. "Sometimes that's close to home, and sometimes people need me a long way away."

She wants to ask what people need him *for*, but she knows this is a forbidden question, like the contents of the brown leather bag. There is a small thrill inside of her at the thought that she might learn something of her dad's work now she is travelling with him. She wraps the sleeves of her dad's jumper around her, burrowing down into the soft wool, which still smells faintly of sweet hay, of warm horse. An old life.

"Who will take care of Grandad while we're gone?" she asks.

"Grandad can take care of himself." Her dad does not look up from the road. He is in shirtsleeves even though it's November, and Sara can see the blackened fingers of his left hand tight around the wheel, the patches of grey creeping down his knuckles. Perhaps whatever is wrong with Grandad is hereditary. She looks down at her own hands: fingers long and pink and narrow, blue-green veins beneath the skin. Perhaps she is too young for it to manifest yet.

"Couldn't we ask Mrs Adams to check on him?" Mrs Adams lives next door. She is old, but not quite so old as Grandad, and far stronger than him; she lives alone with a Yorkshire terrier that breaks into fits of frantic yapping in the night. Her dad thinks keeping animals in the house is dirty. "Or we could ask a nurse to come by, like Malur's family does for his grandma . . ."

"I don't want a nurse in the house. Or anyone else, for that matter." Her dad's fingers tighten. "Grandad will be fine on his own. He's well enough to feed himself and wash himself. He's not a baby, Sara. He doesn't need anyone to fetch after him."

Chided, she turns her face silently to the window. Her face is an ellipse, an off-kilter moon reflected against the deep, marine blue of the oncoming night. She thinks of her grandad's fragile hands. The skin, loose now on his bone-china skull, and the damp rasp of his breathing, in and out like a tide dragged across wet stones. On they drive, ever further from home, towards some nebulous place in the darkening distance where, her dad says, somebody needs him.

⊸

They pull up outside the house just before midnight. Sara rubs her bleary eyes with the back of her hand, clambering out of the passenger seat. "Come on," her dad says, and the leather bag hangs heavy from his left hand. "They're waiting."

The night air is peppermint-sharp in the back of her throat; her breath ghosts white when she exhales. The pavements shimmer with silvery frost. The houses all look the same here: windows frothy with net curtains, neatly-paved driveways upon which gleaming cars are parked. BMWs and Audis and Jags. Rich people cars, her dad calls them, disdainful. She wraps her arms tightly around herself and stands close to her dad as he walks up to the house. It is the only one in the street with lights on.

The door opens before they are halfway up the drive. A woman appears in the narrow gap, backlit. She glances over at the grubby van, looks doubtfully at the tall, unshaven man and his raggedy daughter standing before her. "Are you Dominic?" she asks. Her accent is strange, singsong; Sara has heard people talk like her on TV, but never in real life.

"Yes," he says. "And you must be Rosalia. I'm sorry it took so long. We live in Worthing, you see, and it's a long way to travel."

Rosalia nods, hesitant. Her gaze settles on Sara. She is probably wondering where on earth her mother is. Why she is awake at this ungodly hour, and so far from home.

"This is my daughter, Sara," her dad says. "I'd usually leave her at home, but I couldn't get a babysitter at short notice. I hope you don't mind if she comes in with me."

Sara meets Rosalia's gaze, undaunted by her curiosity. She is not as old as Sara had first thought; she is just very thin, and very tired, and her skin is crumpled like old paper, dark hair sparse as dandelion fluff. She looks, Sara thinks, like a hunted animal; like the hares her dad and uncles used to catch. Cold spring days on the downs, the dogs panting mist into the chill air, lean dogs with long faces and muscle like taut cord. The wild dance of the hare as it ran, serpentine spine and legs like pistons, so elegant in its white-eyed terror. And she would always pray that the hare would escape even as her growling stomach longed for the warmth of the stew it would become.

"No," Rosalia says, looking hurriedly away. "No, of course not. Please. Um." She steps aside, allowing Sara and her dad through. The house is warm, almost unpleasantly so; a myriad foreign scents hang in the fug as though they are trapped there. Coffee and takeaway grease and washing-up liquid. Sour wet-dog stink clinging stubbornly to the carpet. Life-smells. And there, underneath, a smell she recognises from home: a miasma of unwashed skin, fever sweat and alcohol wash. Sweet rot. The smell of sickness.

"He's upstairs," Rosalia says, as they stand for a moment in the hallway. Sara feels as though there is an invisible line dividing this sliver of space from the rest of the house; the demarcation between the world she inhabits and Rosalia's world, which is full of her private things, her secrets. Her dad says that these gorgios—these *other* people, *outside* people, who are not like them and Grandad—are mochadi. They live differently, he says. They live unclean lives. Sara isn't sure what an unclean life looks like. In spite of the discordant scents, Rosalia's home looks as inviting as a confectioner's window: cream carpet and butterscotch walls and crisp white cornicing. Sara is afraid she'll leave grimy marks if she touches anything, so she stands perfectly still, arms tight at her sides. "Will you need anything?"

"I have everything I need." He places a tentative foot on the bottom step. "Shall I start right away?"

"Yes." Dark eyes flit between the bag and the door, measuring the distance between. Sara realises that Rosalia wants to run. She wants to leave this sick-smelling house, away from *him*, this upstairs person her dad has come to see. She wants to bolt into the night and let the dark swallow her. Away from that soul-dirty bag with its bright, glassy voice, and the strange man who carries it. He ascends, and Rosalia tentatively begins to follow, but he pauses, regarding her with solemn eyes.

"You can't be in the room," he says, and she flinches at the sound of him, the chill of his gaze. But his voice is gentle, as if he is scolding a child too young to know the difference between right and wrong. Sara knows this voice. He is not a hard man, her dad; he has always been kind, and warm, but the world is neither of those things, and her dad tries so hard to protect her. "It's not safe for you to be there while I work."

Rosalia frowns. Wrings her bony hands fretfully. "Will I be able to see him afterward?" Then, timid, as though afraid of the answer: "Will he know I'm there?"

For the first time, Sara realises she shouldn't be here. She shouldn't be witnessing this exchange, as intimate as any romance except that instead of love, there is only sorrow, and fear beneath it like black water billowing under ice. And Sara understands that it is not sickness that permeates the air, but dying, slow and drawn-out and painful.

"There'll be time," her dad says, softly now. "There's always a little time."

He disappears up the stairs, into the room at the far end of the landing, and Rosalia watches him, her gaze reverent and afraid. There is the low whine of a door closing. The creak of floorboards somewhere above. Then there is quiet.

Sara does not realise she has been asleep on her feet until the sound of her name pulls her sharply awake. Her dad descends the stairs with a drunkard's unsteady gait. She stands alone in the empty hallway, eyes closed, arms wrapped tight around herself.

"How long have you been standing out here?" he asks. Mumbles, as though through a mouthful of loose teeth. He smells like cold earth, like a night out in an open field, and in the low light the leather bag seems tattooed with a lattice of frost. The air in the house feels different, too; that heavy sickroom stink is gone, and all the life-smells with it, as though an icy wind has swept through the house, stripping it clean like flesh from old bones.

"She said I could go inside," Sara says. "But I didn't want to." She doesn't tell him about the pristine carpet and warm butterscotch walls, too clean to be soiled by her dirty shoes and van-grubby hands. She belongs here about as well as she belongs in school, where the kids call her a *dirty pikey* and keep jealous watch over their belongings. Her dad is right; these people *do* live different lives.

Rosalia must hear them talking, because she appears in the doorway. She opens her mouth to speak, but she pauses, takes in the sight of Sara's dad, heavy-lidded and swaying, and the clean-cold smell in the air, and nothing emerges from her open mouth but a long and trembling sigh.

"He might not recognise you." Her dad's voice is vague, dreamy; he lifts a hand to his forehead, shielding his vision from the hall light. "Not at first. They forget, sometimes. You mustn't take it personally."

Rosalia draws in a sharp breath. "Yes. Yes, I understand. Thank you so much. I, um." She's shaking, now, a full-body tremble like the peak of a fever. "The money is on the mantelpiece. It's all there. You can count it if you like."

"You should go to him. He won't have all that long."

"Of course. Of course." A dull invocation, the sound of defeat. It strikes Sara as strange; isn't this what she paid for? Isn't it what she wanted? "Thank you. For what you've done for him. For me." Breathing deep, she tiptoes up the stairs, one hesitant step at a time, and when she gets to the top Sara turns away. This too is not for her to witness.

"Sara."

She looks up. Her dad is grimacing, pressing steepled fingers against his forehead. His right hand. The tips are a faint, ink-stained blue. "Will you get the money for me?" he asks. The bag rests at his feet, now, and his left arm hangs limp and heavy, like it's gone to sleep.

"Are you okay, Dad?"

"The money, Sara, please." Then, unclenching his teeth: "I'm okay, petal. Tiring work tonight, that's all. I'll be all right once we're home."

She does not want to cross the threshold into that other room, but she does as she is bid. She imagines soot-black marks flaking off the soles of her shoes, indelible on the soft pile of the carpet. Crammed-full bookshelves along the back wall adorned with trinkets: a pastel rainbow of candles; grotesquely proportioned crystal animals which are probably supposed to be cute. An enormous television in the corner, bigger than any television Sara has ever seen. And on the mantelpiece, flanking the brown paper envelope with *dominic* scrawled in Biro, is a procession of framed photographs. Rosalia in better times, face round and sunlit and smiling, and a man beside her: deep brown skin and warm eyes, a beautiful man. He is young in the photos. They both are. Sara stares at the photographs for a long moment, trying to forge a connection between the thin, frightened woman upstairs and this woman, whose bright eyes and full body radiate joy. They are different people, inhabiting different worlds, and Sara thinks that perhaps, when he dies—the dark, beautiful man in that quiet room—then the woman in the photos will die too, and the thin, hollow Rosalia will be the only one left.

She pulls the sleeve of her dad's jumper over her fingers as she reaches for the envelope, careful to avoid the gleaming silver frames, the sugar-white marble of the mantel. Drawing the envelope to her chest, the reassuring weight of the money which, she knows, will only last them so long, and never long enough. As she passes back out into the hallway she glances up at the stairs, where the landing light glows as warm and deep as sunset, and she strains to hear but there is nothing, no sound at all except for the clack-clack of clock hands creeping inexorably towards the morning.

The road home is impenetrably dark; narrow, meandering lanes choked with trees. The fields, when the trees break rank, are blue in the moonlight and dappled with frost, the surface of a still and frozen ocean. Her dad is driving too fast. The van shudders and hops; the bag rattles loud in the back seat.

She clutches the strap of her seatbelt. "Slow down, Dad."

He doesn't hear her, or perhaps he's not paying attention. He has not spoken since they left Rosalia's house, extricating themselves and their van from Rosalia's world, where the streets are clean and quiet. Their estate is never quiet, not even in the smallest hours, and sometimes Sara is drawn from her bed by strange sounds: the chatter of teenagers smoking on the communal balconies, the murderous shriek of foxes. She finds silence as unnerving as the dark; ominous things hide in there, concealed among all the nothing.

"Dad," she says again, insistent now, and reaches out to tug his sleeve, but the second her hands untangle from the seatbelt something large and shadowy appears in the road. They are going too fast, and her dad's reflexes are sluggish. Sara clamps her hands tight over her face as they swerve, too late to avoid the thing in the road; the sick thud of something heavy rolling over the bonnet reverberates through Sara's cold bones, settling at the base of her skull as they hit the embankment and come to an abrupt halt.

"Shit." Her dad hurriedly unbuckles his seatbelt with trembling fingers. The van is tilted at an angle; one front wheel rests atop the embankment, and Sara grinds her heels into the footwell to keep from sliding out of her seat. Her dad clambers out of the van. Whatever they have hit is a vague, grey shape in the unlit dark.

Cold air floods in through the open door, sharp-toothed. Sara unclips her seatbelt, gently lowering herself into the slanted footwell, unbalanced and askew. She wants to proceed quietly but the door swings wide and gravity sends her tumbling on hands and knees to the cold, wet tarmac.

"Get back in the van, Sara." Her dad holds up a protective hand, but it is inadequate; she can see something sprawled in the road, all bent-back limbs and bloodied, foaming muzzle, and it is *breathing* still, tongue protruding from its mouth like thick innards. A deer, broken and gasping.

"Dad."

He looks up at her, penitent; perhaps he has never heard his name spoken this way before, a single syllable imbued with such profound horror. Sara's eyes prickle with hot tears, and her throat seems to close in on itself, denying her speech. Her dad's left hand is splayed out against the deer's pelt, spattered now with blood-flecked foam. He looks so tired, so hollow. He looks so old. "Sara," he says, soft. "It's cold out here, Sara. You'll catch your death."

"You have to help." She forces the words through her clenched teeth. She will not allow herself to cry; she is not a child, she reminds herself, pressing her tongue hard against the roof of her mouth, but she can smell its pain, taste it in the back of her throat; blood and shit and panic, hot and sour, the smell of death rising in a slow, terrible wave.

"It's dying," Dad says quietly. "There's nothing I can do."

"It's in *pain*." Somehow, this is the worst thing. At least when it is dead, it will no longer feel, but it is terrible to watch it writhe, shattered legs twitching with an instinctive desire to run, to escape the pain, a hare in a frost-white field; fine blood sprays from its open mouth as it fights to draw breath. "I know you can help, like you helped that man."

His face hardens. "You don't know anything about that, Sara."

"Yes, I do." The tears are coming, now, and she swipes angrily at them with the backs of her knuckles, furious at herself. Furious at him for hiding it all from her. For pretending, all these years, that what he does is something *normal*, even as he forbids her the slightest knowledge of it. "You help people die. That's why people need you all over, and why you're gone for days, sometimes. Her house smelled like sickness, and when you came downstairs it was gone. You took it away."

"That isn't . . ."

"Then show me." It isn't only the deer, she realises, as she meets her father's dull gaze, his slack shoulders. It's the secrets and the not-knowing. Rosalia's silent, death-smelling house. Her grandad, thin and ghostly, blue skies lost to him forever. Her dad's blackened fingers and that bag, that horrible mochadi bag. It's the bloody foam and the caved-in spine and the rattle of labouring lungs. "Show me what you do."

He could refuse, as he has always done. He could shut her down with a look, that cold stare, treacherous as open water. But he does not, and Sara understands that there is guilt in his acquiescence, not just for the deer but for everything: the years of absence and secrecy, the midnight departures to who knows where, to do god knows what. For shutting her down every time she dared to ask why. His only daughter, caught between worlds.

"I'll need my bag," he says.

From the moment her fingers brush the leather she can sense it; there is a terrible gravity about this object, the malevolent thrum of a cursed thing. And she understands now why her dad has never wanted her to touch it. Can mochadi seep through the skin, into the flesh and the fat? Can it leak into the bloodstream and stain the soul? It is too late to worry, she realises, as she struggles to carry the heavy bag to where her dad is waiting. She chose this.

Her dad pries open the clasp. The bag opens slowly, revealing a faded red lining, the colour of abraded flesh. Something glistens deep within its dark throat. With infinite care, he extricates each individual component, lining his arcane apparatus up on the wet tarmac. A teardrop-shaped glass flask, connected by a length of yellowing hose to an object wrapped in grey-stained canvas. The flask's second aperture—a tap, set low into the body—connects through a second length of hose to a long, narrow jar, which her dad places at a distance; he sets a fat rubber bung alongside it, as though to seal something within.

It's not death I offer, her dad explains, as he carefully cradles the canvas bundle in his left hand, unpeeling the folds like petals. Death is an easy thing to give, if the recipient is not choosy as to the method, but if it is death a person wants, they can seek it close to home; they need not call a strange man from miles away and pay him for the privilege.

The canvas falls away. In his palm, broad and smooth, is a strange, saddle-shaped piece of glass.

You must find the source of the pain, he explains, running a big, dark hand across the deer's flank, exploratory; you must be as precise as you can. The deer is injured in so many places that Sara does not know if precision is even possible. Sometimes it's easy, he tells her; if a cancer hasn't metastasised yet you can pin down the source of the pain, but if it's spread you must make an educated guess. You must choose the place with the greatest concentration, and hope that you are right, because you only get one chance.

I don't understand, she tells him. He is speaking in riddles; he is speaking as though she already knows, as though his world and his work is familiar to her.

Watch, he says.

He lifts the glass saddle to his mouth. A narrow mouthpiece sits adjacent to the opening where the hose connects. His right hand locates a spot along the deer's spine where the bone juts, a sharp and unnatural protrusion. This, he says. This is the worst of it. And then he lifts his fingers from the base of the saddle, and she sees it clearly for the first time: a wicked barb, a sharp glass spire with a black and gleaming tip. For one long moment their eyes meet, and sorrow is etched in the line of his mouth.

He clamps the mouthpiece between his teeth. Lowers his face. She flinches as the barb pierces the deer's flank, sliding with ease into the meat; the animal emits a choked cry, convulsing under this new insult, but her dad's hand remains firm, fingertips caressing the sweat-damp velvet of its hide, and abruptly it calms, as though the barb has delivered anaesthetic straight into its veins. And then he inhales, long and slow, and she recoils unconsciously, expecting blood, *dreading* blood, but what fills the narrow chamber is something heavy and glossy and dark as oil. Trickling through the hose, down into the teardrop flask, fat gobbets pattering against the glass and it just keeps coming, that thick dark matter, red-black in the low light. He sucks it out like venom, more and more until the flask is almost full to bursting and the mouthpiece is clotted with it, staining his lips dark; his eyes are so heavy, his body ragdoll-limp at the joints and she realises, impossibly, that she has not seen him expel a single breath since that first long inhalation.

And just as it seems that the flask might shatter with the pressure, the substance begins to change. Shifting and roiling in the flask like something newly awoken, shrinking down into a dense glut. She steps back, afraid it might explode, that something might escape. He pauses in his inhalation, mouth pressed to the glass, meeting her gaze: *wait. Watch.*

The deer is silent, now, watching him with placid eyes. Its muzzle is caked brown with blood. For a moment there is dead silence, a perfect, sacred stillness. Deer and daughter and dad entwined. Then he exhales. The writhing matter blooms; tendrils burst out and up, dissipating as they rise. The thick, tumorous mass disintegrates into smoke, a churning storm-dark sky. Carried on the current of his exhalation, the smoke spills into the waiting jar until there is nothing left in the flask but a scattering of pale ash. Only then, does he lift his face from the instrument, still embedded deep in the deer's flesh.

A curl of smoke escapes from between his blackened lips. Now you see, he says. Now you understand.

⊸

They sleep that night in the back of the van, parked up on a verge a few minutes from where they left the deer on the side of the road. It will die soon; its spine is shattered, and slivers of ribcage are buried deep in its viscera, cavities filling slowly with blood. It will die, but it will die without pain. This is her dad's gift.

He has sleeping bags and blankets, a mound of musty old pillows. There is a camping stove and a battery-powered lantern. He gives her the biggest sleeping bag and tugs a thin fleece blanket over himself, curling on his side on the floor. "Try and sleep," he says. His mouth sounds full, like it's swollen inside.

"Do you always sleep in the van, Dad?" She huddles in the corner, bone-cold despite the pillows and blankets. The night is still and eerie, and there is only a thin shell of steel between them and whatever might be out there in the dark. She does not want to be here, but her dad is in no condition to drive home. She isn't even sure he'll be well enough come morning.

"Better that than a stranger's home." His lips are the colour of hypothermia. "Used to be lots of stopping places up and down the road. Others'd stop there too, so you'd never be alone. Course, you wouldn't usually be travelling alone in the first place. You'd go as a family, like we did when I was small." Laughter rattles in his chest, liquid. "Wouldn't be travelling in a bloody Transit either."

She's only ever seen her grandmother's wagon in black-and-white photographs: a beautiful round-roofed vardo carved with intricate vines and flowers and birds in flight. Grandad would describe the colours to her, running his finger over the photographs to indicate where the wood was painted red, where the carvings were painted gold. They'd burned it before Sara was born, Grandad told her. It was the way you did things back then. When Grandma died, her wagon went with her.

"This life is in your blood," her dad says.

Sara pulls the sleeping bag around her shoulders, burying her nose in the smooth folds. Exhaustion descends like a heavy weight, but the van is so cold, the floor so hard. This is not the way she'd imagined it would be. "And the other thing," she says. A thrill of fear runs through her, electric. She needs to know. She wants never to know. "Is that in my blood too?"

There is no answer. He is silent save for the low rasp of his breathing. He is asleep, and she is alone now, holding on to a question she may never be brave enough to ask again. Stopping place, her dad had called it, and that sounds so final, so bleak; this dark and quiet lane, where everything has stopped but the wind, whining at the cracks in the door like a wild beast desperate to get in.

⊸

Sara is fifteen when her grandad dies. It feels like he has been dying for a very long time. Before the road, and the deer. It feels like he has been dying forever.

He is delirious in his last few days. He mumbles in a language Sara has heard many times, but understands little of. Her dad responds in kind, his voice soothing, and it feels like another small slight, another cut of a thousand, this language they share which they have never shared with her.

Sara and her dad stand vigil, and though they have been on the road together countless times now he tells her there is no work to be done while Grandad is so sick. "We stay with him until the end," he says, firm, and Sara realises the end must be close. Grandad's decline has been slow and insidious, and she has asked her dad more than once if he can take away the pain but he just shakes his head, grim-mouthed. "It doesn't work that way," he says, regretful. "Not for us."

The night before Grandad dies, he is blessedly lucid. Mostly he sleeps, but his brief waking moments feel like a gift to Sara, who gently places her book face down on the bedside table so she can lean closer. He is weak, and his voice is barely louder than a whisper.

"We never wanted this for you," he says. "Me and your dad." Ash-grey veins mottle his pale skin like marble. "We always hoped you'd have a better life."

"It's okay, Grandad. It's not a bad life."

He smiles. Crumbling teeth jut from blue-black gums. "I wish you could've stayed in school," he says. "Proper school, not just me and a load of old books. You're so clever, Sara. You deserve more than this."

Her heart aches at the thought of school. She'd never belonged, even though her mother had been a gorgio, and she'd tried so hard to be like everyone else. To act and speak the way they did.

"You taught me to read and write." Defiant, now, with her nose in the air, and even in his weakness her grandad turns his face to her, as though seeking the heat of her anger, the fire in her eyes. "You taught me how to count. What do I need school for? I'm going to help people, the way you and Dad help people." She pauses. Looks him carefully in the eye so he understands that she is serious. So he understands that she has thought all of this through. "Please, let me take the pain away. I can do it. I know I can."

He swallows up her hand in the bone-cage of his fingers. "Sara," he says. "I know you want to help me, but you can't. This gift we have. This curse-"

"We *help* people. We stop people suffering. How can that be a curse?"

"Listen to me."

She pauses mid-protest, watching as he lifts himself inch by agonising inch, gaunt as famine and half-swallowed by bedding but sitting, now, pyjamas draped loose like old skin. His body trembles as he holds himself upright; his wasted muscles struggle to recall how it felt to do anything but lay still and die slowly.

"All gifts come with a cost," her grandad says. "No matter how careful you are, the pain will find its way inside you. It'll drift up, and you'll breathe it in. Swallow it down. It'll kill you slowly. Rot you from the inside out, little by little. It's like cancer, Sara. Once it's inside you, it never leaves."

"Mochadi," she says, and he nods.

"Other Rom won't mix with us. Not until their time has come, and even then most of them would rather die in pain than have us dirty their souls. And they're right. Look at me, Sara. I'm only sixty-three." Lips drawn back, more grimace than smile. "It's too late for me. Too late for your dad too, and that's my sin. When you've worked as long as we have your body becomes swollen with the poison you swallow. Decades of pain, deep in the flesh. So rotten with it that it'd kill anyone to try to swallow our pain. You, especially, with your mother's blood." He shakes his head. "This isn't how you want to go, petal."

How cruel, she thinks, as her grandad sinks back down into the bed, exhausted. She has been denied their language, their freedoms: blue skies and stopping places and open fires in the dark, impossible now, for the world has moved on and forced the Rom to march alongside. Her father's blood makes her dirty, strange; her mother's blood makes her weak. She belongs nowhere, to nothing, and perhaps this is freedom too, of a sort, but it feels so lonely.

Her grandad's eyes slip shut. She knows already that they will not open again. He has spent the very last of his energy. This great disappointment is his final gift.

When she looks back on it all, it's not the deer or the photos on Rosalia's mantelpiece or even that first cold, awful night in the van that she remembers most. It's the sight of her grandad's possessions swallowed by fire. Everything he was in life: his books and clothes and jewellery, his multitude of trinkets. Earthly trappings acquired over six decades, blackened and crumbling as the flames licked at the autumn sky. Trees the colour of old blood. And no matter how many homes she visits in the years after his death—sometimes as a child, sometimes as counsellor, holding hands and wiping away tears as her father exorcises suffering in a closed and silent room—she can never acquire enough memories to erase the smell of that bonfire. How unfair it had felt to eradicate every trace of him, as though a single book or pair of shoes might tether his spirit forever to the earth.

It starts with a tremor. An unsteadiness in her dad's left hand which travels, gradually, evolving over months into intense myoclonic spasms. By now his left hand is frostbite-black, and he wears gloves to disguise the dark, waxy skin, knuckles fat and stiff with fluid. It's fine, he tells her, just a touch of the old rheumatism. She knows rheumatism is a disease of the bone, and it does not cause the muscles and tendons to contract with sudden violence so that the arm corkscrews tight against the body, and the pain of it is written in the hard clench of his teeth. It's fine, he insists, and when she eventually takes over the longer drives, it's because of his bad back, his gammy knee, a litany of mundane aches he wears in place of the truth.

All gifts come with a cost, her grandad had said.

By the time Sara is sixteen, her dad's left hand has grown so weak that he can no longer hold the bag, transferring it permanently to his right. He does not stop working. You adapt, he says, though they never talk about why. It hurts her to watch him pretend that he is okay even as his body fails, the rust of his illness infiltrating every part of him; the vicious spasticity of limbs which no longer fully obey him, restless even in sleep. His left eye drifts and wanders, permanently eclipsed now by the half-disc of a drooping eyelid. There is a drunken sluggishness to his gait, his speech, and his clients pause at the door now, as though the arcane magic he has promised them suddenly feels like so much snake-oil. His visible disability is discomfiting, somehow, to these people, for whom pain has become an inextricable part of their lives.

They pay, still. Desperation is more powerful than revulsion.

He sleeps in the passenger seat as she drives them home. His limbs twitch gently in repose, and she can pretend he's dreaming, the way cats dream with their whole bodies; she can pretend he has found freedom in sleep. Perhaps he's riding horses along the lanes, like he did when he was a boy, or hunting rabbits on the Downs, and nothing hurts except the cold wind scouring his dark, unblemished skin.

Her dad is not dying. Not yet. Somehow, this is harder to accept than her grandad's slow death. She thinks she understands those people who stare with ill-disguised disquiet at her shambling father, the sideways droop of his mouth and the greyish pallor of his skin, the starkness of his systemic degeneration. It is easier to accept sickness when it comes with a terminal endpoint; to know that someone's suffering is finite. But suffering as a state of being is a terrifying thought. Her dad has become something horribly symbolic, a grotesque Saint Sebastian reminding those who look upon him not of the glory of martyrdom, nor the beauty of stoicism, but of the destructive power of unremitting pain.

⁂

It is late July and the sky is a molten blue. An oppressive heat fills the empty space between heaven and earth, baked deep into the concrete so that even at night the air is heavy with residual warmth. Her dad finds the sunlight intolerable, and so they travel only after dark, with the windows wound down so that a lethargic trickle of warm air washes through the van's sweat-hot interior. It is impossible to sleep in the van; she has hung dark curtains between the seats and the back so that her dad will have shade to rest in during the daylight hours, but she needs air and sunshine, to stretch her legs after driving for miles. Sometimes, she will find a sunny spot somewhere off a layby, and she will stretch out her limbs so that her body is in full contact with the grass and the earth and the sun, and though the heat is thick and heavy in her skull she breathes in the smell of the cracked, dusty earth, and she remembers doing fractions with Grandad in the park; the spidery scrawl of his handwriting and the warm humour in his smile. Sometimes she will close her eyes and imagine he is there, somewhere, just out of reach.

In the pale, still hours just before sunrise her dad speaks. His body is whippet-thin beneath the woollen blanket; he holds her face in his off-kilter gaze and she loves him, even now, this crumbling shell in which her father resides. She has always loved him. He has raised her and taught her and tried to protect her, in his way, and he hasn't always been good at it, but he has never stopped trying.

"Before we go home," he says. "There's something I need you to help me with. It's about the jars."

Her body is fatigued from hours of driving. Her eyes burn with the strain of her vigilance; she has never forgotten that first night on the road. She wants to crawl into her bed and burrow beneath the blankets, rest her lead-heavy skull on something soft and let sleep steal her away. And yet she cannot deny her dad this request; more than that, she cannot deny her own curiosity, her desperation to seize whatever scraps of their shared history he might offer.

She drives, on his instruction, to the wastewater works a few miles from home. A cankerous eyesore on the coast, stretching industrial fingers out into the dull water; the ripe summer stink of it is vivid in her childhood memories, though there is only the salt tang of the sea as she opens the van door, easing her aching bones out of the driver's seat. The bag rests at her feet, forbidding; it is only the second time she has been permitted to touch it, and its malign aura has not diminished over time.

"There's an old shed about five minutes down the road there," her dad says. "You'll find the padlock key in the bottom of the bag. It'll make sense when you're inside."

"Will you be all right here on your own?" She wants him to come with her. She wants him to explain it all to her in detail, starting at the beginning and on until the present day: to this exact moment, when the stark reality of his illness has finally won out over his desire to protect her from the truth. She wants to know everything and knows that she never will.

"I've been coming here for years, and I've never seen a soul," he says, with a lopsided smile. "I'll be fine, Sara. You don't need to worry about me."

The foliage is thick and lush as she walks down the darkened path, snatching glances of the grey-grubby van over her shoulder; there is a lingering humidity that makes her think of the rainforests she'd read about as a child. Despite the approaching sunrise the birds are silent. The bag is heavy in her hand, and she shifts her grip from right to left. It is too late to worry about the malevolent power imbued within the cracked leather, permeating the flesh as insidious as radiation. She is already mochadi. It cannot be undone now.

The 'shed' is a decaying brick monolith, huge and ugly. Scabrous paint flaking like psoriasis. The small windows are boarded over, and the low-angled roof is thick with moss so dark it is almost black. The silence here feels almost physical. Heavy, like the sky just before a storm.

Opening the bag feels like breaking the final taboo; her fingers hesitate at the clasp, unwilling, but she forces herself to pry it open. Her hands slip into the red-lined throat of the bag, feeling her way tentatively between the sealed jars—soft fingers, so careful—until something small and cold reveals itself, tucked away into one corner. She plucks it between thumb and forefinger, marvelling at its untarnished sheen.

Cautiously, Sara approaches the building. She does not know what she will find in there. All she knows is that she must take the jars inside and lock them away. They have accumulated over the weeks and there is something uncomfortably volatile about them, as though they might spontaneously shatter and release their poison back out into the world. She has never thought to question what happens to the jars once they are filled; by which method a substance as corrosive and mutagenic as pure pain might be disposed of.

The key slips into the lock. A shaft of pale light illuminates the interior, and her eyes grow wide. It is enormous, this place, stretching out into pitch darkness. Row upon row of shelving reaches up to the darkened ceiling. Each shelf is packed tight with jars, crammed full of them, and as she stands there in that silent doorway, clutching the bag tight in both hands, it seems to her, impossibly, that the jars are screaming.

She breathes deep. The smell of industrial rot is strong here; the shelves are thick with blood-dark rust, and the concrete floor is webbed with thick cracks. Nothing lives in here; no weeds or spiderwebs, no fungus sprouting in the dark, damp corners, a hideous sterility. She understands why. The screaming she imagines is not a sound but a sensation, the persistent thrum of a plucked string endlessly ringing out, and she feels it deep in her gut, reverberating in her bones, as though they have cracked her open and are screaming into her. Even the very lowest form of organic life could find no peace in this house of wounds.

The bag feels heavier than it ever has before as she gingerly eases it to the ground. Dust motes dance in the sluggish air. She reaches in and extracts a jar. It is cold to the touch, and as she approaches the shelf the murk within begins to swirl, coalescing on the far side of the jar as though reaching out in desperation to its kin. The sight of it should horrify her, but there is only a morbid curiosity at the way the substance shifts and coils, pulsating like something living. It knows it belongs here. Pain calls to pain, she thinks, as she places the jars on the shelf, where their contents settle once more, placated by proximity.

She walks down the rudimentary aisles, stopping just shy of the places the watery dawn light cannot reach. There must be thousands of jars in here. Decades' worth of them, stacked up to the ceiling and inches from the floor, anonymous in their uniformity. The older ones are coated in a veneer of pale grey dust. She runs a tentative finger through the grime; the pain-mist is still and serene behind the glass. How many years have elapsed since it was extracted? She turns on her heel, dizzy with the extent of it, this repository of human suffering. She remembers Rosalia, so many years ago. The photos on her mantelpiece. The beautiful man with his warm, dark eyes, the man he was before the pain destroyed him. His essence is here, somewhere, distilled and sealed inside an unlabelled vessel like all the others. She is seized with the desire to catalogue all of it; to go back to the very first jar and tell its story in full. To tell all their stories.

She locks the door behind her, takes up the bag, so light without its cargo. The sky outside is shot through with scarlet. A piece of doggerel comes to her; her grandad's voice, singsong: *red sky in the morning, shepherd's warning.*

Her dad is sleeping when she returns to the van. She places the bag at his feet, careful not to disturb him, though he seems utterly dead to the world. He looks peaceful, but his breath comes in short, pneumonic bursts. The breath is curdling in his lungs. Eventually, he will forget how to breathe. How to swallow. He will choke on his own air. Inhale his own spit and drown.

Sara slips into the driver's seat. Turns the key in the ignition. The van starts with a drawn-out, bronchial rattle.

Soon, the sun will come up.

⊸

The summer heat swells like a fever until the horizon is clotted with thick, dark cloud, and the weight of it exerts a pressure so fierce Sara can feel it in the knotted gristle of her overtired brain. She has not worked in two weeks. Her dad has been too ill to travel lately. The fierce heat and relentless, pounding sun have made him fragile, and he struggles to walk, to sit upright, to drag himself to the bathroom. Soon, he will be able to do none of these things, and for him the indignity of his inability will be harder to bear than any amount of pain.

Their money is running out. That, too, is hard to bear.

In the early hours the storm breaks at last with a thunderclap like glass shattering overhead, a concussive blast. Sara is torn from her bed, breathless and sweat-drenched; rain hammers insistently at the window, and somewhere in the house her dad is crying out.

She runs trembling fingers through damp hair, smoothing it into a loose ponytail. Lightning strobes through the closed curtains; she pulls up the sash window a few inches, welcoming in cool air. Rain spatters the desk, the piles of meaningful junk gleaned from charity shops and car boot sales. Gifts brought home by her dad after days on the road. She has thrown nothing away, though she has outgrown most of it. The dead-eyed china dolls and plastic horses and gaudy costume jewellery are relics of a kinder time.

Sara hurries to her dad's room. The depth of the darkness within is almost total; blackout blinds protect him from the ravages of daylight, held firm to the window frame with thick black gaffer tape. Three oscillating fans stand sentinel at his bedside, whirring ineffectually. Her dad is sprawled beside the bed, clawing at the divan with useless hands. There is not enough strength in his pyjama-clad legs to push him back up. She doesn't know how long he's been lying here like this, crying out for help, unheard.

"I'm so sorry Dad." She is small, still, but he is so light, as though beneath his clothes there are only bones and empty skin. Leanness has given way to emaciation. She eases him back onto the bed, pulls the sheet up over him; despite the lingering heat he is shivering, and his teeth rattle in his cadaverous skull. "I'm so sorry." Over and over, because she cannot think of anything else to say; the acute embarrassment of it, the teenage daughter helping her incapable dad into bed, and worse, the shame of sleeping through his feeble cries for help.

"Hurts," he says, through gritted teeth. His arms jitter and flail; the pain and the spasms seem to come in tandem now. His eyes are squeezed tight. Sweat beads at his temples, and his skin is so hot she can hardly bear to touch him at all. Like Grandad in his later years, but devoid of the quiet dignity his slow deterioration permitted him. There is nothing dignified in her dad's suffering.

"I know, Dad." Sharp tears prickle behind her eyes, but it is anger that wells up inside of her, cresting like a wave. She bites her tongue so hard she can taste blood. "Try to rest. I'll bring you something to help you sleep, okay?"

He nods, grim-faced. The rain hammers relentlessly on unseen glass. She gets up. Shuffles into the kitchen, where two weeks' worth of washing up is strewn across the worktops, piled high in the sink. A faint putrid odour lingers in the still air, the scent of decay rising from overstuffed binbags, the remnants of old, crusted food. She wants to sweep it all to the floor, fling the plates and bowls and glasses at the wall until they shatter into tiny pieces. She wants to open the window and scream into the night until she is empty.

She is overwhelmed by her powerlessness. Even if her mother's weakness could be excised from her she would still be unable to take his pain away. This is the hardest thing of all. He has spent his life easing other people's misery; that he must suffer until his last breath is a cruelty she cannot reconcile.

Sara fishes in the cupboard for her dad's pain medication. Gleaming red-and-white capsules nestled in silvery blister packs, the strongest medication the doctor would give him and still almost useless. The thrum of the rain is like distant static. She pops a capsule out onto the table and stares at it for a long time. Tentatively, she picks it up. Pinches the red half with her left thumb and forefinger, the white half with her right. The shell pulls apart, scattering powder onto the worktop like ash. She stares at this for a long time too.

She warms milk in a pan on the hob. Spoonfuls of golden syrup stirred in one after another, because her dad has always had a sweet tooth, and these days he can barely taste at all. She cannot consume his pain. She cannot grant him serenity in these final months. But there is one gift that she can still give.

⊸

Her dad's room is sparse, empty of all but the most essential things. He is not a magpie like his daughter, nor a hoarder of treasures like his father. All he has is his infinity of jars, melting into shadow and swallowed by dust. A mausoleum of untold stories.

"Here," Sara says. She helps her dad sit. His muscles convulse beneath the flat of her palms, an endless dance. His hair has turned the stark white of bleached bones. She picks up the mug of warm milk with her free hand, helps him wrap trembling hands around it and lift, up to his mouth where he fights to swallow it down. He drinks, slow and laborious; she dabs at his chin with the corner of a tea towel, mopping up rivulets of milk. When he is finished, she lowers him gently back down, fussing with his pillows and blankets until he puts out a hand, gentle, his fingers closing lightly around her wrist.

"I'm okay, Sara." Hollow eyes crinkle, a tired and ragged smile. "You don't need to worry."

Her fingers tangle in a loose skein of bedsheet. She stares hard at her own knuckles, at the unmarked skin, the long fingers she inherited from her father. Piano fingers, Grandad had called them, though there wasn't a musical bone in her body. Hot tears burn inside her nose, and she forces them down, swallowing her sadness. Forces herself to meet her dad's gaze so she can burn the warmth of his smile into her memory; the famine-sharp contours of his face and the fevered brightness of his eyes. Love like delirium.

"Thank you, petal," he says.

She stays with him until he falls asleep. Until the twitching of his limbs subsides, and his breathing slows. Until, for the first time in a long time, he is completely still.

The gold coins she fishes from her pocket were salvaged from her grandad's belongings just before they'd burnt it all to ash. She has kept them in her desk drawer, and when she misses her grandad she takes them out, and holds one in each hand, and the weight of them is comforting, as though a little bit of him still lives inside of them. She places the coins gently atop her dad's closed eyes, the way he'd done for Grandad. She doesn't understand the significance of this act, but it feels right. And the words she whispers into the shell of his ear, a language she has never before spoken, but which she must keep alive; those feel right, too. "Kushti bok." Good luck. Goodbye.

Sara stands up. She switches off the fans, one by one, watching them slow and stutter and stop. She reaches out and slowly peels back the tape holding the blackout blind firm against the window. Faint light filters through the gaps, tracing her dad's profile in silver, his eyes shining gold.

The brown leather bag sits at the foot of the bed. She does not hesitate as she picks it up, and it is featherlight in her hand, a faint patina of dust dulling its soft sheen. The chime of glass against glass, a familiar melody. The promise of deliverance. For all her inherited weakness, for all her grandad's warning, nobody had ever told her that she could *not*. What is there left, now, but this? This life is in your blood, her dad had told her.

Her few selected possessions are packed and ready, a scribbled note left on the hallway table: *please cremate him*. She hefts the rucksack over her shoulder, the brown leather bag in her left hand. The keys to the van in her pocket. Outside, the sun is beginning its slow ascent. The rain has washed the pavements clean of dust, and the air is sweet and cool in her throat. All the life-smells are gone, and all the death-smells too. The storm has stripped everything clean, like flesh from old bones. Like the world is starting over.

THE HOPE CHEST

SARAH READ

Hannah walked the half mile from the bus stop, but Grandma didn't meet her at the bus, or on the road, or on the porch. Or in the house. Her mother sat alone at the table, with her hands clutched around a glass of ice water as if it were keeping her warm.

By the time Hannah was close enough to smell that it wasn't water, she was close enough to see that her mother had been crying and that the ice in the glass shook. That her sleeves were soaked to the elbow as if the tears had been a tide, or the glass had spilled and spilled.

"Where's Grandma?"

"Just 'where's grandma?' You're not going to ask me what's wrong?"

It was an eggshell day. A choke-back-the-lump-in-your-throat-and-bite-your-tongue day.

"What's wrong?" Hannah whispered. It was difficult for her to ask with her throat full and her tongue between her teeth.

"Grandma's gone. She got . . . very sick. She's at the hospital. You can't go see her."

Hannah's stomach twisted and her cheeks pricked with ice needles. "Why? I want to go! I need to see her."

Her mother shook her head once, but then looked sick from the motion and stopped, squeezed her eyes shut.

"I want to be with her."

"No visitors allowed. What if it's contagious? If you get too close to Grandma, you'll die. Is that what you want?"

Hannah shook her head slowly, the motion pulling at all the knots twisting down her throat to her heart. "Is she going to die?"

Her mother said nothing. Took a drink. The insides of her hands looked bright red through the glass.

Hannah stepped backwards, eggshells underfoot, even inside her shoes.

It was important to know when to disappear.

"I was stuck here with her all day. Aren't you afraid I'm going to die, too?"

Hannah was halfway down the hall before the glass hit the wall.

⟜

Grandma's dress form stood in the corner of the attic, set to her measurements. Bust, waist, hips, shoulders, neck, height. The hidden network of cranks twisted the padded surfaces into the exact shape of her, the shape of the hole in the house where she should have been.

The air swirled with dust, rafters dotted with cobwebs and dry bees. Shelves of fabric and the feathery crepe of pattern paper lined the walls in a small labyrinth through the attic space.

In the corner sat an antique sewing machine, cast iron set into the dry wood of a desk. The missing drawer knobs had been replaced with brightly colored buttons.

Hannah rested her forehead against the padded curve of the dress form's shoulder. Up close, she could see tiny holes in the fabric, small scars left by decades of pinpricks as dress after dress had been draped over the figure.

Hannah breathed, in out in out, and calmed the shake in her chest.

Between the curved plates of canvas, deep inside the chest of the form, was the network of metal bones and cranks, stiff, rusted.

Hannah looked away. She didn't like to see inside the thing, as if it were Grandma herself laid open.

Have the doctors opened her? Are her insides exposed, examined?

She stepped away from the dress form and over to the cedar hope chest on the far wall. The humidity in the attic had warped the wood so that one side of the lid gaped like parted lips. She heaved it open, the hinges groaning and raising a cloud of dust.

Tissue paper lay over the stack of fabric inside. There were curtains, handkerchiefs and a tablecloth, all treasured, but beneath them—greater treasures.

Hannah pulled the sky-blue satin dress out from beneath the stack of crisp linens. She carried it over to the dress form.

The buttons were small and difficult to manage, but she opened it enough to slip it over the form and smooth it down, and fastened it up the back. It was beautiful. It was Grandma. It even smelled like her. Hannah buried her face into the familiar shoulder. She wrapped her arms around the form. It hugged just like Grandma.

⊸⊷

"No, we can't go to the craft store. We've got hospital bills," her mother said.

They'd cashed Grandma's pension check. Hannah didn't think hospitals took cash.

Liquor stores took cash.

She helped her mother carry the sloshing boxes into the house, then disappeared into the attic as her mother settled in.

Grandma's dress form stood in front of the sewing machine. The small wooden chair lay on its side on the wide floorboards.

Hannah tiptoed across the dusty boards and righted the chair.

The form faced the machine, its buttoned sleeve cuffs resting on the table. A tangle of thread trailed from the bobbin like a cobweb. The thread was bright green, the color of emeralds or Astroturf.

Hannah scanned the rows of cubbyhole shelves. There was a bolt of fabric that matched the thread exactly. She pulled it free and carried it to the cutting table, unspooled it a few turns, and cut a yard exactly as her grandmother had showed her.

She carried the soft cotton to the machine and moved Grandma's form aside, then pulled up the chair so she could reach the treadle. She untangled the bobbin and threaded the needle.

Hannah only knew how to sew one thing: a pillowcase, but she'd made enough of them that she thought she could remember how, even without Grandma here to help.

Maybe she'd feel better with something handmade, from home. Maybe it would help her heal faster, come home sooner.

She ran a tight seam down the edge of the fabric and the needle stitched through the meat of her finger.

She yelped and stood, knocking the chair back. As she pulled away, the thread trailing from her finger pulled against the fabric and puckered her stitches. Blood ran down her wrist as she snipped the thread and pulled it through her wound.

Her breath hitched and she ran to the dress form and threw her arms around its waist, sobbing into the lace at its front.

Her sobs slowed and she leaned away, feeling silly, ashamed. Her blood left a smear on the blue satin of her grandmother's best dress.

Hannah gaped at the stain in horror.

Cold water, she remembered. That was for getting blood out.

She wrapped her finger in a strip of scrap muslin and worked at the tiny row of buttons at the back of the dress.

Hannah raced the dress down the attic stairs and held it under a stream of cold water in the bathroom sink. The water diluted the blood, turning the blue a dingey brown, spreading the stain further in creeping sepia. She kept rinsing till the whole dress had soaked up the water like a thick, heavy sponge.

When it looked clean, Hannah laid the dress in the bathtub. A glint caught her eye and she saw Grandma's glasses curled in the soap dish. They were bent, no longer face-shaped, but Hannah took them and put them in her pocket, hoped she could add them to the form. Grandma couldn't see without her glasses.

Her finger had bled through her soaked bandage. She peeled off the cloth. In the stark light of the bathroom, she could see how dirty the fabric had been.

She tossed the strip into the trash and rinsed the cut, grinding her teeth at the sting, wondering if enough cold water could wash all of the blood from her, if her insides were stained that awful brown.

The needle had punched a ragged hole right through her fingertip. She smeared it with ointment and wrapped a Band-Aid around it.

She looked down at the dress in the tub. It was like Grandma lay there, deflated and empty.

She didn't want to see the bones of the form again. Didn't want to see that skin of it riddled with needle holes, like her finger.

She slipped into the hallway and walked to her grandmother's bedroom.

Her mother's door, next to it, was open a crack. The TV light flickered over the row of bottles on the bedside table. The light shone off her mother's glasses so that Hannah couldn't tell if her eyes were open or not.

Hannah hurried past and ducked into her grandmother's bedroom.

The bed was unmade. Grandma always made her bed, right after her morning bath.

Hannah stared at the depression in the pillow. The pillowcase was patterned with bright green leaves and red ladybugs. They had made it together.

Hannah was still determined to finish a new one.

She went to the closet door and pulled it open.

The smell of her grandmother floated free as if escaping a cage. Tears sprang to Hannah's eyes as she ran her hand over the row of drab everyday dresses.

She pulled down a yellow one that she remembered from an Easter picnic. There was a hat, somewhere, to match. The form would look better with a hat.

She dug through the boxes on the closet shelf till she found it, and the cream shoes to go with.

Then she went to the wooden box where her grandmother kept her modest collection of jewels. She lifted the lid. "Claire de Lune" began to play across the empty red velvet cushions. She snapped the lid shut.

A crash sounded from the next room.

Hannah's breath froze. She rushed to the closet and stepped inside, burrowing her way to the back. She pulled the yellow dress over her face and held her breath.

Her mother burst into the room. "Hannah!"

Hannah huddled, fingernails digging into the shoes clutched in her hand.

The music box began to play again. Then there was a crash and the music slowed, deepened, stopped.

Her mother's steps stormed out and the door slammed.

The wire hangers chimed softly as Hannah shook in place.

She waited. Long enough for her mother to settle, to finish another glass, to sleep.

Hannah slipped out of her hiding place.

The jewelry box lay smashed on the floor. There were no jewels. Hannah knelt by the pieces and ran her fingers over the nap of the velvet. In the plush of carpet, she saw a small sparkle. A single earring, just a plain gold orb, winked at her from the carpet strands.

Hannah pulled it free. She pinched it in her good fingers and hurried back up to the attic.

⊸

It was as if the past had come again.

Grandma's form stood under her wide hat, her Easter dress falling in tiers of yellow polyester, showing only a few inches of the support post, and then the scuffed cream pumps.

Hannah set back to work on her grandmother's pillowcase. Just as she snapped the last thread, a scream rose through the floorboards.

Hannah raced for the stairs, clutching the green fabric in her fist.

Her mother stood in the hall, gripping the bathroom doorframe and panting. She spun to face Hannah. "Did you put that there?"

Hannah stared at her mother's hand and nodded, afraid to trust her voice. *Who else could have*? she wanted to ask. *There's no one else here.*

"What the hell were you thinking?"

There were no eggshells left to walk on, only fine white powder and torn soft membrane.

"I found it. In the attic. It was dirty, so . . . I washed it." A near-enough almost-truth.

"What the hell were you doing in the attic?"

Hannah squeezed her fists and felt the cotton against her palm. She held the pillowcase out. "I made this for Grandma. To help her feel better."

Her mother covered her face with her hands. Hannah thought she might be crying, but when the hands came away, the face beneath was angry.

Her mother snatched the pillowcase from her. "From that dusty old attic? It would make her sicker." She whipped the fabric across Hannah's face.

It stung. It tasted of dust.

Her mother stomped off toward the living room.

Hannah stood in the hall. She looked into the bathroom. The dress looked, for a moment, as if someone lay in the tub. Hannah understood why her mother had screamed.

"I'm going to work!" her mother called out. The front door slammed.

Hannah didn't feel like an Easter picnic anymore.

She slipped back into Grandma's bedroom, stepped over the broken pieces of jewelry box, and went to the closet.

Something grey, maybe. Or black. She pulled a somber dress from a hanger, then a few others. Maybe Grandma would like to decide what she wore. Maybe her mood wasn't as bleak as Hannah's.

She filled her arms with dresses and carried them slowly up the attic steps.

She hung them from the rafters and went back for more, then everything from the drawers, the shoes, all the hats.

Grandma could wear whatever she wanted. She must miss her clothes.

Hannah brought the thick brown wool duffel coat up last and laid it across the floorboards. She crawled on top of it and closed her eyes. The wool itched the stinging spot on her cheek, but she pressed her face in closer. She smelled snowmen and Christmas shopping and ice skating hidden in its fibers. She fell asleep, holding Grandma's hand, gliding across a mirror pond.

She woke to the sound of a car door slamming.

She crawled out from under an old scrap-sewn quilt and peered through the fly-specked glass of the attic window.

Her mother was home, loading her arms with large bags from the trunk of the car. Hannah watched as she struggled up the front steps and though the door.

Hannah turned away from the window.

Grandma had chosen a black dress.

Hannah ran over and hugged the form. "You're as sad as me," she whispered into the dark fabric. The form hugged her back.

There was a commotion downstairs, the tumbling of a half-dozen large bags.

"Hannah!"

Hannah squeezed the form tighter. She wanted to kiss her, but there was no face. She would make one, she decided. It's what Grandma would have done.

"Hannah!"

Her mother's voice had grown closer, nearing the attic stairs. Hannah didn't want her to come up, to see, to start smashing things.

She let go of the form and hurried down the stairs.

Her mother was in Grandma's room. The pieces of jewelry box were gone. The bed was covered in paper bags printed with sharp logos. Bright fabrics and sleek boxes spilled from inside.

Her mother pointed to the empty closet. "Where are my mother's clothes?"

Hannah chewed her lip. "I . . . packed them," she said. "In case she wants them."

Her mother shook her head. "She has to wear the hospital clothes. You know that, right?"

Hannah nodded.

"Whatever. You actually did me a favor this time." Her mother grabbed a fistful of hangers, then dumped the contents of the bags onto the covers and began slipping shirts onto the hangers.

"Did you get her new clothes?" Hannah asked. "For when she comes home?"

"These are mine. She always makes her own ugly clothes."

Hannah flinched.

"I'm staying here, now." She hung the clothes up, tags fluttering from the cuffs. "Here, do me another favor." She handed Hannah a brown paper bag. "Clean the bathroom."

Hannah peered into the bag and saw a bottle of bleach cleaner and a package of sponges.

"But it is clean, I just . . ."

"I didn't ask if it was clean. I told you to clean it."

Her good mood was fading fast.

Hannah took the bag to the bathroom, closed the door, and latched the lock.

She gasped at the sight of a blue body in the tub, choked on the scream in her throat. She squeezed her eyes shut and opened them, and the body was a dress again.

Hannah lifted the dress from the tub. It was still wet on the underside. She draped the dress over the towel rack, wet-side-out so it could finish drying, and turned back to the bathtub.

The dress had left a damp outline of a body at the bottom of the tub. Hannah shivered. She pulled a sponge from the package and wiped and scrubbed, but she could still see the outline of something lying there.

⁂

Even Grandma had struggled to sew spheres. The shape Hannah affixed to the top of the form was not entirely like a head. The muslin was too pale, and the scraps she had used to stuff it showed through as if she were looking at a ghost.

Hannah took a marking pencil from the button-pull drawer and sketched a face onto the fabric. She placed a hat on top to hide the unnatural bulges. A black hat, to match the dress.

She filled two gloves with more scraps and fastened them to the ends of the cuffs with straight pins.

She pushed the post of the single gold earring through the center of Grandma's right eye. Grandma's eyes always twinkled.

Hannah admired her work. It was Grandma—the form of her, so close that Hannah's nose began to tickle and her eyes stung.

She hugged the form and kissed her cheek.

Grandma's kisses smelled like pencil clay, and the pins in the cuffs stuck her when they hugged, but Hannah's heart was lighter when she went to bed.

If Hannah could, herself, make a Grandma, then surely the doctors could make her whole again.

When Hannah woke, her mother had already left for work. There were waffles on the table, still steaming and pooling with butter and syrup. Bacon curled beside them.

Hannah rushed to the table and began to fill her mouth before she even looked at the clock.

She had an hour before the bus would come. She slowed her chewing.

"Grandma?"

She walked down the hall, peering into each room.

Grandma lay in her bed, her form under the scrap quilt from the attic. Hannah rushed to her and threw her arms over her.

Grandma hugged her back, the cuff pins dragging across Hannah's skin.

"I don't want to go to school today, Grandma, I want to stay here with you."

Grandma squeezed her tighter.

"Will you call me in sick?"

Grandma was silent.

I haven't given her a tongue.

The graphite line of Grandma's mouth twisted, but it couldn't open.

"I'll fix it, Grandma, I'll be right back."

Hannah raced to the attic. She grabbed a seam-ripper, a needle and thread, and a short length of red ribbon, then hurried back to the bedroom and leaned over Grandma's form.

She poked the seam ripper into the corner of Grandma's mouth and tore across the pencil line. The muslin sprang back, and the scrap stuffing began to spill from the opening. Hannah stuffed it back inside. She slipped the ribbon between the frayed lips and stitched it in place.

The tongue flopped against the round muslin chin. The frayed lips wriggled to keep the mass of scraps inside. It looked like speech, but no sound came.

Hannah frowned. She didn't know what else Grandma needed in order to speak. Inside parts, of which Hannah had no knowledge.

"It's okay, Grandma, we can look it up."

Grandma's old books filled the walls of the office in the basement. Hannah had browsed through them all at one time or another. The ones that looked the most boring—uniform black covers with plain white print across a dozen identical volumes all along the bottom shelf—were the best ones.

Hannah didn't know quite what she was looking for. Or how, exactly, to spell it. So she pulled out the first volume and began to flip through.

Grandma chose the last volume. Her gloved finger slipped through the pages as the silent fabric of her mouth moved, and colorful threads from the frayed edges of the scraps sprinkled down across the paper.

By the time Grandma handed her the book, the bus had long since come and gone.

The page Grandma held open to her had a black line drawing and a greyscale photo of something that looked both slimy and stringy.

"Vo-cal c-ords," Hannah read. This was the piece Grandma needed to talk. Hannah had never seen anything that looked like the picture. The book said it was a structure in the throat, but Hannah wasn't even certain that the form had a throat. The head was just a ball, closed off, and the neck of the form was sealed on top.

It would be a lot of work. It was going to be difficult and take a long time, but she had to do it.

Grandma needed a voice. Grandma had something to say.

⊸

Hannah hadn't finished by the time her mother came home. She left Grandma with a half-carved hole through her neck when her mother called to her from the kitchen.

Her mother stood with the phone to her ear. She slammed the receiver down. "Why is there a message from the school saying you didn't show up? And what is this mess?"

Hannah's throat clenched so hard she couldn't speak. *Vocal cords.* Hers were trapped in the nervous knot of her neck. She had forgotten about her need to call in sick. Forgotten about her waffles.

Her neck hurt. "I have a sore throat," she croaked. A sort-of truth.

"You should have told me so I could call. Now I'm in trouble. That means you're in trouble." Her mother's voice was creeping louder, well into the range where Hannah knew it was time to disappear. To the attic, the woods, the back of a closet—anywhere. But she was pinned down by her mother's angry stare. If she bolted, this time she'd be chased. Some animal sense in her knew it. A prey instinct.

She stood. A statue, facing the oncoming storm of her mother's rage.

Even with her eyes fixed open, she didn't see the plate coming. The sound of it shattering against the wall and scattering across the floor registered before the pain bloomed on the side of her face.

It came to her slowly, like a thaw. *Hurts.*

It occupied the fullness of her mind, save for a small, indifferent piece of her which registered the pain of her mother's satisfied expression. It was difficult to tell which pain was worse.

One of them would heal.

But the catharsis had uncoiled the spring of her mother's heels and it was safe, now, something told her, to run.

She did.

Up the attic stairs as a voice chased her, "Come back here and clean this up!" and into the close heat of the attic, to the hope chest.

Hannah curled inside and pulled Grandma's most precious linens over her before tipping the lid shut.

She couldn't hear anything anymore. There were no footsteps pounding the stairs, only the pounding in her cheekbone. It stung with every beat of her heart and ached in between. She counted each beat till they slowed, till there was more ache than sting.

Time does not pass in the hope chest. That is its purpose. A capsule, preserving the best things.

Hannah lifted the lid, feeling older, anyway, and climbed out of the chest when enough time had passed.

The sun had sunk lower, and cut through the attic window at an angle that hid everything in contrast. All bright and black, with no familiar shapes.

No familiar form.

Grandma.

She wasn't there—not on the broad cutting table where she'd left her, not by the sewing machine or in the rows of fabric.

Hannah's heart raced again, bringing the sting in her face back afresh.

She forced herself to move slowly, against her panic, down the stairs.

The hall was quiet. The doorway to Grandma's room set mostly closed, the soft light from the bedside lamp showing in a stripe against the doorjamb.

Hannah pressed her eye to the crack, wondering if her grandmother had gone to bed. The wood of the door hurt against the swelling of her cheek.

Only her mother was there, curled on the mattress.

Hannah crept down the hall.

She peered into the bathroom and caught a flash of her reflection in the mirror. She gasped. The form of her face was wrong, the shape unfamiliar, the color strange. She flipped on the light.

Her cheek swelled red and purple, taut as a ripe berry, as if the scraps beneath her skin were showing through.

But her eye was drawn away to the figure in the bathtub. She screamed.

Grandma was there—her form bent into the tub, glasses askew, ribbon tongue rolling from her mouth, which was split wide, wide, wider than Hannah had carved it. Rags spilled from her torn mouth. The unfinished hole in her throat gaped, voiceless.

Hannah screamed for them both.

Her mother came running, stopped behind her, and gasped so deeply Hannah felt a pull at her own lungs. Then she screamed, too.

Hannah felt fingers in her hair tighten into a fist.

"Did you do this?"

"No!"

"What the hell do you think you're playing at?"

The hand in her hair pushed her further into the bathroom, the loud voice driving her forward.

Her feet gave, and she shrieked as the hand suspended her by her hair, briefly, before allowing her to fall.

She heard the slam of a cupboard and felt a roughness scrape past her teeth, tasted bitterness. Her mother rammed the sponge into her mouth.

"Clean it up! Clean this trash away and scrub the tub. Get every trace of her out of there!"

The sponge dammed the sob in the back of Hannah's throat.

The door slammed shut behind her.

She coughed the sponge out of her mouth and vomited over it. She pinched the vomit-covered sponge, stood on shaking legs, and rinsed the sick off it in the sink. And she wondered how anything could ever be cleaned with a dirty sponge.

⊸○⊷

Every trace, every last stray thread from a frayed edge, was tucked safely away in the attic again.

If Grandma wants a bath, I'll bring her a basin upstairs. It's safer.

The fiberglass of the tub shone white, save for the rust stain that never moved no matter what effort Hannah applied.

"What the hell is that smell?"

The taste of the sponge rose again in Hannah's throat. She turned and looked at her mother standing in the doorway. Her eyes were ringed in red and the lines of her face cut deep.

"Look at you. You're filthy and you stink."

Hannah could no longer smell anything but bleach. Her mother reached for an ornate glass bottle in the cabinet that Hannah had never seen before, and sprayed a fragrant, expensive cloud into the air.

"I think . . ." Her mother chewed at a lip that already looked raw. "I think you'd better take a bath," she whispered. Her hands flexed.

Hannah's animal mind wanted her to run, but there was nowhere to go. Mother stood in the only doorway, a look in her eye that set Hannah's rabbit heart racing.

"Turn on the water."

Hannah didn't move. Her mother reached past her and twisted the knob all the way to hot.

"Stand up. Get those filthy clothes off and get in the tub."

Her mother's voice shook, Hannah thought, or else the water beat the sound right out of the air, drowning her voice in the rust-stained basin.

"Get in, Hannah." The voice came firm, then, steadied on anger.

Hannah looked at the water and saw her shadow there, the form of herself, an exact copy pressed to that white depth, stained there, permanent, like the rust. And Grandma's shadow beneath hers, stuck there. Trapped.

"I . . . don't want to go in there." Hannah squeezed her voice past the lump in her throat.

Her mother advanced into the room and grabbed the short hairs at the back of Hannah's neck, lifting her to stand.

"I said get that stinking filthy ass of yours into the tub this second!"

She pushed Hannah toward the water.

Hannah twisted and saw, over her mother's shoulder, Grandma's familiar form in the bathroom doorway. She cried out, a yelp of pain, a call for help.

Her mother's eyes tracked hers.

The fist at the back of her head loosened and she slid free. Hannah backed away till her hand plunged into the steaming water. She pulled it out and clutched her soaked sleeve to her chest.

Her mother began to turn, mouth stretching wide, ready to birth a tirade.

Her mouth froze open when she saw the figure standing there. Grandma's exact form, but her mouth torn too wide and spilling rags.

The limp glove hand rose to the mouth and pulled free a fistful of bright scraps. The hand shot forward and crammed the rags into Mother's gaping mouth.

The other glove rose and reached again past the ribbon tongue to the scraps inside and pulled more free, and pushed them into Mother's trapped shout.

The glove hands picked and plucked every scrap of fiber from inside the muslin shell till it hung limp as wet hair over the form's neck.

Mother stood, stiff and overstuffed, plump with scraps that strained at her seams.

Grandma pulled a crooked needle and a length of black thread from a tuck in her dress, and whip-stitched Mother's lips shut to keep the rags from spilling out.

⊸

They dressed Mother in her new clothes and stood her form in the corner of the living room. Her tall, familiar shape had a view of the mailbox, where Hannah collected the letters.

"Your check is here, Grandma! It came again!"

They could live well, just the two of them, on what Grandma received.

"Do you want to go to the craft store and get some new buttons?"

"Yes," Grandma said, her voice as soft as old linen.

NOR CEASE YOU NEVER NOW

REN WAROM

It was a dark and stormy night . . .

Is that how they want it to start? All these flashcards. These prompts and pieces of paper. *Fictionalise it,* they say, *tell it as a story to find some distance.* But who'd start a story like that? Nonsensical. Self-evident. Night tends to be dark. Why would it not be? The light is gone. The world has turned away from sun, from warmth—submerged in the darkness of space. Anyway, it's irrelevant, because it wasn't night, and there was no storm.

There was only water.

There's no story, either, only fragments scattered all around. Memory is particular and arbitrary. So is trauma. Attach trauma to memory and it chooses what it will cling to at random—but with intent. Witness a car crash whilst eating strawberry ice cream, all those bodies burst like fruit and leaking, and the thought of strawberry ice cream might make you sick for the rest of your life—particular and yet arbitrary. She's not afraid of the obvious, of water. If anything, she's drawn to it. Hypnotised.

She can eat a steak rare, too, and feel nothing. That shocks her parents. They watch her when she's eating, expecting the reaction Luke had—maybe because they're twins or something. Luke's gone vegan. He'll look at meat, look at people eating meat, and go *pale,* swallow like he's fighting the urge to throw up. Memory lives in meat for him. For her though, it's her face. She can't see herself at all. Her face has been stolen by trauma. So there it is . . . Arbitrary. Particular.

In which case, what use are stories?

What use is anything?

Luke's in the back of the corner shop, trying to decide between buying a whole lemon cake or three packs of bourbons. He keeps doing this, spending money on unhealthy crap, food with too much sugar and flavourings, anything to try and erase the taste of meat clinging to his tongue, to the back of his throat. He overhears voices, talking a little too loud. Purposeful.

"Disgusting. I can't believe he's walking around like this. It's blatant."

"I can't believe they let that family buy the cottage in the first place. Bad for the area, it is. For house prices."

"Does Geoff say so?"

"He does. I mean, it's still all over the news, especially with them moving. Especially with that awful accident on the day they moved . . . It can't be a coincidence."

"No."

"I mean, look at what happened. They still don't know why that boat capsized. How those two managed to survive. The *only* ones to come out of the water."

"Too much of a coincidence."

"Exactly. *Exactly.* But do the police do anything?"

"Not likely, they leave us to be around *that*. I won't let my kids stay at the college if they attend, I can tell you that."

"I don't blame you, love, I don't blame you."

Luke *hates* these people. These women and men with their gossip and their curiosity. Their malice. They know he's here, listening, they saw him come in, watched him trail to the back of the shop. They mean for him to hear this. To hurt him. He never realised how *ugly* people could be. That urge they have to poke and worry at something already cracked and leaking. The will to believe the worst, to want it. The hunger for drama. For horror. He thinks of the accident on the motorway. The blackened ruin, the collapse of cars behind; the way people slowed down to look.

It's amazing how fast suffering can pull an enthusiastic crowd. How fast a crowd can turn, screaming for blood.

If they knew the taste of it, the price, maybe they wouldn't.

"Well," one of the voices says, and the sharpness in it is malice and satisfaction both, "they fit in out there, at least, in the sticks. Out on the fens. They say the people of the fens didn't go hungry during the war, during rationing. How do you think they did that?"

There's a shocked, almost delighted silence, and then the other one goes, "Oh my god, Jess!"

"I said it, and I'd say it again."

He leaves without cake. Without biscuits. Without looking at them. Goes home in silence, swallowing again and again at the taste in his mouth. Bitter and strong it spreads all the way down to his stomach, where it wraps around the meat of him and sinks in deep, reminding him that he'll never get rid of the taste of her. She's an accusation built into his body. A memory like a stain, and he's soaked through. Sodden with her.

~

I a a n to ig t

"*Fuck's* sake, what's this?"

Luke, in the passenger seat, his whole body will be tensing forward, as if ready to jump. Driving, Jay will tense too, barely perceptible—he'll want to say something about Luke's language but the words will stick in his throat. They've forgotten how to parent. Is that fear? What is that? In the middle row, Clara will reach out a hand to touch Luke's shoulder but pause, fingers curling on the air, as his eyes catch hers in the rearview.

The car slows to a crawl, then stops. In the back seats, the last row of three, lying down, Laurel's been watching the green blur of the banks roll to sky and cloud and back again. When they stop, she doesn't bother sitting up to see what's happening. Knowing makes no difference.

"It's a car accident." Clara, on her phone. For her, knowing is safety, despite all evidence to the contrary. "Seventeen cars!" She gasps. "Oh my god. This is a twenty-mile tailback."

"Can't we go around?" Luke's knee is jittering now, it's shaking the car.

Jay answers, deep and quiet, in control. Or so he thinks. "We could try, but the next junction is about eighteen miles. Then it's at least a half hour drive to get back to the motorway, and I'd guess we wouldn't be the only ones thinking to do that . . ."

"Shit." The impatience in Luke's voice trips on an edge. He's full of edges.

Clara butts in, conciliatory, voice like syrup, sickly sweet, all calories and no substance. "There's services in five miles. We can check in there for food. Coffee. Make it fun?"

"Cool, cool." Luke doesn't sound like he thinks it's cool, but he won't say more, not with Jay there. Jay will only tolerate so much. That's not parenting, that's just human. Everyone has a breaking point.

Clara leans over the back of her seat. "Hey, Lau, sound cool?" She's all but whispering, always tiptoeing around their feelings.

"Whatever." Miles away, she barely recognises her own voice. She wonders if she'd know her own face right now. Faces fall off. They change.

It takes three hours to get to the services, another hour to get back out. By the time they're back in traffic, Luke's retreated to his headphones, Jay having finally, *finally* lost his cool with Luke's lack of it, and the car is all tension, thick and ugly. For the past hour the view's been nothing but sky, slowly turning grey. There's a tiny patch of white adrift in the middle, fading fast. As it goes the first drops come, like Morse code. SOS.

Laurel lies in the back seat, counting seconds by her heartbeat, her skin thrumming like the metal skin of a car revved too hard. Morse code spatters multiply to a roar, reducing visibility to almost nil, the window a ragged blur of monochrome greys and the spreading yellow haloes of motorway lights. She doesn't want to be here.

She didn't want to come at all.

~

s r ory

They both feel it, the rising tide. The call of water. It's been building within, like the quieting shushing of waves across pebbles, that rhythmic to and fro, the pull and release and pull again, until every scrap of sand, no matter how hard it clings together, is pulled apart and washed away. Even when they understand what it might cost, they can't resist the pull of it, the disintegration. It's like an apology. An offering. One they wouldn't refuse even if they could. The water almost had them once, and it's never really let go. That's why they came here, where the memory of water soaks the earth. Dominates it.

Water has called them here. It has claimed them. And when it comes to take them, it will find them sleeping and fill their lungs to brimming.

I s k n

You try not to give too much of yourself away, hold on to the parts that matter, that feel right, but you end up losing them anyway. Bit by bit, the world steals you away from yourself, leaving you with scraps. Too few pieces, so you forget how to put them back together to make something, anything, resembling you, or who you thought you were. Who you wanted to be. There's just a shadow. A stranger. An outline that loses all resolution until it fades into nothing, into the surrounding dark, and is gone.

Lau stares into the mirror, her eyes pools of black in the darkness, her mouth a circle bleeding into her face. A chasm. She knows the truth now.

The face she almost swallowed was her own.

w dr n o

It's Sunday. Seven weeks, four boxes remaining, all theirs. All left outside their rooms. An unspoken expectation from their parents to move in, move on. They've been mentioning college, leaving prospectuses around. When they go to work, Luke tears them up and throws them in the bin, mainly to stop Lau burning them. They know they won't be going back. Not now. Maybe never. Nothing is the same, and it can't be. It can't. On the screen, his character shoots and runs, runs and shoots. Mindless, his fingers press buttons automatically. He used to be good at this. He used to be a lot of things.

Laurel enters from the kitchen, shoes dangling from one hand. There are circles under her eyes he'd probably have given her shit for once upon a time, when she'd have cared. When he would. Heading to the front door, shoes swinging, she stops to pull them on, and then opens it. Pauses on the threshold without looking back. It hasn't happened for a long time. Knowing. But it happens now. He gets up from the sofa, dropping the controller behind him, barely hearing the thump of it on the floor. Takes her hand at the door, almost dragging. She laughs then, a small sound, like relief more than joy, more than anything.

"Where we going?" He's leading, but he asks her.

In response she moves to lead.

"I've been dreaming of faces," she says, tugging lightly on his hand. Her palm is cold. Damp. "Faceless people."

He swallows, walking faster. "We said we wouldn't say. You made me swear."

"I can break a fucking swear if I want to." Stubborn. This is the Laurel he knows. It's almost reassuring.

"Can you?" No bite in it. He's not arguing, not yet. Temper has faded lately, swallowed by fear. By something darker. A will to drown.

"I know why you went vegan, Luke," she says, so quiet and firm he turns his head to look at her. Her face is solemn. "I was in the water too," she adds, as if he needs reminding.

"That's why we promised, isn't it?"

She shrugs. "Maybe. Probably."

"So?"

"So what are you seeing?"

He doesn't reply until they reach their destination. A miniature wood in the midst of a large furrowed field, a small pond hidden within, and a fallen tree, partially rotted. This was an island once, surrounded by mirror-smooth waters all the way to the horizon, reflecting the sky. It must have been surreal, sky on all sides, above and below. You could jump and think you might float away, only to fall in and drown.

He's been here, so many times. It's like a call, a pull, the same as this twin thing they have, as if that water, or the memory of it, has magnetised him. He's found himself wandering here when he's intended to go to the shop, when he walks just to move and not feel like he might burst apart. They sit on the fallen tree, side by side, hand in hand, and watch the sky, bright blue, ripe with thick cumulus, drifting.

"I ate her," he says, then, like a confession.

"Katie?" She says the name in a rush, but it still hurts. It's Lau though, so he forgives it. Nothing else to do.

"Yeah."

"You're seeing her then."

"Sometimes. In the mist. But mostly I choke her up. Little pieces of her. And then they vanish."

She turns to look at him. "Where do they go?"

"Back inside," he says, and feels something moving in his gut, a tangle of viscera not his own. Foreign matter. "They go back inside."

~

a d k r

It's the usual breakfast in their half-finished kitchen, the cabinets painted varying shades of grey because Clara can't decide which is most sophisticated, and the crappy thrifted table. She insists she'll upcycle it, but the cloth she put down to sand and paint it is still under their feet, and the table hasn't been touched. That's how things are. Untouched. Unchanged. Or changed in awkward ways that stand out too fresh and raw to ignore. Their children are not getting better. He can't say it aloud and neither can she, but they exchange awareness of it when they look at one another. Over breakfast, at bedtime, on the sofa. Things are worse. Everything is dark, and everyone is drowning.

~

w s a d s o h

That's how I remember it . . . muddled. Not just that day, but everything. I used to have this clear timeline, and it's gone. They're like *he has anger issues*, and yeah, I do, I lose my shit all the time. But it's not *them*. It's not their fault. I get mad because nothing stays where it should. Nothing makes *sense*. Not just memory, but everything. Everything. It's all shadows. You know how shadows get distorted? How they don't look like the thing they're made from?

Her family posted photos to their Facebook, you know. I kept going to look at them, but I don't know who that is, that girl. I didn't really know her at all. I mean, I didn't try for that. I wouldn't have. She was sweet, and quiet, and made it easy to be . . . I made her life fucking miserable okay? Because it was *easy*. That's what I did. That's how she knew me. I was the arsehole who made her cry pretty much every day at school.

That was her memory, and now she's gone.

And all I can think of, when I think of her, is that I *ate* her. And they tell me that it was an accident, that it might not have been her at all, not when so many of them . . . not with so many remains in the water. But that's all I can think of, and that it's not her, in those pictures. They're a lie.

All of this is a fucking lie.

~

I s a k n o g

If I imitate the reflection, I will become the image, she thinks, resting her hand lightly on the surface of the water. Breaking it. Her face stares back at her as the ripples smooth out to a mirror. Nothing has changed. Water, mirror, it makes no difference, her image is blurred, a fuzz of colour and darkness where her features should be. She can't make it come to focus, as if a soft and constant rain is falling on the water, disturbing the surface tension. Water upon water. Water into water. That makes sense. It's all water, always.

In the mirrored surface, her reflection ripples and vanishes, replaced by bland blue sky. Lurching up, she stumbles back blindly, reaching for something, anything. But there's nothing to hold onto. Everything has vanished.

~

t s a a r y

"Tell me what you're feeling. I'm not here to judge. Everything said in this room is in confidence."

Clara smiles, a touch uneasy. She clears her throat, looking at Jay for support, he reaches over and grabs hold of her hand, squeezing. Nods.

"It's just," she starts, then stops, looking down at her hands, her shoulders hitching once, and then again. When she speaks again, her voice is thick, heavy. "You get your children back, but they're no longer your children, you know? And . . . and you don't know what to do with these traumatised strangers, and they're, oh my god, just *breaking your heart*. I look at them and I *ache*. I don't have a clue how to help them, or what to say, and I'm scared of pushing them. I think . . . that would be bad."

"Jay?" Amanda, their bereavement and trauma counsellor, looks at Clara's husband and presses gently, "Do you feel the same?"

"I . . ." His jaw tenses. "I don't know how I feel. Helpless? I keep looking at them and wondering where Luke and Laurel are."

"That's perfectly understandable." Amanda looks between them, her face filled with compassion. "Trauma can have a profound impact on a personality. They're grieving, dealing with almost dying, with surviving, with the particular horrors of that survival. They'll improve, but it will take time, and patience, a great deal of patience. Normality is the best medicine you can offer them. Let them know nothing has changed, that there is stability they can trust."

"I try that. I do," Clara says. "But, I look at them, and I find myself wondering sometimes . . . would it be better if they'd died? And then I wonder if they can tell I'm thinking it and I feel so guilty, so *awful*. Like I've betrayed them."

The second it's out there, in the open, she's horrified to have said it, her hand over her mouth, her eyes wide, staring at Jay. He smiles, and it's painful. Lifts her hand to his mouth and kisses it.

"I think it," he says, softly. "I think it, too."

t s ~ o gh

They've been here a week, and he's spent most of it out of the house, unable to bear himself, the way he snaps at anything and everything. How it makes them react. The tension flooding the house is his doing, he drags it with him like a tidal wave, washing away any chance of peace. Even Lau won't speak to him half the time, but maybe that's not his temper. He's lost the ability to be calm, she's lost the ability to care. He's walking the roads between the fields today, he likes the endless emptiness of it all, how it stretches on forever, dragging the eye with it to hazy distance merging into sleepy blue sky. It makes him feel.

He's stopped to breathe it all in when she appears on the horizon, flickering in the heat haze like a ghost. Her hand is rested lightly on the rail, her hair blowing behind her, a tangle of agitated brown. She's laughing with her friends, holding back her hair as it whips into her mouth. Minutes later—or was it seconds?—their laughter turned to screams as a whining, grinding roar came from below, the boat pitching, sudden and steep, water splashing over the rails. Their whole class was there, some in the cabin, some on the deck.

Everyone on the deck died, apart from him and Laurel.

He watches as Katie and her friends tumble down, hitting the waves with violent slaps of sound. They fell together, churned to pieces by the engine blades as they spun through the water. He slid down the deck after them, hands scrabbling for purchase. He remembers the cold shock of the water, the screams, the blades spinning over his head in slow motion, the force of their movement pushing him down in a whirlpool of remains. Hers. He had no idea he would scream until it happened, and when he opened his mouth, she flooded inside, coppery and warm.

He rubs his hands over his eyes. When he looks again, she's back on the horizon. This time her gaze is on him, and when the wind whips her hair into her mouth, she doesn't reach to pull it away. She opens wide, and swallows it.

a d r̃ t y

They were late on the day they moved in. I was handing over the keys in person for the cottage, because they came from so far away, you understand? Oh, it was convenient. Better than having them stay in a hotel overnight, and the moving van was coming early. 6am, I think. So I was stuck waiting, in the middle of that storm . . . Patricia, or whatever it was. Thunder so loud you could shout and not hear yourself, lightning illuminating the whole fen, all the lakes flaring white. Beautiful really, but torrential rain and no signal here for texts to reach me to say they were delayed, so not their fault. Couldn't be helped.

No, I didn't meet the twins then. Jay and Clara came in for the keys alone when they arrived. I didn't meet the twins until much later, a week or more perhaps. In the cafe it was. Well they seemed quiet, somewhat withdrawn, but that's hardly out of the ordinary considering what happened to them, what they went through . . . As for what happened, it's awful. Awful. Gut wrenching. I can't imagine how Jay and Clara must have felt, how they're feeling now. But yes, we all knew things weren't right. We could all see that family was falling apart. Those poor kids, and people didn't help. They gossip, don't they.

I hope some of those nosey old bints are suffering guilt. They ought to, god knows.

No, no. Look I know what was *said* about how those kids died, but it must have been out on the fens. I'm telling you. Well because, no one drowns in their bed, it's not possible, and it wasn't homicide, they ruled out any possibility and I believe the verdict. No reason not to. What am I saying? I'm saying that they were off wandering a good deal, sometimes too long. I saw that. I witnessed it. Gave Luke a lift home once, close to midnight. He was exhausted, miles from home. Soaking wet. You understand me?

What I think is . . . I think they were missing that night, when Jay and Clara got home. That Jay and Clara went looking for them and found them like that out on the fens. And I think they couldn't bear it. You understand?

They wanted them to be sleeping. Only sleeping.

~

I a r n

Laurel leans up to watch when they pass the line of wrecked cars, illuminated red by a succession of taillights. The front car is nothing but a black skeleton. Perhaps the engine exploded, the firemen driven back by roaring flames and flying metal. Bodies roasting. The road is wet, but there are puddles of darkness she imagines must be blood. They died hard, these people. How many? So many cars ruined, concertinaed behind the black skeleton of the first into a single entity. Vividly, she can imagine the bodies inside, woven together.

She lies back down and closes her eyes.

Water roars in her ears—the chaos and screams above mute and fly away, so very far. Part of her wants nothing more than to let go and sink deep. Deeper. Give in to the lull, the roaring in her ears. The weight of water. But when she opens her eyes for one last look, imagining the blue vault of it above flickering with the reflections of flames and sunlight, the water churns red, and there is a face floating in front of her. A face without a body, eyeless, the mouth a gaping window to red water.

It flies into her mouth when she screams, tangling around her tongue, warm and rubbery. Metallic.

This is not her first kiss.

Breathing in, she opens her eyes. Bites her lip until thin copper leaks onto her tongue. Watches police lights, blue and red, flashing in the drops on the window, melting and merging. Floats in the stillness, in the rain, in the quiet water of her body.

~

t r a o ht

Luke wakes choking, a familiar taste in his throat, thick and metallic. There's something stuck inside, filling his entire throat, impeding breath. Sour spit flooding his mouth, he lurches up, knocking the headboard against the wall. The lump shifts and he lets out a sound—rough panic. Curling over his tangled sheets, he gags, violent, his entire gut wrenching, acid rising hot and heavy to lap against the obstruction. He gags again, tearing up from the force of it, the burn of the acid, and the lump slides free, over his tongue, flops out onto the pale yellow of the candlewick spread.

A chunk of something, slick and purplish, stinking of water and rot. It soaks into the soft fabric, a spreading circle of brown liquid.

Rearing back, he smacks into the headboard, the back of his skull colliding with brick, roaring white noise into his ears, distant ringing pain. He hears screaming, muffled by water, the slap of bodies hitting the waves, the waves hitting the sides of the boat. His chest constricts, too tight. There's water pressing down, pressing in, and she's in his mouth again. She's always in his mouth. And on his sheets, her scrap still there, the circle of brown growing ever wider. Sobbing, he stuffs hands into his mouth, trying to drag the taste of her from his tongue. There's blood and acid. Salt and filthy water.

Meat and memory. Nothing more.

—◦—

He wakes in buttery daylight, pain locked into his shoulders, the back of his neck. His head hurts, a slow, dull hurt like a headache. Wincing, he lifts a hand to rub it away, smelling spit and the sour edge of vomit on his skin. His gaze slides to the candlewick. The wide brown stain marring the soft yellow fabric, soaked through. Her remnant is gone, but it was there. It was there.

He can feel the shape of it lodged in his throat, slipping back down.

~

s t m i

The fens are mostly drained, turned to arable land, but the land here remembers water in the same way her body does. It leaks out of the ground and surrounds her, mirror-smooth, mist rising from its surface like breath in cold air, rippling into strange reflections. Building pictures—worlds made of water. Ghosts in water vapour. People walking in lines, careful, across boggy land, leading cattle and children. Or cottages, smoke winding its way up into cloud, or drifting down in light wind to melt into the mist and be lost. Doorways. Worlds over the world.

On bad days, the mist writhes into bodies without faces, faces without bodies. Water follows her on those days, leaking out beneath her feet, leaching from the walls, from her skin. Leaving her smelling of copper and salt, that cool brackish scent of ocean mingled with blood. The mist rises from her skin then and forms eyeless masks, screaming mouths that open wide, wider, gaping to vast holes the wind howls through. Worlds and ghosts, all screaming at her.

~

ws r o n

After. There's a word with new meaning. Loaded. It's like a line has been gouged, separating his life into two pieces, then and now. If he squints he imagines he can see it, an ugly black line, a barricade. But is he trapped inside or outside? He can't figure it out. The world feels distant and too close, too raw, too loud and full and suffocating, but he can't touch anything, or nothing touches him. Everything he feels is inside. Trapped. Waiting to come up. He may choke on it.

Lights out. The dark laps like water.

He sits, unable to sleep, shivering, his gut churning around lumps and scraps. In the dark, nothing is familiar, even his body is a stranger. He's floating too far away, needs to find something solid to stand on before he disappears completely. There's nothing beneath his feet but water, boiling red. He throws off the covers and goes to find Lau, his twin, who's always been that. Who must be, even now.

They've told him where she is, that she's doing well, but they tell his parents that he's doing well too.

It's like they don't even know what the words mean.

-<o>-

Her room, like his, is private, and she's awake. Of course she is. Sat staring at the television, the sound off, light and colours playing across her face, across the walls. She looks around when he closes the door and her expression, tight before, relaxes just a little.

"You're here," she says.

"Yeah."

"Watch with me."

He drags the big chair from the corner and they sit in silence, watching the show, a re-run of some old '80s sitcom. At some point he reaches out to take her hand and she clings to him like they're both still drowning. Or he clings to her. Perhaps they cling to each other, pretending that's what happened in the water, when neither of them really remember, not really. The only thing they know for sure, because they were told, is that they were far apart, that one of them almost wasn't found. They won't say which one.

Luke thinks it's both of them.

The sitcom finishes. There's a movie then, black and white. He watches without watching. All he notices is her hand in his, too warm, trembling. Halfway through, her grip tightens to the point of pain and she whispers: "Don't ask. And don't tell me. We should never say. Swear to me."

⊸

He wakes in his own room, disorientated in the darkness, the quiet hum of the hospital at near rest. Did he find her? Was that real? It seems unlikely, not here, not with so many people watching them, so many worried eyes tracking their every move, every expression. But they must have found one another somehow, because no matter what else is gone, the promise remains, as clear as the line between before and after. Sworn.

We should never ask. Never tell. Swear to me.

I s ñ g

There was a storm on the day they arrived. Patricia. She escorted them in. Storm Edda is escorting them out in bursts of thunder and lashing rain.

Clara's not sad to go. This place has stolen from her. Everything. She could happily see it burn to ash, see it smashed to dust. They came here so hopeful, their children rescued from the water but still drowning. They believed this place might save them, instead it offered them to water—like sacrifices. How did she not see the water beneath the soil, waiting, predatory? Filling their footsteps until it became an ocean, vast and unfeeling. And so hungry.

She watches out the window, hating every inch of this place. Her heart clenches within her, an aching knot of muscle. It will never unfurl.

As they approach Ely, the cathedral rising through cloud like a judge, two hares, pure white, emerge from between the trees like darting lights, will-o'-the-wisps. They race the car for what seems like miles, appearing and vanishing, fleet of foot and fanciful. Edda grows fierce around them, pounding them with rain, with jagged forks of lightning clawing down from the heavens, lighting the clouds, those jagged billows, those hungry mouths, those weeping eyes. When their light fades, the hares have vanished. The storm has swallowed them whole.

Or perhaps they've fed themselves to it.

PLAYSCAPE

DIANA PETERFREUND

You weren't friends; not really. She was one of those mom friendships, the cohort you drift into by dint of your children being born around the same time. Parenting astrology, entwining your fates.

People call you, when they see her on the news. "Don't you know her?" your mother asks, her voice dropping over the phone line as if someone might overhear this secret. "Didn't I meet her with her baby at the playground once? *That* playground?"

Yes, you admit. It had been her. And it had even been that playground. You stare at the news broadcast with grim fascination, same as everyone else in the country. How tiny she looks on the screen, stating nonsense in a clear if quavering voice. Her child had been on the playscape, near the top of the slide. She'd been right there. And a second later, she had vanished.

Complete fabrication, of course. Children don't just disappear, though some days, when your own is being troublesome, you wish they would. The theories fly fast and furious around the stroller set, across back fences and on the neighborhood email list.

She must have been preoccupied with her phone. These days, people are more interested in whatever's happening on social media than in their own children's safety. And there had been that creepy fellow sleeping in the woods lately. Didn't she know about him? There'd been dozens of concerned posts.

Or maybe it was something more sinister entirely. Maybe she had never taken her tyke to the park at all. Had the police checked her house? Her shed? The trunk of her car?

Your husband shakes his head incredulously over dinner that night. Hadn't you wanted him to be friends with *her* husband? You'd tried to arrange a double date on three separate occasions. Thank goodness the timing never worked out.

That was before, you insist. Back when you were on maternity leave, and you were desperate for any kind of conversation that wasn't about the bodily functions of a squalling infant. When your mind was so addled and sleep-deprived that any fellow sufferer was a sister-in-arms.

You look at your onetime sister-in-arms on the TV screen, her tear-streaked face, her terrified eyes, and wonder why you were ever friends.

You turn to your toddler, playing with blocks on the carpet. His nose is running with some fresh cold—that daycare is a germ factory, really—but at least he's safe. You both are.

⊸o⊷

That had been the end of the nascent friendship, if you wanted to be perfectly honest about it. Your maternity leave ended. You went back to work. She hadn't. You never met at the playground anymore, or on the street, in strollers clammy with morning dew, baby spit-up drying stiffly on the front of your comfy maternity shirt.

The things you'd shared back then. Cracked nipples, sleepless nights, painful sex, even the looming specter of postpartum depression. Neither of you knew the line between *cranky and overwhelmed* and *let's try some medication.* You remember her bringing it up once, bashful.

"My doctor asked me if I ever have those thoughts, like I'd be better off without the baby. And I know you're supposed to answer 'of course not.' But really. Think about it. I haven't washed my hair in ten days. Wouldn't we all be better off if we could just run away to Bermuda?"

You'd nodded and laughed at the time, understanding exactly what she meant.

Now you look at her on TV, crying as they lead her up the steps to the police department, her arms pinned behind her back. Is her hair washed? Do you detect a swipe of lip gloss?

They searched the woods; they searched the house; they put out an AMBER Alert. They gave onesies to the dogs to try to track the child's scent. Media personalities in New York and Atlanta commented on the case. "Stay off the internet," your husband warns the next day. "You don't want to see what they are saying about her."

No, you don't want to see it. And also, you already know what they are saying.

You can't sleep, and though you know it's playing with fire—heaven forfend your little light sleeper hear the nursery door open!—you check on your child one more time. He's passed out in his crib, one hand clutching the corner of his ratty old blanket. He looks so big in there. You should really consider transitioning him to a toddler bed, but he just can't be trusted to stay put. It's safer this way. Easier, too. Despite months of sleep training, he still cries himself to sleep most nights.

You do, too, those nights.

Downstairs, you turn on the computer screen, letting the blue glow bathe your face in the darkness, and see what they have to say.

⟜

What kind of monster would murder her child?

That's what it boils down to, in forum after forum, comment section after comment section. And then there were the neighbors, under screen names you don't recognize. Your neighbors, telling these strangers on the internet what a mess she has always been. Her hair ratty, her kid grimy and unkempt. Always, they pointed out, there'd been something not quite right.

Had you noticed it, when you saw her around? You remember waving when you drove by and caught a glimpse of her out with her stroller or in the yard. You remember sometimes being envious of her faded yoga pants and bare feet as she played in her garden with her mop-headed moppet, while you faced a morning commute in stilettos and a suit jacket. She'd wave back, smiling sheepishly and shrugging as her kid turned the hose on. You'd laugh and rush off to your real job.

You'd both been a mess in those early days. Who had time for hairdos and manicures with a newborn in the house? They shouldn't be so hard on her.

But you also remember the children's last playdate. You'd dropped by with your son and a bottle of wine. There were tubs of unfolded laundry all over the living room, and pasta from the previous night congealing on the stove. Her husband was away, you remember, and she'd admitted she was indulging in squalor.

"I just don't have time to keep up with it," she'd said, pushing a load of towels out of the way so you could both perch on the couch and watch the children's parallel play. But really, what was she doing all day?

There wasn't much to talk about. She was having problems with toilet-training and asked you for advice. You had very little. Your child was so motivated, though. He watched what the older kids at daycare did and emulated them. Perhaps if she got out a little more often? Maybe if her child spent more time around other kids?

She'd looked at you then, as if to ask, *Where*?

Surely there were moms' groups, around. Playdates with other stay-at-home families. And didn't that church down the street run a program a few mornings a week?

You watched your child share the toys with her child, tall and slim in his big-boy underwear, while she still toddled about in pull-ups. You were so proud of him. What a little man.

"Every baby's different," you'd said by way of apology. "Your child is not mine."

Was that the last time you were over at her house? You wonder as you stand at the end of her front walk, a casserole dish balanced awkwardly on the canopy of your child's stroller. You haven't knocked yet, though you can see their cars in the driveway. The curtains are all drawn, and you don't blame them. The media has been relentless. You wonder if that white van parked across the street holds reporters, lying in wait.

Maybe this was a bad idea.

Is that a flutter of movement from the living-room window? Too late to turn back now. You leave the baby in the stroller on the walk and climb the porch steps. Maybe you shouldn't have brought your child.

No, you definitely shouldn't have. You know it at once when her husband answers the door. His hollowed-out eyes go right past you to the stroller, and the chubby legs sticking out from under the canopy.

"I brought you a casserole," you say, holding forth the offering.

He glances at the dish as if he's never seen one before. As if the very concept of eating is somehow foreign. He certainly looks like he's never had a meal in his life, this new, strange life he now lives.

His hands are stiff and dry and cold when they take the dish from you. "Please tell her . . .tell her that we're so sorry."

The look he gives you now is suspicious, calculating. Hard.

"I know the neighbors haven't all been supportive," you say, wavering. "But . . .we're thinking of you."

His gaze shoots to the van. "This isn't a good time."

"Of course. Of course." You're already backing away, as if the house is infected with the plague. You can't imagine losing a child.

What's worse is you can. It's all you can think of, every minute of every hour.

You grab the stroller and somehow make it down the block without breaking into a run.

◆

It's not as if you never go to the park anymore. You just haven't been in weeks. Months? Work is getting so busy, and there are always chores to do on the weekend. You can't have the laundry pile up. But this morning is lovely, sunny and brisk, and your toddler has been bouncing off the walls. It's the park or the dreaded screen-time—and you know what they say about that!—so you load him up in the stroller and head over.

You can't even remember the last time you went to this park. Do you not take him out enough? He gets plenty of playtime at the daycare. That part you made sure of when you picked the place that would look after your precious little one while you work. They have a beautiful facility with a lovely, well-maintained playscape. And your son adores it.

The park near your house is nice enough. Swings, a sandbox, the playscape with its ladders and climbing grids and platforms. There are two slides on the playscape. The low one, meant for toddlers, where caregivers can hold on the whole time, and the high, corkscrew one at the far end, with its little cupola at the top.

The park had been closed for a few days after the child's disappearance, while the police combed for clues among the wood chips and fallen leaves. There was nothing left to mark it as a crime scene, no scraps of yellow tape binding the playscape, no officer left behind to keep an eye on things.

Someone on the internet had scoffed at the woman's cover story from the start. The playscape was in the middle of an island of mulch. There were no trees for potential abductors to conceal themselves behind, no way for a toddler to run off unnoticed.

Another had taken issue with the entire activity. For what kind of person would let a toddler on one of those things alone?

You are that kind of person. At least you still have that in common with her. Your child, like hers, never wanted help to climb or run or go down the slide. From the time he could walk, he'd insist on climbing the playscape by himself. "I do it!" he'd scream if you so much as put a hand out to steady him on the slide. And that was a year ago. Now he can climb so high and so fast, you've given up entirely.

You park the stroller and undo the straps keeping him safely inside. He scrambles out of the contraption and takes off toward the playscape eagerly. You laugh and follow at an easy gait.

It really is a beautiful day. The light is lemony and almost wet as it plays through the leaves of the trees around the park. The wood chips are dark with dew and you brush tiny puddles of water at the base of the slides away with your hands. He only likes the little slide, though. He barrels up the ladders and pounds across the bridges. He has a system. Up the ladder, over the bridge, down the slide, then around the playscape to the ladder again. Over and over again. He doesn't need a companion. He doesn't want your help. And no matter how many times he does it, it's not enough. By the time he skids to a stop at the bottom, he's impatient to get going on the next round. He doesn't even take a second to enjoy the thrill of the moment. Up and over and down and around. It's hypnotic.

Or boring, after a minute or two. You try to induce him to try the sandbox, or even the swings, but no. He just wants the playscape. For five minutes, ten, twenty. Who knew he had so much energy to burn off?

Imagine if this was your life. It's pleasant enough for a Sunday morning, but imagine every day like this, standing on the wood chips and watching him, like a hamster on a wheel. Up and over and down and around. Up and over and down and around. Would you go mad?

Would you go mad, too?

There's no one else here this morning. No parents. No nannies. No teenagers playing soccer on the adjacent field. Just light in the trees and the distant buzz of insects.

"Mommy!" he calls, and you snap out of your reverie and look at him. He's on top of the platform—the high part, near the cupola over the big, corkscrew slide, and he's holding his arms out to you. "I all done."

"Okay," you reply. "Come on down the slide."

He stomps his little foot. "I all done!"

Oh, this attitude thing again. He's been pulling it a lot lately. "Well then, come down. You can do it."

"No!" he whines, his little face screwing up. He starts to cry. "I. All. Doooooooooonnnnne!"

Your husband says you baby him, you and the old ladies at the daycare. That he cries and you snap to do his bidding. But you're relieved he's done with the playground for the day. You reach up to swing him down into your arms, and he wraps his little limbs around you, monkey-like, and clings tightly as you head back to the stroller.

"I'm putting you down now, to walk."

"No . . .I want up."

"Buddy, you have to walk."

"Up. . . ." he whines, and his eyes fill with tears. "Please?"

You kind of have to reward politeness.

Poor little guy. He tired himself out. He can really turn on a dime, from whirling dervish to wrung out. You strap him into the stroller and kick off the brake.

"Did you have fun at the park?" you ask as you head down the block toward home.

"Yeah." He's already distracted, blinking up at the sunlight dappling through the leaves. If you circle the block and stop talking to him, he might fall asleep before you get home. "Look, Mommy. The sun is raining!"

Kids are so cute sometimes. "Mm-hmm."

Your phone buzzes in your pocket. It's a text from your sister-in-law. *Do you know that woman*?

"I climb climb climb the ladder."

"You sure did, buddy!"

Yes, you text back. *Terrible, isn't it?*

"And then I go down down down on the slide."

"Except that last time, right?" you ask, before realizing that if you keep talking to him, he's never going to fade away.

"Yeah." He rubs his eyes. "It was scary. There's a hole in the slide."

Well . . .do you think she did it? your sister-in-law asks via your screen.

It's hard to text and steer the stroller. But you can't stop thinking about it. *What kind of monster would murder her child*?

⊸o⊷

Your mother can't believe you went to that playground. *That* playground, as if it's cursed. Your husband rolls his eyes, hearing the story. There's nothing wrong with that playground. It's the woman.

"She didn't *do* it!" you exclaim over dinner, appalled that he'd even say such a thing about your . . .well, your neighbor. Because you weren't friends. Not really.

"Honey," he replies, with that tone that means he can't even believe he has to explain this. "She either did it, or she lost her daughter at the park. You were just there. How could you lose a kid at that place? It's not like it's a crowded shopping center. It's not being prowled by wolves. It's just a park. Where would the kid go?"

You have no answer for that. You were just there, and you thought the exact same thing. Then again, you watch your child closely there. Boring as it was, you never took your eyes off him. Maybe the people in the neighborhood were right. She hadn't paid attention. She hadn't been careful enough. And someone had gotten him.

But if that were the case, then there was someone still out there. Someone who stole your children right out from under your nose.

This time, when you check on the baby in the nursery, he wakes up and screams until you take him out of the crib and sit down for a cuddle.

Your husband finds you asleep in the rocker after midnight, still holding on tight.

⊸o⊷

Her house is dark and the curtains are still drawn the next time you walk by. The flowers in the yard have gone dry and brown with no child to water them. You found your casserole dish, scrubbed clean, on your porch this morning.

The van is still there when you come around the corner with your child and you pause, half-expecting it to vomit out reporters to ask you how you could bring a casserole to a child murderer. Because that's what you did.

Either that or you are blithely strolling your precious progeny around a neighborhood where a kidnapper is running loose, snatching toddlers off playgrounds. She is a monster, or nobody is safe.

And today you are going to the park.

When you arrive at the mulch border, you put on the stroller brake and go to unbuckle your child. He lingers in the seat.

"What's wrong, buddy? Don't you want to go play?"

He nods, with that faraway look he sometimes gets. You watch carefully, surveying the trees at the perimeter of the park like a trained sentry. But no one is there, lurking, waiting to strike. No wolves, no monsters.

"Off you go," you instruct him.

And off he does go, clambering out of the stroller and across the park to the ladder. And then it's the usual, up and over and down, again and again.

Sure, it's boring, but it's also your child. Your darling, perfect little boy, for whom you put up with pain, and boredom, and monotony, and whining, and a thousand sleepless nights.

It's like you told your husband this morning. You never really know someone, even your neighbors. Even your friends. For what kind of monster would murder her child?

"Mommy?"

You look up and he's standing at the top of the corkscrew slide, near the little cupola.

"Ooh, are you going down the big one?" you ask.

He nods, so serious.

"Okay, I'll watch you!"

He sits down, deliberate in that way he sometimes has, lining up his little legs so his sneakers stick straight out.

And you realize you can't watch him. Not completely. There's that first quarter-turn at the top where the cupola blocks your view, right there where the sunlight stutters and skips.

"Wait—" The words strangle in your throat.

Because he pushes off, and disappears.

A hundred thousand years pass. You stand in front of TV cameras and cry, saying you don't know what happened. One second he was there, and then he was gone. You scream it to anyone who will listen, but no one will, and there are strange looks and midnights in jail cells and pity casseroles and empty rooms and your husband is hollow and hateful and why why why won't anyone believe you? Why won't anyone help you find your child?

And then he's there, coming around the turn, a smile plastered on his chubby little baby face. By the time he reaches the base, you've snatched him up and cuddled him close, and then you spare one more look at that spot, that twisted, hungry spot where even the air is wrong.

For a second, you see it. There's a hole at the top of the slide.

And then you're at the stroller, and you don't even buckle him in as you stride away.

"I did it!" he crows in triumph. "I went down the big slide."

"Yes you did, baby," you say, and you start to jog. Back home, maybe, or just as far as you can get, as fast as you can get there.

Could it have been you? Could it have been you?

ADRENALINE JUNKIES

RAY CLULEY

"Carpe the fucking diem."

I'm thinking about Suki when Cate pats my arm and gives me the thumb-to-forefinger okay. For a moment I think she means we're ready to jump but the door's still closed and everybody else in the plane is triple-checking their harnesses and packs, pockets, cameras. She means the sign as a question, I realise. I don't want her to think I'm worried about the jump—I'm not—so I smile, and return the sign with a nod. She gives me a thumbs-up, grinning. She's excited, adrenaline already working its magic. This is her first freefall, no static line, and I can't be looking sad when I know she's probably as nervous as she is excited. She doesn't know much about Suki yet, just the little she's heard from the others and maybe a tiny bit more from a well-meaning Kit. I'll give her my version after we've landed. Or tonight. I'll tell her tonight.

"You okay, pretty lady?" Todd shouts. We're flying in a tiny prop and the cabin is loud with its noise. I have no okay sign or thumbs-up for him, just a middle finger, and he laughs. He's called me "pretty lady" ever since Quintana Roo where one of the barmen kept trying his luck, complimenting my dress, my hair, no gaydar whatsoever. Cate had joked I should kiss her so he'd get the hint and a few tequilas later I did, but it wasn't for the barman's benefit. I'm not sure what I was trying to prove. Or who I was trying to prove it to.

There'd been tequilas last night as well, and a morning wake-up so early that we may as well have not gone to bed. It had left most of us silent at breakfast, even though it was jump day. For the other stuff, the climbing and kayaking, we'd fill up on oatmeal and protein snacks, but a jump day breakfast was whatever you wanted it to be. I opted for brown toast, scrambled egg, and half an avocado because that was what Suki used to have. Todd noticed, I could tell, so I stole a spoonful of baked beans from his fried breakfast and spread it over mine and he'd laughed, pretending to protest, and everything was okay.

"Come on, come on," Måns urges, sweeping his arms to bunch us together for a pre-jump selfie. He's got his phone on the end of a selfie stick. He actually owns a selfie stick. Maybe it's a Swedish thing. He leans into us, arm outstretched, and Todd rubs at Måns' bald head as the picture's taken. "Makes me more aerodynamic," Måns says, and although it's an old joke, we all laugh. We're all excited. Pumped.

Måns retrieves his phone. He's taken a good picture. Four of us huddled close, Måns in our laps. Cate where Suki used to be, right beside me. She's made rabbit ears behind my head, fingers sprouting from my helmet. A sign for two. A sign for peace.

I wonder if the others feel Suki's absence as strongly as I do. There's a quiet moment after the picture when everyone's lost in their own thoughts, and I like to think they're all remembering her. But maybe they're not. Maybe they're just suffering what's left of their hangovers, or thinking about the jump, running through a mental list of everything they've done in preparation.

Måns is flicking through the pictures on his phone. They're old ones. He stops at one of him and Suki; she's in profile, a curve of glitter garish around one eye, planting a big kiss on his painted cheek as he grins at the camera. A club in Rio, almost two years ago. Måns notices I'm looking and turns the phone so I can see better and I smile at both of them.

"Okay," says Todd. "Okay, okay, this is it. We ready?"

"Yeah!"

"I said, are we ready?"

"Yeah!"

"Wieslander. Helmet."

Måns reaches to Kit and she slings it to him. He straps it on, knocks the top of it with one fist, and Kit copies. We all copy. Even Cate, who hasn't been told, realises the ritual of it and does the same. I catch her exhale a few hard breaths, looking at the door, then Todd yanks it open and the wind tears in.

Nothing wakes you up or blows away a hangover like squatting in the back of a light aircraft with the slipstream rushing in around you. I do my best to take slow, deep breaths. Kit crouches in the opening. She's flexing her knees, rocking on the spot, pulling and pushing at the doorway, back and forth, back and forth. Todd crouches beside her, looking down, then he pats her on the shoulder three times—go-go-go—and she's gone.

Måns is next. He stands long enough to put his head to Todd's and they bump, then he squats and rolls forward out of the plane in one quick movement.

"Cate."

Todd beckons her and she shuffles to him, squatting. I follow her. She glances up at where she would normally hook onto a static line and then she looks at me. I sign the okay, nodding. She puffs out another breath then Todd's patting her, go-go-go, and she's gone.

It's a good clean exit. We've timed the jump especially for dawn and the light is breaking out over the jungle below. I can see her as she falls. She's holding a stable position, her body open like a giant starfish, arching into the force of the wind.

"She's all right," Todd yells.

I can't see anything of his expression behind his face shield, but I can see his eyes and they are like mine. I know what he really means and yeah. She's all right.

"You ready?"

I give him a nod. He gives it back to me.

I bend my knees to crouch lower. Hold the sides of the door. The wind tugs at me from the front, pushes at me from the back, and passing below is the vast green carpet of jungle canopy. Between me and that is 13,000 feet of sky.

"Carpe the fucking diem!" Todd shouts, then he's slapping at my shoulder: go-go-go!

And I'm gone. Plucked out into a sky Suki never got to see.

⊸

I first saw Suki in a waiting room. Not my practice, a colleague's. And as important as that meeting was, as striking as she'd been, sitting there in one of those god-awful plastic chairs, the memory that always comes first when I think of how we met, my preferred memory, is of her walking a slackline at Malham Cove. We were meeting there to climb Upper Terrace, but I was late thanks to some unavoidable overtime, and when I'd arrived at the site there was something of a low-key party already in progress. Nothing too wild; a night of drinking before jumping out of a plane isn't genius but the night before a climb it's a definite no-no, even if the climb is supposed to be an easy one. Low-key party meant only a couple of drinks, a bit of a smoke (courtesy of Kit), and some music (courtesy of Måns). Someone had strung up a rope between two trees. Suki was barefoot, toes scrunched around the line as she walked a metre above the ground, arms out for balance. She had a line of stars tattooed on her foot, I noticed, and she'd changed her hair since I'd last seen her, her head shaved on one side while the rest of her hair swept over in a deep purple wave. This is how I always see her first when I remember her, balanced between a beginning and an end. Laughing, and giving Todd shit about something he'd said. My heart had expanded into a feeling far more intense than the attraction I'd felt in the waiting room, turning into something far more powerful and needy. I wanted to be with her, and belong to her, and all of that happened right there and then while she balanced on a taut tightrope.

"You'll never make it," Todd said. He turned to Kit and said, "She'll never make it." He called over to Måns, "What do you think, Wieslander?"

Suki raised one leg out to the side, oh so carefully, and brought it around slowly to the front. She did the same again with the other leg.

Without looking up from his guitar, Måns said, "She'll never make it."

Suki had her arms out to balance, but she made fists of her hands and turned them to raise a middle finger both sides, moving slowly forwards as the others laughed. That was when Måns looked up from his guitar and noticed me. He stopped playing to raise a hand in hello and the others noticed me too. They were quiet, taking me in. Kit nodded hi and looked to Todd, smiling. Suki must have picked up on the mood change, or maybe just the new quiet, because she looked up from the rope to glance at them, left quick, right quick, and then at me. "Hey."

"I love your hair."

She wobbled on the rope, "Fuck," and adjusted her balance as the others made dramatic noises. She stepped quickly now, rushing to beat her fall, but even I could tell she'd never make it, much as I wanted to believe otherwise. She was moving too fast. She slipped from the rope about a metre away from the opposite tree.

The others laughed and clapped and cheered, and Todd declared, "Told you," to all who would listen, saving his grin for Suki who told him to fuck himself. She'd done better than anyone else.

"So far," said Kit, stepping up onto the rope and immediately stumbling off again on the other side, much to everyone's amusement. "That doesn't count!"

Suki came over to me and I had a moment of, oh shit, how do we do this, a hug, a handshake, what? She swept her hair back and exaggerated tossing it, a shampoo model, and said, "Part of my 'alternative' phase. You like it, then?"

"I love it."

I love.

"Sorry about that just now," I said. "I distracted you."

She put her hands on my arms, just below my shoulders. She looked at me for a moment, then came in to kiss me on each cheek. Afterward she opened her arms to the group at the rope. "These are my friends," she said. "And Todd."

Todd smiled like she'd complimented him. "You must be the hot doctor lady."

I've often wondered what Suki'd said about me prior to that meeting, and Todd probably would've told me if I'd asked, but I never did.

"Yeah, Todd," said Suki, "thanks for that." But she barely looked embarrassed at all. "Come on, I'll introduce you properly."

She took my hand to lead me to her friends and she held it the whole time we exchanged hellos and little bits of background. She smiled with me, and laughed with me, and by the end of that night I was hers forever.

You don't jump out of a plane: you drop. You hold the doorway and somehow you convince your brain that it's okay to let go, to pull yourself out of a perfectly good, fully functional airplane. You tuck in tight. You plummet. There's no better word for it. You might even experience a few moments of sensory overload while the mind tries to figure out what the fuck has just happened, sorting through all these new sensations while the whine of the plane fades and wind rushes up and all around you. Some people even black out for a moment. But your brain figures it out soon enough and maybe you scream because you're scared or because it's fun, maybe both. The wind pushes at your clothes and at your face and if your mouth's open then it rushes into there as well and flaps your cheeks. Your thoughts roar with the sound of your falling.

I'm falling in silence this time, feeling the fullness of the rush downward and thinking it's apt, thinking this is how I've been feeling for nearly a year now. I'm waiting to stabilise so the chute can get a good clean wind when I open up, but I don't know if I'll ever stabilise. Don't know if I'll ever open up again.

Below me: Kit, Måns, Cate. Kit's rolling, knees tucked to her chest to spin around her own axis, head over heels. Måns is spread wide, looking left and right. He has a GoPro mounted on his helmet and he's catching as much of the experience as he can because memories are all anybody ever has, something I wish I'd realised a lot sooner. And there's Cate, her arms and legs open wide in an X that marks the spot. Somewhere safe to land, maybe. Or maybe she's just a shooting star, bright and brief like all of us are. Not much more than a kiss in a jumpsuit.

I could lean, if I wanted to. Could tilt forward, streamlining myself, and choose to fall faster. I could urge the winds to take me closer.

Instead, I pull the cord to release my chute and force a greater distance between us.

⊸

"So there I am, bungee-jumping over crocodile-infested waters—"

"They weren't crocodile-infested."

Todd was standing to tell his story, *grand*standing, you could say, for the benefit of the new group we'd joined for the night. He was lit from below by the campfire that cast classic eerie shadows up his face. We all saw him scowl at the interruption, though.

"They bloody well were crocodile-infested, mate."

Måns shook his head. He exhaled smoke and said, "The crocodiles live there."

"Like I said."

Kit passed the joint up to Todd as if to calm him. "He means if they live there then it's not infested."

Todd puffed once, twice, and said, "Whatever," with a tight voice. "Smart-arse."

Of all of us, Todd had travelled the most. He had a world map outlined on his back, and he added a flag to the tattoo for every place he visited. There were a lot of flags. He'd done it all, and done it almost everywhere, and he had plenty of stories to prove it. I think that's one of the things Suki loved so much about him. His eagerness to cram as much as he could into life. Carpe the fucking diem, as she put it to him once. They'd kayaked the Congo River together, at the turbulent low end, and they'd gone BASE-jumping in Hong Kong, leaping illegally from the International Finance Centre. The Grand Canyon was the one big one Todd still hadn't done, the flag he most wanted to add to that atlas on his back, but he was caught between desperately wanting to thru-hike the canyon to completely avoiding it as too touristy. Never mind that more people have walked on the moon than have thru-hiked the GC.

"So there I am, bungee jumping over this, fucking, crocodile *residential area*, right? Fucking, croc central . . ."

I'd heard the story before, so I tuned it out to focus on Suki. She was looking into the flames of the campfire and I doubted she heard Todd's story either.

"You okay?"

Suki smiled. It was one of the gentle ones I'd grown to hate, a token gesture rather than one of her typically vibrant smiles. The fire was bright in her eyes, but it was only reflected there. Used to be they lit up with a light all of their own. They drew you to her, those eyes. Pulled you along for whatever wild ride she had planned next. Before meeting her, the craziest thing I'd done was go trampolining with my nephew, but since Suki there'd been plenty, starting with that first climb at Malham Cove. There'd been abseiling, zip wires, hand-gliding, skydiving, an awful attempt at surfing, and the whole time I felt like I was trying to catch up. It was exhilarating. *She* was exhilarating. Or she used to be. Those days near the end, she spent a lot more time in her own head, and I couldn't blame her for that, though I still did. Just a little.

"You remember the first time I came back to yours?" I asked her quietly while the others listened to Todd. It worked; I saw a proper Suki Smile. She leaned into me. Nudged me.

"*Yeah*, I do."

She was referring to the sex, but for me it had been a much bigger step than that. No adrenaline rush has ever come close to what I felt that night, stepping into that private space where she lived. There had been ropes everywhere, loops of it draped over furniture or coiled on the floor, with metal clasps and caribiners and hooks. I made some terrible joke about her being kinky. Then I saw the mountain bike held on a wall mount, the collapsed sail of a windsurf board leaning beside it like a bright limp shark fin. There were skis and a snowboard. In the ceiling, sitting across the beams, was a kayak and paddle. She was a cooped-up city girl in a tiny flat surrounded by all the things she enjoyed going elsewhere to use. It was overwhelming, seeing so much of her so clearly on display, and not in some pretentious way for others to appreciate: this was what she loved. What was familiar to her, the equilibrium she moved about in, was to me an exciting presentation of her personality, and it brought with it a lightness to my stomach, a shortness of breath.

She took my hand and led me to her bedroom. There was a helmet on the dresser next to her vanity mirror, a headlamp attached. She draped a vest over it and switched the headlamp on, then went back to the other room to turn the main light off.

"Sorry about all the mess," she said. "Romantic, hey?"

It its own way, it really was. The light shone back out from the mirror at an angle that diffused it. The décor here, if you ignored the safety gear and the wetsuit draped over a chair, was a nod to her Indian culture that she otherwise ignored. And the bed looked very comfortable.

"It's very comfortable," she said. I laughed at her mind-reading, and with nervousness, and because I had clearly been staring and waiting, expecting. She laughed with me and pulled me to the bed, and to her.

Afterward, hearts pounding, we'd talked about adrenaline.

Todd was trying to do the same now, in a roundabout way, but Todd's adrenaline-fuelled stories were always about Todd. Where he'd been, what he'd done, what he'd dared. Stories were what he told so he had something to hide behind.

"Look, do the crocodiles eat you in the end, or not?" someone asked.

"Hey, if you want stories about being eaten, you—"

"Don't you go there," Suki warned, and people laughed. I tried to, but I'd just seen my attempt to cheer her up surpassed by a crude joke.

Todd held up a hand to accept the warning. "Okay, where was I?"

"Heart hammering, blood pumping, something melodramatic like that."

Adrenaline does lead to an increased heart rate. There's an increase in blood pressure, too, thanks to the kidneys producing more renin, and the blood is redistributed to the muscles, increasing the power for muscular contraction and altering the body's metabolism to maximise glucose levels, all of it happening very quickly in anticipation of fight or flight. I remembered, when Suki and I had talked about it in bed, that I explained how fear was healthy in its own way, thinking I was being clever and talking about us, the excitement of a new relationship, but having no fucking clue what she was going through at the time and how scared she must have been.

"A lot of people think adrenaline is a kind of fear," she'd said, "like there's a good kind of fear, right? But the adrenaline is what you get when you say 'fuck you' to fear. That's what it is for me, anyway."

She used to say fear was subjective, that you could choose whether to be scared or not, but thinking back, I realise she was scared all the time and did whatever she could to shift it elsewhere. Fight or flight. You couldn't fight what she had, not really, and there's no running from it either, though she tried for a while. Not so much flight as falling at high speed.

"You okay?"

She wasn't, but it would be a long time before she told me. In the meantime, she would distract me.

"Are *you* scared?" she asked.

"What?"

"It's just . . . How did you put it? The airways to the lungs expand." She leaned closer; quickened her hand. "Or, to put it in normal language, you're breathing heavy."

I smiled. "Because of what you're doing right now."

"And your pupils have dilated."

"Because you're so fucking beautiful."

"Yeah," she said, slipping away from me, farther down the bed, "keep saying things like that . . ."

I did. I said things like that all the time, through all of that night and all the others after. It's just that, as it turned out, there weren't as many of them as either of us would have liked.

⊸⊸

Nylon and rope spews behind me, unravelling above, and suddenly the chute is forced full. On TV you'll see the body jerk upwards as if yanked by the parachute, but that's bullshit. I've seen it myself in some of Måns' films, but it's just the camera falling faster than what it's seeing. The slider slows the opening of the chute, and you get an intense deceleration, but that's it. A jolt. It's a little abrupt, but not severe.

Below me, one, two chutes blossom open. Three.

On TV, you also see people suspended gently beneath their parachutes, floating like fucking dandelion seeds in a breeze, but the truth is you're still falling and you're falling fast. You've got more control, and you're able to guide yourself by pulling on the toggles left and right, snaking long Ss in the sky, but you're still buffeted and tossed about by the wind. The lush green canopy of the jungle might look like some giant moth-eaten green blanket plumped up thick and soft, but it won't be. It'll be hard and sharp if we haven't timed this right, and we'll hit it with force. If we miss the clearing, we'll be shredded by the trees or jerked dead with a sudden neck-snap crack. We might all look pretty from down there, flowers falling slowly, but thousands of feet up it's a different story, and that's fine by all of us. That's the rush. The adrenaline. The reason why we do it. One of the reasons, anyway.

I can see a gap in the trees. And there, taking up most of the clearing, is a vast sinkhole. A cenote. Godzilla, we've been calling it, but it's Zotzil-aha or Zot-hilza, or something like that. Aligned with it, the ruins of a Mayan temple, a relatively new discovery far off the tourist trail. We'd all been to Chichén Itzá and marvelled at it, glad we'd missed the equinox when tourists descend on the place to watch the light snake its way down the pyramid, but it had still been a little too crowded for us. Godzilla was ideal. We'd look around the site then abseil down into the cenote. Todd had wanted to drop right into it, wipe away our primary sense for a moment, namely our sight, and plunge into sudden night for that extra rush. But there was daring and there was stupidity. We'd hit water in the dark and our next adrenaline rush would be trying not to drown in a tangle of parachute ropes.

I glance at Cate below, wondering how she'd liked her first proper freefall. At this altitude we had a whole sixty seconds of it. How's she feeling?

Is this how Suki used to feel, watching me?

The wind I'm falling in changes abruptly and a sharp riffle of the canopy overhead has me yanking hard left to compensate. Then the canopy flaps wildly as the wind suddenly drops and I plummet twenty feet faster than a moment ago before lurching into a steadier stream.

Todd falls past me. He twists around onto his back as he passes. His face shield is gone and he's so stricken with terror that I think I know what's happened, I'm sure I know: his chute has failed. And for a moment I see it's tangled around him somehow, and I'm thinking ditch it, cut it loose, pull your reserve, come on Todd. Except it's not his chute at all. Whatever it is wrapped around his legs, his waist, it slithers up and around him in a quick tight coil and a wing, a fucking *wing*, long and leathery and brightly feathered, unfurls from behind him briefly before snapping shut again against the wind.

"Todd!"

The wind snatches that away.

A head appears behind Todd, at the nape of his neck. I see only the squat shape of it, only for an instant. The dark colour. The open mouth. It snaps at him. Then a splash of something hot is on my face and I shut my eyes, twisting away. I wipe the blood away with my forearm as best as I can. Blink my eyes clear. I've arced away in my S shape but hurry to twist back and look behind, look down, look for where Todd falls. Something that's not his parachute unfolds around him, a mottled rainbow of colours spanning left and right, and just like that he's carried away out of sight on beating wings.

What the fuck? What the *fuck*? What the actual *FUCK?*

Coming in from the right, something too snake-like to be a bird, too bird-like to be a snake. It dives right into where Måns hangs suspended. Folds its wings away a moment before impact and strikes him like some scaly torpedo, disappearing beneath the canopy of his chute and snapping it sideways.

"Måns!"

He's carried away somewhere out of my sight. His chute has whipped free, some of the ropes severed, and drags behind him like a bright streamer.

There's no way he'll hear me, but I scream for him anyway.

⟜⟝

Måns collected trinkets wherever we went. Kit collected postcards, sending them home to herself as mementos, Todd collected tattoos, and Suki would pick up a rock, or some sand, or a shell, something like that. She had jars filled with these bits and pieces. We all had our things. For Måns, it was the trinkets, and the local stories.

Two nights ago, we'd been sitting around the fire, listening to it pop and crackle, while behind it, somewhere in the dark, the sea hushed up the sand and washed it away. Måns had pulled a pendant out from under his shirt. He held it up to us, as much as the length of cord would allow, and said, "Look at this, eh?" before ducking out of the loop to pass the necklace around.

It was a wooden carving, impressively intricate, about the size of a pen. A nearly-naked man stood in front of a column or cylinder. He was wearing what I thought was a feathered headdress, wonderfully detailed, and part of it had a long beak coming down over the head. But I noticed, too, talons at either side of the figure's waist and turning the pendant saw a scaled tail running down from the head and snaking around the column. A very elaborate headdress, then, I thought. Or some weird lizard-bird thing standing behind him. In which case the beak wasn't decorative at all. It was coming down to scrape at the face and throat of the man, talons ready to rip at the stomach.

"What the hell, Måns?"

"Grim, huh? Bit weird."

"Just a bit." I passed it on.

"There were these Mayan heroes—"

"Oh, here we go," said Todd, settling back into the sand. "Story time."

"They were twins," Måns said. "These heroes. And they were put in a cave filled with bats."

"Why?"

Måns shrugged. "Punishment for something, probably."

"What were their names?" Cate asked. She was already pretty good with the banter. For some reason I liked her a little less for that. Or maybe I liked everyone else a little less for letting her fit in so easily. I don't know.

"Come on, guys, just let me tell it."

We pretended like we were doing him a favour, but the truth was if it wasn't for Måns our only local knowledge would be geographical and alcoholic, nothing cultural. He was the one who told us about Chaak and other gods, the Quetzalcoatl, the ancient Aztec sacrifices. All the fun stuff.

"These two brothers," he said, turning to Cate to add, "whose names I've forgotten because they're probably unpronounceable with lots of Qs and Xs and Zs, they were put in a cave with these creatures called Camazotz and—"

"I thought you said bats?"

"These are like bats. Camazotzare are, like, bat creatures. Or bat-gods, or something."

"You remember that name, then?" Todd said.

Cate laughed. Måns gave them both the finger.

"They have these noses, these long snouts, like blades. Like a beak. And these giant leathery feathery wings. They're like birds and bats mixed together. Flying around in the dark of the cave."

Måns lunged at us all in turn around the fire and we humoured him with shrieks and flinches. I clutched playfully at Cate in mock-fright, and perhaps lingered longer than I should have afterward. She felt good.

"So to get away from these Camazotz, the bat-things, these brothers hid inside their blowguns—"

"But—"

Måns silenced Todd with a warning glare, exaggerated into cartoon proportions. "They hid," he said again. "Inside their blowguns." He waited, but there were no more interruptions. "And the whole time, these creatures tried to attack them while they hid inside, all through the night, until, at dawn . . . nothing. Not a sound. So one of the brothers looked to see if it was safe."

Cate said, "I'm guessing it wasn't."

"As soon as he poked his head out . . ." Måns looked around, choosing someone, and lunged at me suddenly, clapping his hand together at my face. "No more head!"

"Well that *does* sound terrible."

Cate grinned at me. I smiled back, politely. Quick and then gone. I've never been very good at flirting, except with Suki. Suki was the queen of flirting, pursuing it with the same eagerness for new experience as she did her shots of adrenaline. It made me worry about losing her, the same way I worried about slipping off a cliff face and smashing myself on rocks, or the way I worried about drowning upside down in a capsized kayak. Which is to say, I was always careful to pay attention, just like she taught me. Never become blasé, because complacency could end everything. It was how accidents happened. "Always be, like, super aware of where you are and what you're doing at all times. Live in the moment," she told me, "be right there, in it, all the time." So that's what I did with her. Seized every moment I could until suddenly she was never there at all.

"It's hollow," said Kit. She was holding the pendant horizontally to the fire. She put it to her mouth.

"It's a whistle," Måns said.

"It's a blowgun." Kit mimed shooting it at him and he collapsed back into the sand.

"They've got a lot of bats here," Todd said. Kit feigned a blowgun shot at him as well and he clasped it to his chest with a groan of pain. "Makes sense that they'll tell stories about them. Southern Mexico, Bolivia, Brazil, Paraguay even, and Argentina. All these bats."

"Vampires?"

"Meat-eaters."

"When the fuck did you suddenly become David Attenborough?" It was the sort of thing Suki would've said, and I was glad to have said it because of how he laughed.

"I got to talking to some guy and he said as soon as the sun goes down, the whole sky around the Yucatán Peninsula comes alive with bats. Regular ones, vampire ones, these meat-eater ones. All of them out to feed. He was probably exaggerating, trying to sound smart or scary of something. He was probably coming on to me. But yeah. Lots of bats."

Måns had his pendant back. He gave it a long look and said, "Pretty fucked-up bat," and ducked into the loop of its leather cord, tucking the carving back under his shirt.

"Hey," said Kit, rummaging in her bag, "I've got one for you. Why did the Mexican push his wife off the cliff?" She produced a bottle for her punch line and we all cried, "Tequila!" and cheered.

"Okay, I have a story," Cate said.

Everybody settled into quiet for her because, well, she was new. There was no getting around that fact, although we all did a pretty good job of pretending otherwise. I saw Kit and Todd share a look and I thought, don't fuck this up Cate. You've just volunteered for an early make-or-break moment, created an audition for yourself, and the spotlight is bright on you right now. We're all looking, and we're all listening. Don't try too hard, but do try.

"I got this from some tourist in—"

"Tourist? There are no tourists out this way, just people like us." Todd glanced at me and I knew right then he was judging her as hard as I was, and testing her a bit, but mainly hoping she'd pass. I think.

"Those are the tourists I mean. The extreme sports kind. Anyway, out here, tourist is just another word for foreigner, right?"

There was some agreement.

"Well, some of these people, they disappear. Nothing all that unusual, I suppose, when many of them are a little off the radar anyway, and doing crazy shit like jumping out of airplanes or swimming with crocodiles or whatever. People fall, they drown, get eaten."

"This is one of those cheery stories, yeah?" Kit said, passing the bottle.

"I can add kittens and lollipops if you like?"

She was doing well.

"Anyway, if they just disappeared, that would be one thing. But sometimes they'd turn up again in crazy places. The bodies of white-water rafters found in the treetops, miles from the river they disappeared from. Skydivers found years later in cenotes, their chutes still packed. Things like that. This one group, they were climbing, although fuck knows what because there aren't many mountains around here, maybe it was one of the ruins or something? Whatever. Three of them were climbing, one of them wasn't. The climbers all vanished. The one on the ground, he heard them scream but that was all. By the time he got to where they'd secured their lines, there was nothing, not even rope. They had a guide with them, some local boy, but all he could do was say, '*¡Lo vi! ¡Lo vi!*' I saw it! I saw it! Pointing up. But there was nothing. No one. They were all there one minute, and the next minute—" She clicked her fingers. "Gone. Just like that."

I knew exactly what she meant.

"There was a full-on search, but nobody found them for days. When the bodies eventually did turn up, they were ten miles away. And all of them were cut open."

"Cut open," Todd said.

Cate nodded. She made a slashing motion across her abdomen. "Same for all the others that turned up, the kayakers and the skydivers. Their kidneys, gone."

There was some groaning at this, a collective sigh of exhalation.

"The black market thing? Selling organs?" said Kit. "Basic urban myth stuff."

"I know, I know," Cate said, "but these weren't clean excisions or anything. More brutal. Ragged." She settled back, a little deflated. "From what I heard."

"Wieslander's bats got 'em," Todd said, and Måns swooped at her, screeching while we laughed.

"It's interesting," I said. "The kidneys are where you'll find the adrenal glands."

I suddenly had their full attention. They liked it when I went doctor on them. Sometimes because of the gruesome stories, sometimes for the more exotic ones, like how the parasite *toxoplasma gondi* can make its host take greater risks, they loved that one. Humans can catch it from cats, but cats pass it to each other through rats—an infected rat becomes reckless, daring, gets caught and eaten and that's that: toxo-cat. A cautionary tale if ever I heard one. They also liked to be reminded that as a doctor I could patch them up pretty good if I had to (and I often had to). But I wasn't looking to reassure them right now.

"Yeah," I said. "The adrenal medulla. And from the sounds of it, the victims all had one thing in common—apart from the missing kidneys . . ." I paused just enough to make it dramatic. "They were adrenaline junkies. Like us."

I watched as each glanced at the other, Todd eventually making an ominous "*oooh*" noise. Cate smiled her gratitude at me, but I hadn't really done anything. Whatever fixing her story needed had been achieved by Todd and Måns joking about bats. She was part of the group now, and she was smiling at me, and I was okay with that.

-o-

Below me, Cate is spinning. Whatever's happened to her, I missed it, but her chute is tattered and her body swings around beneath it. An occasional flash of colour suggests one of the things is on her, too, or close by; she doesn't seem to be entwined yet, but there's an irregularity to her spinning that suggests something more than momentum has her moving like that. One of the creature's wings is beating while the other is held upright, caught in the ropes of her partially ruined parachute. Some sort of tail lashes around as if to balance or steer and—

I'm hit hard in the chest. It knocks me swinging in a direction that deifies that of my falling. I feel a sharp line of pain in my thigh as something clawed takes hold there, and suddenly I'm wrapped about the leg. A muscular pulse and the coils spread upward, enveloping my abdomen. A head rises to look up at me from there. It is both snake-like and bat, squat-faced but with fangs, sabre-toothed and red-fleshed where its mouth opens. The fangs are so close together as to be almost one tooth, like a curve of beak. It tilts its head in an effort to sink these into the softest part of my body, uncoiling slightly to allow it more movement.

Somehow, I get my hands under its jaw. The flesh is scaled but it feels leathery, with ridges to hold onto as I try to redirect its attack, shoving its face away from my body. Two monstrous wings unfold and beat . . . beat . . . beat, controlling our descent. I flail with the sudden shift in direction and speed. With one leg still free, I kick at the creature wrapped around my other. With my elbow I smash at its puckered snout before grabbing at what I can find of the nearest wing. I slap at it, push at muscle and pull at scales, at feathers, but it constricts tighter. The wings fold around me with the smell of something wet and dark, and something snags at my back, yanks at the pack I wear.

This close to its body, I can smell meat, alley-meat, something spoiled. I'm too close to strike it now, arms crushed to my chest. But I can reach the cut-away. I yank at the handle on my harness and detach the main chute. I'm not thinking of how it might help, only that it has to.

And it does.

Whether it's caught in the main chute, or simply surprised by the sudden change of circumstances, the creature parts from me at the same instant I jettison the main parachute, one claw raking a line of pain across my abdomen. I see the thing only in snatched glimpses as I spin, falling. Its wings are open at full span to arrest or maybe steer its descent as I plummet. My chute flutters away above us both.

I turn from the sight. Lean myself into a headfirst vertical arrow, streamlining my fall to get away. To get to Cate.

I can see someone else below me. Whoever it is, they're being tossed from one creature to another like a toy, parachute nothing more than a tangle of torn colours pulled after them. They spin spread-eagled, and even from this distance I see, or imagine I see, lashes of blood thrown out from the body. Because that's all they are, now. A body. That, or they've passed out.

I think it's Måns.

It is Måns. I recognise the colours of his jumpsuit.

The flying snake things with the bat faces, they're strikingly colourful from above. The wings are a combination of blue, red, orange, like twin skies at twilight. They're not beautiful, I've seen too much to think that, and the length of body that whips around denies them the majesty of birds. The sound they make is a high-pitched screech but short, like the quick scrape cutlery can make on a plate, only louder.

I don't dare look above to the one that had me moments ago. I've no doubt that it pursues, or readies itself to, spiralling in or diving on my fall. I'm flooded with adrenaline—seeing Todd, the attacks, falling without my chute—and I keep thinking of that story, that stupid fucking story, and I'm thinking that'll make me a tasty breakfast for them, all that adrenaline, and I'm thinking that's what we'll all be now, nameless victims in a tale told with beers around a fire, and I'm thinking I'm going to die, we're all going to die. Even as my heart tells me not yet, not right now.

I've got a reserve chute. I can control this descent.

I'm gaining on Cate. I am controlling this descent.

Above me, behind, something makes a series of shrill sounds. A shriek of noise. A stuttered *reek-reek-reek-reek*, each syllable louder than the last.

I'm not going to fucking die. I can't die. Not yet.

⊸o⊷

"You hear a lot of near-death experience stories doing the adrenaline-junkie stuff," Suki told me once. We were in bed, which was where we spent a lot of our time when we weren't pursuing some sort of outdoor adventure. Not always for the sex, you understand, but the intimacy. It was our private place, our safest space, where the rest of the world disappeared and there was only us.

"I bet," I said. "Near-death experience stories, and actual real-death experience stories, too, no doubt."

"Fair enough. That's true. But I'm talking about the whole, 'life flashing before your eyes' moment. You believe in those?"

"I'm not sure. You?"

For a moment, I had forgotten about her cancer. I was thinking of rock climbing and freefalling and BASE jumping and all the other crazy shit she'd done and continued to do. She could tell I'd forgotten, or rather she could tell as soon as I remembered—which was almost immediately—because she kissed my shoulder. "It's okay," she said.

"Suki."

She kissed my neck and then leaned over to kiss my mouth. She'd told me about the cancer a month or so prior to this conversation, but any time I tried to talk about it she kissed me to close the subject before it could begin.

We were only allowed to talk about it on her terms, which had seemed fair at first but less so as time went by.

"When the doctor first told me," she said, "I had something like one of those near-death things, only instead of seeing my life so far flash before me in a series of snapshots or whatever, it was more like a flash forward. I saw every little thing I hadn't done yet, it felt like. Every part of the life I had left to live, if only I could've lived it. The things I could've done if I'd been brave enough. When I realised I was thinking in the past tense, like my life was over already, I decided, fuck it. I'll do it all."

"Carpe the fucking diem."

She nodded against me. "Damn right. Carpe the fucking diem. I started taking greater risks, travelling farther abroad to try things, racking up the credit card bills. But it changed the nature of it for me. I thought it would be like, I dunno, more of a 'fuck you' to death or something, right? But it was weird. First time I jumped out of a plane after getting the shitty news, I kept thinking of that Tom Petty song. Fucking, 'Free Fallin'" Just the chorus, over and over."

"I don't know it."

She sang, dramatically grabbing at the air above us and pulling it down to her face with, "Because I'm freeeeeee . . . Free fallllling."

I laughed a lot at the abruptness of that. The kind of laugh that leaves you breathless. She watched me, smiling.

"You know, that one."

"No, I don't know, you'll have to sing it again."

She pushed me lightly. "I felt it, you know? Free. Rushing towards something that would kill me, i.e. the ground, but having control enough to stop that from happening, right? Like, I'm the one that says, that's enough now, let's slow it down and live for a bit longer. Up in the clouds. Yank the cord and all is well." Her lip trembled. Her chin. "Except when I land I'll still have cancer."

"Baby."

"The ultimate fucking c-word, right?" she said, and she was crying now. "What a cunt of a disease."

"Baby, hey. I'm here."

"I *know*, and that makes it even worse, because now I've got so much more I want to live for, and it's not *fair*. I've only just met you."

I held her for a long time, and wiped away tears, kissed away others.

Eventually she settled, and the first thing she said was, "You know, it's fucked up, but if it wasn't for that c-word bitch fucker, I never would've even met you."

I was stroking her hair by this point, her beautiful now-blue hair, but I stopped at that.

"Yeah," she said, and sniffed. "Exactly. Fucked up, right?"

"God, then I wish you'd never met me."

She sat up then, suddenly, and said, "No. No fucking way, don't wish that. Not ever."

"Are you angry?"

"Yes I'm fucking angry. You're too fucking perfect for me to ever wish I never met you, okay? I'm so stupidly happy."

"I thought you were angry."

"Fuck off."

"I can't take your anger seriously when you're naked."

"Shut up, I'm trying to be serious. And you know what else? You're too perfect to be wasted on just me, so when I'm gone—"

"That's it, this conversation is over."

"No. When I'm gone—"

"Come here."

I tried to kiss her, pulling myself up to her, pulling her down to me, but she shook me off.

"I'm going to be gone, that's just medical fact, doc, and you need to find someone else quick before your beautiful body gets all old and decrepit."

"Suki—"

"I mean it." She relaxed, and she touched my cheek, and she said again, "I mean it. You're too good to go to waste. Someone else should get to experience you like I have. Fall for you. And you for her. Promise me."

"Suki, I'm not—"

"If you don't promise, I'll end things right now."

"No you won't."

She didn't say anything. She just held my stare. And I realised, with absolute certainty, that she wasn't kidding.

"All right. I promise."

"Okay," she said. "Okay. Good." She laid back down beside me. "That's good." She nestled close, resting one arm across my chest, and kissed my shoulder. My neck. My ear. "If she's too pretty, I'll haunt you."

I wanted to make her promise, but all I did was kiss her.

I'm hurtling towards Cate. It isn't going to be graceful, like with a team jump, gliding towards each other to hold hands. I don't even know if Cate's done one of those, and she won't have seen me coming anyway, so she can't prepare for it. Her chute's open, but only partially effective, damaged as it is. I'm heading right for her.

For all I know, there's something heading right for me, as well.

Closer, I can see the creature on Cate is as much caught around the ropes of her parachute as it is around her. One wing buffets them both back and forth, the other tugs and drags at the chute, claws it with talons.

Cate's conscious. She's kicking at the length of tail or scaled body that curls first one way and then the other, whipping around her as the thing struggles to free itself.

I tilt into a more horizontal position. Doing it slowly. I even sweep at the air like I'm swimming, for all the good that does. I'm only going to get one shot at this, and after that we're both on our own.

"Cate!"

It's pointless, but I scream it anyway.

She's still moving erratically, but for a moment it looks like I'm going to fall clear of her chute and manage to latch onto her. It doesn't go that way. I strike a taut edge of her canopy and am engulfed by it. Briefly. It whips over me with burning speed as I fall past, though I've collapsed it enough that Cate drops quicker for a moment. A suspension line slices the inside of my wrist and face but then I hit her and grab her, and grab something of the creature, too. I yank them with me before Cate's parachute takes a fuller shape again and by then I'm holding her suit, her harness, I think a handful of her skin as well. The creature slips away from her body, tearing as it goes. She screams. She tries to buck me off, too, still screaming, and panicked.

"It's me! It's me!"

Above, still caught in her ropes, shaking us around like marionettes, is the fucking Camazotz or Quetzalcoatl or whatever the hell is fighting to free its wing.

I grab at Cate's helmet, not too softly, and pull her to face me. "The cut-away!"

She screams again, this time in surprise, in recognition. Her eyes are cartoon-wide, pupils so dilated there's almost no colour, only blackness.

"Your cut-away! Pull it!"

She nods.

I tighten my already white-knuckled grip on her.

She pulls the cut-away and clutches at me simultaneously. The lines fly free of her, seem to whip up above us. I look up after them to see the creature become more tangled in its attempts to escape. But there's no joy to be felt in that: another is bearing down on us in a dive. Its serpentine body is straight. Its wings are folded back like dart-flights. It comes at us with its mouth open wide, twin fangs bared.

"Hold on to me!"

She's got handfuls of my clothing and harness like we're about to fight. I wrap my legs around her like we're about to do something else. "Don't let go!"

I pull my reserve chute. Immediately as it deploys, I'm freeing my hook-knife. I've never had to use it before. I pray it's sharp enough to do the job quickly; a reserve chute doesn't have a cut-away.

I slash at the lines just as the chute puffs full, setting it free to envelope the fucker coming at us. The thing streams past us like a fiery comet, a bulk of red nylon and a thrashing tail.

Cate and I are freefalling again. I'm holding onto her like my life depends on it because it really fucking does.

"You need to pull your reserve," I tell Cate, yelling into her ear, "but not yet."

She nods and reaches for it.

"Not yet!"

She nods again, just holds her hand ready. Her other is holding onto me. She's wrapped some of my harness into her fist. I still have my legs around her. I've got one arm around her, too, wedged between her back and her pack. The other I've forced under the harness at her front so that the straps cross my forearm and I'm able to hold a handful of her clothing. I can't be separated from her. Cate's reserve is all we have.

But she can't release it too soon. We're turning, rolling. She can't release the chute until we can hold a decent position. Also, releasing it will slow us down, make us easy targets. We'll need to alter our course, too, if we're going to make the clearing and not smash ourselves into the trees. That'll slow us down, as well. She needs to wait as late as possible.

I worry about the AAD; the Automatic Activation Device automatically opens the reserve chute at a pre-set altitude if the descent rate exceeds a certain pre-set speed. We must be nearing those parameters.

I catch glimpses all around us. Shapes in the air. Colours that are the bat-snake things, colours that are torn chutes and limp jumpsuits. My friends. Below, the lush green carpet of jungle, coming up at fast. The clearing, with its ancient stone. I want to point it out to Cate but with no chute of my own I'm too scared to let go for that kind of movement.

"As soon as we land, run for the rainforest!"

I can't tell if she's heard me.

"We'll get cover from the rainforest!"

The wind is trying to wrench us apart, whipping our hair around, ruffling our clothes, sharp and loud. Cate's hand, the one pressed closed to her chest for the release pull, finds mine and grips it hard without forcing it away from where it clutches at her. She nods at me.

Even hurtling towards the ground with weird monsters in pursuit, the world turning topsy-turvy around us, it's a strangely intimate moment. I think, yeah. I can do this again. I'm sorry, Suki. And thank you, Suki.

Then there's a *beep-beep-beep* and a sudden unravelling and Cate's reserve chute releases.

"Hold on!"

I'm not sure which of us yells it. I think maybe we both do.

Above, the parachute billows open and fills. It's a good, clean deployment. We're blind to any dangers directly above us, though.

Can't think about that.

Cate begins to guide us. No long, snaking S moves, but quick pulls that correct and re-correct our course in short circles. I can't tell if it's calculated or panicked. Sometimes there are trees beneath our feet. Sometimes the ruins. A short distance away I can see another gap in the trees and the dark open pit of the cenote.

Drifting across the jungle canopy, caught in a breeze, are the ragged remains of someone's parachute. It's snagged on something, or it's still tethered to someone, and before I can help myself I'm straining to see who, turning my head each time Cate changes our course, moving to see around her without lessening my grip. If there's a body, it's caught in the lower branches somewhere.

Above, the shrieking screech of one of the creatures coming at us from a blind spot. There's a moment I think I see it in silhouette through the chute.

The ruins are right there. Right fucking there.

The creature hits our parachute, claws it into a bunch of nylon and lines, and pulls us away with it. Yanks us off course at the last moment.

Cate gives a short scream. I'm wrenched along with her.

For an awful moment it looks like our legs are going to get dragged through the treetops, but they're not as close as that and suddenly the trees are gone altogether. We're still dropping fast.

"Oh, shit!"

We pass across the gaping hole of the cenote, then swing down into it. Collide into the side of the opening. Cate takes the brunt of it across her shoulders and grunts with the impact. We smash our heads together with the force of it, too, and I'm shaken loose. Thrown from Cate to grab at the ground's edge, at air, at nothing.

I'm falling again, this time into the dark gloom of the cavern. Cate's legs kick for a moment and are gone, dragged out of the light above, out of my sight.

Looking up, I tumble into icy water, back first. The sudden cold dark closes over me and pulls me down, farther down, settling over and around me and closing out everything else and this, I realise, is what death feels like.

We were going to go to China. That was the plan. A last trip together, climbing and caving, mostly.

"I'll show you Crown Cave, which is all handrails and elevators, now, probably, but after that we'll see some proper caves."

Suki had been excited about the trip. She'd been several times already, but she loved the place. China has a huge concentration of karst, which makes a decent playground of rock columns and sinkholes and rivers that just disappear into nothing, swallowed up by the ground. She wanted to show me The Stone Forest, a vast area of limestone eroded into a variety of column formations with beautiful names like 'stone singing praise to the sun' and 'tiger roaring at hawks', things like that. Geographical poetry.

"Karst areas hold loads of chi," Suki had told me. "You know, life energy."

Suki loved all that spiritual stuff. A lot of travellers do, I've noticed. Maybe they're more open to other possibilities, having seen more of the world and accepted their own very small part in it. Near the end, as the cancer took a firmer hold on her, tightening its skeletal grip around her organs, so she grasped harder at a range of religious beliefs. Some she'd been brought up with, others she'd picked up on her travels the same way Todd collected tattoos. She liked to point out that there was plenty of weird shit out there that no one knew or noticed, whatever my science might say. *My* science. She pulled away from me at the end, you see. Only a little, but it hurt. I understood it, though. I represented those who couldn't help her. And she didn't want me diagnosing her, seeing her only as someone to be cured. She didn't like that I would know how hopeless it all was, or that I would pretend otherwise for both of our sakes.

But China, with its wonderful caves and all its life force, all its glorious chi, never happened.

You know what they worship in Mexico? Death.

⊸o⊷

I see a light. A tunnel of dark, and a circle of light. I reach for it, pull at it. Chop my legs back and forth and sweep my arms to get to it. I pull. I kick. And with a sudden gasp of air, I'm there. Inhaling lungfuls of breath, sucking up my own echo, head back and arms splashing to stay above water.

The cenote is deep. The few I'd seen already were tourist spots, with steps carved into them, or laid with wooden boards and rope rails. This one, though, is natural and untampered. Above—far above—is a circle of morning light surrounded by stalactites. The walls around me are twisted thick with the roots of the surrounding rainforest.

I swim for them. I unclasp my harness and refasten it around one of the lower roots, freeing my hands so I can pat down my body, checking for injuries. The lacerations on my wrist and face are minor, but the gash across my abdomen feels serious. I fumble for my headlamp; the LED light will give me about 150 feet of clear sight. Only it doesn't work. I can feel that the helmet is cracked right through, too, probably from when Cate and I hit each other. I leave it on, though. If nothing else, it will help keep my hair out of the way.

I feel lightheaded, as if simply acknowledging the possibility of a head injury has created one, made me aware of a concussion.

I want to rest. Sleep.

"Can't, baby. You've gotta climb."

"Suki."

She's treading water, looking around at the walls. Looking for decent handholds. Suki used to free solo, climbing with nothing but rock shoes and a bag of chalk, daring the world to kill her. Something like this would be easy for her. I'd seen her dancing across rock faces, leaping from one outcrop to another like she's playing fucking hopscotch.

Not me, though.

"They used to throw people into these as sacrifices," I tell her.

"That's nice."

She turns a circle, looking for the easiest route.

"Cenotes were home to the ancient Mayan rain god, Chaak. Or Chuck, or someone. He was very important to the Mayan people because he was a rain god. He poured the rain from jars he smashed to make thunder. I don't know how I know this."

"Måns told you."

"Mm. That's right. He also told me that cenotes are entrances to the underworld."

She glances at me, but that's all.

"Yeah. An open mouth that devours the living, that was how he put it. And you know what else he said? He said, sometimes it spits out the dead."

"You believe that?"

I sigh. "There's some weird shit out there."

"Karstic rock, doc. It sucks the rain down to groundwater level. Cenotes are where the Mayans got their drinking water, that's all."

"Karstic. Like, with all the chi?"

"Exactly. Now come on, climb."

Sunlight angles in from above. It holds Suki like a spotlight.

"I just want to rest for a minute."

"You can't." She slicks her hair back in the water. "Come on. Jam your hand into whatever crack you can find."

I smile, remembering how she'd made that into an innuendo before. She doesn't smile back, though, not this time. She points up, and I remember the guy in the story, '*¡Lo vi! ¡Lo vi!* I saw it! I saw it!'

"You're not here. I'm seeing you, but you're not here. You left me."

"Did I?"

I've hit my head. That's what this is.

"Cate's up there, and she needs you."

But I'm already unclipping my harness from the root that had been supporting me. I pull myself upward with one arm and reach with the other. Taking hold.

"Yes. You can do it."

I look up at where the sunlight of a new day forms a circle far above me and I think, carpe diem. Carpe the fucking diem. I try not to remember what happened when one of the twins poked their head out of the blowpipe.

And suddenly there's Suki, leaning out of the light, offering her hand.

Below me, the water of the cenote is empty, but I hear her voice down there. "She's pretty."

From above comes my name, and I look again to see it's not Suki silhouetted against the daylight but Cate. She's lowering the lines from her parachute.

I grab for handhold after handhold, eager to reach her.

Eager to climb out of the dark.

WATCHING

TIM LEES

I follow Carmen up the stairs.

There's a sweetish, sickly smell comes off him, like bad fruit, and it strikes me, if I'm smelling that, there must be tiny molecules of Carmen drifting through the air between us, little pieces of him, filling up my nose, my lungs.

His dirt, his sweat, his stink.

What's worse, I get the feeling that he knows I'm thinking this, because we reach the landing and he swivels round and grins at me, his teeth all worn to stumps.

I don't grin back.

Carmen wears earrings and a long, grey braid, a worn-out leather jacket, like some geriatric rock star.

Carmen thinks he's cool. He thinks I worship him.

He's wrong, both counts.

He slips the keys from out of his pocket, swings them on the lanyard. Counts to the fifth door. There's a stale, locked-in heat, a stink of bad things here. I think I should just turn away. This is the last place I can do it, the final chance. Just shake my head, turn around and go, never come back.

I think about it, think hard, those few seconds, so hard it almost seems that I could really do it. But he puts the key into the lock, and looks at me. His eyes are slitted now, his fever squeezed down to a cold, hard glare.

I'm here.

He turns the key.

⊸

The boy's waiting inside. But he doesn't know he's waiting. Doesn't know what's still ahead.

Carmen looks at me, says, "There," and, "See," and, "Don't tell me you're different. Don't tell me you're clean."

Except I am.

I watch. It's all I ever do. I don't even take pictures, bar that time he put the camera in my hands and made me. All I do is watch. That's all.

⊸

The boy is small and thin, with short, red hair. Cheeks and eyes all coloured up from crying. Pale around the flush, all pink and white.

Still fresh.

It's strange, seeing him like this, still human, still a person, full of thoughts and feelings and ideas.

That's going to change.

His fingers twitch. They scrabble at his thigh. A sound leaks through his teeth, the barest, briefest sob, and *whump!* Carmen hits out, knocks him sideways, right across the floor. He's quiet, after that. He's learned.

Always the same. Their voices are the first to go. He won't last long, this one, I know.

Carmen chews his braid. His face is slick with sweat.

He eyes the kid, looking to wind him up a little, just before we start. He turns, pretending he's lost interest, taps his foot, hums tunelessly a while. Then spins, lunges, roars out, "Yaaar!" and the boy jerks back, pulls his knees up, shakes his head in fear.

I see his spirit seeping out, hanging off him, loose and empty.

He's gone already. He just doesn't know it yet.

⊸

We took the room last year. Docherty's idea. The best ideas are Docherty's. He spent a month, checking the place out. Checking the neighbours. Winos, derelicts and welfare dregs. Another month for soundproofing. No-one can hear. It's easy, really. We could do it anywhere, in any town, in any city in the world. Who'd ever know?

⊸o⊷

You get a little pop, sometimes, a little sound, the moment that the spirit goes. A cork out of a bottle. I wait for that. I watch the way their eyes get wide, their hands reach out, grasping for a thing they never even thought they had. All they know is something's gone, something they can't get back.

I watch it all.

Remembering.

⊸o⊷

Come here come here come here. Come cuddle with your Uncle Rigsy, hey?

I think I see him sometimes. On the street, or in the subway train. For two, three seconds I'll be sure it's him, then realise the man I'm seeing can't be more than forty, fifty at most, and Uncle Rigsy is old, if he's alive at all. A white-haired, fat old man. Or shrivelled, eaten up inside, the way they get sometimes. It's only in my head he doesn't change.

Come here come here come here.

I watch. That's all I do.

⊸o⊷

We look for boys. Lost boys, loner boys. Boys out on the edge of things. Boys who want to fit but never will.

They cheer the team, and maybe do it louder, bolder, bigger than anyone, trying to prove they're part of things. Maybe they love their mums and dads, or think they do. But under that, there's emptiness. A hole. You learn to see the signs, that little split-second delay, while they work out what they're meant to do.

Shifting. Nervous. Always looking round, wondering if they got it right.

It's never who you think it's going to be. It's not the slutty convent girl, it's not the kid runs weed for bigger boys. It's never them.

It's the quiet ones. The ones that no-one sees, there and not-there, both at once.

I dream about them sometimes. Like I'm trying to cross a river, and their faces are like stepping stones. They never make a sound, they barely even flinch. But in the dream, I know them, and I move from face to face, each face a life, each life now long, long gone. And I never reach the other side, no matter how I try. I get closer and closer, and I think I'll get there, always. But I never do.

⟜○⟝

With Rigsy it was different. Trips to the pier, the big wheel where we rode and then he'd push his liquor face at mine and hold me so I wouldn't fall. Ice cream and elephant ears and cotton candy. There were marks on his hands. White lines, all over. Scars. Scars like little ridges, scars that you could see and feel. Then his mouth pressed to my skin. The rocking. Filling me. His body, huge, his belly coarse with fur like matting, how it puckered and the flesh would fold in on itself. *Who's Uncle Rigsy's little boy? Who's Uncle Rigsy's little man?*

The shadows on the ceiling. Dizzy. Turning. Sick now, tumbling like an acrobat, and something breaks inside me and I tear like paper. I hold myself, trying to hold myself inside myself.

Old Uncle Rigsy.

Dead or else in jail by now, I guess. I think I see him sometimes, but I don't, I only think I do.

His breath, his sigh.

The way he'd blow the air out through his lips.

Breath like a fart.

⟜○⟝

Now Docherty's arrived. Grey suit, smart shiny shoes, clean blue shirt. Docherty works for the city. Cool, respectable. Very polite. He looks around, sees Carmen, guessing he's already had a taste. He looks at me. He's ready. I could leave. I could, but still I don't. I can always leave. Any time. I never do. I sit down on the stool next to the kitchen counter. Carmen rolls a joint. There's a stink of petrol from his lighter, then the sweet aroma of the weed, and he and Docherty just pass it back and forth. Carmen says, "Shit," and shakes his head. You almost think he'll let the poor kid go, only he won't. We all know that.

⟜○⟝

The boy has wrestling books. They're in his bag. The weirdest thing. Three, four big books, library books, filled with pictures of these heavy, angry-looking guys: the Blade, Mysterio, Brock Bennar, Underworld. Pictures of supermen, with heavy, swollen muscles, iron jaws. Like that's the body he was looking for, the body he was wanting to grow into, and I picture him, all lonely in his room, straining to do push-ups, or bench-pressing some big encyclopaedia or something. Dreaming of the day he'll stroll back into school and kick that bully's ass, oh yes he will, oh yes, yes yes!

That's never going to happen now.

⊸

I get a little high from off the weed. I feel the sweat go running down my neck except it doesn't feel like sweat, it's like some animal that's slipped inside my shirt, and I don't try to move or swat it out, I let it run. Docherty goes over and he sits beside the boy. He's talking very quietly. He wants the boy to smoke a cigarette with him. The boy says no, but he watches while Docherty shows how its done, letting the smoke drift from his lips then, whoosh! sucking it all back in. Docherty's lips are full and fleshy, purple in the dim light, his mouth looks like some big, fat, rubber sucker, swelling and shrinking as he breathes. A button's gone from off his cuff. It doesn't matter. Tonight, he'll get exactly what he wants. The boy trusts Docherty. Docherty's not hit him, scared him, or done anything that's bad. He's calm and quiet. He knows to save it up, to spin it out, and wait.

The boy asks when we're going to let him go.

"Soon," says Docherty. "Very soon."

⊸

Carmen, another joint half-rolled. The sweet smell rising off him. Ferret eyes, head thrust forward, ugly and impatient now. "Come on, come on!" under his breath.

But Docherty won't rush. He's slow and gentle. That's how he likes it. Puts his arm around the soft, pale flesh. The boy is like a ghost in his embrace. Docherty's voice, soft and lonely, like a lullaby, the memory of a lullaby. The boy looks half-asleep. He only shivers slightly at the start, as Docherty takes out his knife and starts to peel him, gently, delicately, comforting him: "Hush now. Soon be over. Soon be done." It's fascinating, watching it, hearing the silence. That heavy, heavy silence. Like a single word could shatter it, deafen us all.

I only watch. That's all I ever do.

But I remember how it used to be, back in the old days. Trying to run, trying to catch up with the other kids, calling out, "Hey! Hey! Wait for me!"

Back in the old days.

In the days when I was whole.

MR. AND MRS. KETT

SAM HICKS

You might say I couldn't have been dead. But I accepted that my fight was over as I drifted like a feather, down into the soft spread of darkness. Then the darkness jolted from my lungs. There came the growl of a dog and distant words:

"It's Catherine, isn't it? There, there—you fell into the water but you're fine now. You know who I am don't you, Catherine? From Saint Jude's?"

Life was burning back; I felt it scorch me. Something made of cloth was being rubbed against my skin.

"Careful does it," said a different voice. "Just look at her arms."

I could see the Reverend Wilfred Lowe more clearly now: his big, familiar face hovering somewhere over mine. "Time for that later, my love," he said to the woman. "Just making sure she's safe, that's the main thing."

I pushed myself up on my elbows.

"Now, don't be scared, Catherine," the reverend said. "We'll help you. Not to worry, my dear, not to worry."

But he spoke too late; I was on my feet by then, swaying in rhythm with a world swimming sideways. My two saviors edged towards me, but their kind faces and their soothing words filled me with sudden fear and I staggered back and half-fell, half-ran into the leaning gray reeds that spread out from the water's edge. If I can reach the hawthorn trees, I thought, they'll never catch me.

When I came to the road and was in sight of home, I still didn't understand I wasn't dead. I didn't see how I could be alive.

⊸

I'd been sent away to boarding school the year before, just after my fourteenth birthday. My father had been promoted to manager at the local bank and he'd asked me, what was money for, if not to give your only child the best? So that was that: out of the blue an exile, and expected to be grateful to leave my friends and everything I'd ever known, in exchange for extra Latin.

That Easter when I arrived at the railway station for the holidays, my parents weren't waiting with the car. Instead, a man approached and introduced himself as the taxi driver they'd sent to collect me: I asked him why they hadn't come themselves, but he couldn't say. They could at least have warned me, I thought. But maybe something had happened; was Granny ill again? There'd been a stroke a few years before and you couldn't help being afraid. Or could something have happened to them—my parents. What would I do then?

We drove past the floral display outside the church and the driver waved to Reverend Wilfred Lowe, who was standing by the gate like a guard. It was a small town, and so the reverend must have known he wouldn't be seeing my family for the Easter services. My father was an atheist, for one. He didn't advertise it for fear of offense, but he betrayed his lack of faith in the Deity by avoiding His institutions and His celebrations and by staying silent whenever He was praised. My mother's beliefs were a more movable feast: a mess of palmistry and tea-leaves and color-illustrated myths; she'd even been to a séance once. It was as though, for her, the spiritual realm fulfilled a need for outré entertainment. But I don't want to give the impression they were unconventional types; in fact, they went to great lengths to conform to their small society. They played tennis and golf and bridge, ran cake sales and charity events, and my mother was a keen gardener who'd won first prize for her flowers at the annual summer fete. Mummy didn't work—this was fifty years ago—but she looked after her mother-in-law, who lived with us, and she looked after me as well, in a slightly more careless way.

That afternoon, the taxi stopped outside our house and I looked out, searching for my mother's face. All the curtains were drawn, making me doubly sure that something had happened and so recently that no one had

had time to tell me. At the best of times our house had an unapproachable look. It stood on its own a mile from town, backed by fields of fenced-in pasture, beyond which were woods and the many-forked paths that led up to Coldhill Pond. The house's dark windows looked down beneath a gray tiled roof, which on overcast days seemed to slide straight out of the sky. Its brick walls were dingy and mottled and its door, with a knocker like a small clenched fist, was the grim, unshining black of iron dug from a grave. In summer, when the roses in the front garden lifted their bright heads, the look of the house would jolly up, but that day was one of those when it turned a cold shoulder to the outside world.

After the taxi driver had helped me with my luggage and left, the front door opened: it seemed like my mother had been standing there, waiting for him to go.

"Mummy! You made me jump," I said as I went to step inside, but she held me back with a hand on my arm.

"I didn't have time to tell you, Catherine," she said in a rush, "but we've got some guests. I know you'll be on your best behavior, won't you?" She turned her head. "Look—there they are."

I looked past her down the black and white tiled hallway. At first, I thought they might be medical people, or undertakers.

"Oh. Yes. I see them . . . is Granny all right?"

"Yes, dear," she said. "Granny's fine. She's doing very well. Now go in and say hello to Mr. and Mrs. Kett."

The couple made no effort to approach me, so it was I who walked down the hallway to where they stood, beyond the last angle of the staircase. The only daylight entered from the glass above the door, and, that afternoon, theatrically steep white rays sloped down towards these strangers, Mr. and Mrs. Kett. Only someone who'd seen them would understand when I say that there was something undefined about their faces. The planes and contours seemed to sweep away, as if they couldn't really be contained. Their cheekbones, their foreheads, their eyes, pitched forward, whilst remaining at the same time still. They were tall and slim, their hair fair and long, and they wore pale, loose clothing; the woman a long dress, and the man a shirt and trousers, possibly silk. But this was only an impression: it would be hard to give details or to be definite. It was like looking at a pencil sketch with highlights and unfinished lines, where forms are hinted at as they blend into the background paper. I'd never seen anything like them. It was the 1960s, but where we lived, you'd never have known. No one stood out, no one had glamour: no one glowed like Mr. and Mrs. Kett. How on earth had my mother found them?

"I'm very pleased to meet you," I said and held out my hand for Mrs. Kett to shake. Her mouth was a small shadow in her unfixed face. She made no move to take my hand so I let it drop, but neither she nor Mr. Kett took their eyes from me as they silently, just perceptibly, shifted their heads. I didn't find it at all rude, this unwillingness to small talk. Instantly, it won my admiration. They were wonderful, completely captivating, and I was very, very impressed. Then my mother's voice broke the spell, calling to them from the kitchen, and they moved away, like beautiful wraiths. I wanted nothing more than to follow them, but I knew my grandmother would be expecting me; she'd be waiting in the living room, whose door stood open across the hallway. I'll find them afterward, I thought, when this is out the way.

The living room ran the length of the house, and that afternoon, with the curtains drawn at the front and only partly open at the back, it wasn't much brighter than the hallway I'd just left. Despite its generous size, it was a room with a closed-up, shut-in feel, crammed with furniture and thick-shaded lamps and too many paintings in heavy, ornamental frames. Granny was sitting at the end in her usual chair, looking out at the back lawn. Although her speech hadn't fully recovered since the stroke, her mind had stayed keen, and I saw with some relief that she'd taken up knitting again: from her thinnest needles, a fine lace shawl was growing, falling in red filigrees across her lap. She looked at me eagerly as I leaned to kiss her, and kept her eyes fixed on me as she strained for speech. I knelt by her chair and waited, holding her hand, until she said: "Help me . . . with this."

"Oh, Granny," I said. "You know I can't knit like you can. I'd be no help, would I? Anyway, you're doing so well without me. You're so clever at things like that."

She looked at me with bemusement, and for a moment I wondered if she knew me, or if she thought I was someone from the past. Clearly frustrated, she felt around again for words.

"Catherine . . . undo . . . this."

I squeezed her hand. "Oh, Granny. It's so beautiful, I can't. I'd ruin it."

Her eyes grew wide, as though amazed. Why on earth was she talking to me about her knitting? She knew I was hopeless at it. Had she forgotten?

"Have you seen our guests?" I asked. She closed her eyes and shook her head. "The Ketts?" I tried again. But the change of subject didn't help; tears escaped from beneath the crinkled eyelids and slipped into the hollows of her face.

I didn't know what to say because I didn't know what I'd done to upset her, and I was thinking it would be best if I just left, when my mother came bustling into the room. She looked at me accusingly. "What's wrong with Granny? Catherine—what on earth have you said?" She fussed across and started stroking my grandmother's hair.

"I only asked her if she'd met the Ketts."

"Of course she has. She loves them just like we do. Don't you, Hilda?"

Granny's head had fallen forward. Somehow, within seconds, she was asleep.

"I'm sorry. I honestly don't know what I did to upset her," I said, and then, softly: "Mummy, I wanted to ask—how did you meet them, the Ketts?"

She didn't look at me as she absorbed my question. Her top lip thinned and then she said, in the voice she used to close inquiries down. "Through a friend. Now, why don't you go into the garden and say hello to Daddy?" She gave me a quick smile. "He's taken the week off, so we can all be together. Isn't that nice of him?"

⤙⊙⤚

I found him at the end of the long walled garden, where the apple trees were. He was standing over a pile of junk, emptied from the tumbledown brick outbuildings which my mother used for potting seedlings and storing tools. She must be having a re-design, I'd thought as I walked down; there was bare earth in the borders where the perennials had been, and shallow trenches dug into the lawns and vegetable beds. She'd always liked to move things around from time to time, although I'd have expected to have heard about a major plan, as this one seemed to be.

My father kissed me and then slumped down on a packing crate. "Oh, it's a job, clearing all this," he said. He had a thin, bloodless sort of face, but he was very fit, what with all the tennis and golf he played, so it surprised me that this not very heavy work had left him hot and breathless.

Around the open doors of the two small buildings were heaps of flowerpots and trays, watering cans, baskets, coils of wire, battered tins of preparations.

"But doesn't Mummy need all this stuff?" I said, starting for the first door.

"No!" he shouted, as soon as I moved. "Leave it alone!"

I turned around, startled.

"Why's that?"

"We can't disturb them. Can't you see?" He nodded at the little building.

"What am I meant to be seeing?"

And then I did see something through the cobwebby window; a smudged movement, the sort you catch at the corner of your eye, the kind a small, fast animal makes.

"Is something in there?" I said.

"The Ketts. We really shouldn't interrupt them. They're cleaning that one up for more guests. They don't need us getting in their way. They have to do things how they like them."

"The Ketts?" I felt myself flush as I spoke their name. "But I thought they were inside the house? Why would guests want the shed?"

"Better ask your mother," he said. He shifted on his crate and looked up at me with shining eyes. "So you've seen them, have you? Aren't they wonderful?"

"Oh yes. I've never seen anyone like them. Where ever do they come from? I asked Mummy but she wouldn't say."

He gave a short laugh and raised his eyebrows. "You know, I didn't think to ask her that. But I'm just very glad they came, to tell you the truth. It's been such a pleasure having them around the place. Yes, last week, I think it was, they came. Such marvelous people. You know—there is such a thing as the perfect guests. People say there isn't, don't they, but there is."

I took another, newly curious look at the old building, at its missing roof tiles and mossy bricks, finding it hard to picture what the Ketts could hope to do in there. And then, behind the dirty glass, I glimpsed another movement, which could have been anything; the loose flutter of a dress, or a silky sleeve, or the turning of a face.

⟜

For the rest of the afternoon I lay in my bedroom, getting up every now and then to fetch a glass of water. My parents were somewhere outside, working on the sheds, and so, I imagined, were the Ketts. I didn't want to interfere. I didn't want to upset them in any way, however small or unintended. Really, if I were such a considerate person, I should have spared some time for my grandmother that afternoon, instead of lazing around on my bed; I could even have tried to help her with her knitting if she liked. But her outburst earlier had scared me. How could I know what might make her cry? What was the right thing to say? I even convinced myself it would be kindest not to disturb her later by going in to say goodnight. So I lay there, thinking about the Ketts, trying to hold the image of them in my head.

At eight that evening, my mother called all of us except Granny into the dining room and, with some ceremony, lit candles in her best silver candlesticks in honor of our guests. The table was polished to a mirror sheen, and my father sat at its head, with my mother and I at either side. The Ketts sat at the other end, separated from us by empty chairs, which seemed to me to be a gesture of politeness, a shy reluctance to impose. The table made an island in the candlelight, framed by a fitful darkness from which our guests' faces arose, part-concealed and indistinct. Small reflected flames quivered in our cut crystal glasses as we drank, and we drank a lot (for the first time ever I was allowed wine) because we had no appetite for food. We spoke sometimes: we must have chatted away quite happily, because I have a memory of easiness, lightness, of feeling that we were basking in the fascinating company of the Ketts. I do remember asking my mother about the new guests that were coming and her telling me. "We'll always keep a welcome for friends of Mr. and Mrs. Kett." And we raised our glasses and drank toast after toast to lasting friendship.

I wasn't at all resistant to alcohol of course, and after dinner I went straight up to bed. The room spun when I lay down and then an annoying restlessness, a kind of twitching, nervous pain, built up inside me until I couldn't bear it any longer. I hopped up and bumped around my room, hoping movement might ease the horrible feeling, but after a few circuits came to rest at the window that looked down onto garden at the back. My parents and the Ketts were out there, standing on the soil where the grass had been. Our guests were making wide, languid gestures, like people turning in their sleep, and my parents, rooted to the spot, were watching and listening, caught in a kind of rapture. It was so predictable, normally, life at home, and my parents never seemed to know quite what to do with me, but now we were all coming together, all doing new and interesting things, due to the inspiring presence of the Ketts. It felt like the deepest honor anyone could ever receive had been bestowed upon us.

-<>-

When I got up the next morning, I went to the window again. They were out there already, at not even seven o'clock. My parents were marking out lines with sticks and string, while, with their backs to me, the Ketts might have been Roman emperors directing their slaves, as they sipped their wine, and watched. But that's not to say there was anything imperious about them, not at all. My parents' shining faces, their giddy, rushed actions, showed them to be as excited and willing as children on Christmas Eve.

A delicious thought occurred to me as I dressed: I could have a quick look in the spare room, where the Ketts were staying. Here was my chance, now the coast was clear, to see something of their secret selves. Just a look, just a peek at the little things they kept about them. I'll only be in there a few seconds, that's all, I thought, as I crept along the landing. They'll never know, I said to myself, as I pushed open the door. But there was nothing there, no sign of them, no clues; no socks, no scarves, no hairpins, no books, no magazines. They'd brought nothing with them, and didn't even seem to have slept in the bed.

I had no appetite for breakfast when I went downstairs, so I drank a cup of tea and more water, which I tinted pink with the dregs from an open bottle of wine. On my way out to the garden, I looked round the living room door: my grandmother turned her unsteady head and for a moment I thought the look in her eyes was not frustration at her efforts to speak, but hopelessness.

"Help . . . with this," she said.

I laughed an uncomfortable refusal and told I'd see her at lunchtime, but that now I had to go outside because we had guests. I knew how condescending I sounded, how weak my excuses seemed, but I really intended to make it up to her later, when I had more time.

It had rained during the night and the freshly dug earth smelled of rot and leaves and mushrooms. A grid of taut green string stretched out before me over the remains of the grass and as I looked, it seemed to levitate, rising and rolling into a slowly spinning maze. Of course, that's what it was—a maze: lines joining and dividing, dead ends, reversals.

"Why didn't you tell me what you'd got planned?" I said when I reached my parents, who were busy shoveling soil into a wheelbarrow. "What a wonderful idea! And you've got to let me help."

"Oh, darling, would you?" my father said. "You know, it's a big job with just us."

A few feet away, the Ketts seemed to be smiling. They leaned against each other, loose and relaxed, drowsily sipping their red wine. I didn't ask, but I knew this project must have been their idea. It was so adventurous, so daring.

"And then we'll have to get the stones to finish it. We'll need all our strength for that," my mother said. "There's going to be walls. Walls all around it, so you can get lost."

"That'll be even more incredible," I said and I jumped down into the trench they'd dug. As they handed me a shovel, I looked to check if the Ketts were watching, but they were drifting away, down towards the outbuildings at the back, behind the trees.

"Are the Ketts all right?" I asked. "Mightn't they get bored?"

My mother stopped digging for a moment. Her curled hair was bound up in a spotted scarf, and her chin was smeared with dirt. "Oh no," she said. "They've got lots to do today. They're getting things ready for the other guests."

"And when will they be here?"

"Oh, I don't know that yet," she said, and I knew, by the way her top lip tightened, that it would be futile to question her further.

At midday, or thereabouts, we stopped for lunch, but none of us were very hungry and we made do with a crust of bread left over from a previous day; but we had water and several glasses of wine, which was what we felt was needed. Then we went back to the garden, with me forgetting the promise to look in on Granny, although I'd made it only hours before.

It was hard to gauge our progress from ground level, but as we dug, Mr. and Mrs. Kett would appear from time to time and by the subtlest of signs, they let us know that we were doing well. I would see the blur of their flowing clothes, the slow expressive gestures of their hands, the eloquence of their hazy eyes, and understand how truly glad they were to see people so committed and hardworking. And we worked at a breathless rate, my father wheeling the earth we'd removed round to the front of the house, where he tipped it over the rose beds and the gravel path. We'd see to it later, my mother said, when we had more time. I reveled in the simple pleasures and discoveries of our task: the hair-like roots ripped from the turf, the round brown stones that tumbled from my digging blade and the fat worms that flipped about in panic when I lifted them away. We didn't really talk, so deeply were we focused on our work, so determined to complete it as quickly as we could, to impress the Ketts.

By the evening, we'd dug out half the former lawn, the borders and two of the vegetable beds. I went upstairs to change before dinner and was astounded when I looked down and saw the intricacy of what we'd created. It was going to be stupendous, like nothing I'd ever seen.

That evening, when we gathered in the candlelight around the smooth and shining table, I suppose we were all too tired to eat. Instead, we lifted the cut crystal glasses in shaking hands and drank toast after toast with our guests. To friendship, we said. To getting the job done, we said. To dreams, we said, again and again, as the exhilarating hours fled by. Sometimes our guests seemed to retreat into the dark, but then the candle flames would straighten and briefly reveal them, bathed in snowy, moving light. Eventually, so overcome by intense emotion that I could hardly speak or see, I left the table, embarrassed at myself, not wanting the Ketts to know how weak I really was.

I should've been exhausted, but my heart was beating so fast, and my limbs were aching and twitching in such an uncontrollable, internal way, that I passed the night in a fever of restlessness, my waking thoughts as unlikely and confused as the dreams which suddenly took me. It's possible I was genuinely ill, because in the morning I couldn't remember how I came to be standing outside the old brick outbuilding, my hands pressed against the misted glass, my eyes unblinking, fixed upon the dark interior. My mother found me and told me to come away, and soon, after forgoing breakfast, we started digging again.

What about Granny, I thought as we got near lunch. Did I see her last night? No—I'd forgotten. With everything going on, the usual routine had just fallen away. And what were the odds of finishing the maze anytime soon? Perhaps we had overestimated our abilities. I had the feeling that the Ketts, who had seemed so happy with us before, were starting to think the same way. I started to feel that they were disappointed with our progress, that they expected more. They came into sight less frequently, and there was a different quality to the movements they made, a touch of impatience in their graceful limbs, a reproach in their inscrutable gaze. They lit a fire at the end of the garden, presumably to burn the stuff from the sheds, and I could see the flames, intensely red, rising up from the pile of rubbish. Please don't let them leave, I thought, please never let them leave.

We drank water for lunch and at a quarter past four, my father fell forward into the trench, and lay there, panting, his eyes wide and trying to turn backwards in his head like a stricken beast. He brushed my mother and me away and pulled himself up.

"I'm sorry, girls," he said. "What an old fool. Overdone it a bit, that's all. I'll go and sit inside with Granny for a while, and leave you to it. What d'you say?"

An hour later, my knees gave way. My mother said she thought it was probably time to stop, and, mainly because I couldn't face the stairs, I went to join my father and Granny in the living room. They were sitting in their chairs by the window, staring out at the garden. They're as tired as me, I thought, as I dragged over a chair to sit beside them.

⊸⊙⊷

It seemed they had forgotten about us, my mother and the Ketts. I could hear my mother talking to our guests as she moved around the house; sometimes her high-pitched laugh, sometimes murmured words, from the dining room, or the hallway, or moving upstairs.

"Help me with this," Granny had said when I'd taken my seat, and I'd answered: "How can I do that, Granny, when I can barely lift my head?"

Her hands trembled, white against the lacy red knitting that fell across her lap.

"Well, perhaps you'd like to help me instead, Catherine?" my father said. His voice was strange and I leaned forward, trying to read his face, but it was becoming as vague and unknowable as the Ketts'.

"Daddy, I'm not making excuses," I said. "I don't think I can move. I'm so exhausted."

He looked at me with the same bemusement as Granny. Was it his idea of a joke, a way of saying I was being selfish by not helping with her damned knitting? Was I supposed to say yes just to please her, and then make a mess of things? I would've gone up to my room, but I didn't have the strength to move.

The evening darkened, but not one of us rose to turn on a light. Outside, the sky was solid, black marble streaked with gray, but the house around us was fragile, whispering with breath. The whirr of a moth in another room, the slow drip of the kitchen tap, seemed as near as the echoing tick of the glass-cased clock that sat upon the mantelpiece. Every so often, I caught a glimpse of gossamer movement which barely registered on the air, and I would anticipate the appearance of the Ketts, but each moment of anticipation seemed to rob me of that wished-for possibility.

Moonlight gleamed on the carved wooden arms of our chairs, and fell across my grandmother's white hair and my father's open eyes. It glinted on something lying in the garden; the steel of some tool we'd left behind. The light fell across my feet, which I noticed were bare.

When the birds began chirruping at dawn, I seemed to hear them as through an illness; queasy, garbled caricatures. The thick pile carpet lapped wet against my feet: when I tried to move my toes, it released an odor of decay, and I closed my eyes in fear of filaments and spores and green clouds of dust. Help me, I thought, and something moved inside me. Was that a voice, or the sound of something walking, shuffling, through dead leaves?

"Get away from here," I heard.

It couldn't have been my father's voice, could it? No, it was the sound of something walking through dead leaves, imitating speech. They were still asleep in their chairs, my father and Granny, their faces in shadow, untouched yet by the faint morning light.

"Get away from here," I heard.

But I was only dressed in shorts and a T-shirt, summer clothes, and my cold arms and legs were covered with marks, like rust.

"Get away from here," I said out loud, but to move those limbs would be to dislocate them, to move them would mean excruciating pain. But I had to breathe; I had to breathe air beyond the boundaries of our house, if only for a short while, before the work started again.

I moved those screaming limbs; I left my chair and went into the hallway, where the black and white tiles tilted and the walls bubbled beneath their skin. The door swung open to reveal the earth mounds where the front garden had been.

I ran up the path that skirted the cattle pasture and onto the one which led up through the thickets of hawthorn and larch. At the banks of Coldhill Pond, I stopped. I hadn't intended to run so far, but now that I had, I gulped the morning air like a person who'd been suffocating. The pond looked black, yet it glittered with light and suddenly, a breeze split its surface into a thousand freezing beads and I looked down and saw, in the deep, what I knew at once was the face of a corpse. Without a thought, I jumped.

⊸

Reverend Wilfred Lowe's wife bent down to where I knelt. She peeled my fingers from my grandmother's legs, which were deathly cold and streaked with dried blood; like her hands, they were tied to the chair. Mrs. Lowe put a blanket over my shoulders. I knew she didn't want me to look at the other chair by the window, the one where my father sat staring out with frozen eyes to where, I'm told, my mother lay.

"What about the Ketts?" I said to Mrs. Lowe as she led me away.

I asked everyone that. I told them all: you need to speak to the Ketts. They'll tell you how happy we were. They'll know what happened, and when they explain you'll see that it must have been someone else. Because how could they ever have done what all of them said they had? Only someone who'd never met them would think that. It made no sense. If they had, why not kill me too?

What do they look like, they said? Where did they go? How do we find them? Where do they live? They don't live anywhere, I should have said. They visit.

⊸

Yesterday, after fifty years, I saw them again. They haven't changed: why would they? I was on a train bound for the coast, when, just outside a town, we slowed to a stop behind an isolated house. I saw the pale circles of their faces, the mysterious luminance of their forms, and as we gathered speed again, I saw a hand rise as if to acknowledge me. I raised my own hand in answer, to let them know I'd seen them and was grateful, even now, to be remembered.

BELOW

SIMON BESTWICK

Manchester's a city of layers; over the years it's been knocked down and built over, again and again. Now and then, something comes to light. They dig a new building's foundations, find an old one's. Coins, earthenware and glass, mixed in sand and clay.

If you're lucky, that's all you find.

Of course, you can find other ways in, too. And sometimes—sometimes it's what's down there that finds a way out.

⁂

I was walking to school along Dunham Road in Altrincham, one cold misty morning in November 1986, when Martyn called out to me. We walked in together sometimes, depending on whether or not he was late, getting a lift, or just not bothering to turn up.

"You all right, Stumpy?"

From someone else, that might have been an insult, but I knew Martyn didn't mean it that way; by then I had a pretty good radar for insults, subtle or otherwise.

"Yeah," I said. "You?"

"All right." He leant against a lamppost. "You going in?"

"Yeah," I said. "Course."

I didn't *want* to, but playing truant was as unthinkable as murder to a good little boy from a middle-class South Manchester suburb. Martyn didn't care. He was always in and out of trouble—bunking off, fighting, keeping girlie mags in his desk. He'd even told Mr Briggs the Games master to fuck off. We'd thought Briggs' head was going to explode.

Martyn had caught hell for it—as always—but didn't give a shit. I dunno how he escaped expulsion, but he did. He was a big lad, athletic, successful—for a thirteen-year-old—with girls, and nothing scared him. He was everything I wasn't.

"What for? Just gonna get the shit kicked out of you."

Not if you stop them, I wanted to say, but didn't. When Martyn helped me out it was because he felt like it; other times he couldn't be arsed, or he was busy making one of his famous non-appearances. He was something I was grateful for when it happened, not something I expected, much less took for granted. Besides, he'd have had to be nearby every minute.

I didn't want to go in that morning, or any other; it's a shit feeling, to hate and dread going somewhere but having to. Every morning I dragged myself in, wanting to stay in bed, or take a bus into the countryside, wander through a field. But I couldn't.

Martyn looked at me and shrugged. "I'm not."

My stomach clutched; the worst days were the ones Martyn wasn't in school.

He saw my face. "Don't go in then," he said.

"I can't."

"Why not?"

Because, I wanted to say, but didn't.

"Come with us," he said. "I'm going town." *Town*, if you live near Manchester, means the city.

"Can't," I said.

He scowled. "Don't be a poofter."

I just looked back at him miserably. He snorted. "Fuck off, then."

When you don't have any power, those who do are scary. Like gods: you live or perish by their whim. I could say that's why I called after him—I was scared of losing whatever favour he held me in, and with it the little protection it gave me. But that wasn't it. Just for a second, I'd visualised the possibility of a day away from school. Another path. One where I wasn't picked on. Being a goody-two-shoes hadn't got me anywhere; maybe I'd be luckier as one of the bad boys.

"Hang on!" I said, and ran after him. Martyn looked back at me and grinned.

*

About three months before, Barry Rigby had been duffing me up while one of his mates emptied my schoolbag out all over the yard. Martyn had dropped Rigby with two quick punches; when he did that, his mate ran away.

Afterward, he'd helped me pick my stuff up. I had a Douglas Reeman book—one of my Grandpa's, who'd been in the Navy in the War—and it turned out Martyn liked Reeman too. Maybe that'd been why he waded in. Or maybe it was just because he could.

I dunno why he liked me—if that's what it was. It wasn't a friendship as such, but now and then he told people to fuck off when they bothered me. I was grateful but scared too. Martyn Barrett was the kind of lad they meant when they said *loose cannon*; you never knew which way he'd go.

*

We caught a double-decker into town, bagsying the front seats on the top deck.

I spent most of the journey staring out of the window. Back then, I went to Manchester maybe once or twice a year with Mum and Dad, so it was like a voyage to an unknown land. The 108 bus route from Altrincham led up through Fallowfield and Moss Side into the city centre, but they might as well have been Outer Mongolia or the surface of Mars for all I recognised them. It was another world.

It was the first time I'd ever done anything like this. I was the one whose Mum and Dad would be shocked when it came out. Mum would shake her head and be disappointed; Dad would bark and glower. Never mind the teachers. But I didn't let myself think about that. Instead, I thought about the view from the bus's top-deck window, about where the streets that bled off from the main road went, who might live in the tall Victorian town houses along Princess Road as we went into Moss Side—anything but what would be waiting for me later.

"What we gonna do?" I asked Martyn. He slouched in the corner of the other seat; he was looking out of the window too, but I don't know if he saw anything much. He glanced at me and shrugged.

"Dunno," he said. "We'll see."

Every morning I was given bus fare and dinner money; I'd a little of that left, while Martyn had a fiver—a small fortune by our standards. I didn't ask where he'd got it. We'd find some use to put it to.

We got off at Piccadilly. I'd stuffed my blazer and tie into my backpack; Martyn had pulled his tie off and zipped up his parka against the cold.

We bought some chips and ate them in Piccadilly Gardens. Nearby were a bunch of scruffy-looking homeless types, and a few punks in studded jackets. When one of them looked at me I looked away: I was afraid of both groups, but at the same time I was excited. This was living; this was adventure.

We finished eating. Martyn crumpled up his chip wrappers and tossed them away. "Let's go to Shudehill," he said. "They've got nuddy mags in the shops there."

I followed him, stopping only to chuck my chip wrappers in a nearby bin. I had a good-boy instinct to pick up his and dispose of them too, but resisted it.

Shudehill's different now. There's a shiny new bus station and Metrolink stop there these days, but back then it was just a grubby stretch of dirty-fronted shops laid beside the Arndale Centre. And the Arndale then was a dull squat box of grimy-looking beige tile that looked more like the world's biggest public toilet than anything else. Stayed that way till 1996, when an IRA bomb wrecked the place; after that they rebuilt it as the shiny steel-and-glass thing it is today.

I followed Martyn into one of the second-hand bookshops and a smell of old paper folded round me. A couple of books caught my attention: science fiction, horror. But I was trying not to look at the stuff on the other side of the shop. There were cardboard boxes of glossy magazines; the tops of girls' faces peered over the rims of the boxes, eyes warm and inviting. Dyed-blonde hair, black eyebrows. Above them were shelves, some of them with magazines facing out.

Then as now, Shudehill was full of second-hand bookshops, half of each one given over to girlie mags. Some dealt in harder stuff, and if you knew who to ask you could buy actual videos—usually grainy, third or fourth (at least) generation copies. Today, of course, there's no act you can't view at the click of a mouse on the internet, but back then sex still had something of the air of a sacred mystery. Was that better or not? I couldn't tell you, but back then getting hold of a picture of a girl with nothing on was like finding the Holy Grail, never mind anything else.

I'd seen a couple of dog-eared second-hand magazines at a friend's house one afternoon the previous year; it'd left me with an ache in the groin I still hadn't yet found the means to get rid of. But here it was all on display. I went over to the shelves; couldn't help myself.

"Would you come away from there, please?" said the man behind the counter. He probably wasn't much more than twenty-five, but to me he was a giant with all the authority of adulthood. "That's for over-eighteens only."

I mumbled an apology and drifted back to the bookshelves. I saw a Douglas Reeman book and smiled. Maybe I could buy it for Grandpa. But that just made me think of what would happen when I went back home and I stopped smiling, feeling my stomach clutch again.

"Oi!"

The man behind the counter bellowed it—a full-throated blast of adult rage—and I knew Martyn had done something stupid, something really bad.

I probably knew what it was even before I saw, of course—what else could it be? He ran past me towards the door, shouting "Come on!"

I saw the magazine clutched in his hand, and I ran after him. Behind me I heard the counter flap flung back as the man came after us. I hadn't taken anything, but that didn't matter; I was playing truant, after all, so I was already Martyn's partner in crime.

We burst onto Shudehill and Martyn tore across the street. Normally I looked both ways before I did that—I'd been raised on the Green Cross Code adverts—but I was bloody terrified at that point. The counter-man yelled behind us.

A horn blared—a big orange and white GM bus, coming straight at me. I ran away from it, heard tyres screech as an Austin Montego coming the other way braked. Somehow, I didn't freeze up but ran on to the far pavement, trying to keep up with Martyn.

It wasn't easy. Martyn ran with the school cross-country team, while I was about as far from being "sporty" as you could get; PE and Games held a special kind of terror for me, above and beyond even what school normally had to offer. Still, I was scared shitless, which helped.

Even so, as he cut down one of the narrow side-streets that squirmed off from Shudehill, my lungs were burning and I was starting to flag. I couldn't even tell if the counter-man was still behind us—we might have lost him when the bus roared past, darting down the side-street before he had a clear view of the street again—but I didn't dare look around.

The back streets off Shudehill—well, most of them are called the Northern Quarter now, and a few years later they'd be full of quirky little shops and bars, but back then they were a hive of grim pubs, run-down shops and derelict buildings. Narrow, cobbled streets, filthy with dogshit and puddles of stagnant water. I saw a rat scuttle out of my way as I ran, following Martyn around a corner.

Around the corner—and the side-street was empty. I looked around, still running, close to tears now: if the counter-man was gaining, I'd be left alone to face the music. *Bastard*, I thought.

"Stumpy! In here!"

I swung round; the board covering what had been the doorway in a derelict shopfront had been prised back, and Martyn's face showed in the darkness inside. I wondered if the counter-man had heard the nickname. It was the kind of thing, I suddenly thought, that criminals called each other. We *were* criminals now, both of us.

"Quick!" Martyn hissed.

I stumbled over the threshold; he grabbed my arm and let the board flap back into place. "Shhh," he whispered.

The inside of the shop was black and the air so damp I felt it settle on my skin. It reeked of piss and decay, stale smoke and other things I couldn't name, but which made me want to tear back the boarding and run out into the street, gulping air.

Martyn gripped my arm tighter, as if he knew what I was thinking.

From outside came the slap of running feet, a gasping for breath. "Little shits!" roared a wheezy voice. "I'll fucking have you!"

The counter-man. I heard him huffing and puffing—right outside the shop, by the sound of it. "Fuck!" he yelled, and there was a thud as he kicked a wall. There was a soft rattle and hiss from above us, as if the blow had dislodged something. I shrank back; there was no knowing how stable or solid the building's structure was. It might fall on our heads any second.

Outside, the counter-man wheezed. "Bollocks," he muttered again. He spat. Then, after the longest time, we heard his footsteps recede.

"Let's get out of here," I whispered.

"Shhh," Martyn whispered back. "Not yet. Give it another minute. Make sure he's gone."

He was right; I knew that, even though all I wanted was to get out of the place. So I waited, breathing that poisonous-smelling air. I could hear my wristwatch ticking in the dark. It seemed ridiculously loud, all of a sudden; I couldn't believe that counter-man hadn't been able to hear it.

"Can we go now?" I whispered.

"Yeah, okay," said Martyn, but even as he said it there was another noise. A creaking, cracking noise, then a splintering: wood giving way.

I realised where it was coming from at the same moment that the floor buckled and sagged under us.

"Fuck!" said Martyn.

I tried to jump for it, but it was already too late. The rotten floorboards collapsed, and we fell.

⊸

I know I screamed. I know, too, that I had time for a moment's surprise at how long the fall was: even a basement wouldn't be this far down. Then there was just the scream, the fear sweeping everything else away.

I knew I was going to die, and that I didn't want to. A silly, childish thought, as if not wanting to would change a thing. I would hit ground and then—

Except that I didn't hit ground, not exactly. What I landed in was thick, wet and deep, and I plunged through it, but it cushioned me. I *did* sort of hit ground in the end—my hip cracked hard against something solid, and I screamed in pain—and the thick cold wetness covered me, but I coughed and flailed and broke free of it and there was air. It was colder and damper and smelt worse than the air in the shop had, but it was air.

"Fucking hell. Fuck. You okay, Stumpy?"

In the dim grey light, I made out Martyn; he was slathered with filth. We were in some sort of round chamber with earth walls. The floor of it was awash with mud; sitting down in it, it came up almost to my neck.

I realised I was crying. "My hip . . ."

"Bad?"

I struggled about in the mud and managed to stand, groaning in pain. "Fuck, that hurts. Think it's broken."

"You couldn't fucking walk if it was." Martyn floundered upright too. We peered up; the shaft we'd fallen down vanished into the dark above.

"Help!" I shouted.

"Shut up for Christ's sake! You want that fucker coming back?"

"Do you wanna stay here?"

Martyn scowled. "Don't want either," he said. He chewed his lip, then spat mud. "Well, he'll have fucked off, anyway."

"Maybe someone else'll come past, then."

Martyn squinted around, dug an old lighter out of his pocket and flicked it into life. The flame's glow crept up the walls. "The fuck are we?" he said.

"Maybe a well?" I said.

"Nah." He pointed at the walls. They were mostly earth; bits of brick and wood poked out of them. "There'd be bricks or tiles or something. Wouldn't there?"

"Dunno." I didn't much care either, not right then. I was cold, wet, scared and my hip was throbbing where I'd banged it. Even school seemed preferable right then.

Martyn started shouting for help. I joined in too. But none came. There was only the rustle in the dark above us; bats and rats and creeping things.

Martyn flicked the lighter on again and inspected the walls. He dug his fingers in experimentally, and loose wet earth crumbled and fell to the floor. More slid down from above and spattered us. "Bollocks," he said. "Not getting out that way."

"*Where*, then?" I could hear the whine in my voice and despised it, but I couldn't seem to make it go away.

"The fuck should I know?" he shouted. I cringed from it, and hated myself for cringing. But I couldn't help it; for the second time that day, I was thinking that I was going to die—this time slowly, starving down here.

I turned away, looking at the greyish mud we stood in. Puddles of water had formed on its surface; they gleamed in the light.

What light?

"Hang on," I said.

"What?" Martyn snapped.

"Put the lighter out," I said.

"What you on about?"

"Please," I said.

He did—and there was still light there. Of course there had been; we'd been able to see each other even before he put the lighter on. We could see each other down here, but I hadn't been able to see a thing up above.

"See it?" I said. "Where's it coming from?"

"Fucking hell." Martyn crouched down; so did I. When I did, I saw there were holes in the walls—big round ones, just above the surface of the mud. They were deep, stretching away from us, and the pale silverish light gleamed on their damp earth walls.

"They're *tunnels*," I said.

We stared down them. The question of who'd built them never really occurred, not then. Of course there were tunnels. You got tunnels underground, didn't you?

There was a shallow slope from the bottom of the nearest tunnel mouth to the mud-pool. I got on my hands and knees and tried to climb up it but slid back. Martyn grabbed me so I didn't fall. "The fuck are you doing?"

I pointed down the tunnel. "There's light down there, right?"

"Yeah, so?"

"Where's it coming from?"

"Well how I should I fucking—oh. Right."

This time, Martyn helped push me up, then clambered up after me with a grunt. The tunnel was pretty low, but I could stand almost straight; he had to stoop down. The floor was sludgy, but not as bad as what we'd just left.

The light, wherever it was coming from, still glistened on the damp of walls and floor. We started down the tunnel towards it.

⊸

There was no sign of any supports, nothing to shore the tunnel walls up; they were just round passages of hard-packed soil that snaked through the earth. The air was stale at first, but soon I could feel a very faint breeze, cold but comparatively fresh.

We kept trudging towards the light. I'm not sure how long for, as my watch had broken in the fall. I began to wonder if we shouldn't have stayed back at the bottom of the shaft and called for help. Sooner or later, someone would have heard us. Wouldn't they?

We were both bitterly cold and shivering, teeth chattering: shock, coupled with the dip in the cold mud bath, followed by the traipse through the damp, draughty earth tunnels.

Something changed. It took me a few moments to realise what it was, because it wasn't one thing. The ground underfoot was becoming harder, more solid, and the air's cold dampness less. Something about the light up ahead had changed too.

A few more steps and I saw why; the walls of packed earth were giving way to reddish-coloured stone. I reached out and touched it; it had a gritty, sandpapery feel, and was dry. Sandstone.

"We're getting somewhere," I said.

Martyn grunted. He didn't sound convinced, and that made me wonder if I was wrong. But we went on.

"Listen," he said suddenly.

"What?"

"Listen."

I did, and then I heard it too; a distant thumping and clatter of machinery. I twisted round to look at Martyn and he grinned. I found myself grinning back. He clapped me round the shoulders awkwardly. "You're a genius, Stumpy. A fucking genius!"

I didn't feel cold any more as we pushed on; a warm glow lit me up. A *genius*, he'd called me. Till now, I'd always been a follower, a hanger-on, like one of those pilot fish that hovered around the sharks as they swam, picking food from their teeth. But now *he* was following *me.*

The noise got louder and the light brightened with each bend of the tunnel; soon the racket was deafening. Martyn looked back.

"What's up?" I shouted—I had to, over the noise.

He shrugged. "Thought I heard something."

I shrugged too. An echo, running water, rats; could've been anything. Didn't matter, anyway; we were nearly out of here.

One more bend, and now the light was sharp and bright, the noise thunderous. Even shouting at the top of my lungs, I'd have struggled to be heard. God knew what we were coming out into—a factory of some kind?—but there'd be people surely, somewhere near.

Only as we rounded the bend did I stop to worry—what if the tunnel ended in a grille, something we couldn't get through? Even if there were people on the other side, how would we make ourselves heard?

But the tunnel opened straight out into a huge, wide room. I saw a white-tiled floor and ranks of tall machines. Long strands of some material stretched up over frames, and shuttles whizzed back and forth across them.

Weaving machines; warp and weft. We'd had a school trip to Quarry Bank Mill in Styal the year before, and they'd had a machine a bit like these running.

Martyn prodded me in the back, and I went forward. There was a two-foot gap between the tunnel mouth and the floor, and I was already feeling stiff from the cold and the walking, so I climbed slowly down. Martyn jumped down and landed flat on his arse.

I laughed weakly—I don't think he heard it over the racket—and looked around for a person. I saw several; small figures in white smocks and black trousers, tending the machines. I started towards the nearest one, but even as I did, I realised something was wrong.

Partly it was the light. At first, I'd thought there were fluorescents, but the ceiling was bare sandstone, and the light seemed to come from everywhere and nowhere. And there were huge skeins of cobwebs stretched out between the tops of the machines—years' worth, it looked like.

I told myself it was just a scruffy basement, somewhere where they weren't fussy about appearances. The important thing was that there were people here, and we'd be able to get help. I was so sure the worst of our problems were over that I found myself worrying about what would happen when we got back to the surface, over the stolen magazine and our bunking off school.

But as I came near the figure in the smock, I realised that it wasn't just the surroundings; there was something wrong with it, too. It was no taller than I was. And its hair was pale—not white, like Grandpa's was, but *faded*—and dry, like straw. Its feet were bare and looked like splayed white claws.

And then it turned towards us.

Its head was a papery bulb. That's what it looked like; damp paper that had dried, brushed with a thin layer of muck like that which coated Martyn and me, only dried and cracked and flaking. It didn't have a face, that was the horrible bit—no nose or mouth, just taut empty skin. It had no eyes either—just black empty sockets, but the worst thing of all was that they seemed to see us, and they seemed to beg us for help.

I took a step back, bumping into Martyn. I heard him say something—I don't know what it was but felt him move backwards. The child—I suppose that's what it was, or had been—moved towards us, but was pulled up short. I saw that it couldn't move away from the machine, because its hands were being pulled into it. I don't mean that they were crushed—the substance of them seemed to be pulled and stretched, like chewing gum, dragged into the machinery's churning guts. I looked up at the threads being woven.

"The tunnel," I heard Martyn shout, and I nodded. We backed away. All along the line of machines, other children like the first turned to stare at us: empty faces, holes for eyes.

We reached the entrance we'd come through, and Martyn started climbing in—but then I grabbed his arm. A moment later, he saw what I'd seen; shadows moving at the bend in the tunnel. Something was coming down it.

I turned back to the machines. The children were staring at us. Shadows disrupted the pale light, moving across the ceiling and spilling across the floor; something was moving between the ranks of machines, coming our way.

"Oh *fuck*." I heard Martyn shout that even over the machines. "Come on."

We ran away from the tunnel, past the row of machinery and staring eye-sockets. Martyn yelled and pointed—I saw another tunnel entrance, up ahead.

He jumped straight inside and ran in—it was lit by a pale glow, the same as the other had been—but I hesitated. What was going to be down *this* one? What if something was coming the other way, the same as there'd been in the one we'd come in through? But when I looked back, I was just in time to see something else emerge from between two weaving machines and turn to look my way. I don't know what the hell it was, but it wore long dark robes with a hooded cowl, and it was very thin and very, *very* tall; its head almost brushed the ceiling twenty or thirty feet above. Inside the cowl there was only darkness, except for two eyes—I assume they were eyes—glowing palely.

"Stumpy, come *on!*" yelled Martyn, and I did as he said, scrambling down the tunnel. I didn't dare look back again. I didn't want to know how fast that thing could run.

The thunder of the factory—or whatever that place had been—died away as we ran. As it did, there was a humming in my ears that slowly faded.

We ran until we collapsed; for the first time ever, I kept up with Martyn. Then again, I was well-motivated. Tall as it was, the thing in the robes had been thin enough to fit inside the tunnel if it crawled on hands and knees. Assuming it had either.

"Jesus. Jesus." Martyn was shaking. "Jesus."

He didn't ask what it was. Neither did I. An adult might have, but we were still young enough for much of the world to be an unknown place. A monster, a bad thing; that was explanation enough.

"We should have stayed in that fucking well," he said, glaring at me. But his lips twitched, and his eyes were wet: to see Martyn Barrett nearly crying was almost more frightening than what we'd seen in the factory. Almost.

"Well we didn't," I snapped back. He glared, and I thought he was going to swing for me, but then there was a noise from back down the tunnel and we both shut up. We froze there, waiting, but nothing came.

Martyn tugged my arm, and we moved on.

The light grew brighter, but we didn't hurry towards it this time. It was the same silvery glow we'd seen before, and we'd seen what had been at the end of *that*. Unfortunately, what we'd seen was right behind us and possibly gaining, so we hadn't much choice but to move.

The air became colder again; I could see my breath in front of my face and began to shiver once more. The walls glistened with moisture, and soon the sandstone was giving way to packed soil. Water trickled along the tunnel floor and seeped, icy-cold, into our shoes.

There was a smell too; stagnant water, sewage, rotten things. The light brightened, and the tunnel opened out.

What we could see beyond wasn't pretty. A flagged stone floor, brick walls blackened with soot and slimy with moss, and water trickling down them. There was an archway almost directly opposite us. I could see a table laden with filthy, mould-covered pots and pans and wooden chairs green and spongy with rot.

I glanced at Martyn; he didn't look any happier about the place than I did, but then he looked back down the tunnel, and so did I. We hadn't heard any more noises from behind, but that didn't change the fact that our only way now was forward.

Martyn took a deep breath and jumped out, landing with a pained grunt on the flags. He turned back to help me down, and we looked around us.

The brick walls curled up overhead, but not that far—the ceiling was seven or eight feet high, at most, and the cellar or undercroft or whatever it was we'd found couldn't have been more than twelve feet wide. I breathed in and gagged on the stink, despite the cold.

"Breathe through your mouth," said Martyn. "Come on."

As in the "factory," the pale silvery light seemed to come from everywhere and nowhere at once. It didn't light the whole chamber, though; thick shadows filled its corners and could have hidden anything.

The chamber through the archway was the same size as the first, but the floor was unflagged, just raw earth, wet and soft and oozing. The worst thing was that there were blankets spread out on straw on the ground, each with a bundle of rags at one end. Beds and pillows for whoever or whatever slept down here. Across the chamber was another archway still. If we were lucky, I thought, the undercroft might lead out to a way back. Assuming we could keep going; my teeth were chattering, and my toes and fingers were numb with cold.

Martyn stopped. "What is it?" I said.

"Listen."

I did. "I can't hear—"

"*Listen*, Stumpy."

I did, and this time I heard it: a very soft, wet sound that came from behind.

We turned as it moved to fill the archway we'd come through. My first thought was that it was a maggot, a huge maggot; it was pallid and pulpy with a body of soft, mealy-looking segments, and its face was a white, featureless blob, except for two round black eyes. But the shape of it was manlike—or perhaps apelike would have been more like it. It had a hunched back, huge shoulders, long arms with massive hands that almost dragged along the ground.

We backed away as it slouched through into the second chamber. There was something boneless about it; I thought that if punctured with something sharp it might deflate in a gush of warm fluid, but didn't feel confident enough to test it. Its long, flabby fingers flexed and clasped, clenching tightly; I didn't want to test the strength of their grip either.

"Come on!" Martyn bolted through the archway at the end of the chamber, but braked to a halt on the other side and I nearly cannoned into his back.

The third chamber was flagged like the first, and also featured a table and chairs. But these chairs were occupied; three creatures like the one we'd just fled from turned slowly to face us and rose to their feet, shambling forwards.

"Fucking hell!" I ran back through the archway, but stopped again; the first creature was halfway across the chamber and closing in.

Martyn jostled into me, also retreating from the family of flabby creatures. We stumbled back into the unflagged chamber; closing in on us, the first creature lifted its head and a wet, gaping hole slowly tore in the featureless pulp of its face. A slow hollow moan rang out; it was echoed behind us and I looked back to see the other three squeezing through the archway, similar maws yawning open in their faces.

"Shit," said Martyn. "Oh shit shit shit."

I looked around for an exit, but there wasn't one.

Except that there was.

In one of the brick walls was a large round hole. Beyond it, the same silver light gleamed down another sandstone tunnel.

"Martyn!" I shouted and ran for it. He overtook me on the way, jumped as he reached it and landed on the hard stone with a yelp of pain. I jumped too and landed inside the tunnel in a crouch. I had to laugh; Briggs wouldn't have believed his eyes if he'd seen some of the feats I'd managed today, bruised hip or no—the pain of that had faded almost to nothing.

The four pallid ape-maggot things lumbered towards us, moaning, arms outstretched—and then stopped. They lowered their arms and stood there, staring at us. But their mouths stayed open, and the moaning didn't stop.

I looked back at Martyn; he'd already retreated several yards down the tunnel. I looked back at the moaning creatures and backed away too. We kept backing away till they were lost to sight.

The tunnel became earth and then sandstone once again, drier and even a little warmer. My teeth stopped chattering, and feeling seeped back into my fingers, although my toes stayed numb.

It didn't do much to lift our spirits, though. Neither of us had spoken since getting out of the undercroft, but I didn't doubt Martyn was thinking much the same as me: wherever this tunnel led, there'd be something else waiting for us. We'd been lucky the last couple of times, might even be again next time or the one after that, but sooner or later we'd be too tired or slow to outrun whatever we encountered.

The tunnel shivered; at first there was a gentle vibration, then thin dust fell from the ceiling and it shook. I steadied myself against the wall.

"What's going on?" I turned and stared at Martyn; there was a quaver in his voice and he looked as if he'd start crying any second. "What's *happening?*"

The tunnel shook harder, and Martyn opened his mouth to cry out. I don't know whether he did or not, because there was a cracking, splintering sound. It wasn't like the noise the floorboards in the old shop had made—this was harder and *louder.* The tunnel jerked and shifted—and then, as in the shop, the ground under us gave way and we were falling.

I was screaming, and heard Martyn doing the same. But this time it was different. We hit solid earth almost at once but continued falling: we'd dropped through the sandstone tunnel into an earth one below it. This was steeper than any of the others, though, angling sharply downwards. Wetter, too—the floor was a river of slippery mud so that we shot down it as if was a log-flume.

The same silvery light bathed everything as we went down. Even if there'd been anything to grab hold of—and there wasn't—we'd gathered so much momentum there was no arresting the descent. At this rate, we'd be killed whenever we reached whatever was at the end of the tunnel—we'd be fired out of it like bullets.

But the tunnel was levelling slowly out. By the time the small disc of light that marked the tunnel's end showed, we were slowing down, finally coming to a halt about a dozen yards from the entrance ahead.

Martyn gripped my shoulder to push himself to his feet. I could feel him shaking. "Bloody hell," he said, and gave a weak laugh. I stood up; my legs felt wobbly. We couldn't see what was beyond the tunnel yet.

"What do you think?" he said.

"How do you mean?"

"I mean, what do you think we should do?"

I didn't say anything. I mean, what was there *to* do? Climb back up the way we'd gone? We'd have only come slithering back down. And even if we *had* been able to reach the sandstone tunnel, that would have led us to some other buried pocket of old lost things.

Martyn sighed. "Yeah," he said. The quaver was back in his voice, but then he pulled himself up, stuck his chest out and said: "Right then." His voice was as hard and steady as he could make it. He strode past me towards the entrance.

The cold here was worse than it had been anywhere else; my teeth started chattering again within seconds. The tunnel entrance was set into a damp stone wall, and that wall looked . . . *old*.

Overhead—fifty or sixty feet above us—the light gleamed on stone buttresses and slabs. Thin white stalactites hung down from them. At ground level was a narrow, cobbled street. I don't think it could have been more than five feet wide. On either side were buildings with mullioned windows—houses, or maybe shops. There was faded black and white paint on them; I thought they might be Tudor. Rats scuttled along the street, but they were different from the ones I'd seen up above: they'd been sleek brown-furred things, while these were hump-backed and jet-black. Black rats, I realised; I'd seen pictures of them in a book. The kind that used to be everywhere in Britain but had been displaced by the brown rat hundreds of years ago.

The buildings had iron-bound wooden doors that looked ready to fall apart from rot, the stonework was cracked and the windows filthy—but lights gleamed inside them nonetheless, yellow and greasy-looking.

Shadows moved on the cobbles too, from inside the houses. Dark things moved close to the windows and peered through at us. The windows were dirty and foxed; the faces behind them were just blurs.

And then, with a creak, the door of one house swung open. The light spilled out across the damp cobbles; rats scattered from it, squeaking. A shadow stretched out, and inside the house something began to move.

It was silhouetted against the glow from inside, so I couldn't make out its features, but its clothing resembled that of a seventeenth-century Cavalier. A wide-brimmed hat with a bedraggled feather in it; a heavy rapier hanging at its waist. Leather boots that clacked loudly on the cobbles; breeches, a faded sash. Long, dead-looking hair fell around its shoulders. It wasn't completely made of bones, but the light shone through its dry, papery skin as it turned to face us. It didn't move after that or make a sound; it just stood there, watching.

Another door swung open; another followed, then one by one the rest, till washes of yellow light illuminated the entire street. More men dressed like the first, women in bonnets and dresses. There were at least a dozen of them, and still the yellow lights flickered as shapes moved in the windows.

They didn't move or make a sound, but I felt a greater sense of threat from them than I had from anything else we'd seen down here.

Even the rats now made no sound. The only thing I could hear was water dripping somewhere. And a very muffled, distant sound that might have been machinery. Perhaps we'd gone full circle and ended up near the factory. But then the Cavaliers stepped forward; they moved as one, in a mass, and in complete silence.

"Shit," said Martyn, his voice going high. We both backed away but were up against the wall in two or three steps. I peered up the tunnel—if the mealy things in the undercroft hadn't been able to follow us, maybe the Cavaliers couldn't either. But the tunnel was gone—all but the first few feet, anyway. Beyond that was only a mass of wet earth.

I turned as there was another sound from the street—it was a sort of dry rustling, like the wind blowing through leaves, but with a kind of *rhythm*. I'm not sure, even today, but I thought then—and now—that it might have been laughter. I don't know which of them made that sound. All of them, maybe. Then it died away, and the Cavaliers, still in silence, took another step down the street towards us, all together.

Martyn grabbed my shoulder. He was pale. "Gotta go through them," he said.

"What?"

"If we can get past 'em, there might be a way out."

A way out to what? Surely the best we could hope for was another tunnel, which would lead us to somewhere else like this. But I decided I'd rather take my chances with the factory or the undercroft than these. "How?" I said, as the Cavaliers took another step.

"Rush them," he said. "Knock 'em down or dodge 'em."

It sounded ridiculous, but what else could we have done? "Okay," I said.

"On three," said Martyn. "One, two . . ."

The Cavaliers took another step. Martyn didn't speak, his grip on my arm tightening. They took another, and then he found his voice again. "Three!" he shouted, and ran at them, head down.

I ran too, not at them but at one of the gaps between them. One moved sideways to close the gap, but in doing so opened another gap between himself and his neighbour, and I veered left and plunged through that. Then

I was in amongst them; they stank of dust and age. A bony hand clawed my shoulder; I screamed, tore free and ran on.

Martyn screamed too, but he didn't stop.

I wasn't the fastest runner in school, far less the strongest boy, but I was good at dodging things; it was a skill I'd evolved out of sheer necessity. I dived and rolled to the cobbles to avoid another clutching hand, then scrambled to my feet as bony fingers snagged my hair. I screamed again as I pulled one way and they the other, till the hair came out and I went charging up the street.

"Stumpy!"

Almost at the far end, I looked back. Martyn hadn't stopped screaming, and now I saw why. Most of the Cavaliers formed a line across the street, now turned towards me, but behind them was a knot of a half-dozen, male and female, who had hold of Martyn and were shepherding him into one of the houses. I couldn't see all of their hands—I'm not sure, and I keep trying to tell myself I *couldn't* have seen it, but it looked as though some of their hands were *in* him, rather than *on* him.

He had an arm free, and was reaching for me with it, and he kept screaming my name until they bundled him through one of the doors, which swung shut behind them with a dull, final *thud*. Even then, I could still hear him.

The other Cavaliers stood in silence for a moment, then took a step towards me.

I turned and ran—but all I found in front of me was a blank wall. I clawed and pounded on it, but of course nothing happened. I looked for something, anything, even another tunnel entrance, but there was nothing. And when I turned around, they were only a few feet from me. I could see their decayed, half-mummified faces. Their hands reached out.

And the wall beside my head exploded.

I screamed. I don't know if anyone else did. But light burst through the hole, and it wasn't the same light as before. I registered that but didn't understand what it meant as I fell to the floor, curled up and screaming. I'd reached my limit. I just wanted to be somewhere else. Away from here. Even if it was only in my head.

I vaguely registered the light getting brighter, heard voices shouting. But I was still past understanding what they meant, and when hands touched me, I screamed and fought them, till finally someone stuck a needle in my arm. And no matter what happened, no matter what anyone said, I wouldn't open my eyes.

⊸⊷

I never went back to that school. I enrolled at a new one in the summer of '87, after some home tuition to help me catch up on what I'd missed. I was a quieter kid than I had been, and no one picked on me; when I hid inside myself from the Cavaliers, not all of me came out again. At least not then. There'd been a lot of therapy, of course. To help me get over Martyn.

I don't know if they found a body. If there was a funeral or memorial service for Martyn, it happened while I was still hidden away inside myself. Martyn and I, I was told, had fallen down a disused drainage shaft under the derelict shop, got lost in some maintenance tunnels before emerging partway across the city near Cateaton Street, where as luck would have it some workmen had been digging a new gas main.

Years later, someone told me that there are stories of an old cobbled street, buildings and all, under Cateaton Street.

Part of the tunnel had collapsed, burying Martyn, but the workmen had broken through into the area where they found me.

No one believed me about the factory, the undercroft, or the Cavaliers. A hallucination, they told me, caused by a terrible trauma.

I almost came to believe that. In fact, I *did*, for years; I suppose it was the only way I could get through the rest of my school years and all that followed. By the time I'd left University, you couldn't see the join any more between who I was and who I'd been. It was later that it came back.

I keep trying to push it away, with work or drink or drugs. I've have had all the associated ups and downs along the way, and I've come out in reasonably good shape, all things considered—but it's never stayed gone for good. And the last year or two's been particularly bad. That's why I've written this down; hoping it gets it out of my system. Gets the factory and the undercroft, the cobbled street and the Cavaliers, out of my dreams. And Martyn, too; Martyn most of all.

I keep seeing stories on the news, you see, about sinkholes opening in Manchester. It could be anything, of course, but I keep thinking about how that sandstone tunnel gave way under us. How the floor of the old shop did, come to that.

Like I said: sometimes it's what's down there that finds a way out.

MY NAME IS ELLIE

SAM REBELEIN

My name is Ellie, and I like figurines made of ceramic.

Not the little angels or the ones based on paintings, but the ones that are just little people.

Which I know is not what most 10-year-olds are into, but I like them.

Which is something my mom says I picked up from my grandma.

Which is my mom's mom.

Which is funny because I also got my name from my grandma, whose name was Ellen.

Which, for a while, was pretty much the only thing I knew about my grandma, who died before I was born.

Which my dad once said, at a party when he was very drunk, is a good thing.

Which is because she scared him.

Which my mom told me is only because my dad is intimidated by women who know things he doesn't.

Which she said is all women.

Which my dad said isn't true and she knows it, that's not why he was afraid of her.

To which my mom said, "Shut up or I'll dip you in glaze and pose you myself."

Which I didn't really understand.

"Intimidated" isn't really a word I understand either.

Anyway.

The only other thing I know about my grandma is that she lived in a large lonely house in the middle of the woods.

Which my mom says smelled very nice when it rained.

Which she says was one of her favorite things about living in that house when she was my age.

Which always makes me wish I'd gotten to meet my grandma, and see her house.

Which is gone now.

Which is sad, because my mom says it was beautiful and had lots of stained glass and "gables."

Which sounds fancy even though I don't know what a gable is.

My mom says that the house was surrounded by pine trees, and that the air was always misty so you couldn't see the tops of the trees, and that the house was so high up in the hills that when you couldn't see the tops of the trees, it felt like you couldn't see the very top of the world itself.

Which my dad says is horseshit.

Which my mom says is a bad word, and whenever he says it, she makes him put a dollar in a jar on our counter.

Which my dad always does without grumbling.

Which my mom says is because he's actually very nice (and he is!); he just gets scared when she talks about my grandma, that's all.

Which Mom says is also why Dad won't go in my bedroom at night, and why he sometimes won't even go in there by himself during the day.

Which can be annoying sometimes, if she asks him to go in there to get my laundry, to help her with the chores, or something.

But which she also understands, because of all the ceramic figurines in my room.

Which he says he's never liked, ever since he met my grandma.

Which my mom says was in college, during a winter break.

Which was about a year after they'd started going out.

Which I think is gross to think about—my parents going out.

Anyway.

My mom says that my dad really liked Grandma's house, too, and that he even liked all the figurines at first.

Which was good, because Grandma Ellen had lots of them on the shelves all around her house.

My dad says there were hundreds. All standing around in suits and fine dresses, waving to each other or playing games or doing other simple poses. All over the house. On shelves, in cabinets, on the mantel, on tables, on the stairs, and just standing on the floor. At Christmastime, they hid three Christmas figurines in the house, all wearing Santa suits, and whoever found them got a candy cane.

Which my grandpa never approved of, because he thought candy was the devil, but which is one reason why my mom says I would have liked Grandma Ellen's house.

My mom says I also would have liked the house because everything was a dark, rich wood, and all the ceilings were carved into arches, and all the rooms echoed if you yelled, and you could stand in one corner and whisper to someone in another corner and they'd whisper back, and the wallpaper was very pretty, and there was a library filled with books (which sounds like heaven to me), and because there were people who lived inside of the walls.

Which my mom says she told my dad about before he visited for the first time.

Which she says she was really nervous about—even more than him meeting her parents.

Which she says is because she thought he might think she was crazy.

Which, my dad says, he did.

At first.

My dad says he thought the house was too big. He hated all the open space. He didn't like how lonely it was. And he says the "altitude" (which means it's very high up, which I said already) messed with his head and made him dizzy whenever he climbed the stairs. He didn't like looking out the windows at the trees and not knowing where the trees ended. He says the mist made him nervous.

Which my mom says is only because he doesn't have a sense of mystery.

Which I understand, because my dad is always the one who plans everything and keeps track of stuff.

Which my mom calls "being grounded."

Which she likes about him.

But which she also says can be a bad thing, because it means you're not open to new and weird stuff.

Which is why my dad didn't believe her about the people in the walls, and why he still doesn't like all my figurines. He's just not open.

To which my dad says, "That's definitely a way to put it."

Which he says without looking at Mom or me.

My dad says he figured my mom was just hearing mice in the walls, or some other critters. He says she must have been scared sleeping as a little girl in a big lonely house in the middle of the woods.

Which my mom says is wrong because the woods never bothered her, and the sounds she heard were definitely people sounds.

Which she says included things like laughter, utensils clicking against plates, bootsteps, teeth-brushing, and whispers.

Which she says would only happen at night, and only after everyone else was asleep.

That's when she'd hear them wake up.

Which she says sounded mostly normal—like people yawning and shuffling around and making coffee and making that sleepy murmuring you hear people do in bed just after they wake up—except smaller.

Which she says is because *they* were much smaller—only about a foot tall.

Which meant their days were shorter.

Which she says always started with them making tea.

Which she always thought was terrible because she could hear the kettle on the stove whistling, shrill and loud, through the wall.

Which was then followed by the sounds of the people going about their day.

Which included them reading the paper, playing games with each other, two meals, and a snack right before dawn, when they would go to sleep.

Which my mom says she heard every single night, for years, ever since she was a very little girl.

My dad says she told him this, and he thought she was kidding.

But then, he says, he heard it, too.

The first night he stayed at my grandma's, my mom fell asleep right away (forgetting about the people in the walls, she was so used to it), and my dad was left alone to listen to their sounds all night long, scared stiff.

He heard them make tea.

He heard them read the paper.

He heard them play chess.

He heard them laughing.

He heard them dancing.

And then, at dawn, he heard them pick one of their people and tear them apart limb by limb with their bare hands.

Which he's only told me once or twice, and both times it made his hands shake.

He says he could hear all of it.

He says he *knows* it happened because he could hear, through the wall over the bed, the skin bursting and the joints ripping and the screams of the one chosen and the chant of the ones doing the killing.

Which went, "This is our choice. This is our choice. This is our choice."

Which my dad says he could hear all over the wall.

Which he says must have been filled with hundreds, maybe thousands of people.

"This is our choice. This is our choice. This is our choice."

Which they said over and over as they did the "butchering."

Which my dad says is the only word for it.

Which he says was then followed by all the people in the walls, very formally, saying good night to one another.

Which was followed by silence, as dawn slid through the window.

In the morning, Grandma Ellen smiled at him and asked him if he heard the people in the walls.

Which my mom says she'd forgotten about, she'd been so tired.

Which she said she was sorry about, because she'd meant to stay up with him so he wasn't scared.

My dad said he *did* hear, and did they know the people in the walls killed each other?

My dad says that this was the worst part because Mom and Grandma Ellen just laughed and told him that was normal. They'd always thought the people in the walls were just regular people, except that they were smaller and they made "sacrifices."

Which we learned about at school when we were talking about the Mayans.

Who made sacrifices all the time.

Which didn't make them bad, just different.

Which my mom and grandma explained to Dad.

My grandpa said the people in the walls didn't have jobs, and called them "communists," but I don't know what that means.

My mom says none of this made my dad feel better.

My mom says he spent the rest of the day staring at the walls, jumping when anyone said his name.

My mom says she caught him scratching at a rip in the wallpaper once.

My mom says he didn't want to go to bed.

My mom says they lay there together in the dark, talking, and she promised she'd stay up with him.

My mom says she feels bad about it, but she drifted off again, leaving him alone, staring at the ceiling.

My dad says he thought about shaking her awake, but something told him not to.

My dad says he didn't move a muscle all night.

My dad says he heard them again, and he could hear them so clearly that he could picture what was happening in his head, step by step, when they did the butchering.

They'd chant, "This is our choice. This is our choice. This is our choice."

They'd tear and break and crush and twist and rip.

They'd press the sacrifice's eyes back into the sockets until the eyes popped, then they'd tape the mouth shut (he says he could hear the peel of the duct tape).

They'd saw open the neck and then tape that shut, too, so the sacrifice bled into their throat and drowned in it, and because their hands were already twisted off, they couldn't take off the tape so they'd just wriggle around like worms until they died.

Then the people in the walls all said good night, very formally, and went to bed.

My mom says he didn't need to tell me that part.

My dad says it's the only part that matters.

Which always makes my mom angry.

Which makes my dad stop talking.

My dad says, at the time, he didn't know why they killed their own, how they chose the sacrifice, or what they did with the bodies.

Which he says he imagined simply piling up behind the walls, for years and years, slowly filling the house until the walls warped and small person parts began sliding out through cracks in the wallpaper.

Which he told my mom.

Which she was nervous about, because she was scared that she was scaring him away.

Which she tried not to do, by assuring him that the people in the walls just had a very different way of life.

Part of which must have been eating their own.

Which must have been where the bodies went.

Which she assured him is perfectly natural—lots of cultures eat strange things, including dogs and people.

Which my dad says he asked my grandpa about.

Which my grandpa denied, because the small people sounded much too polite to eat their own, despite all that killing they did very regularly.

Which my grandpa almost said more about, but stopped himself.

Which made my dad *really* wonder where the bodies went.

Dad says he spent several days sitting in a chair in the corner while Mom ran around the house, trying to find the Santa figurines.

Dad says she asked him to join her, but he couldn't.

Dad says he was too scared to even think.

A few days into the trip, he went looking for Grandma Ellen, who he found in the attic.

Which is where he found her kneeling by a small metal latch in the wall.

Which was about three inches tall, and which was in the wall right by the floor.

Which he says she had open, and was scooping something out of.

Which, when he got closer, he saw was parts.

Arms. Legs. Heads.

Small person parts.

Which made him want to throw up.

Which made my grandma get a chair and tell him to sit down.

Which he did, as he waited for her to get him a glass of water.

He stared at the small open door, and at the little basket of parts she'd been scooping (all the fingers and feet sticking out), until she came back.

Which she did, carrying a glass of water he was too scared to drink.

Which is when she explained about the limbs.

Which started, she said, when my mom was in middle school.

Grandma said, one day after my mom came home from school, she and my mom were wondering about the people in the walls and wanted to know what they looked like.

"They seem so sweet," my grandma said. "Saying good night so politely every night, and making tea."

My mom, who hated the sound of the kettle when they made tea because it woke her up (which I said already), only half agreed.

"But," she said, "I *do* think I'd like to meet them one day. Maybe peel apart the walls and look inside."

Which gave them both the same idea at the same time.

Which led to them tearing apart a wall in the kitchen that very minute, giggling and looking around with flashlights.

Which revealed hundreds upon hundreds of people, each about a foot tall, hanging from beams like bats, arms crossed over their chests, fast asleep. They were dressed very nicely, in vests and trousers and house dresses and pant suits and gowns and tuxedos and all kinds of things. Even a monocle or two.

Which my mom thought was just adorable.

Which is why she took one.

Then they covered up the wall hole with cardboard, nailing it in place.

The person she took screamed and squealed and kicked, even bit. My mom tried to keep it in a glass jar but it suffocated (which my dad says means "ran out of air"), so she had to get another one.

Which she did by peeling up the nails in the cardboard, plucking another person out of the wall, and putting the cardboard back in place, holding in one hand the still-sleeping person.

Which, according to my grandma, she kept in a terrarium.

Which lasted a while, until the small person broke their head against the glass wall and killed themselves.

Which led to my mom taking another. And then another. And another. All of them killed themselves, or died by accident. One made a rope from her little pants and hung herself in the cage.

"Some people keep guinea pigs, or fish," my grandma explained to my dad. "They die all the time. It's not any different. Pets are hard."

But my grandma started feeling really bad that my mom couldn't keep any of them alive.

So she took the most recently dead one, fixed it up, and dipped it in glaze, then baked it, turning the person into a little ceramic figurine. Keeping it locked in the same little position forever.

My grandma surprised her with the first one, and then dipped the next dead pet (which came a few days later) in the glaze, too, so the first would have a friend on the shelf. They posed them together on the mantel, my dad told me. Two little figures waving at each other. Then my grandma and mom started taking people out of the walls and making figurines together, which became their favorite thing to do together.

But the small people got tired of this. They got tired of losing people at random all the time. So every morning, they chose one of their own and served them up in the attic.

"Isn't that a hoot?" my grandma said to my dad, laughing.

He wanted to know why they killed each other so violently.

Grandma Ellen said the butchering was actually very helpful because it made turning the people into figurines much easier. This way, my mom and grandma didn't have to scoop out the blood or the eyes or try moving the limbs through "rigor mortis" (which is when a dead body gets too stiff to move). They just had a bunch of parts they could adjust like they wanted. The people in the walls did it to "appease" Mom and Grandma Ellen, which means make them happy.

"They think we're gods," Grandma Ellen told my dad.

Which I understand, because of the Mayans.

I asked my dad why he was never really into the figurines, and he gave me a strange look.

I asked him why he decided to stay with Mom if he didn't like them so much.

Which is when he told me that my mom told him that if he tried to leave, she'd sacrifice him to the giants.

"You're *my* choice," she told him.

He said that made him nervous.

I asked him if she meant she'd sacrifice him just like the small people did.

Which is when his eyes got really wide and he said, "Yes, but Ellie—*everybody* is the small people."

"But we're not small," I told him.

"Yes, we are," he said.

"But we don't live in walls," I told him. "There aren't any giant people around."

"We *do* live in walls," he said.

He told me that every so often, the giants pick someone. They bring them up out of the wall, they fix them up, and dip them in ceramic. They pose them however they want. Sometimes, if the giants are taking too many people, it's easier to sacrifice someone. If someone's really old or really sick, we sacrifice them to the giants.

My dad says that's what happened to my grandpa.

My dad says he had Alzheimer's, which is when your brain rots before your body does.

My dad says he asked to go.

My dad says they all got together in the living room and cut him up. Dad couldn't do it, so he was the one who handled the duct tape.

Which he also almost couldn't do.

My mom popped the eyes, he says, and Grandma Ellen twisted off the hands.

Which he says is the worst thing he ever saw.

Which he says was only made worse by my mom and my grandma chanting as they worked.

"This is our choice. This is our choice. This is our choice."

He says he felt watched by the people in the walls. He says he felt their fingers wriggling at the boards, pushing their faces against the wallpaper and trying to see. He could feel hundreds of curious faces looking at him from all around the room.

He says once they'd butchered my grandpa, they got all the pieces in a basket and then hauled the basket outside.

He says they carried it into the woods.

He says they got the basket on a rope and pulley on one of the trees.

He says they worked the rope and hiked the basket up the tree.

He says that after ten minutes of work, the basket disappeared into the mist.

He says that they could feel something tugging on the rope, up there, beyond where they could see, at the very top of the world.

He says that when they pulled the basket back down, it was empty.

Which is why, he told me, he went nuts and burned my grandma's house to the ground.

Which he says was terrible, because he had to make sure he didn't get caught, and because he could hear all the little voices in the walls screaming.

He says he could see their little hands flailing outside the wallpaper.

He says he could hear their bodies burning.

He says he could see them tumbling out of the walls as they died.

Melting, bleeding, and popping like cooked sausages.

He says he felt bad that Grandma got trapped in the fire, too.

He says he doesn't feel *that* bad, though.

All of which he says I am never allowed to tell my mom.

Ever.

Ever.

Ever.

Which I told him I wouldn't.

Which is also why he doesn't like to go in my room.

He doesn't like to think about the figurines in my room.

He doesn't like to think about where my mom keeps getting them.

He doesn't like to think about how I get one every year for my birthday, and how sometimes my mom will surprise me with one at random.

But my mom just says that's because he's not open to new experiences.

Because he's "grounded."

My mom says that when I hear our house settling at night, it's not the house at all.

She says it's the people in the walls.

My dad says that's not true. He says it's the house moving of its own accord, and his hands shake when he says this.

My mom says that's ridiculous because no house does anything of its own accord, and there are no accidents, there are only things that the people in our walls do not want us to see.

My mom says that *every* house acts according to the people in its walls.

That even *our* house acts according to the people in its walls.

That Dad should be careful, or she'll sacrifice him to the giants, and feed his parts to them in a basket, which they'll haul all the way up a tree so someone larger than us can scoop them out of a latch in the attic.

Just like Grandpa.

Which my dad never says anything to.

Which makes my mom laugh, and then she ruffles his hair and says she loves him.

Which she also says to me. "I love you."

Especially when she gives me a new figurine.

Which is all the time.

Sometimes, I stay up and try to hear the small people in *our* walls.

Sometimes I listen very hard.

But I never hear anything.

My dad says this is because they're scared, and don't want to be found.

My dad says they're scared of people like Mom, and Grandma, and me.

My dad says I shouldn't like the figurines.

My dad says it's cruel.

But I think Mom's right.

I think he's not thinking about it the right way.

Plus, Mom says I'm almost the same age she was when she started.

Mom says, soon, she'll show me the hole in the attic where she gets the parts.

Mom says she'll show me how to use a knife, so I can help take care of Dad when he gets old and sick.

Mom says she's excited to show me how to make my own figurines.

Mom says it's like having a Mr. Potato-Head, and you always have new ones to play with.

Which I'm excited for, too.

I like Mr. Potato-Head.

And I like ceramic figurines.

SLIPPER

CATRIONA WARD

It's a dark and stormy night and I drink three in quick succession. This combination of dark rum and sugar has always been particularly effective. I do not want to retain detail, this evening– want to be nicely blunted for the conflict that's sure to come.

"We leave at nine sharp tomorrow morning," Rachel says. "How much did you have before I got here?" Her fingers play nervously on the stem of her wine glass.

"Not enough. I hate the countryside."

Rachel's finger strokes the back of her ear, the old sign of her irritation. We know how to irk one another, how to hurt. Brothers and sisters do. "You could lay off just this once, Henry," she says. "Couldn't you?"

"I could," I agree. I order another. The waitress comes quickly, as if she had been waiting eagerly for just this moment. It is that stagnant time in August when town is as hot as an empty hell. Surprisingly, the drinks are served correctly, in a highball glass.

"It's a disease," I explain to Rachel. She shakes her head. "You used to be fun. Once upon a time."

"You used to be kind," she replies.

She has come to London for me, I know. She will do her best to ensure that I arrive at the funeral and remain upright throughout.

⟜

As we go into the night, the sky tears open. Rain descends in rippling sheets, great drops of it fall plosive on the cobbles. Thunder cracks the air and then comes lightning. Rachel catches my hand and for a white-lit moment we are small again, frightened animals under a spring storm. Strands of dark hair cling to her wet face as if painted there.

"I don't want to go, R," I say.

"I'm glad," she says. I can scarcely hear her over the hammer of the rain. "Be good for you to do something you don't like, for once."

I lean in close and speak into her ear. "You look much older than you did a year ago," I say. "That sour expression is settling in. You should keep an eye on it."

⟜

There is of course no question of me driving. I fall asleep in the passenger seat as we are leaving London, and I wake just as we are turning into the gates of Monkshood. It gives me a nasty jolt of immediacy, as if the house is following me around.

Monkshood is square, white, built on the remains of a medieval priory. It has a cheerful air that belies its name and late inhabitant. The house is surrounded by little woodlands, filled with banks of nodding aconite, the flower they call monkshood. I don't know whether the house was named for the flowers or the monks, or for both.

I wonder, as I approach the front door, if something will happen when I enter the house; whether it will expel me, send me flying across the lawn. Perhaps I will be consumed by flame. But nothing does happen, and I go in. I sort of wasn't prepared for that.

"You have been busy," I say to Rachel. The house is almost stripped bare. Packing crates and cardboard boxes stand against the walls, filled with books and lumpy bundles of newspaper which I suppose are fragile items—china, ornaments, the mantle clock. I'm to have the contents of the house, and Rachel will have Monkshood itself. She agreed it all with Father, and I couldn't give a damn. She has an affinity for this place, for its ways and moods that borders on the eerie. I wondered whether she might stay, but it seems not.

You could interpret her packing everything up as a generous gesture – to save me trouble. If you didn't know us better, you might indeed think that.

"Here's hoping some fool buyer comes along, and quickly," I say. "Then you and I don't have to see one another again."

I go down into the bowels of the house. I've got to face it sooner or later; it may as well be now.

The basement is cold and white under the glare of the bulb. The shelves that line the walls are empty, exposing the dusty plaster behind. In the south east corner, there is the bricked-up arch that once led to the old cellars, which are all that is left of the priory. I watch the arched doorway, as if something might come through from the dark place beyond, through the brick, through time. I can almost feel Father here. That won't do. I take the bottle from inside my jacket and drink, eyes watering. That helps.

As children, Rachel and I loved the cellars. They were a maze of old passages and little rooms. There were mice and snails and beetles down there. Sound didn't behave the way it should. We convinced ourselves that the air still smelled like the wine that had been stored there once. But it was probably just damp. We lit candles, made hoods out of sacks and formed a procession of two, walking through the narrow passages, intoning in the guttering light. We did not know any Latin, so we chanted nonsense words.

It was fun to be down there together, the unease walking pleasurably up the back of my neck with its light insect legs. The monks built the cellars, but they had been used by others in the long years since. We found treasure in dark corners. An old silk shoe with a kidskin sole, almost entirely rotted away. A fine length of chain, a ration book.

I never went into the tunnels alone. That would have tipped the balance between pleasure and fear. Rachel wasn't the same. She would spend hours down there, exploring the long stone passages. When I was sent to call her for supper I stood uncertain under the arch, watching the semicircle of light thrown on the uneven flagged passage, and beyond, the dark.

"R," I called, as quietly as possible. I was always afraid, at those times, that something else would answer. The walls threw back my voice in a weird echo. *R, R, R.* Sometimes it was minutes before she replied.

"H." The sound of her footsteps multiplied, became that of a slow army shuffling towards me in the black. When she appeared, dusty-headed, pupils big with the dark, I was so happy to see her.

"Sorry," she said, stroking my head. "I went too far, that time."

"Don't get lost," I said, clinging to her. "Why do you like it here so much?"

"It teaches me things," she said, thoughtful.

Rachel was fifteen then, I remember that, and it was shortly afterward that she began sleepwalking.

I was in that elastic place between sleep and waking. I heard footsteps on the landing, passing my door. The tread was far too light to be a person. *Oh, it's just the cat*, I thought. Then I sat upright, because we didn't have a cat.

I seized a torch from the bedside and opened the door. I saw Rachel going down the stairs. I hissed her name and when she didn't answer I followed, feet curling on the cold stone of the entrance hall. She vanished through the little iron-bound door in the corner. I hurried after.

The torch beam danced weirdly over the cluttered basement, showing objects in momentary alarming clarity. I found the opening to the cellars in time to catch Rachel's pink pyjamas disappearing into the dark. I went to the dark mouth and called her name but I knew it would be no good. There was only the empty echo of my voice. It was as if she had been eaten.

I knew, miserable, that I had no choice. I couldn't go in after her. I just couldn't be alone in that place. So I went to wake Father.

We searched all night but it was not until morning that I found her, curled up behind an old barrel, eyes blank. She was as cold as the dead and something had gnawed at her fingernails, biting them right down to the quick. Her socks had also been eaten through, and her toenails nibbled on. I realised with a little icy shock that it must have been mice.

That was the first time. After the second, Father had the archway filled in and the cellars were closed off for good.

Rachel watched the old gardener do it brick by brick. Later, after they had gone, she stayed, dark eyes still fixed on the glistening, freshly plastered wall. "I don't think that was good idea," she said, shaking her head. "He shouldn't have done it."

"Come up to bed, R," I said.

Her words rang a chime of unease in me. There was something blank and frightening about the solid white place, the door that was not a door, the silent dark behind. The cellars had been eerie when they lay open and crumbling. After Father had them closed off, they became terrifying. Even upstairs, in the hallway on a sunny day, I could still feel the vaulted spaces there beneath our feet, the lonely passages echoing.

Father saw my fear of course. He had an innate cunning, a way of putting his finger on your vulnerable places. I am sure that is why he began to bring me down here to do it.

It still looms in my dreams, his face, the expression it wore at those times. *That will earn you a slippering.* He took it from his foot, burgundy to match his dressing gown. *Bend over, old boy.* The slippering part was over quickly. It was just a rehearsal for the other thing. *Come here, old bean.* It was always *old boy* or *old bean.* He never called me Henry, then. We each became someone else at those times.

Afterward I would go to the woods. Rachel always found me there.

"He doesn't mean to hurt," she would say. "He never had kindness from his own Papa, you see, so it's not natural to him." She held me tightly. Her arms were warm about my shoulders. Rain dripped from the green leaves and the scent of the earth was all around. It can't have been true, but in these memories the aconites are always in bloom, their delicate purple heads pearled with rain. I wished I could tell her what the slippering really was, but I didn't have the words for such things back then. Perhaps I still don't.

Enough. I shake myself free of memory. Even the here and now is better than that. There's something wet on my face, and my breath keeps catching with a *click* in my throat.

This is exactly what I wanted to avoid. I go upstairs quickly. The packing cases loom in the quiet dusk. To make myself feel better I take something out of a nearby box, wrapped in newspaper. The china makes a grinding sound as it breaks under my foot. It is to be mine, after all. I can do what I like with it. I put the package with its shattered contents carefully back in the crate. Then I go to father's study.

"You're out of luck," Rachel says. She sits in the window seat, swinging her leg. Her hair falls long and dark down her back. There is grey in it, I see now. I was just trying to rattle her, last night, but I wasn't entirely wrong. She looks worn away, like her face is being eroded. "The decanter, the glasses, the whiskey, the brandy," she says. "They were the first things I packed up. Sorry, H. Kill yourself if you like. I won't be a part of it."

I mime despair. It is infuriating that she has anticipated me—but after all, we have always known to expect the worst of one another.

I have an emergency bottle in my bag but I'm not going to tell her that.

⊸

I sleep on a mattress on the sitting room floor. All the bedrooms are full of boxes, the beds broken down into pieces, leaning against the wall. I can't help but suspect that this is Rachel's way of delivering her message—that I have no place at Monkshood. Really, she needn't have bothered. I was born in this house but I never felt at home here.

Images drift through my mind. A red spaniel's tail, Father's silver headed walking stick. He lost his leg in the Great one, which didn't stop him going back for the second. I think they let him sit behind a desk for number two. He must have hated that, almost as much as he hated being a parent. Perhaps we could all have been perfectly happy if Mother had lived. He could have shot and walked the dogs and drunk brandy and soda and never seen us at all. But she died and by some terrible mishap the money died with her, or at least it went back to America, which was just as bad. So he couldn't pay for help or the kind of school that would take us out of his sight.

I don't remember her. I think Rachel does, just.

⊸

They wake me in the night, the long shining needles of pain. I set my teeth and manage not to make a sound. Real pain is a private thing; I won't have Rachel's eyes on me. It sweeps through again, stabbing at my eyes, my head, my heart and along the length of my limbs. My jaw clenches so hard that I feel a shard of molar come away on my tongue.

The vodka trickles into my mouth through my teeth. It's the worst thing I could do for the pain, of course, but it is the only thing that helps. At length the agony recedes, or maybe I get used to it. It is a recent development, the alcoholic neuropathy, a sign that matters are reaching a crisis.

⊸

I wake to the sound of the world breaking. It's so loud that it seems to almost be inside me. I raise a bleary head. The noise comes again from below.

At first, I think that the basement is filled with fog. Actually, the air is white with dust. It tickles my nostrils with its dead chalky scent. Through the swirling clouds I can see a figure clothed in white overalls, wearing goggles like the eyes of a great insect. I call out and the figure pauses mid swing, jackhammer raised above its head.

"What are you doing?" I ask again, although that is fairly clear. The hole in the cellar wall is like a jagged mouth, rounded in surprise or a scream. What I meant to ask was, *why?*

The white figure lowers the jackhammer to the ground. It raises the goggles to show Rachel's brown eyes, ringed with plaster dust. "Go and help yourself to coffee," she says. "It's in the kitchen."

"It's something to do with probate," she says, spreading butter on toast with a shaking hand. There are blisters on her palm where she gripped the hammer. The morning light is cruel on her parchment skin. "Naturally, Father didn't have permission to brick up that arch. The surveyors will have to get in and look at the foundations to value it. This house is built on a bloody honeycomb."

She eats the toast in three quick bites, teeth clicking, and then rises. Her old black dress is too big for her now, the neckline shows her sharp, carved-out collarbones. "Are you ready?"

⟜

The important thing at funerals is not to allow oneself to feel too much. You've got to be careful, or you will leave a piece of yourself in the grave with the dead. My feelings aren't about father, of course, but that won't save me.

We aren't the only ones in church, but almost. The solicitor who drew up the will is here from the village. He has a comically old-fashioned little moustache, like a neat pair of apostrophes painted on his top lip. He is nervous and his eyes are young. There are two neighbours, women, who I don't know. They must have moved here since I left. They have come for curiosity, I suspect, rather than affection. We don't go to the graveside after the service, Rachel decided that. And suddenly, it's over.

The young solicitor comes back to Monkshood, as do the curious neighbours. The day is beautiful, flooded with sunlight. Along the drive, the aconites are coming into bloom.

Rachel has made a clearing in the forest of boxes and crates, large enough for us all to stand with a tea and a biscuit. It is cramped and there is nowhere to put our cups down so we talk and drink, hunched over them.

"I'm Tom Orland," the solicitor says. "Of Orland and Orland." I can't take my eyes from his little moustache. "Your father's executor. Will it be convenient after tea?"

I shrug. "I refer you to my sister," I say. "She's in charge. None of this has anything to do with me."

One of the women tells me how beautiful the house looks today. "My father was keen on local history," she says. "Monkshood was fascinating to him. Nothing was ever built here,due to some old protection about common land—I can't remember exactly what. Such a waste, it's a lovely position. Then your grandfather got around the bylaw somehow and built the house."

"Well, there was the priory here before all that," I say. "Monkshood stands on its foundations."

"No," she says, puzzled. "There was certainly never a priory in these parts."

"How strange," I say politely and excuse myself to the lav. It is unwise to leave it too long between nips.

The women leave reluctantly after an hour or so, craning brightly round corners, eyes guessing the shapes of shrouded furniture, wrapped objects. "What a lovely scent," one of them says. "Is it potpourri?" She's right, I can smell it too: something heavy and rich, like wine.

We perch awkwardly on the boxes in the study and Tom Orland takes out the will. He reads slowly and stumbles a little. I have already had rather a lot from my emergency bottle today, and I'm sitting in a patch of warm sunlight. I find my mind drifting, moving outside, lightly borne on the summer day, over the tops of the apple trees in the orchards. Below me the young green grass, the rushing stream, glimpses of blossom.

I am brought back by Rachel's scream. She is pale and trembling, one hand over her mouth, staring at Orland. "That cannot be right," she says.

"Those are the terms," he replies. "The contents of the house are yours, but Monkshood is left to Henry."

"Damn you, Henry." Her voice is a high rasp. "This very last thing, you couldn't help taking it too."

"I am as surprised as you." To the solicitor I say, "It doesn't have to change anything. We can sell it, just as Rachel was planning to. I'll give her the money."

"You aren't permitted to sell, or leave it vacant," Orland says. "I'm terribly sorry, but unless you agree to live at Monkshood it will go to a trust for wounded soldiers."

My brain is fogged with surprise and vodka. "I don't understand," I say. "Why would Father want me to live here?"

Rachel stares at me. Then a smile spreads across her face. It is too wide, like a cut made by a knife. She begins to laugh.

"Stop," I say. "Please. God, Rachel."

"I see it now," she says. "He's not giving the house to you. He's giving you to Monkshood. What's left of you, that is." She makes for the door, gasping with tears. When I try to stop her, she shoves me and I lose my balance and fall hard among the boxed remains of Father's life.

I find Rachel at our place in the woods. She is hugging her knees and staring into nothing. The birds sing in the trees around us, a riot of life.

I sit down beside her. "Let the soldiers have it," I say. "We'll manage somehow. You could come back to town with me."

"No," she says,

"Oh, come," I say. "How much would it really have fetched, this old pile?"

"I wasn't going to sell it," Rachel says. "I was going to burn it. Do you never wonder why the aconites are always in bloom, here?

"They're not," I say. But I stop for a moment, struck by doubt. Perhaps she is right.

"Oh, H," she says, furious. "You are wilfully blind. You never want to face up to things."

"Steady," I say. But I have a numb feeling like the creep of frostbite.

"It lives in the cellars," she says. "Though they're not cellars, not really. It is old and it doesn't understand that everyone it knew is dead. If you decide to live in the house, you're going to have to give it things. People. Father offered up mother, and after that he gave you—at least, the part of you that mattered."

"No one gave me to anyone," I say. "I'm right here."

"Are you?" Rachel's touch is cool on my cheek. "Don't be so sure, H. It eats all kinds of things."

I feel very drunk, and I wonder if perhaps this is all a hallucination. But I have a horrible feeling that it's not. It seems like something I have always known. "What is it?" I ask. "Does it have a name?"

"I don't know," she says. "Maybe. I had my own name for it. It always spoke to me when Father took you to the basement. I could hear the beating and the sound mingled with its voice. So, when I was very little, I called it Slipper." She takes my face in her cool hands and looks. Her eyes are long and dark. "The thing is H, what's left for me, even if I get free of it? What is there for you? Where do we belong?"

And here we are at last in the final place; the secret that lies at the heart of us both.

It was after one of those times, when Rachel was comforting me in the woods, that it first happened between us. I was sixteen, she seventeen. I could sense that I was growing too old for Father. He called me to the basement less frequently, but it had the violence of disappointment. It had been a bad one, that day. I remember rising above my body. I felt my limbs flying apart, each to a different corner of the room. When I got to the woods I was still weeping, and all the feelings were running into one another.

Rachel found me there. She held me and cried a little too. She asked me again and again what was wrong. I couldn't tell her. So I did the next best thing and tried to speak to her through touch. The curve of her cheek, the long sweep of her lashes, the mole on her wrist – her body is mapped forever in my mind. A long-ago journey, which we never speak of. When I came to the glade that day, I felt that nothing about my person belonged to me anymore. But the moment I touched Rachel, I owned myself again.

I started it, I know. But it is something we did together. It is still the best thing that ever happened to me, and I suspect to her too, which is why we cannot forgive one another.

"You're right," I say, and take her hand. "We only belong together." Is this happening now, or then? The past and the present overlie one another. The blinding blue of the aconites is painful to my eyes, my heart. We are enclosed in a circle of us. It has the feeling of something written long ago, and out of our control.

-o-

We stand before the crumbling archway. Piles of broken brick litter the floor. The scent of wine is rich in the air. I don't know what time it is, or even what day. We were a long time in the glade. Stars wheeled overhead, and dawn came twice, I think. But now it is time to act.

"We have a gift for you," Rachel says to the dark. "It's the greatest gift you can be given, because it is surrendered willingly. And in return you have to promise to go to sleep for a long, long time." She looks thin and frightened, and very young. I take her hand.

"Do you promise?" Rachel asks. The dark seems to pulse. It reaches out like a hand towards us, its breathing deep and long. How did I not hear it all those years?

"Was that a yes?" I whisper to Rachel.

She shakes her head. "It doesn't matter," she says. "It lies."

I flick on my torch. We walk hand in hand into the dark. As we go through the tunnels, the old walls breathe about us. I tighten my grip on her hand.

"Not just yet," she whispers. The scent of wine is strong, now, it encloses us like smoke. I can smell what is underneath– the liquid stench of rot.

We reach an open space in the deepest part of the tunnel. A cave. This is further, deeper than I have ever been. Or perhaps it wasn't here when we both came exploring as children. Maybe this part of the maze is just for Rachel. The chamber is lit by some unseen source. I turn off the torch. The paintings on the uneven rock walls seem to dance, the men with spears chase the great deer through the flickering light. Many crude wooden racks are scattered across the cave floor, hung with drying skins. Pelts are stretched across tables. Some are the hides of animals. Some are not. I can see the flattened outline of a nose, the creased skin of a knuckle, the light down of a young man's chest.

In the centre of the chamber there is a hole. It is from this hole that the breathing comes. As we approach, the sweet rotten scent intensifies until I am choking with it. I can hear its voice, now—it is filled with the sound of beaten flesh and my father's grunting. *Slipper.*

I take the matches from my pocket, and my emergency bottle from beneath my coat. There is a petrol-soaked rag in the neck of the bottle. I light it and throw the flaming bottle into the dark hole. There is a roar and then comes a noise so great that it sounds like silence. Rachel and I look at one another. The world grows wide and white and we are truly together at last.

HOW TO STAY AFLOAT WHEN DROWNING

DANIEL BRAUM

Montauk, New York

I figured slipping away to the bar would be a good way to escape the table's cringe-inducing conversation, but I can still see Uncle Roy and Alison, laughing it up with the Client and our hired boat captain among the litter of cracked lobster shells and half-eaten fish platters.

The bartender sees me coming and is ready with another rum and coke. The night wind blows a gust of clean ocean air into the dock's aroma of fried food and cigarette smoke.

"Enough fishing talk for you, buddy?" the bartender says over the miasma of tables full of high-season out-of-towners here for something the fast-paced Hamptons can't offer.

He knocks on the wooden bar top and collects the dollar bills pinned under the tea light burning in a thick shot glass.

"I prefer my meals without talk of buckets of blood and guts," I say. "Thank you very much."

From over my shoulder a laugh joins the murmur of lapping waves audible in the second before the next classic rock song kicks in on the tinny speakers.

The bartender and I both turn to look at the woman on the stool next to me. She's in a long sun-dress and a green army surplus jacket despite June's warmth. There's no make-up on her young face, but she doesn't come across as young; the way her lithe frame is comfortably parked on the bar stool speaks of years. I think there's something unusual about her forehead but it's just the glow from the light strings hanging above the bar flashing on and off her face.

"What's so funny?" I ask.

She's staring past me at the water. I don't think she's going to answer.

"Everyone knows the real way to chum for sharks is to cut yourself from nape to navel and let your guts spill out," she says.

I expect her to laugh again, or at least smile. She doesn't.

The bartender winks at me and steps over to serve an old Italian man who has come up to the bar.

"We're uh, talking metaphorically here, right," I say. "Spill as in, spill into life? Your life, my life? Not into the water, right."

"Sure. Yeah sure," she says, blankly.

I feel like I've disappointed her and she's searching my face for a hint of the answer she wanted. I know I should be uncomfortable with the way her gaze remains on me but I'm flush with excitement.

"Come on, you know what I mean," she says.

I *don't* know what she means but I smile like I do.

"I'm not really one for chumming," I say.

"But you're bleeding all over the place."

There's a splash from baitfish jumping below.

"*You better look out . . . there may be* sharks *about . . .*" I half-sing.

It's her turn to smile at me with no idea of what I'm talking about.

"Sorry. My singing's terrible, I know," I say. "The real lyric is *dogs* not *sharks* though . . . never mind."

"I get it," she says. "Sharks smell blood like some people smell weakness."

At the table the Client and Uncle Roy are pretending they're holding rifles and aiming into the air.

I try to fight away the memory that comes. I'm surrounded by a mob that's pulling a six-foot thresher out of surfer-crowded waves and I'm squeezing Nina's hand.

"Fear isn't strength, it's just . . .thrashing," I mutter.

"Strength is in truth. The real kind of truth vulnerability brings," she says.

"Not too many people feel that way or would even comprehend that."

"You do," she says. "But you're here to hunt?"

I'm not here to hunt. There's no way I'm going out with Alison and them in the morning. There's no way to tell her without spiraling into everything I don't want to talk about. I almost say 'I'm just here to get through the day', but even that intentionally casual answer leads to unwanted paths.

"I'm only here for my family," I say.

She laughs again.

"What?"

"Tell me something true," she says.

"That is true. That's my sister sitting over there with my Uncle Roy. She runs the surf apparel distributorship our parents founded. The guy next to her is the purchaser for a big group of stores. So yeah, the point of the weekend is to land his business. The other guy is the boat captain my sister hired to take us out tomorrow. He told us his full name but he insists we call just him Captain Mike. He's a *bit* too serious about the Captain part of it too, if you ask me. Boring stuff."

"Then tell me something else."

"I don't know, like what?"

"Do you surf?"

"Never been on a board. Yeah and my family's business is surfing, go figure."

She swirls the ice in her glass, slides a few cubes through her lips then covers her mouth as she shifts her lower jaw. I think I hear a little pop.

"I . . . lived out here one summer," I say. "Feels like a lifetime ago. It was."

"What *was* it like?"

"Nothing like now, the town's grown up so much since—"

"No. What was it like for you?"

"Me? I was young, though I didn't feel young at the time. I felt alone and far from home. Then I fell in with someone. We were sort of engaged and . . . what can I say, we ran away together. That's what it was like."

"Almost sounds romantic," she says.

"I wish it was. It should have been. It wasn't."

"Are there really any good places left to run to?" she asks.

"We found a place in the middle of nowhere. Costa Rica. They have bats down there we wanted to see. This kind that grab fish right from the water.

We had to take buses, and a little plane, and then a boat. The boat had to go . . . well the whole thing was a mess. Did you know whirlpools were a thing? I never knew they were real. And a thing to worry about when you navigate into the mouth of a river from the ocean. That's how I know. For a while there we thought our boat was going down. I'm not the praying type but I swore if we got out of it alive I'd never leave sight of land again."

"Wow, careful," she says.

"Don't worry. I'm not going out tomorrow. No way."

"I meant careful, keep being honest and vulnerable like that—"

" . . .and I don't know what I'll attract."

"I guess that too," she says. "I was going to say careful, you might get used to it."

We stare past the diners and drinkers at the crescent moon and the red dot beneath it. I wonder if she's going to speak. I like that she isn't about small talk, that she dives right into the heart of things.

"Can I get you another drink?" I say. "Better yet, I'm dying to get out of here. You up for a change of scenery?"

"It's late."

"Yeah, the days start so early around here. How about just one more?"

"It's not that," she says. "I'm here for my family too."

I want to ask *her* to tell *me* something true but it feels like the moment to ask that has passed.

"If I stay I'm going to have to go back to that table and talk about fishing and brand name wet suits," I say. "So I'm gonna walk these drinks off. If you're feeling like company and want to walk and talk with me, just say the word."

"I've already stayed too long. I have to find my sister."

She stands. I awkwardly wish her good night and mumble something about how I understand family comes first instead of asking her name and if I could see her tomorrow. She weaves through the tables and disappears into the door leading to the inside part of the restaurant and the parking lot and road beyond.

The bartender returns and shakes his hand like he's just touched an oven.

"Now that's a keeper if I've ever seen one," he says. "For a second there I thought you were going to reel her in."

I pay my tab and ask him where else is open around here this time of night.

"You could count the places on one hand," he says, then tells me.

I return to the table. Captain Mike and Uncle Roy are lighting cigars. Uncle Roy implores me to join them.

I politely decline, remain standing, and announce that I'm hitting the hay.

Alison whispers in my ear as I peck her cheek and wish her goodnight.

"You look pale. You okay?"

I nod and smile to let her know that I am.

"Goodnight," I say to the table. "See you all in the morning."

I don't mind lying to them though I'm kicking myself for not having the presence of mind to ask the woman for her name. I hope it's not too late to catch up.

Headlights from the road briefly light up the neighboring dock as I make my way through the tables. One of the busboys is standing on the shore having a smoke.

Somewhere in the dark a night bird calls.

⊸

The dock where I spent so much time with Nina isn't far from here. Salt air smells the same ten years on and isn't easily forgotten. I try to conjure the feel of her hand against mine. I'm not sure which memories are of real sensations and which are just fabrications dulled by the years. Wind rustling the sea grass brings the sense of vast open stretches of sand back to me. The night bird's honking cry echoes over the water . . .

⊸

The ocean breeze has tussled Nina's black bob into a wild tangle framing her sun-touched face. I can smell her last cigarette, though she swears she's quit. She leans in and rescues our melting ice cream cone with a well-timed lick followed by a big sloppy smile that transforms her. She ceases to be the depressed soul who thinks and talks so much about Art School but never paints. I no longer see the street-wise girl, running away from school, from the city, from what she calls 'conformity and everything' but instead she is an ethereal, sensual, carefree being, here watching the waves and afternoon surfers with me. Me. The would-be surfer who's never stepped on a board. With the afternoon sun warming my shoulders through my t-shirt and her sticky hand around mine I think maybe this is all life is, pairing up and running away from whatever it is you are running away from. Together. Like this.

The end of the pier is crowded with people fishing, holding hands, and wave-watching like us. The break isn't so hot but there are still surfers out there hoping the left will develop.

Someone in the water is yelling. Nina and I push over to the railing to look with everyone else. A young man has hooked a thresher shark on a line. The panicked fish spins and spasms as it is hoisted from the waves. A half-dozen people have their hands on the line helping bring it up. The shark swings and manages to smash itself into one of the concrete support pylons. The people pull and pull and bring it up all the way to the rail. A woman leans over and gets her arms around it. Someone holds her waist and pulls her in. The crowd grabs hold of the shark, lifts it over the rail, and drops it on the pier. It flops and twists, its open mouth revealing a maw of dangerous teeth and the steel hook that snared it protruding from its lower jaw. No one wants to go near it now. A widening circle of space forms around it as everyone backs up. The woman who first grabbed it emerges, brandishing a baseball bat. Her blow connects with the shark's side, right under its dorsal fin. It flips, landing on the steel hook, driving it deeper. The woman slams the suffocating thing again, then the mob is all over it. This isn't fishing. This isn't protecting anybody.

Our ice cream splats onto a puddle of blood and salt water. The shark is beaten into an unrecognizable shape. I realize Nina has never seen tears in my eyes. In the chaos of kicks and bat swings and skin and scales it dawns on me we're drowning. We're drowning here.

"Let's go," Nina says.

"I'm with you."

"No. I mean it. I mean let's really get out of here."

"Anywhere you want," I say. "Anywhere at all."

The silver setting reminds me of a wave curving around the small blue opal and two tiny diamond dots. The plan is to ask her to marry me at the lodge, at night, after we see our first fishing bat.

"Maybe I'll draw a bat while we're down here," Nina says, all the bouncing on the dreadful road making her voice vibrate funny.

The awful bus ride doesn't dampen her spirit and she kisses me as we lug our bag from the bus stop to the shore. The roaring ocean and clean air are so welcome. We're warned by the two boatmen not to go in while we're waiting for all the passengers. After ten minutes or so they decide there are no other passengers. There's water in the bottom of the wooden boat. The older man pushes off the beach and jumps in. The boatman on the motor guns it as we crash through the wave line. The boat catches air and lands with a heavy thunk. The older boatman leisurely bails water with a half of plastic jug.

We motor to the estuary at the mouth of the river which is the only way to the lodge. Swells lift and drop us. I don't like the look of the waves we're going to have to pass through nor the way the boatman are bickering in Spanish.

"It's rough," the younger boatman says to me. "We may have to go back and try again tomorrow."

"But it's almost dark," I say. "Where are we going to stay?"

"Don't sleep on the beach," he says. "The sand flies are not very nice."

The men speak to each other in Spanish.

"We're going to try?" I ask.

The boatman guns the engine. I grasp Nina's hand. The water in the bottom has soaked our packs. The older boatman is bailing in earnest now.

A big swell lifts and drops us. We spin and spin and wind up with our port side facing land. The boatmen men yell at each other as the boat is dragged along parallel to shore. Waves hit from all sides, the water fills up faster than the old boatman can bail.

"Can you swim?" the boatman asks.

"What's happening?" I ask.

"Kiss your wife and pray."

The older boatman stops bailing and throws a small wooden crate overboard. Then a full jug of something, motor fuel maybe. Then a bag of oranges he has fished out of the calf deep water. He grabs my pack and I stop him. We watch the jettisoned stuff spin away in the current. Large dark shapes are moving beneath the surface; I spot a lone dorsal fin heading toward the crate.

Nina is perfectly calm though she is squeezing my hand as hard as can be. Behind her a big wave is coming up on us sideways. Her look of resignation inspires a burst of sadness and anger. The boatman guns the engine. The wave slams us. We're soaked but somehow we don't go under and emerge from the blinding spray shooting towards the shore.

⊸○⊷

The sweet woman who runs the lodge escorts us to our cabin which is on a secluded rise nestled into tall palms at the edge of the rainforest. Through the big window taking up most of the far wall we can see the water that almost dragged us down. There is an assortment of pots and pans, a hair dryer, a small electric radio, towels, a flashlight and a can of bug spray lined up on the counter next to the sink in the kitchen area. A thick extension cord runs through the front window bringing power. The shower runs on rain water. We thank her and flop our bedraggled selves onto the big bed. When the woman leaves Nina cries softly. We fall asleep in our soggy clothes; the distant sound of waves no comfort.

We wake in the night. The waves have quieted. The tide has receded. A coral reef and fish are visible in the clear water, their tropical colors illuminated by the full moon. The balcony outside the window is bigger than my apartment. A metal tub, a coal grill, and bucket are the only things on it. We peel ourselves out of our clothes, heat up buckets of water, and fill the metal tub.

From our bath we watch the fish in the water below and spot bats flying by grabbing insects. I rub Nina's shoulders gently and whisper "we made it". This inspires a fresh round of sobs.

"What is it? What's wrong," I ask.

"People don't get it."

"Get what?"

"They don't understand the only thing that's real is how we treat each other. Nothing we do is going to be remembered."

Nothing I say comforts her.

After an hour I decide to trek down the cliff to the main area to see if I can find ice cream or anything that might cheer her up.

⊸○⊷

I return to the cabin and notice the big window is open and the power cord is running through to the balcony. Nina's stopped sobbing. I don't like the low-pitched buzz coming from outside.

"Nina?"

She's motionless in the tub. Her head's tilted back, staring at the sky with that same awful resignation that came over her on the boat. I'm confused at why the cord is out here until I see the submerged hair dryer. A blue arc jumps from Nina's bruised skin joining the pink and orange bolts that crackle over the water every second or two. The awful sound is coming from the radio floating by her feet. The reek of ozone and burnt hair hits me and I understand that what she has done was no accident.

⊸

I told myself a lot of nevers that night. Never leaving sight of land is the one I've kept. I must not have truly meant the rest. I spot the woman from the bar on the bend of the dark road up ahead. I walk faster to try and catch up.

⊸

The shape I thought was the woman is not a person at all but a big owl perched on road kill on the shoulder where the road turns onto Main Street just past where a bunch of cars are parked. The owl sees me, opens its wings and silently lifts into the air.

A man ambles out from behind the nearest car and crosses the road. There's something wrong about his face. He stumbles into the brush and beach scrub on the other side. I realize there's a path to the beach there and I follow him.

A dozen surfboards are half-buried in the sand forming a circle around a small bonfire. Dozens of people, surfers, are drinking and smoking and milling about in the fire-glow. The man stumbles towards them. In his path, I see the woman from the dock standing just outside the ring of light.

I run over.

"Holy shit, you scared the hell out of me," the guy says.

The woman is nowhere to be seen. I spin around looking for her on the beach and in the crowd of surfers.

"Sorry. Uh, hey, did you see which way the woman who was standing right there went?"

"I didn't see anybody," he says.

His face is a patchwork of healed-over burns and scars.

I point to the sand. There's an indentation that's much too big for footprints. It looks like a person or two had been laying there.

"She was right there."

He shrugs and fishes a bright pack of cigarettes out of his pocket. He takes one out, lights it up and pulls deeply. I introduce myself and ask if I can bum one.

He hands me the pack and motions for me to take. Words on the wrapper say *BusaBukaBaki*. The cigarettes are cloves, wrapped in thin white paper. In what far-away place were these purchased? What a life he must have. They all must have.

I scan the beach looking for her again. I spot another of those big indentations in the sand a few yards away.

A tall surfer breaks away from the pack by the fire and comes over.

Every inch of his lean swimmer's build is sun tanned. His hair is bleach blond and he's wearing board shorts and a T shirt like the rest of the young people but the lines on his face show he is older than me.

"Everything alright?" he asks the scarred guy.

"Yeah, sorta, this guy scared me but everything's cool."

"This is a private party," the surfer says to me. "Do we know you?"

"No. And sorry, I didn't mean to crash. Or startle anyone. I'm just looking for my friend."

"You see her?" he asks.

"No. But maybe I can have a look around? To be sure."

A big splash at the shore carries through the darkness before he answers.

"Hey, Danny, I think someone's out there," someone by the fire calls.

The surfer and the scarred guy go to look. I palm the pack of smokes and slide them into my back pocket. I used to lift smokes the same way for Nina; even though I didn't want her to smoke, I knew she would and we couldn't afford it.

There's no one there, just the sets of waves coming in. People are leaving the fire-lit circle to check it out anyway. There's no thrill being here for me. I've come so far from the time I so desperately wanted to be a part of something like this. I return to the road and trek back to my hotel room.

Despite the hour, I cannot sleep. I wish I had told the woman at the bar that I didn't come to hunt; I came for Alison. I did think there'd be something here for me. That I'd be full of memories of Nina. The ache is so dull and far away it is almost not real.

I take a clove from the pack and smoke it. When it burns down I light another one. Nina thought stealing was wrong so I never told her where the smokes came from. I sit and smoke and imagine what it would be like to connect a swing of a bat into the sides of each of the surfers out on the beach. I know it's terrible but I don't care. Nina thought killing the shark was wrong. She'd probably think it was wrong to beat that mob who did it in. I never had the chance to tell her how I much I longed to do that.

⊸⊷

I used to believe there would always be good places left to run to. Now I'm not so sure. Determining if there are any good places left to come back to seems more important.

⊸⊷

Our warehouse was in Hauppauge, less than two hours away when the traffic's right. It was more like home than our house ever was . . .

⊸⊷

There's a hint of saw dust and vanilla pipe smoke in the air, which means Dad's in his workroom shaping a board. Mom is gathering all signs of our domestic activity in the conference room the four of us have made our de-facto dining space and finding hiding places to obscure them from visiting eyes.

"Go get your father before you leave for class," Mom says. "The buyer should be here any second. Tell him it's the Professor, he'll know who."

The whine of the motor on Dad's wonky power sander grows louder as I walk through the rows and rows of stock, shelved wet suits and shoe boxes, towards the corner of our warehouse Dad has claimed for his personal workspace.

I push through the hanging plastic barrier into Dad's world. Remnants of past projects, experiments, and abandoned works in progress fill the small, square space; a test section of planed hardwood, a rack with two shaped but unvarnished boards, dozens of fins.

Dad's at the machine in the center of the room grinding a piece of wood that will one day be a surfboard. His long, dirty-blonde hair is tied back. Oversized safety goggles mask his clear blue eyes. He clenches his stubble-covered jaw in concentration.

The fins fascinate me the most. Dad could easily make standard designs. Easy sells to buyers but he makes all kinds of crazy boards with all sorts of fin positions.

"What kind is this one going to be," I say to announce my presence. "Single fin or double?"

One style is all the rage right now but I can't remember which.

"Neither. When it's done, I'll know."

"Mom says someone's here for you."

"A buyer? This late?"

"Mom said you'll know who."

This inspires Dad to stop the machine. He flips his goggles off.

"It's almost done, want to try it with me?"

"Now?"

"No better time."

"I dunno. I'm heading to class. I'll walk with you up front."

I know he's not pushing. He's trying to instill in me the notion to take on the world, on my own terms and at my own time. I grew up with him telling me you don't know if you can surf until you try and I love him all the more for it.

He shuts the lights and the power and together we walk through the rows of inventory towards the front. He's muttering to himself as we walk.

"When you are taken by the undertow, if you are lucky you realize you are but a river in this dark sea," I discern him saying.

"What's that?"

"Something for this meeting."

"What's it mean?"

"It's something surfers say."

"Come on, tell me."

"If I could I would."

Mom has transformed the conference room back into a showcase for our business. I grab my book-bag and leave Mom and Dad talking about waves.

As I'm getting into my car an old gray fiat with an empty surf board rack on top pulls up.

"Going to school, young man?" the man in the car, who I take to be the buyer, says through his rolled down window.

"Yes, sir."

"Good," he says. "All my best surfers do, I like that."

-o-

When Mom and Dad did not show for work the next morning Alison and I realized they were gone.

The police and the insurance investigators pointed out that the bank accounts were untouched and no valuables, personal items nor a single piece of inventory was missing. Except for whatever Dad was working on. His surfboards and parts and experiments were the only things unaccounted for.

Alison kept the business going fueled by the belief they'd be back. Later that summer, right around when Uncle Roy showed up to help her, I left. I'd only gone out East, but the East End might as well have been the ends of the earth when it came to the warehouse and my sister.

Knocking on the door wakes me.

"Come on. Time to go," Alison is calling from outside.

I get up and crack the door. Morning light leaks in.

"I'm staying behind, sis," I say, pretending my best to sound ill.

"You okay?"

I open the door more so she can see my face, to let her know that I am. The door pushes inward; the security chain stretches taught preventing it from opening. It's Captain Mike.

"That's not how you treat family, son," he bellows. "Get your ass out here. Your client is waiting down at the dock."

Alison maneuvers him out of the way.

"It's okay, I got this," she says.

I'm about to say thank you when I realize she's talking to Captain Mike.

"Can I come in?" she asks.

I let her in. We sit on the edge of the bed. She takes my hand in hers and I know she is asking me to come on the boat.

"I'm not leaving sight of land," I offer as an explanation. "I promised myself after . . ."

"I know," she says. "It must be so hard for you to be back here."

"I'm fine," I say.

"The Client won't go without you," she says.

"Why the hell not?"

"How am I supposed to know, he just won't. Bad luck. Superstition. Misogyny? All of the above?"

"Tell him to fuck off."

"Believe me, I want to. The point of this weekend is to land his business though."

I realize how little I know of her. I know who she *was*. When we were a family. Before I left. From the few times we spoke I remember she'd broken someone's heart or had her heart broken, maybe both. Her life, as far as I know now, is keeping the business alive. And I don't think there's much else.

"Are you going to be okay if he doesn't sign with you?"

She shakes her head, no.

"Uncle Roy thinks I should give up, cash out, and sell the business."

"Why'd you even invite him to come?" I say.

"I wasn't sure you would."

We sit in silence.

"Where's the Client now?" I ask.

"On the boat, with Uncle Roy, waiting for us."

I grab my clothes and take them into the bathroom to get dressed.

The sensation of being pulled sideways in waves comes over me while pulling my shirt over my head. I stumble into the shower curtain.

"You okay in there?"

"Yeah, I'm okay. I'm coming. Just give me fifteen minutes to get coffee."

"Maybe you're not a pussy after all," Captain Mike grumbles under his breath as I leave the room.

"Does your boat hold water?" I ask in reply.

"What the fuck kind of a question is that," he says to Alison. "Where's he going?"

"To get coffee," she says.

I head for the diner Nina and I used to go to on Main Street, next to Lisa's bait shop. Most of the fishing boats are already out. There's no break and the waves are free of surfers. I turn onto the street and join the early-riser tourists walking leisurely from storefront to storefront. The only vehicle traffic is the knife-grinder truck crawling along, announcing its presence with a song on its old-fashioned bells. The truck gives a gentle honk as it passes the hardware store, which I'm amazed is still open for business. I see old Harvey Levitin behind the wheel and give him a wave. He returns the wave without any expression of recognition. A young mail guy is delivering to businesses that have sprung up since I was last here.

The diner next to Lisa's has been replaced by a frozen yogurt shop. It doesn't sell coffee. I wonder how long it will take me to find some and make it to the dock. I look to see if a new place has opened up and see the woman from last night walking my way.

"Hello," I call.

She doesn't respond. I walk over and match her pace.

"Hello. Good morning," I say. "I'm so glad I ran into you. I went looking for you last night. Right after you left. I didn't ask your—"

Her mouth opens into a smile revealing a maw of jagged, triangular teeth. They are sharp and pointed and much too big. The edge of each tooth is serrated with small barbed notches.

I stop and squint, her face now showing no sign of the sharp-toothed monstrosity. She continues walking. I watch her pass the bait shop then double back and go around the side. She's not the woman from last night. Her hair is slightly shorter and she holds herself differently, otherwise she looks exactly like her.

An ambulance turns on to the road and speeds towards us; lights on, siren silent. It gives a brief chirp; the tourists move the minimum distance to give it space. The mailman crosses the street to my side after it passes. I walk to him and ask, "What was that all about?"

"Someone was killed," he says.

"What? Here?"

"Late last night. Beach's full of cops."

"What happened?"

"Who knows? We'll know when they tell us, right?"

We watch it turn left towards the beaches and docks and the path I came upon last night. I want to follow the ambulance. I want to follow the woman. There is no time for either.

⟜

The Captain's forty foot convertible, the Lady Luck, is the only fishing boat remaining at the dock. An American flag attached to one of the antennae on its cabin tower flaps in the breeze. Alison, Uncle Roy, and the Client are on deck watching me approach. I can see Captain Mike inside the open cabin fiddling with the gear and switches on the console.

I step off the dock onto the boat's weathered rail, then onto the cushion of one of the built-in seat benches, then the deck.

"Hey, coffee boy," the Client says. "What happened, no coffee?"

His playfulness is grating. He's so chipper I wonder if he's still drunk. Uncle Roy puffs on a cigar, watching for my response. Is he wanting everything to fail?

"Who needs coffee when we've got eels," Captain Mike says saving me from having to speak. He exits the cabin hauling a white five-gallon bucket in each hand.

"Ready to land some Stripers? Don't let anyone tell you they like squid. This is my 41st summer doing this and I know the bass love this eel."

The edge is absent from the Captain's voice when he directs us to help by untying the ropes holding the boat to the dock. I think he might actually be trying to be pleasant.

"Hold onto your hats," he says. "It's a fine day for fishing."

I hope it is. The Lady Luck leaves the inlet and speeds into the Atlantic.

I'm not happy when the last glimpse of Long Island disappears from view.

The steel gray ocean water is mercifully calm. The sky is clear. The sun is warm. I imagine it is a fine day for fishing. Captain Mike has classic rock playing on the radio. We can hear him singing along over the sound of the engines and gulls hitching a ride in our aerial wake.

He spots something on the fish finder and stops the boat.

He secures our rods in metal holders attached to the rail and helps us bait them. We're told we're over a school of striped bass. Within minutes I watch Alison land the first fish, then every few minutes someone is pulling a two or three-footer from the water.

Captain Mike brings two coolers from the cabin to the deck. One is for storing the fish. The other is full of iced beers. Uncle Roy and the Client each crack open a can. Alison waves her hand-held video recorder in front of them asking them what they've caught. They raise their beers proudly and hand one to me and the Captain.

Captain Mike declines because he is driving the boat and "on duty". I make a show of drinking one with them though a hundred beers aren't going to help me feel any better.

Captain Mike steps in front of the camera.

"I was driving the boat that pulled the world record 70 pounder out of the Sound. There are seventy pounders out there. Who wants a world record?"

We boat farther and farther out following schools on the boat's fish-finding sonar. The Client tells us stories of how his family brought him fishing when he was young and he doesn't seem like that much of a dick. Uncle Roy joins in by telling stories of how much Mom and Dad loved to surf and fish and finally pulls his weight by working in how they were such geniuses in business.

After we fish the next school Captain Mike adds heavier rods and reinforced line into the holders.

"Ready for more or ready for lunch?" he asks.

"We're drinking our lunch," the Client says.

They are such children.

"I suggest you put some grub in your stomach as there's no yakking on Lady Luck," Captain Mike says.

He breaks out the sandwiches he has packed. We sit on the deck benches eating his deli meat sandwiches wrapped in wax paper and foil and throwing bait to the gulls who grab it in the air. The boat rocks in the gentle swell. Alison seems carefree. For a second I almost forget how unhappy I am to be here.

⊸

Something strong is pulling on the Client's line. His rod has bent into a shepherd hook.

Captain Mike scrambles from the cabin.

"Pull 'er in, pull 'er in," he gloats.

"I'm trying," the Client says.

His reel is spinning.

"Okay, give it some, give it some. Let her take it. Wait for her to stop."

About half of the line goes out.

"Now crank," Captain Mike barks. "Want me to take a turn?"

Captain Mike and Uncle Roy and the Client take turns giving line and pulling in.

The client insists Alison take a turn. She passes me the camera. I get a shot of Uncle Roy against the rail trying to spot the fish.

About fifty yards out something jumps from the two-foot waves. A shark. The unmistakable dorsal remains above water for an instant before disappearing.

Captain Mike yells a mix of "hell yeahs" and indiscernible hoots before he switches to English.

"That's a ten-footer, out there," he hollers. "At least."

He instructs the client to take over the rod and reel from Alison.

"You want this fish?" he says to the Client.

"Yes," the Client says.

"Then dig in, this is going to take a while."

"You want this fish?" he asks to Alison and Uncle Roy in turn.

"Then put down that camera and get ready to fight," he yells. "Now we're fishing."

The damn guy is actually trying to give Alison her money's worth.

The Client yells a pathetic imitation of Captain Roy's hooting.

"Now we're fishing," I whisper.

They've wrangled the tired shark up against the side of the boat. Each section of rail is five feet long so we know the fish is over ten feet.

The shark is sleek and streamlined. The silver skin of its pointy head has a blue sheen from the sun and sky.

"Keep your hands away from its mouth," Captain Mike says.

He produces two sticks that look like broom handles tipped with a sharp metal barb. He drives one hook into the side of the shark and instructs the client to hold it. He sinks the other in the fish a few feet away and puts Uncle Roy on it.

"Hold it there. Just a few more seconds."

He lifts the cushioned top of one of the built-in seats and retrieves a short-barrelled shotgun.

The shark slaps its tail sending up a spray of ocean water. I taste the salt on my lips.

He pushes the barrel down, drops in two slugs, and pumps barrel back, chambering the first shot. Then he places the gun about a foot behind the shark's black eye and tries to hold it steady. The gulls on the tower take to the air in a noisy cloud when he fires.

My shoes are soaked with blood. All of our shoes are stained dark red. If Nina could see me now I would tell her I would do anything for Alison just like I tried to do anything for her.

When we reach the mouth of the inlet we can see the small crowd of people from the newspaper and fishing rags waiting at the dock. A crew of two men and a crane-necked hoist help Captain Mike get the Mako from the side of the boat onto the measuring gallows. It is almost twelve feet. The people from the papers are taking photos of the Client and Captain Mike with the shark hanging behind them.

I'd kiss the ground, for real, if everyone wasn't around. The Client is on cloud nine and thanks Alison for it, so at least I didn't break my word for nothing. The guy operating the hoist gives me the business card of his brother who is a butcher and the card of a friend who is a taxidermist. The small town doesn't feel as small as it used to.

A police car pulls up in the lot. Two officers get out and walk directly to us. They ask if they can speak with Captain Mike in private and escort him away from the hubbub to the soda vending machine under the extended roof of the shack that houses the restrooms. I watch the excitement of the day vanish from his face as they speak. Then he doubles over and drops to his knees. The officers help him up. One of them tries to embrace him. He pushes the man away and tries to hide his tears as he runs to his truck.

The surfer killed last night was Captain Mike's son. Someone opened him up the middle from neck to navel. The area on the beach where they found him is still an active crime scene. The Client insists on taking us to the bar and grill on the dock again to celebrate the catch anyway.

A thing like a death is not going to stop people, mostly out of towners like us, from eating and drinking on a weekend summer night. Uncle Roy and the Client are drinking and smoking and holding court at the table for the seemingly endless amount of people who want to congratulate them on their catch over lobster and shrimp cocktails. The Client is flanked by two women he brought to dinner. He says they are his cousin and her friend on summer vacation but they are obviously two escorts from the city. Uncle Roy is in hog heaven. The bartender has named a cocktail for the occasion; he told me he did it under orders of his boss. Alison's downed several of his Mako Madnesses and I don't blame her because she's the one who is really stuck in the shit show.

I escape to the bar, again, to fetch another cocktail for her.

"Too bad it isn't September," the bartender says. "That fish would have won the shark derby for sure."

"How many sharks do they land in the derby?"

"I dunno. A lot. Real shame about Mike's son. I'm not fond of his Dad but Danny was a good guy. I hate what his stupid beach parties do for business but when he's here he always tips proper. Way back when he taught my kid to surf."

"Was he tall and blonde?"

"Like every other surfer, right? No surprise to anyone he was forty-one and never settled down. Speaking of which, whatever happened with that young lady from last night?"

"Oh, I never caught up with her."

"That's a shame."

The Client and Uncle Roy get up from the table, receive a few last back-claps and handshakes, and then depart with the two women. Alison joins me at the bar and lets out the biggest sigh.

"He's going to sign," she says. "Thank you."

"I'm going to celebrate with a clove," I say.

"Cloves. Where'd you get them?" she asks.

"All the surfers smoke them," I say.

"I'll join you."

We go over to the busboy who's taking a smoke break on the beach where the neighboring dock begins.

"Off the record, Captain Mike is a dick," the busboy says as we smoke. "Harsh to hear about his son, though. There's a memorial bonfire going on tonight."

"Want to walk?" I ask Alison.

"Sure," she says. "I'm going to need a week to decompress from this."

We head away from the restaurant lights into the dark. Alison takes off her shoes and walks in the wet sand.

"Thanks for today," she says.

"I'm glad it worked out."

"He's happy as can be. This trip might become an annual thing, but I'll take that as it comes. You okay? You've been thinking about Nina all weekend?"

"Strangely no, something else. Something Dad once said to me."

She doesn't ask what. I don't blame her. It's been a hell of a long day.

"Need any help back at the warehouse?"

"Sure," she says without hesitation. "I'll need the help more than ever now."

"I've been thinking about sticking around. Count me in for Monday morning then."

I don't ask if she ever feels like she is sinking. She's too busy moving and keeping everything going to contemplate such a question.

"You ever wonder why Dad's stuff was the only stuff that went missing?" I ask.

I spot the bonfire up ahead. Even more people than last night are silhouetted in the glow.

"I still have Mom and Dad's boards," she says. "Their personal ones, from the house."

The smell of smoke and sound of rock and roll reach me together.

Someone between us and the fire is walking our way in the wet sand. We step away from the shore to allow her to pass by us easy. She changes course to keep right toward us. A woman. I recognize the elegant contour of her face. Is it the woman from last night? Or this morning?

The woman's lower jaw drops. In the dim light I discern those horrible teeth much too big for her mouth. Her arms do not end in hands but tapered triangles.

I push Alison towards the road. "Go," I say. "She's coming for me."

"What the fuck?"

"Go."

She sees my fear and takes a few steps.

The woman veers for Alison. I try to get between them and I trip on uneven sand.

The woman continues for Alison with only a glance at me. Her skin is rough and grey and full of texture. Someone emerges from the darkness.

For a second I think I am seeing double and that there are two of the same person standing before me.

The first woman tries to side step around the second, but the second woman matches her step. She pushes Alison's attacker preventing her from getting around her. She is the woman I met last night.

"Go, get out of here," the woman from last night says to me. "This is my sister."

Her sister lunges for me. All I see are teeth.

⊸⊙⊷

The two sisters step side to side, their grappling an almost elegant dance. Alison reaches the end of the beach and disappears into the sea grass and dunes.

"I want her meat," the sister says. "Let me—"

"No," the woman from last night says. "Blood from sea for blood from land is not what we do."

The sister tucks her head and throws herself at her sister.

The woman from last night darts aside and her sister thuds down on the spot where she had been standing a second ago. She reaches for her sister's legs. Her thrashing throws up sand and shells and a spray of liquid that I hope is water.

I'm not certain of what I'm seeing; they are two women fighting but their shapes are not right, something more than the almost darkness. I am sure the woman from last night is easily evading her sister's wild swings and thrusts, and that she's speaking, almost singing as she does. With each heave and thrust and bite the two of them wind up closer to the sea. When they reach the wet sand the fighting has stopped. The singing has stopped and I'm watching the two women walking into the water side by side. The receding tide pulls one of them out, leaving the other standing there, watching. I run to her.

"You saved me," I say.

I reach my hand around her back and pull her to me to kiss her. She pushes me away with one hand. The force causes me to stagger backwards and fall. She retreats from the water and stands over me looking down with only disdain on her beautiful face.

"I'm not here for you. I told you I'm here for her," she says. "To stop her from making a mistake."

Her face is the most beautiful I have ever seen. Her sleek, pointed head. Round black eyes. Silver skin with that hint of deep sea blue.

"I understand now."

"What do you think you know?" she says.

"Everything. Life. The currents. Tides. You showed me—"

"I showed you nothing," she says. "There is only one thing I want you to know . . ."

She takes my hand to her face and places my right index finger just inside her thin lips. A quarter inch slit opens in my skin where I touch her human incisor.

" . . .always remember the sharpness of our teeth."

Something jumps from the water at the wave line. A fish. A shark? The shape is larger than I have ever seen in the shallows.

She moves her face close to mine. A raised notch pushes through the skin between her eyes. I try to look away. A single spiny antenna unfurls from the center of her forehead.

⊸⊷

The spine ends in a pleasing shape, a fascinating shape, the shape of something to eat, a source of soft, gentle light in the darkness I cannot look away from.

I see water and waves; there are surfboards in the waves.

V-shaped gills open in a long, elegant neck. The mob carries a shapeless bloody carcass from the pier to the beach. Nina's face, happy and unblemished, dissolves into soft, yellow light, then all fades to darkness.

⊸⊷

I wake up on the beach in the middle of the night. Sometime later, Alison finds me and helps me back to my hotel. I'm overcome with an aching emptiness, I don't know what from. There is only the terrible yearning, so terrible, but I don't know what for.

Monday morning, I show up at the warehouse as I promised. I get myself an apartment out East. On weekends I return to the town and watch waves like Nina and I used to.

—

-o-

The night wind blows a gust of clean ocean air into the dock's aroma of fried food, cigarette smoke, and miasma of tables full of people. The glow from the light strings hanging above the bar flashes on and off the face of the young woman sitting next to me.

"Here for the shark derby?" I ask.

"Yeah my husband's going to get a record breaking Mako this time."

"How?"

"I just know it."

Her husband sees us talking and comes over from a nearby table.

"I was just telling him you're going to win the shark derby, honey."

"You a fisherman," he asks.

"Kind of," I say. "I try. What's your secret?"

"You can't ask that," his wife says. "A magician never tells his secrets. He's got the right lures though, I know that for sure."

She plants a kiss on him and runs her hands along his back.

"It's all in the chum," he says.

"Everyone knows the real way to chum for sharks is to cut yourself from nape to navel and let your guts spill out," I say.

They look at me like they expect me to laugh, or at least smile. I don't.

THIS WAS ALWAYS GOING TO HAPPEN

STEPHEN GRAHAM JONES

There's no traffic out this far, so the only real danger when the tire on your trusty Accord blows is that you might panic, wrench the wheel over, plummet a few hundred feet down. You don't.

Instead you slow, ease over to the shoulder, then scooch a little closer to the guardrail—as close as you can get, since there's a blind turn up ahead that Porsches with ski racks can come whipping around. If they have to overcorrect from that hairpin situation, it might point them right where you're sitting. No thank you, mountain gods.

Really, you consider it lucky that that rear tire went when it did. Ten, twenty seconds later and you'd be changing it in the cool shade of those giant red rocks, and every car coming down the mountain would only be seeing you at the last possible instant.

But then . . . luck? Real luck would have been the tire not blowing at all.

Anyway, you call Marcy because that's the safe thing to do, but of course, cell service being spotty all up and down this road, you can't get through. The faster you swap the flat for the donut in the trunk, the faster you can tell her about all this in person, you figure. It's not like you haven't changed a tire before.

So.

Five minutes later the back of the Accord's hiked up on the scissor jack. You're just cranking on the first lug when a slow crunch turns you around.

It's a cyclist in full-bib tights, bright white with orange and yellow stripes and accents, one of those helmets made to reduce wind drag, his legs hairless because smooth skin slips through the air that much faster. He's doing that balancing-on-the-pedals thing they all do, like the ground's lava, and if they just make it two more seconds they'll be safe.

His mirrored sunglasses are nearly ski goggles.

"What is it?" he asks, more chipper than anybody should be after the climb he just has to have made.

"Flat," you tell him, kind of obviously.

He pauses like rolling through response options, then says, "You got it, then?"

"Old hand at this," you say, the lug wrench loose by your thigh.

"Well if you need anything," he says, and nods bye or good luck or . . . it's hard to tell, actually.

He pedals off, continuing his classic ride or Sunday afternoon burn or whatever it is he's crazy enough to be out here doing. More power to him.

You're rolling the spare around from the trunk when a flash up at the jumble of red rocks catches your attention.

It's the cyclist, coming back, whipping in and out of the yellow stripes on the faded asphalt.

He pulls to a soundless stop, feet down in the lava this time, and works what he's found down off his shoulder, along his arm.

A cast-off air filter, its accordion paper packed with seed heads and dirt.

"Thought this might help," he says, and sets it by the flat tire.

You consider it, come up to the cyclist again, consider him all over again. Is this what counts for humor at eight thousand feet?

"O-*kay*," you say.

He throws a jaunty salute your way, flashes a perfectly symmetrical grin, his leathery cheeks crinkling up from it, and pedals easily away. This time you watch him until he disappears around the red rocks.

You don't get it. Not even one little bit. In an *effort* to, you inspect the air filter, but it doesn't hold any answers, was completely content with its life in the ditch before being hand-delivered back to you.

Marcy is going to love hearing about this one.

You're on your stomach, your arm shoved as far under the Accord as it can go after a gotten-away lug nut, when you realize you're not alone. Again.

You roll to the side, see two high-dollar road bike wheels, tires that are weighed in grams.

"Found this," the cyclist says, grinning wide and eager.

It's a two-gallon gas can, its plastic body faded from a season in the sun.

"I have a *flat*," you can't help but reiterate, watching his mirrored lenses for a sign of—of anything, please. Any sort of clue.

"Just thought you might need it," the cyclist says, and sets it down on the shoulder of the road like the most delicate vase, the most sacred artifact.

"Thank you?" you say.

He nods sagely, almost reverentially, and hauls his bike around, pedals uphill.

You study the road behind you this time. There's no one to witness this, whatever it is. You're alone out here. With this crazy person.

You edge over to the gas can, toe it over onto its side. It's empty, light, probably brittle. After checking the road both ways, you step out into it, take a running start, and kick the gas can with everything you've got. It sails over the guardrails, hangs like a cartoon for a moment, then drops.

You've got to get off this mountain.

You spin the three lug nuts you *do* have onto the studs and walk around to the other side of the Accord, the long fall past the guardrail taking your breath away a bit. Don't look, you tell yourself, while completely looking. Your prayer was that the lost lug nut had rolled this far, that it would be there waiting for you.

Nope.

With your luck, it's probably dead center under the car—right under the muffler, which wants nothing else in the world but to sizzle into the skin of your forearm.

You *could* tighten down the three lug nuts you didn't fumble away and roll the Accord back, expose their missing brother. But what if one of the studs, carrying its weight plus a third, snaps off? And then you're stuck up here?

No, better a burn on your forearm than having to walk down for enough bars to call for help.

When you come around the car to get that lug nut, damn the consequences, the cyclist is playing his balancing game again, turning the front wheel of his bike this way and that way, pedaling forward degree by degree.

He looks up like surprised to see you.

"Oh, hey," he says, "found this, thought—"

It's a bezel. Thin, aluminum, all twisted up and dull. In a former life it probably framed a tail light. In its current life, it's just trash.

"Um," you say, "yeah."

"Got to look out for each other up here, right?" he says—or, recites?

"Thank you," you say, sort of chilled even though it's hot. He shrugs like it's nothing, like pleased with himself—that's it: it's like he's a dog, isn't it? And dogs don't understand flats, or cars. They just know to bring you stuff. It means they get petted.

He nods, accepting your verbal pat, checks the road both ways, and hauls his bike around, stands on the pedals to make this climb a third time.

Marcy is going to *flip* for this.

And you really need that fourth lug.

You lie down, reinvigorated, can *see* the dull glint of the lug nut now, can . . . *just* touch it with the leading top of your middle finger, and then, your eyes pressed tight now so you're fingers can feel better—a thing happens.

The cool lug nut is placed on the back of your straining hand, and then held there until your forearm figures out how to rotate in that tight space, let your palm accept this gift.

Except.

You reel your arm in, open your eyes, have to look.

It's the cyclist, shimmied under the car from the passenger side, the muffler smoking against his cheek but not messing with his grin one iota, his mirrored lenses absolutely unreadable.

You jerk back, dropping the lug nut, and roll fast away, stand.

"What *are* you, even?" you bellow, having to back up to try to keep a line on him under the car, which is when a horn blows and tires scream and you realize you're standing in the middle of the road.

At least for about a hundredth of a second longer.

THE BUTCHER'S TABLE

NATHAN BALLINGRUD

I. Devils by Firelight

The Englishman stood on the beach, just beyond the reach of the surf, and stared out over the flat, dark plain of the Caribbean. A briny stink filled his nostrils. Palm trees heaved in the night wind. Overhead, a heavy layer of stars, like a crust of salt on Heaven's hull. At his back, the small port town of Cordova gabbled excitedly to itself: fiddles and croaking voices raised in raucous song, like a chorus of crows; the calling and the crying of women and men; laughter and screams and the rumble of traded stories. It sounded like life, he supposed. No wonder it made him sick.

Martin Dunwood was very far from home.

Approaching from behind came a heavy expenditure of breath, feet shuffling in sand; he turned to see a shape lurching from town: a small man, fat and stumbling, a rag-wrapped something clutched in his left hand. The smell of rum blew from him like a wind.

"Mr. Dunwood," said Fat Gully. "What're you doing—" His words trailed off as he caught his breath.

"I'm taking some air," said Martin. "Please go away."

"No you don't," Gully said, his words sliding together and colliding. "No you fucking don't."

Martin controlled his voice. "No I don't *what*."

Fat Gully meant to muscle up to him with his broad chest, but he miscalculated his footing and toppled back onto his posterior, air exploding from his lungs like a cannonball. His dignity, however, remained undamaged. He gestured with whatever item he held in his left hand, which Martin noticed was caked in dark blood. "No you don't take on no high-borne airs with me, you fancy bastard. I'll peel you standing, fat purse or fucking not."

Martin wore his rapier, but he had seen Gully and his wicked little knife in action as recently as this afternoon, when they had been surrounded by four shipless sailors, attracted by Martin's moneyed appearance and anxious to settle the question of his worth. Fat Gully had acted suddenly, with a grace utterly at odds to his toad-like aspect; before a breath could be drawn, two of the men were attempting to keep their innards from sliding through their fingers and onto the filthy street. Martin was not eager to test him, even in his drunken state. Instead he turned his gaze to the gory rag in Gully's hand, leaking a thin black drizzle onto the sand. "What in God's name do you have there?"

Gully smiled and climbed slowly to his feet. The lights of the town cast him in shadow as he extended his arm and opened his hand. He looked like an emissary from an infernal province, bearing a gift.

Martin inclined his head forward to see, raising an eyebrow. It took him a moment to make sense of it: a tongue, freshly pulled from its root, saliva still glistening in the moonlight.

"The Society told me what you're here for," Gully said, a dull smile moving across his face. "I brought a snack for your new friends."

"I don't know what you mean by showing that to me, but I assure you I have no use for it Nor do the people I'm going to meet. Get rid of it."

"You'll learn not to bark orders at me, Mr. Dunwood," Gully said, tossing his dreadful trophy onto the sand. A dull anger set in his face. If Martin hadn't known better, he might have thought his feelings were hurt. "Oh yes you will. You'll change your tune when we get there, I'll wager."

He'd met Rufus Gully at the London docks. Gully, no stranger to the cut-throat world of the Spanish Main, had been hired by the Candlelight Society to function as a bodyguard, seeing him across the Atlantic to Tortuga, where they now stood. From here they were to secure passage aboard a pirate vessel to the middle of the Gulf of Mexico, where they would rendezvous with a second ship, and the purpose of his journey. They had crossed the Atlantic in nearly complete isolation from each other; Martin had been provided a room near the captain's quarters—not the fine appointment to which he was accustomed, but the needs of the moment demanded certain concessions—and Gully among the rats and the scum before the mast. It seemed he had emerged with fresh ideas.

"We have to get there first," Martin said. "This Captain Toussaint is a day late, and I'm beginning to doubt that he'll show up at all. He's either been sunk, or he's a coward."

Gully smiled, his teeth a row of crooked headstones. "Never you fear, Mr. Dunwood. I've come with good tidings."

For the first time in many days, Martin felt something inside himself lighten. "*The Butcher's Table* has arrived then, Mr. Gully?"

"It has indeed." Gully turned about and made his tentative way back into brawling Cordova, with Martin in tow. A pistol cracked in some ill-lit alley and a cry of pain rose above the cacophony of voices like a flushed bird. Gully lurched into the heated maw of that place, his purpose steady. "Come and meet our benefactors, Mr. Dunwood. We ship with the tide."

~

Gully slid into the city like an eel into a reef, steering his round body through the nooks and crannies of the crowd with a nimbleness which Martin both hated and admired. It was just another reminder that he could not allow himself to underestimate this squat little man. He was ungainly but quick, unintelligent but cunning. A sharp, murderous little villain.

Cordova was a ghastly place, alive with pitched debauchery. It was a constant maelstrom of noise and stench: roaring and howling, gunpowder and piss. Taverns spilled garish light. Women were passed around like drinking mugs from one lecherous grotesque to another, some cackling with abandon, some with the affectless expressions of dolls or corpses. He found himself surrounded by more black faces than he'd ever seen in one place, a fact which made him decidedly nervous. He understood that most were free men, though he found that hard to credit. A free black man was as alien to Martin's experience as a crocodile or a camel, and he stared like an idiot as Gully hustled him along.

A dim glow marked the docks: fires and lanterns alight on the shore, ship windows radiant as business of one sort or another was conducted within. The masts were like pikes struck into the earth; arrayed alongside this lurching little town, they gave an odd appearance of order. Gully crossed a muddy street, shouldering aside a man nearly double his size, and made his way to a two-story wooden structure across from the docks. It was an inn, and a busy one at that. A sign hanging above the door identified it as *The Red Mast*.

"Mind your manners now," Gully said. He pushed his way into the building, and Martin followed.

The interior was close and hot. Several small round tables collaborated to make up a dining area. An arched doorway led into a kitchen, where dim forms toiled. A fire grumbled to itself in a vast, grimy hearth. The flue was insufficient to its task, and greasy smoke trickled up the wall and gathered on the ceiling like a dark omen.

Gully approached a table of three men, their backs against the far wall. His demeanor was much reduced, and when he spoke, it was with none of his usual bluster.

"I brung him, Captain Toussaint, like what I said."

Martin knew the men immediately for what they were: pirates. They were not likely to be anything else, here in Tortuga, but the shabbiness of their bearing would have made it plain besides. The man on the right was older, his gray beard hacked short and his face a jigsaw puzzle of scars. One eye sat dully in its socket like a boiled quail's egg, pale and yellow. The man to the left—a Chinaman, Martin thought—was slender and quite young, his gaze unfixed, his attention flitting through the crowd. Sitting between them was the man who could only be Captain Toussaint: a black man, broad-shouldered and broad-featured, his skin as dark as any Martin had ever seen. His beard was a shaggy bramble, and his hair grew in a dark shock around his head; Martin imagined the fear this imposing figure would strike into the hearts of his fellow Englishmen as he came leaping onto their decks, clutching a knife in his teeth and raging with all his barbaric energy.

They wore shabby, loose-fitting clothing, and they were armed with steel. The Chinaman held a blunderbuss between his knees, and he tapped his fingers against it, as though eager to bring it to bear.

"Oh my, look at the pretty thing," the captain said, and the older man produced a chuckle, a sound which seemed unpracticed and awkward from him.

Martin stood straight, determined to suffer whatever insults to his person they might deliver. He knew he'd be travelling with base men, and he was prepared to acclimate himself to their lifestyle. "Captain Toussaint of *The Butcher's Table*, I presume."

"The very one. And you must be Mr. Dudley Benson, of the Candlelight Society."

"I'm afraid Mr. Benson took ill, and was unable to make the trip. He sent me in his place. My name is Martin Dunwood, also of the Society."

Captain Toussaint's eyes flicked between Martin and Mr. Gully. "Ill? How unfortunate. I hope the old fellow will recover. He seemed a lovely chap in our correspondence. You have a signed letter from him, vouching for your identity, no doubt?"

"I do not. I did not think it would be necessary."

"You were in error. It seems our business is concluded. How disappointing."

Martin's stomach dropped. All his plans, undone by such a stupid oversight! He struggled to maintain his composure. "Captain, don't make a mistake. You cannot proceed without my participation. Only a member of the Society can contact the Order of the Black Iron, and only a monk from that order can provide the map you need."

Toussaint seemed to consider this. After a moment, he said, "There's the small matter of payment to be addressed. You'll be eating from our stores, after all. Only fair that you should contribute. Surely Mr. Benson will have told you, despite his unfortunate illness."

"Of course," Martin said. He had no doubt this wretch was exercising a crude revenge for being caught off guard. However, he was in no position to object. "I'm quite willing to contribute coin to the endeavor."

"Then produce it, Mr. Dunwood. Produce it, please."

Martin withdrew his purse and placed it onto the table, taking care to keep his hand steady, fearing one of these bastards might cleave the fingers from his hand for the simple joy of it.

The older man with the bad eye spilled the coins onto the table, where they thudded dully in the dim light, and counted them. All the while the younger man kept his eyes roving about the room. The blunderbuss, of course, was not for show. Meanwhile the captain's gaze had not wavered from Martin. When the sum of money was announced, he waved a hand idly, as though such concerns were beneath him.

"It seems I am forced to take you at your word, Mr. Dunwood, at least for the moment. The Society has a fine reputation, for a pack of diabolists, and right now that is all you have to support you. Be thankful it is enough. See that you do your job well, and we shall part as friends. Otherwise I will bury you at sea. Are we in agreement?"

Martin swallowed his pride. To be spoken to like that by this man—a thug who should be lapping water from a puddle in Newgate Prison—caused him a pain that was nearly physical in its intensity. But Alice awaited him further along this journey, and he could not afford the comforts of his own station. Not now. He would remember this wretch, however, and he would see him suffer for this display. That much he vowed.

"Yes, Captain. We are in agreement."

Captain Toussaint clasped Martin's hand and gave it a vigorous throttling. "You make me glad. Now Mr. Johns will show you to your berth"—he indicated the one-eyed man—"where you and Mr. Gully can nibble crumpets and giggle like ladies while I conclude the ship's business in town. Will that be fine?"

Mr. Johns permitted himself a chuckle.

Martin pulled in a long breath, and nodded his acquiescence. "That will be fine, Captain."

"Mr. Johns, make sure *The Butcher's Table* is prepared to depart the moment we return. We won't want to linger." The captain rose and quietly departed, the young Chinaman in tow. Mr. Johns, however, made no move to rise from his chair. He reached a grubby finger into the coin purse and liberated a few shillings. "Sit your arses down," he said. "I mean to be well and truly drunk before I take you devil-worshippers aboard."

Martin and Gully had no choice but to comply.

⟜

Captain Beverly Toussaint and his first mate Hu Chaoxiang pressed their way through Cordova's crowded lanes as a cool wind blew in from the bay, carrying the sharp tang of lightning, the promise of rain and thunder. They made their way to a ramshackle warehouse which stood a little too far from the docks to be considered of much use to anyone.

The warehouse was owned by a man called Thomas Thickett—known locally as Thomas the Bloody, due to his penchant for sudden, furious nosebleeds. A refugee from the Buried Church in the Massachusetts Colony, he'd won the building in a card game when he arrived in Tortuga several years ago. The man he'd won it from laughed as he signed over the deed, wishing him good fortune in housing cobwebs and rats. But Thickett, born in a cage and destined his whole life for the dinner plates of wealthy men, was accustomed to turning shit into gold. And there was no better place for that than a city of pirates. He capitalized on his particular knowledge of the Buried Church and its cannibal cult, making himself valuable to the men who did commerce with them. He stored their unmarked cargo for extended periods, and he provided specialized sails and timber to the quartermasters who came to him when they had to refit their vessels for unique purposes. As long as he did these things well, he was assured a livelihood in Cordova.

Captain Toussaint in particular had found him useful. He disliked dealing with the Buried Church; like the Candlelight Society, it was a pack of Satanists. But while Society members tended to be toothless storytellers in gentlemen's clubs, congregants of the Church commanded genuine institutional power—to say nothing of their cannibalistic appetites, kept sated through their hidden farms of human cattle. As a fugitive from one of these farms, Thickett proved an invaluable source of information. So Toussaint paid him handsomely, and fostered a camaraderie with the man over shared drinks and wild dreams of the future.

Tonight, it was going to pay off.

The warehouse was dark. The windows were shuttered, the door closed. The door was unlocked, and they pushed their way inside. The place was densely packed with mildewed crates, rolled canvas, bags of grain. A single lantern, balanced on a wooden barrel full of God knew what, cast a shallow nimbus of orange light, throwing strange, wide-shouldered shadows against the wall. Beside it was Mr. Thickett's closed office door.

In the quiet, Captain Toussaint could already hear the hoarse whispers, a dozen or more voices attempting speech in the strange tongue of a different world. The voices crawled over the walls like cockroaches. He felt a thrill of excitement.

A small door opened to their right, and Thomas Thickett emerged from his office, where he had been waiting in absolute darkness. He looked frail and sickly, older than his thirty-seven years—that's what hiding from the

Cannibal Priest would do to you, Toussaint assumed—but tonight there was a flush of vigor in his cheeks.

"Thomas the Bloody," said the captain. "Bless my bones."

Thomas nodded deferentially. "Captain. It's fine to see you again. Yes. I have the cargo right here, sir."

Captain Toussaint and Mr. Hu exchanged a glance. "Right to business then, is it? All right, Thomas, all right. Show it to me."

Taking the lantern in hand, Thomas Thickett guided the two men through the maze of crates to the other side of the warehouse. There was a large door here which would swing open to admit carriages drawn by mules or oxen, but it was secured fast, shutting out the din of the town. The whispering voices were louder here; Captain Toussaint felt steeped in ghosts. An old memory crowded his thoughts, and he forced it back.

The voices emitted from a crate about waist-high, sitting in the middle of the aisle. It was segregated from the rest, like a diminished little temple.

"I've secured a carriage. It'll be waiting outside," Thickett said. "At my own expense, of course."

"Of course, Thomas. Always reliable." Captain Toussaint nodded at the crate. "Open it."

"... Captain?"

"I want to be sure."

Thomas glanced at Mr. Hu, as if seeking a better opinion. Finding none, he fetched a crowbar from a shelf and set to, his body sheened in an icy sweat. Nails squealed against wood. After considerable effort, the top of the crate popped off. Thomas peered inside, and the pirates came up on either side of him. Together they leaned over, studying the contents like learned judges of the damned.

Inside was what looked like a huge anemone, its wide base crumpled and folded against the confines of the crate, resting in a thin gruel of blood and gristle. Its body tapered into a stalk which culminated in a flowering nest of glistening tongues, moving like a clutch of worms. Little channels of teeth and ridges of gum wended through the cluster, as though a single mouth had been turned inside out like the rind of a mango, yielding this writhing bounty. From this mass came a chorus of whispers in a language unknown to them.

Captain Toussaint clapped Thickett on the shoulder. "Seal it, Thomas." His demeanor was much reduced.

Thomas complied, nailing the lid back into place with trembling hands. The voices were muffled beneath the wood, though not sufficiently to suit any man present.

A lotushead. Captain Toussaint had experienced one once before, five years ago, when he was first mate to Captain Tegel aboard the ship he now commanded. They'd put it to good use: it enabled Toussaint to buy the ship, and it made Tegel a king. Or something very much like a king.

"I'll help you haul it out to the carriage," Thomas said, his voice elevated over the sound of his hammering. "I trust the next time I see you both, you'll be rich men!" He laughed nervously. "And perhaps you'll make me a rich man too."

Captain Toussaint put away thoughts of Tegel with relief. "The next time? My dear Thomas, you won't have to wait so long. You're coming with us."

Thomas paused, one long nail poised between his fingers. A dark coin of blood dropped from Thomas's nose onto the crate's lid.

He knew what that meant. Captain Toussaint wrestled down a sudden surge of self-loathing.

"Captain," Thomas said. He blinked tears from his eyes. He remained facing forward, away from the others. "I arranged this whole thing. I procured the lotushead. I told you about the hidden cove. This whole venture is thanks to *me*. I'm sorry to be blunt about it, but it's true. Now, let's just load this into the carriage and you men be on your way. We had a deal. Let's just keep to it, shall we."

"Working with the Cannibal Priest comes with certain costs. You know that better than anyone, Thomas. This time, that cost was you."

More blood spattered onto the crate, and Thomas pressed a handkerchief to his face. The horror of the underground pens came rushing back to him: the thick stench of blood and fear, the close press of flesh, the chanting of monks. The sound of cleavers in meat.

"Who told them? How did they find me?"

"I did," said the Captain. "I needed someone from the Candlelight Society. They were the ones who put me in contact. As long as I promised to deliver you to them."

Thickett turned to run. Perhaps he thought he could catch them off guard, and make the exit before they had time to react. Perhaps he hoped they would kill him outright, and he would be spared his fate.

But Mr. Hu had anticipated this, and he swung the stock of his blunderbuss into his temple, dropping him to the floor. Thomas moaned and made a feeble attempt to crawl away. Mr. Hu trussed him while Captain Toussaint looked on.

"I'm genuinely sorry, old friend. If it's any comfort, I'm told they have grand plans for you."

Once Thickett was immobilized, Captain Toussaint slapped the crate. "Let's get it all on board, and smartly. I want to be gone before the jackals arrive."

Outside, it had finally started to rain.

Alone in the second mate's quarters, which had been surrendered to him without a twitch of protest by the one-eyed Mr. Johns at his captain's order, Martin Dunwood lay in the cot suspended crossways across the tiny room and tried to acclimate himself to the deep pitch and tumble of *The Butcher's Table* as it pushed its way across the cresting waves, bound for the open sea. Somewhere above him rain drummed over the ship. The lantern light stuttered as the ship plummeted down a steep trough. Martin snuffed it out before it could spill and light the room on fire. The sudden darkness was oppressive, as though someone had thrown a weight over him. The sounds of the water smashing into the hull mingled with the raw voices outside shouting to be heard over the storm, as the crew worked the lines and the sails with the precision—or lack of it—one might expect from a congress of pirates. Below, the carpenters worked on constructing a new set of rooms for himself and their future guests. It seemed as though the whole ship's complement had suddenly crowded into his cabin and began knocking things about. Martin did not care to speculate on their abilities; he felt sick enough already. Instead he entrusted his fate to Satan's judgment and focused his attentions on better things.

Alice.

The promise of Alice pulled him across the sea, from the polluted stink of London to Tortuga and now to this criminal's vessel; he would have let it pull him across the whole of the world, if necessary, but he was struck again by the continually surprising thought that he would see her again in a matter of days, at which point a year's careful planning might at last come to fruition.

He remembered the first time he ever laid eyes on her: she had been standing on a corner outside a grocer's shop. Her fine clothes and her red hair were disheveled and there was a placid beauty in her expression, her face as pale as a daylight moon. Blood matted the expensive materials of her dress, caked heavily near the lower hem and arrayed in a pattern of sprays and constellations further up her body, as though she had just waded through some dreadful carnage.

Martin, a newly minted agent of the Candlelight Society and a virgin to London itself, stood transfixed. He didn't know what catastrophe had befallen her but it seemed she needed immediate help. He waited for a carriage to pass before he stepped out into the muddy thoroughfare, but immediately came up short—an older gentleman stepped out of the grocer and joined her at the corner. He too was well-dressed, though his clothes were free of blood. He threw an overcoat around her shoulders and hailed a carriage. Within moments he bundled her into it, and with a flick of the driver's wrist she was whisked away, leaving behind an ordinary corner on an ordinary street. The drabness of the image seemed to reject the possibility that she had ever been there at all.

It was not until years later that he saw her again. By that time he had solidified his position in the Candlelight Society through a series of successful missions, and had graduated to a more elevated social stratum. His success precipitated his invitation to a party thrown by a fellow Satanist, one who occupied a seat in the House of Lords. As Martin lurked unhappily in a corner of the glittering room—he was acutely conscious of his humble origins, sure that they were as plain as a facial disfigurement—he saw her again.

She was standing amidst a crowd of men, young and eager for her attention. She smiled at one of them as he gestured to illustrate some point, and Martin knew at once that none of the fools had a chance with her, that she was only wearing them like jewelry. He pressed his way through the crowd until he joined her little retinue.

If she noticed him as he approached she did not show it. He stationed himself in her outer orbit and just watched her. Although she was properly demure, and maintained the comportment of a young lady of her station, something set her apart from everyone around her. She seemed carved from stone.

Martin could immediately tell that these men were normal, God-fearing Londoners, unaware of their host's secret affiliations. He was afforded a new confidence. At the first break in the conversation, he said, "Didn't I see you once outside a small grocer's in the East End? It would have been a long time ago."

Her pale blue eyes settled on him. "The East End? I rather doubt it."

"You would remember this," he said. "You were covered in blood at the time."

She betrayed no reaction, but even in that she revealed herself. No shock, no disgust, no laughing dismay. Just a cool appraisal, and silence.

One of the young men turned on him, his blond hair pulled back harshly from his forehead and tied into a bow. "I say, are you mad?"

"Not remotely," said Martin.

"It's all right, Francis," she said. "He's right. I do remember that day. It was quite dreadful. A horse had come up lame and had to be shot. It was done right in front of me and I think it's the worst thing I ever saw."

"Odd. I don't remember a dead horse," Martin said.

"Perhaps you weren't paying attention," she said. "So much occurs right under our noses."

Within minutes she had dismissed her pretty men and Martin found himself sitting some distance from the party, talking to this remarkable woman who seemed to fit amongst these people the same way a shark fits amongst a school of mackerel.

"Why did you say that to me?" she said. "What did you think would happen?"

"I had no idea. I wanted to find out."

"Hardly the environment for social experiments, wouldn't you say?"

"On the contrary. I would say it's the ideal environment."

She offered a half smile. "What's your name?"

"I'm Martin Dunwood. My father owns the—"

"Are you an anarchist, Martin Dunwood?"

He smiled at her, his first genuine smile of the night. "In a manner of speaking."

In minutes they were in the banker's bedroom, fucking with a furious, urgent silence. Thereafter they met often, and always clandestinely. She was even more contemptuous of the world than he, prone to stormy rages, and he found those rages intoxicating. They were wild and different and echoed his own sense of alienation from the world. Their illicit sex was as much an act of defiance as it was a hunger for each other. After a month of this she introduced him to the Buried Church, and he saw what she did there.

It was when he watched the blood drip from the ends of her long red hair that he knew he was in love with her, and that he would break the world to keep her.

—o—

Hours after *The Butcher's Table* had left, the carrion angels arrived in Cordova. There were four of them. They emerged from a lantern-smoked alleyway, building themselves out of shadows and burnt rags. Seven feet tall, their thin bodies wrapped in fluttering black cloth, they listed back and forth as they walked, their bones creaking like the rigging of ships. Their faces jutted forward in hooked, tooth-spangled beaks, their eyes burned like red cinders, trailing smoke through the rain.

They stalked the avenues of the town with deliberation, keeping to the shadows, sending those that witnessed them shrieking and scattering like frightened gulls; some stopped and fired a few wild shots before running. The carrion angels were oblivious, their bodies accepting the violence the way a corpse accepts the worm. They swung their great heads at each juncture of road and alley, lifting their snouts and huffing deep breaths as they tracked the scent of their quarry.

They followed it to a darkened warehouse. The scent of the lotushead was strong here, but a quick inspection revealed that it had gone. Thwarted, they creaked slowly out of the warehouse, emerging from the interior like dim lamps.

The trail wended down toward the docks. The town had erupted in panic. Word of the carrion angels' presence spread fast. Narrow lanes were choked with men fleeing for their ships. Pirates and sailors careened drunkenly: lurching, stumbling, and trampling the fallen. Throughout the town, panicked men shot and stabbed at shadows, and the road to the sea was marked by the bodies of the dead and the dying. The angels came upon a fallen man lying across their path, the back of his head a smoking hole and his brains festooned across the packed earth. The stink of it made them drunk and they permitted themselves a brief respite, hunched around this glorious fountain of scent, this unexpected confection. They ate with a grateful reverence, the sound of wet meat and cracking bone rising in syncopation with the driving rain.

Most of the townsfolk stayed inside, shuttering the windows and locking the doors. Some followed the pirates to the docks, forgetting in their fear the true nature of these men, and remembering only when they were beaten back or shot as they tried to climb the gangplanks to safety.

The ships were alight with lanterns, riggings acrawl with sailors making ready for the sea. Boats were dropped from the side, towing the vessels away from port. Gunsmoke hazed the air. The bloom of violence was a grace upon the town. The carrion angels walked in their slow, swaying gait through it all, like four tall priests proceeding safely through Hell, confident in their faith.

The scent ended at the docks. The lotushead had been taken to sea.

It was a small thing to sneak passage aboard a ship. The carrion angels dissolved into rags and dust, blowing like so much garbage in the wind, carrying over the water and into the rat-thronged hold of one of the several pirate ships, called *The Retribution.* They settled amidst the refuse there, lying as still as the dead.

The captain of this ship was a hard old man named Bonny Mungo. He'd seen creatures like this once, several years ago, in a half-sunken stone church he'd stumbled across in a Florida swamp. There had only been two; they'd killed most of the men he'd been with, and wore another like clothing, too small to properly fit. Catching a glimpse of them now, he was moved by an extravagant fear. Once *The Retribution* achieved some distance from land, he ordered it to turn about, offering its broadside to the town. At his command the ship fired its full complement of guns in a devastating volley, sending cannonballs smashing through weak wooden walls and bringing whole buildings to the ground. Another ship took inspiration from this and fired as well.

Within minutes, Cordova and its luckless residents were reduced to broken wood, and smoke, and blood. The pirates, satisfied by their own efficiency, rounded out to sea, disappearing into a curtain of rain.

The carrion angels slept in *The Retribution's* hold. The scent's trail was a road, even over the sea. They were sure of their way.

II. The Last Meeting of the Candlelight Society

Martin had only just achieved a precarious sleep when he was awakened by the harsh voice of a bent, pinch-faced man in his nightclothes. He stood in the narrow door and held a lantern at his side, casting his own face into garish shadow. "The captain wants you," he said. "Sharp-like."

He pulled himself unhappily out of bed and fetched his trousers from the floor, noting the slow, easy roll of the ship over the waves. He must have fallen asleep during the storm. Perhaps he would make a seaman of himself yet. Still, an unbroken sleep would have done him good.

"Who are you?" he asked brusquely, reaching for his jacket.

"I'm Grimsley, and I cook your meals for you, mister, so mind your tone. I also see to the captain's whims. Which is you now, so be smart about it. Look at you fussing over your clothes like a proper lady. Leave off and do as you're bid, before his mood turns."

As it happened, Captain Toussaint's mood was generous. His quarters were at the aft of the ship, and the windows were open, affording him a salty breeze and a king's view. The clouds had dispersed, and although there was no moon to light the waves, the stars burned in great, glittering folds. Toussaint sat with his back to it, a shadow against the sky. He looked like an illustrated figure from the Old Testament. The table had been set up between them, with a kettle of hot water and two mugs.

"Did I interrupt your sleep, diabolist?" said the captain.

Martin took the seat opposite. He heard the steward shut the door behind him. "I know this is your ship, and you're lord of the high seas and all that, but I will thank you to call me by my proper name."

"I see your sensibilities are as delicate as your tender little hands." He leaned forward and pushed the mug closer. "Perhaps some tea will soothe your English heart."

"Thank you, Captain." Martin poured the tea into the mug and held it under his nose, breathing it in. He sipped, and found it surprisingly good.

Captain Toussaint smiled. "Privileges of the wicked life," he said.

"I suspect the privileges are many. Including summoning gentlemen from sleep to sit at your table upon a whim. What need do you have of me, Captain?"

"I have need of your context, Mr. Dunwood. I would like to know your business here."

"It is the same as yours, of course. We shall goad the lotushead into speech, and we shall cross into the Dark Water. Then I shall contact the Order of the Black Iron, and we will sail to Lotus Cove, where the Cannibal Priest will have his precious Feast. You'll fill your hold with lotusheads and I'll get my atlas. Everyone is happy. Is this a game, Captain? Why do you ask me what you already know?"

"It is not a game, Mr. Dunwood, but you continue to treat it like one. You are hiding something from me. Tell me what it is."

All the warmth generated by the hot tea dissipated. Martin put the mug back on the table and concentrated on maintaining his composure. The captain, damn him, watched him as carefully as he would an opponent in a duel; if that's what this was, Martin was already being pressed into a disadvantage. "Mr. Gully has been indiscreet," he managed to say.

"Mr. Gully has the eager tongue of a dockside whore, but I don't need him to tell me what's already plain. Something about you smells rotten, Mr. Dunwood. You're a pup, and I expected a grown man. The Candlelight Society does not send children to do men's work. I did not have time to question you before the carrion angels arrived, but now we're at sea, and time is something I have in abundance. So allow me to ask you again. And if you avoid my question one more time I shall summon Mr. Hu into the room, and he will do the asking on my behalf. Do you understand me?"

Martin's sense of control had evaporated. He was now simply afraid. It was a new and unwelcome emotion. "Yes, Captain, I think I do," he said quietly. He took a breath to steady himself. "There is a woman."

Captain Toussaint sighed, easing back in his chair. The ship crested a wave and through the great window behind the captain's head Martin watched the sea fall away; for a moment he was staring into the starry gulf of the sky. The cups on the table between them slid a few inches. "A woman. You mean *the* woman, of course. Alice Cobb."

"Yes. I do."

"So it's a love story then."

"If you like."

"All men of the sea enjoy a proper love story, Mr. Dunwood. Maybe it's because our own always end so badly. Tell me."

"I met her in London, some time ago. I was new to the Society. I'd had no dealings with the Buried Church; I'd only heard stories of it. I wasn't sure I even believed. When I met her, I . . . well. We fell in love, Captain. It's as simple as that."

"I doubt anything about it is simple. I'm shocked the Priest tolerates this. She is his daughter, after all."

"He doesn't know. Alice and I would very much like to keep it that way. At the Feast, he will come to understand."

"I see. But Mr. Benson not only approves, but is so moved by your plight that he sends you upon the excursion of a lifetime in his place?"

"'Approves' would be putting it strongly. But we in the Society are storytellers, Captain, and it's in our nature to encourage the passions of the heart. We are romantic creatures, after all."

Captain Toussaint regarded him carefully. "So they send me an untested boy with a hidden ambition, so that he can run about my ship like some plague-addled wharf rat, with love corroding his blood like a disease. What's more, he has a secret which, if discovered by the Priest, will not only scuttle the purpose of our voyage but very likely result in blood being spilled aboard my ship. Do I understand it correctly?"

Martin said nothing. Despite the cool air blowing in, the room felt close and hot. The pitching of the ship made a tumult in his gut; that, along with the new and very real possibility that this brute might interfere with his and Alice's plan, made it a struggle not to spew his last meal across the table between them.

"I love her, Captain. We are going to wed, there on Hell's shore. We will do this with or without her father's approval."

"A wedding at the lip of Hell. You amaze me, Mr. Dunwood."

"Love drives one to extravagant behaviors. Have you never loved anyone?"

Captain Toussaint fixed him with a searching look. "In fact I have. It too would have provoked disapproval, had it been widely known."

Martin pressed his advantage. "And if what I've heard of pirates is true, you would not have let something so small deter you."

"Not even death would deter me, Mr. Dunwood." The captain sipped from his tea. He seemed to consider for a moment. The stars heaved in the sky behind him. Finally, he said, "All right. Your story does not set me at ease, but it does rouse my sympathies. We'll go on as planned. You may return to your bunk."

Martin nodded. "Thank you," he said, and rose to leave. His hand was on the door when Captain Toussaint stopped him.

"A word of caution: it's not *my* discretion you should worry about. That little villain you've hired to do your dirty work will sell you for a tuppence. You know that, surely?"

"Fat Gully," said Martin. "He's a creature of brute impulse, nothing more. He'll behave as long as he's paid."

Captain Toussaint smiled. "It's my experience that we all have a secret heart. Even brutes." He leaned back in his chair, drawing in a deep breath. "But perhaps you're right. Let's see what tomorrow brings us, shall we? Good night, Mr. Dunwood."

Martin retreated to his cramped quarters. He slept fitfully, and he was plagued by dreams of the Buried Church. He watched a cleaver rise and fall, over and over again, lifting bright red arcs into the air. He saw a stunned human face pressed against the bars of a metal cage. He heard a shriek so piercing that it launched him from sleep, upright in his swinging cot at some unknowable black hour of the night, panting and listening. He heard only the sound of the waves against the hull, the groan of wood straining against the deep. He closed his eyes again, and if he dreamed further, it was only of the abyss.

⊸

Six hours earlier, aboard *The Retribution*, Bonny Mungo stared at the creature looming over his bunk and understood that he had only moments remaining before it extinguished him from the earth. He had fallen asleep perusing charts outlining the Hispaniola coastline, and so the lantern suspended over his head still shed a dim light. The carrion angel fluttered silently in its glow, its hooked beak opening, its red eyes spilling thin smoke.

If anyone had thought to ask him about the condition of his heart, Bonny Mungo would have said that it was bountiful with love. He had answered the call of his passions, leaving behind the diminished lifestyle of his parents on their Scottish farm and turning instead to the pursuit of his desires. He lived in a hot climate now, he waged glorious war in the ocean, and he indulged in women and drink on shore. What did not come to him willingly he took by force. The world was a heavy fruit. Life was the long satisfaction of impulse, and he would be a sorry man to complain about any of it.

He tried to set himself on fire. He would prefer to burn alive then let the carrion angel take him. His lunge for the lantern was too late, and his reach too short. The angel seeped through his skin and oriented itself in his body, fitting its eyes to Bonny Mungo's, cracking his joints and splitting his skull to accommodate itself more comfortably. Most of what made the pirate the man he was dissolved in the holy heat of the angel's presence, but enough rags of himself remained that he appreciated the smallness of his life's purpose until this point.

A new hunger grew in Bonny Mungo's heart. It was like gravity, bending every thought toward it. The passions of his former life were like a child's whims. Now he wanted only to eat.

The carrion angel guided Bonny Mungo like a clumsy puppet. He lurched from his cot on his new, broken legs, the knees snapped and bending haphazardly with each step. He maneuvered out of his cabin, the breach in his skull smoking, black rags fluttering from it like hair, his eyes sizzling like fat in a pan of oil. The angel opened its mouth to speak in its new tongue, and syllables spilled out like teeth. To hear them was to bleed. It would take some getting used to.

Down the hall, there were screams. The other angels were claiming their hosts. Following that, they'd have to spill some blood, but hopefully not much. The crew would obey. They wanted to live, after all.

The lotushead was somewhere ahead of them. The smell of it hurt Bonny Mungo in his bones. It turned his belly into a yawning hole.

⊸

Martin awoke early the following morning, roused by the commotion of work. The day was already warm. A crisp wind filled the sails, driving them west. He found Captain Toussaint standing aft, holding a spyglass to his eye. Martin squinted, but could see nothing through the glare of the early sun.

"There's a ship back there," said the captain, still watching. "The lookout spied it an hour ago. They're steering from the sun, hoping to buy some time before we spot them. A standard tactic."

"An enemy, then? How can you tell?"

"I can't for sure. But I'll wager it's the carrion angels, sniffing out our cargo. Once they get a scent they're bloody relentless."

"But they're beasts! Can they pilot a ship?"

The captain glanced at him. "Never seen one, have you."

"No."

"You will." Captain Toussaint left him, striding back to the deck and barking orders. Some of the men scampered up the rigging and started untying sails. Canvas dropped and billowed. The man at the helm adjusted the great wheel a quarter turn to the right, and the ship surged forward, sending white foam crashing over the bowsprit.

Martin lingered at the railing, eyes locked onto the horizon. Though he still couldn't see anything, the sense of threat soured his stomach. He'd heard of the carrion angels in Society meetings: holy cockroaches, gorging themselves on anything from Heaven or Hell which might have become lost in the mortal world. The lotushead would be a fine morsel, no doubt.

Not for the first time, Martin doubted the wisdom of this venture. The captain was right: he was too young and too inexperienced. Here he stood, sturdy as a fencepost, and still he felt a consuming fear. He wished to be home in London, with its dark libraries and lantern-lit alleys, with his pipe and his brandy, surrounded by the Society's flickering candles and devil-haunted shadows. There he would feel safe. Out here, in this briny, sun-wracked environment, he felt exposed and bewildered. A moth lost in a delirium of light.

After nearly an hour of waiting and watching, he could still see nothing on the horizon. If this was a chase, it was the dullest one he'd ever heard of. He made his way below decks, and found the galley, where the man who had woken him from sleep a few hours ago—Grimsley—toiled over his fire. Beside him was a small table covered in chopped vegetables, strewn with cured meat. The kitchen would be freshly stocked from the visit to Cordova, and the food was as fresh as it would be all voyage. Martin heard the clucking of chickens coming from some way off, and a barnyard stink—two pigs and a goat—mingled with the welcome smell of cooking meat, and coffee.

The steward cast him a glance over his shoulder. "His Highness arises."

"I'm hungry. Give me something to eat, Cook."

"You've missed vittles, so you can make do with a biscuit and a slice of pork." Grimsley threw the items onto a plate and pushed it toward him. "Sorry—not the type of meat you're craving, I gather. I know some pygmy tribes in the Pacific could help you."

"I am no cannibal."

"Of course not, Your Highness. You just share a table with them, is all. Why should one draw conclusions?"

Martin tamped down a flash of anger. "Coffee," he said.

Grimsley directed him to the pot with a lift of his chin, and then turned his back on him once again, resuming his chore.

"Wretch." Martin took his meager breakfast to the mess hall next door, which was empty save for his own Mr. Gully, lounging like a lord with his back against the bulkhead, digging a nugget of food from his teeth with a fingernail. Gully winked, and presented an unsightly grin.

"We're going to have a party soon, so I hear," he said. "Another ship stalking us like a hungry shark. Best stick close to me, if it comes to a fight, lad. I've got to earn my keep, you know."

"There will be no battle. The captain is quite competent." In fact Martin had no idea if this was true, but it made him feel better to say it.

"Did he pry your secret from you last night?"

"How did you know I spoke to him at all?"

"Why, I'm your protection, ain't I? It's my business to know what you're up to, Mr. Dunwood."

Martin passed a hand across his face. "I told him what I needed to. He gains nothing from betraying my confidence."

"Maybe, maybe not." Mr. Gully took another bite of his biscuit, chewing as he spoke. "He has secrets of his own, our captain does."

"What do you mean?"

"He's got a man locked up in the hold. Weeps throughout the night."

Martin smiled, enjoying the opportunity to display his superiority over his awful companion. "You're like a child sometimes, Mr. Gully. It's almost charming. That man is no secret. That man is the Feast."

Something like thought seemed to pass across Mr. Gully's face. "Him? But he's nothing. He's a nobody."

"For once, I agree with you. Congregants of the Buried Church are an odd lot, though. They care about the nothings, or at least they claim to. For them, the Feast is the ultimate expression of love, and Satan is egalitarian in His appetites. Even a beggar may suffice."

Mr. Gully considered this in silence.

Martin, pleased, enjoyed his coffee in peace.

⊸⊷

The final meeting of the Candlelight Society's London branch remained one of the signal moments of Martin's life. Six gentlemen convened, as per usual, in the Brindle Mare Club. They retired to a private room prepared according to their specifications: the table polished to a high shine, reflecting the light of fifty candles arranged in clusters throughout the room. The curtains were tied open, and through the window one might watch the streets of London at night. Coats and wigs were hung by an employee of the club, who retreated from the room immediately, and who would not return until summoned. A decanter of brandy waited on a serving table in the corner, and Mr. Dunwood—at twenty-four years of age, the youngest member present—assumed the duty of filling each man's snifter before addressing his own. Pipes were lit, and conversation eased into life.

The Candlelight Society met bi-monthly, and at these meetings it was a selected man's duty to relate a story to the other members, recounting what he had done to further Satan's cause in society. Often these stories involved considerable risk to the teller of the tale; if there were occasional embellishments, well, surely they were only symptoms of enthusiasm for the cause. The atmosphere at these meetings was unfailingly collegiate and warm, and the men had forged a familial unity over the years.

Conversation was permitted to wander for a time before Mr. Benson summoned everyone's attention with a gentle clearing of his throat.

Martin's heartbeat increased, and as he held his snifter, he studied the level of the brandy inside, to see whether he could detect a tremor in his hand. He found none.

"Gentlemen," said Mr. Benson, "I'm afraid we shall have to forego the stories this evening. I know it's a disappointment."

In fact, it wasn't. Mr. Withers had been scheduled to speak tonight, and his stories were always a chore to sit through. The events were all well enough, but he spoke without pause or inflection, as though he were reading market reports on Turkish figs. Anything that might delay that experience was to be welcomed.

"At our last meeting Mr. Dunwood surprised us all by telling us a wonderful tale of his visit to the Buried Church. The friendship he struck with Miss Alice Cobb facilitated an exchange of letters between myself and her father,

Abel Cobb. London's own Cannibal Priest. Because of that—indeed, because of your initiative, Mr. Dunwood—the Candlelight Society is presented with its grandest opportunity since its acquisition of the Damocles Scroll, some two hundred years ago."

"Hear, hear," they said, and glasses were raised all around. "Greater even than that," offered one of them, and there were murmurs of agreement.

Martin smiled humbly, raising his own glass. "Thank you, gentlemen. All I seek is to bring honor to the Burning Prince."

"I shall speak your name to Him," assured Mr. Benson. "This I promise you."

Martin smiled. Mr. Greaves, a portly, middle-aged man sitting directly to his right, clapped him on the shoulder. "I know you wanted to be the one to go, Dunwood. Very good of you to understand."

"I defer to Mr. Benson's authority, of course, and to his many long years of service. If any man here has earned the privilege of being the first member of the Candlelight Society to tread Hell's shore, it is he." He waited for all the tedious affirmations to settle before he continued, "I only fear that the journey may be dangerous."

Mr. Benson made a dismissive gesture. "Never fear. I don't trust the Buried Church any more than I trust those southern pirates. I've hired a bodyguard to accompany me. I am told he's quite capable."

"What's the name of this fellow?"

Mr. Benson paused, and chuckled. "Do you think you would recognize it, Mr. Dunwood? I daresay you travel in different company."

Martin produced a laugh. It sounded sincere, even to him. How easily the lies came, these days. "Not at all. But should anything happen to you, I would like to know whom to hold responsible."

"Risk is a natural component of our endeavors here. We all know that. Should I fall in my duties, I trust the Society will continue its business unflagged. Nevertheless, if it will please you to know it, the man is called Rufus Gully, and I am told he can be found lurking about Whitechapel or at the docks. You may deliver whatever retribution seems appropriate. Now, if that's settled, I would like to move on to the question of Miss Alice Cobb."

Martin compressed his lips, unable to hide his discomfort. He felt keenly the scrutiny of the others. "What do you mean?"

"I know this is uncomfortable, Martin, and I'm sorry for that."

The sudden informality caught him off guard, and he felt a curious wash of goodwill toward Mr. Benson and all the gentlemen here. They were the best family he had ever known, and the few years he'd spent doing the Devil's work at their side had been the proudest of his life.

"I know you feel strongly for the girl," Benson continued, "and the Society has always honored great passion. The Burning Prince is not called such after a simple fire, after all."

Someone said, "Hear, hear."

Martin nodded, acknowledging this.

"I only wish to remind you of what's at stake. Miss Cobb, enchanting as she may be, is the daughter of a Cannibal Priest, and therefore in pursuit of a different cause. We may all bend the knee to the same lord, but we honor him in different ways. I go in place of you not only because of my position in the Society, and not only because of your youth, but because I know I will not be distracted by my heart. Do you understand?"

Martin nodded, the goodwill of a moment ago entirely evaporated. "I do."

Mr. Benson gestured to his depleted glass. "I wish to make a toast. If you would, please."

"Of course." Martin rose and turned to the decanter. Behind him, Mr. Benson addressed the group.

"Multiple purposes are converging here, and if every man is honorable there will be no difficulties. The pirate wants to fill his hold with lotusheads, so he can cross into the Dark Water at will and do trade with the cities on Hell's border. The Cannibal Priest wishes to hold a Feast there, and hopes to entice Satan Himself to the table. I admit I hope very much that he succeeds. I can imagine no greater honor than to sit at that table. And I, of course, have my own purpose." He waited until Martin had finished replenishing the brandy snifters. Once this was accomplished, he raised his glass. All followed suit. "I shall bring to the Society an Atlas of Hell," he said. "I shall bring to us the means to study the true face of our Lord."

"To your success, sir," said Mr. Greaves. "And to the Candlelight Society."

"Hear, hear," they said, and all but Martin drank.

Mr. Benson beamed. "Hail—" His throat closed around the phrase. He brought his hand to his neck with an expression of bewilderment. The others sputtered and coughed briefly, and then a gravid silence spread over the group. Their faces turned a turbulent red. Blood flowed from their noses, their eyes. Their faces, Martin thought, looked like holy masks.

He overturned his raised glass. The brandy spattered onto the table and ran off the edge. He met Mr. Benson's bulging eyes, and held them for as long as it took for the light within them to expire.

"Hail Satan," Martin said.

III. The Cannibal Priest

They sailed a week without incident. Martin browned in the tropical sun. He dined at the captain's table in the evenings, but kept as much to himself as was possible during the long, bright days. His only true moments of apprehension came when he observed a crewman training a spyglass behind them, reminding him of their pursuer. But Captain Toussaint surmised that that ship had laden itself with stores for a long raiding campaign, while *The Butcher's Table*—with only the lotushead and the unfortunate Mr. Thickett in its hold—carved a quicker path through the sea. They kept an easy distance.

So it was that the first ship Martin beheld with any clarity was not their pursuer, but a colonial schooner called *The Puritan*, its Union Jack fluttering crisply in the southern breeze.

Martin leaned over the railing, straining his eyes to see if he could make out anyone on the deck. He felt the proximity of Alice in his blood, and if he'd believed he could get to her more quickly by swimming, he would have jumped overboard on the instant. The thought was already half-formed in his mind when a hand clasped his shoulder, startling him so much that for a moment he thought he had actually done it.

"It'll be a few hours yet," said Captain Toussaint. "She'll wait for you."

"Hours?" They appeared so close; it seemed outrageous.

"Indeed. The eye travels faster than the wind will carry us. We'll meet with them before the sun goes down, be assured. I'm only grateful for the reinforcements." He cast a glance behind them, where the other ship lurked on the horizon like a mote in the eye.

Martin followed his gaze. "Surely they won't attack all of us together? They'd be mad."

Toussaint cast him a sidelong glance. "It's past time you became accustomed to madness, Mr. Dunwood. But don't fear. They are far enough behind that I believe we'll make the crossing before they catch us."

"But *The Puritan* won't be crossing with us. What of them?"

"They shall have to fend for themselves. If their captain is intelligent, they'll be rigged for speed."

Unsettled, Martin retreated to his cabin, hoping to pass the hours going over the particulars of his task. As much as he looked forward to seeing Alice, and as much as he anticipated the thrill of the passage into the Dark Water, he was already feeling nostalgic for the past week's quiet journey. He'd grown used to the rolling waves and the slapping of the water against the hull as he settled in for sleep each night. He fancied himself becoming a proper man of the sea.

He opened his valise and removed a package wrapped in oilcloth, which he set beside him. He felt a nervous flutter in his breath, and took a moment to compose himself. He unwrapped the cloth, exposing three tall, inelegant candles, dull yellow—more like some waxy excrescence than things designed by human hands—with long black wicks like eyelashes. He should not have them out; they were as crucial to the success of the mission as the lotushead, drowsing somewhere below him. He had taken all three from the Society's stores, as a safeguard against accident, but even that seemed a brazenly small number.

The door opened and Martin jumped in alarm, though every man aboard knew what he carried.

Fat Gully stood framed in the door, staring with naked interest. "That's them, isn't it? The hellward candles."

Martin wrapped them carefully again. It seemed somehow grotesque that Gully had seen them—as though they'd been sullied. "Yes."

"Ugly little things."

Martin slid the oilcloth back into his valise, which he tucked beneath the cot. "They are not meant to please the eye, Mr. Gully. What do you mean by barging in on me?"

"We've nearly arrived. We're in shouting distance."

Martin felt a pulse of excitement. Still, that did not justify the intrusion. "Thank you. I'll be up presently. You may go."

Mr. Gully moved fully into the room then, shutting the door behind him. The quarters were close at the best of times; with his wide and malodorous presence, they became oppressively small. "It's time we spoke clearly, Mr. Dunwood. I was going to wait until later, but what with that other vessel coming on behind us, it seems there might not be time."

Martin shifted uncomfortably. "Why don't we go above and—"

"We'll stay down here, Mr. Dunwood, where it's nice and private, ay?" Gully leaned over him. Martin couldn't leave without physically pushing past the man, which he did not wish to attempt.

"Very good, Mr. Gully. What's on your mind, then?"

"It's about your lady, sir. It's about Miss Cobb. I want you to arrange a meeting between us."

Martin flushed, both angry and frightened. "You have no business with Miss Cobb."

"Oh, I do."

"*What* business? Is it the Society? Did they give you some instruction?"

Martin was unable to hide his frustration, and Mr. Gully made no secret that he enjoyed it. "No, it ain't the Society, Mr. Dunwood. And even if it were, you took care of them, didn't you? Nothing they told me matters anymore. No, it's just me. Just dear old Gully. I got something I want to ask of your precious lady, and you're going to make sure I get the chance."

"You're mad. Of course I won't do it."

"You will, sir."

Martin attempted to stand, but Mr. Gully shoved him roughly back onto his cot, where he swung wildly, nearly spilling backwards. As he struggled to right himself, Mr. Gully gripped his throat and dug his fingers in. Terror overwhelmed Martin; he gripped Mr. Gully's thick forearms, but he was too weak to do anything but clasp them tightly, as if he were grasping the arms of a welcome friend.

"Now look here, dog. I've got you to rights, I do. I know all there is to know about you. You do what I say or I tell the Cannibal Priest about your designs on the girl. Her father's the top man, ain't he? Won't he be fascinated to learn what became of the Society, and that the whelp who done it is here to fuck his daughter right under his nose. You'll be keelhauled, Mr. Dunwood, or worse. You do what I say or I make sure you're dead before the sun sets."

". . . bastard . . . you bastard . . ." Martin struggled to breathe. His face was going red.

Mr. Gully smiled. "Are you questioning my parentage, Mr. Dunwood? Why, I've never been so insulted. What *shall* I do." He relaxed his grip just slightly, allowing Martin to haul in a ragged breath.

"You've crossed a line, Gully. You were paid to protect me. You have no idea what—"

Mr. Gully cut him off again with a squeeze of his hand, like a man turning a valve. "You're nothing to me. You've always been nothing. The Society was just a bunch of wanking old men telling dull stories to each other because no one else would bother to listen. You're all as threatening as a litter of kittens." Martin felt a sharp pain near his groin; Gully had slipped the blade of his knife through his trousers and pressed its edge against the pulsing artery. "You'll say nothing to anyone. You'll do what the fuck I say and you'll be quick and quiet about it. Tell me you understand."

He loosened his grip. "Are you going to hurt—"

"Tell me you understand."

"I understand."

Gully released him completely this time, leaning back, and Martin slid to the floor, curling into himself and coughing. The pitch of the ocean, a soothing rhythm only moments ago, tried to wrestle the breakfast from his belly.

Before the rage had time to bubble up, Mr. Gully addressed him from the door. "I've no doubt you'll be performing your little ritual after dinner tonight, so there won't be much time. Arrange my meeting before all that happens."

"Perhaps I'll just have you killed before we get there," Martin said. He regretted it immediately, but the threat gave him satisfaction.

"Aye, you might. Who would question a gentleman condemning a scoundrel like me? But let me tell you something, Mr. Dunwood. If your friends in the Candlelight Society thought there was safety aboard this ship, my contract would have expired once you were taken into Captain Toussaint's care. But it didn't, did it? Has it occurred to you the captain doesn't need you at all, once you've performed your duties tonight?"

Martin shook his head. "We have an arrangement. I've even paid for passage."

"You put a great deal of stock in your 'arrangements,' don't you? As much as Mr. Benson did, do you think?"

Martin said nothing.

"Once you've crossed into the Dark Water, there's nothing to stop them from dumping your carcass overboard. Nothing but me, that is. The Society knew it. That's why Benson paid me for the whole journey. So you can turn me over if you like, Mr. Dunwood, but if you do you'll be joining me down a shark's gullet soon enough. Do what I tell you, though, and everything will continue as it was, pretty as you please."

He departed, leaving Martin shivering on the floor.

⊸

Late afternoon found *The Butcher's Table* joined with *The Puritan* in the calm Gulf waters, sails furled and launch boats plying the short distance between them. Stores and personnel were ferried from the colonial vessel to the pirate ship in preparation for the crossing. Captain Toussaint stood on the aft deck, in the company of Mr. Hu, Martin, and Fat Gully, where they received Abel Cobb—the Cannibal Priest himself—accompanied by his bodyguard, a Virginian soldier called Randall Major. Abel Cobb was an older gentleman with a heavy white moustache, his round belly an indication of his wealth, his white clothing crisp and smartly tailored. One might imagine he'd just stepped out of a club, and not spent a week at sea.

Cobb grasped Captain Toussaint's hand and shook it coolly. These were two men who, under any other circumstance, would be happy to watch the other hang. Then he turned his attention to Martin, whom he greeted with genuine warmth.

"Mr. Dunwood, it's a pleasure to have a member of the Candlelight Society join us at the Feast. I believe it's been more than fifty years since the last time such a thing has happened."

"I believe it's been that long since an invitation has been extended," Martin countered, and the two men permitted themselves a chuckle. In truth, though they ultimately served the same master, certain doctrinal differences forced a rivalry between their organizations, to which bloodshed was not unknown.

Captain Toussaint interjected. "You do not seem surprised to see Dunwood, whereas I had been expecting old Benson. I do not like feeling shut out, Mr. Cobb."

Abel smiled indulgently at the Captain. "You have not been shut out, I can assure you. Mr. Benson sent word along to us that he had fallen ill. You, well . . . your particular business makes you rather more difficult to reach."

"And yet here we are," Toussaint said, but he let the matter rest. "Enough pleasantries, I think. Let's attend to business."

"Why the haste? We have an abundance of time."

"Mr. Cobb, we are pursued."

Abel Cobb peered into the horizon beyond Toussaint's shoulder. The sea appeared empty and quiet.

"They are perhaps a day out, but they are not under a natural command. It would be a mistake to linger. Come below, and I'll show you what we've rigged for you."

The Captain led Mr. Cobb away, followed by Hu and the Virginian. Martin and Gully lingered on the aft deck. The afternoon was hot, and the sun cast bright shards over the waves. They watched as Mr. Johns supervised the intake of materials, much of which seemed to be rare foodstuffs, spices, and animals, in preparation for the Feast on Hell's shore. Finally, though, he saw what he had been waiting for. She seemed a jewel in the sunlight, the launch that carried her lifting and dipping over the gentle waves, six men laboring hard at the oars.

Interminably long minutes later, Alice Cobb was assisted aboard *The Butcher's Table.* Her hair was done up in a bun, and she wore a somber black dress. She navigated the crowded deck gracefully, and she seemed to Martin as out of place on this ship as a nightingale flitting through an abattoir. Not a single head turned; every man aboard this ship kept to his duty, and he wondered at the fear she instilled, that she could quiet their grosser instincts. She mounted the stairs to the aft deck and approached him, her smile radiant, her skin ruddy with the sun. Martin felt as though every inconvenience, every crime, every humiliating slight had been nothing more than prelude to this heart-filling justification.

"Alice," he said. Every impulse in his body urged him toward her, but he resisted. Though no one would stare at this woman outright, he knew that the corner of every eye was attuned to them.

"Mr. Dunwood," she said. With her back to the crew, she was free to give expression to her joy. "It is fine to see you again." She looked at Mr. Gully. "And who is this?"

"This is Rufus Gully. He is my companion on the journey."

She arched an eyebrow at the little man. "Surely not the whole journey?"

Mr. Gully stepped forward and executed a clumsy bow. "Absolutely the whole journey, Miss Cobb. Martin and I are the dearest of friends. Isn't that so, Martin?"

Martin stiffened. "Mr. Gully was hired by the Society to serve as my protection."

"Protection? Not from us, I'm sure!"

Martin shook his head. "Of course n—"

"From everyone," Gully said, presenting his full, gap-toothed grin. "We don't know what awaits in the Dark Water, after all, and you lot might get hungry."

Alice smiled down at him. All pretense of warmth had gone. "I do like a plain speaker. If we do get hungry, I daresay there's more meat on your bones than his, rancid though it may be."

To Martin's horror, Gully giggled shamelessly at this, as though she'd just performed the most outrageous flirtation.

Alice was indifferent to him. To Martin, she said, "I regret we do not have more time, but there is still much to be done before tonight. I shall see you again at dinner." She nodded politely, letting her gaze linger with Martin's for a delicious moment, and then turned away.

She'd gone a few steps when Mr. Gully turned to Martin and fixed him with a cold stare. "Don't you dare test me, sir."

Martin, face flushed, called out to her. "Miss Cobb. If you please."

She turned and paused.

"Mr. Gully has a point of business he must discuss with you."

"Does he now." Her face was unreadable. "Spit it out then, little morsel."

Gully grinned again, but this time he maintained his composure. "In private, if you please."

"If you think I'm going to be shut into a room with you, you're mad."

"Right here will suffice. Give us a moment, Mr. Dunwood."

Presented as an order. Martin felt lightheaded. He considered that if he acted quickly he might surprise the man and wrestle him overboard. If it became a struggle, perhaps others would come to his aid. But he knew there was no realistic hope of this, and that such an action would only result in his own guts spilling onto the deck, there to cook in the hot sun. Worse, the same fate might come to Alice. So he swallowed his anger and said, "Be quick."

He walked to the railing and turned his back to them. From this vantage point, he could see *The Puritan* poised nearby, its own decks alive with activity. The traffic between the two ships had slowed. He peered into the southeast, but there was still no sign of the pursuing vessel. Perhaps they'd given up.

He would not have time to spend with Alice before the crossing, but he consoled himself with the promise of her company afterward. In a few days' time, they would be married. With a little good fortune, perhaps they could even secure her father's blessing, though they would certainly proceed without it. He did not think Abel Cobb would find cause to refuse him, even considering their natural animosities. He felt confident that the ritual following dinner tonight would put any possible objections to rest. It was all very well to call the Candlelight Society a toothless gathering of storytellers, but let him see Martin work with a hellward candle, and he would adjust his thinking.

"Come on then, Mr. Dunwood."

Mr. Gully stood at his side. Martin turned in time to see Alice wending her way through the crowded deck and disappearing down the ladder into the interior of *The Butcher's Table*. She did not spare him a glance. Martin grabbed him by the shoulder and shook him once. "If you've threatened her in any way, I will kill you for it!"

"Take your hand away. I did no such thing. All I did was ask for a place at the table."

Martin needed a moment to understand what he'd just heard. "A place—you mean at the dinner tonight? Preposterous."

"Not tonight's dinner," Gully said. "Another one."

Martin's mind reeled. He meant the Feast. Even under normal circumstances, it was remorselessly exclusive; few outside the diabolist circles even knew of its existence. The notion that some miscreant from the gutter might be welcomed tableside simply by exhibiting a bit of bluster offended him on a foundational level. "You don't even have the right clothing for it," was all he could think of to say.

"I don't think it'll be a problem." He patted his employer on the arm. "Now let's get below and get you ready, Mr. Dunwood. You done what I asked, and now God help anyone who crosses you while I'm about." He considered a moment, then gave him a wink. "Well . . . God, or whoever."

⊸⊷

Fifty leagues to the southeast, what remained of Captain Bonny Mungo stalked the decks of *The Retribution*, calculating the time it would take to catch *The Butcher's Table*. The captain existed as a fluttering scrap of thought in a body which had once been his, but was now broken and expanded to house the carrion angel that lived there. The bones in his face had unlocked and pushed outward to accommodate the angel's presence. The flesh was swollen and bruised black; occasionally some pocket of trapped blood would find its way out and trickle down his face in an oily stream. When the captain issued orders to his crew, his Scottish burr pushed through altered vocal cords to create a sound which terrified them, and left them wholly subservient.

The other three carrion angels had surrendered their hosts as soon as the crew had been tamed, and now roosted in the masts, black silhouettes fluttering against the hot sky, occasionally drifting down to feed on one of the bodies spread like a red feast on the decks. The crew had been trimmed to its barest essentials. Everyone else was provender.

Bonny Mungo retained enough of himself to remember Scotland, to remember standing atop a seaside cliff and watching the ships leave that cold rock for adventures under a foreign sun. He remembered a childhood spent thieving from the shops, waylaying passing carriages and unfettering the fops inside from the bags of coin weighing them down. The years spent in and out of gaols, escaping the hangman's noose long enough to finally find passage aboard a ship full of bloody-minded young men like himself, brothers all. He hacked and beat and bought his way to a position of prominence among them, to a captaincy, to respect and fear and a rolling home thousands of miles from the fog-clapped cliffs of Scotland, in a part of the world where the sun hammered its devil's eye onto hot sand and clamoring Spanish ports. Bonny Mungo retained enough of himself to remember all of that, and to provide the angelic cockroach splitting his body like a too-small jacket with the requisite knowledge to keep enough men alive to sail his ship, and to point it in the direction of its prey. After that, he and all that remained of his crew would just be gruel in the trough.

The scent of the lotushead drew them across the waves. It was getting closer, but the rag that was Bonny Mungo knew that it was not quickly enough. Because he knew it, the angel knew it too.

It spoke a word that fractured the jaw of its host, registering the pain as a curiosity. Upon hearing the word, one of the roosting angels took flight, rearing against the sun in a flare of black feathers, and plummeted into the sea, where it sank from sight like a corpse weighted with stones. The angel descended quickly, a dark-feathered ball, until it passed beyond the reach of sunlight and the water grew cold and black. It fell more deeply yet, oblivious to the atmospheres pressing against its body, its eyes pulling from the lightless fathoms darting shapes, shifting mountains of flesh.

It found a host, made a bloody gash and wriggled into it, and filled the beast with its holy spirit. Skin split in fissures along the length of its form, and it jetted forward with fresh purpose, its tentacles trailing in a tight formation behind it, its red saucer-shaped eyes incandescent with hunger.

"Tell me," said Abel Cobb, as Captain Toussaint led him through the cramped corridors below.

Toussaint bulled his way toward the ladder which descended into the hold. He spoke over his shoulder as he walked. "I believe we're pursued by a carrion angel. Perhaps a host of them."

If this rattled Cobb's resolve, he disguised it well. "I suppose it was to be expected. Tracking the lotushead, no doubt."

"No doubt."

The hold, lit generously with lanterns, bustled with activity as crewmen filled the larder with the meats, spices, and vegetables that would supply the Feast, and afterward sustain them on the short journey back to the colonies, where all parties would go their separate ways. Beyond this, toward the aft, were the rooms the carpenters had added to house Abel and his retinue. The scent of recently cut wood filled their nostrils. Abel peered into his own room and sniffed with disdain.

"These are barely adequate."

"Your other option is the open deck. I'll leave that decision to you."

Cobb turned away. "Show me the runner."

Toussaint gestured further down the passageway. No lantern hung there, and it ended in a swell of shadow.

Cobb hesitated.

"Don't be nervous, now," said Captain Toussaint. He smiled.

Cobb proceeded without a word. About twenty feet ahead the corridor ended in a closed and locked door. Sound was muted here; the loading activities behind them seemed to come from a more distant place, and the chill of the water, so near to them, shivered their blood. The captain gestured to the door. "In there, Mr. Cobb. Would you like to see him?"

Cobb only nodded, and the captain shouldered by him with a key. He couldn't shake the unpleasant notion that he was taking orders aboard his own ship. Abel Cobb was one of those men who inhabit power the way other men do a suit of clothes.

The door pushed open and they discerned a shape on the floor, which slowly materialized into the crumpled form of Thomas Thickett, lifting his face into the meager light. He blinked and held out a hand to block it out. "Yes? Yes?"

Cobb swelled as he drew in a deep breath. "There you are at last," he said.

Thickett froze as he recognized the voice. He scrambled back into his cell's darkest corner. "No."

Abel Cobb knelt at the room's entrance. When he spoke, his voice was gentle, almost kind. "You are the most fortunate of men," he said. "Do not flinch from this honor."

"NO!"

Cobb backed out of the room and shut the door. Captain Toussaint locked it again, muffling the sound of Thickett's sobs. They were an assault on his heart, and it took him a moment to harden himself against them again. He passed the key to Cobb, formally transferring custody.

"You feel sorry for him," Cobb said.

Captain Toussaint straightened himself and walked back down the corridor, not sparing the man a glance. "He's made his own fate. I have nothing more to do with it."

"I've heard rumors that you're a sentimental man," said Cobb, following behind. "I just wasn't sure I should credit them."

"Sentiment is a dangerous quality on the sea, Mr. Cobb. So is a credulous nature. Be wary of rumors."

"Ah, then the stories about Captain Tegel and yourself are lies, invented to destroy your character. What a relief, sir, I must tell you. So there will be no sentiment, then, to spoil the Feast."

They arrived at the door to Cobb's new quarters. Captain Toussaint stopped there. "I will not be dining with you at the Feast," he said.

Cobb smiled beneath his moustache. There was no warmth in it. "I thought your kind were less discriminating. Do you tremble at the thought of tasting the human animal? He was bred for this, after all." He flicked his eyes over

Captain Toussaint's solid form, as though sizing up a slab of beef. "I assure you, you are as different from one another as a dog is from a pig."

Captain Toussaint felt a familiar heat rise in his chest. It had been growling like a low fire since the Priest had boarded the ship. He'd expected to dislike the man, and was not disappointed on that front. But he did not know how long he'd be able to keep the fire banked if Cobb insisted on making provocations. "I want nothing to do with your barbaric Feast. I am not one of your cultists."

"'Cultists,' is it? We are an old order, sir. Older than the Candlelight Society, older than whatever groveling thing you Haitian beasts fashion your altars to. We are bound by traditions. A man like yourself may have no regard for such things, but I assure you they are the very bedrock of civilization."

"'Captain.'"

"I'm sorry?"

"You will address me as 'Captain,' sir. You're aboard my ship. You will address me properly. You will not attempt to recruit me or any of my crew into your brutish practices. And what's more, you will not speak the name of Josiah Tegel again. You're not fit to. The rumors you've heard are true. I loved him. I still do. You may titter behind your handkerchief in private, but do it where I can see you and you'll learn what punishment looks like to a pirate crew."

Abel Cobb nodded absently, seeming to consider. His eyes shone in the lantern light. "Thank you for your candor. Allow me to return it. A man like you can only give orders to white men aboard a ship which has already surrendered itself to chaos. No vessel in the Royal Navy would tolerate it. Not even the colonists would endure such a thing, and they are known to fornicate with savages. I need your ship, *Captain* Toussaint; I don't need you. You would be wise not to forget it."

Captain Beverly Toussaint smiled. "And now we understand each other. Good day, Priest." He turned his back to the man and made his way to his own quarters, where a mugful of rum would help calm his anger. That, and the knowledge that he would see sweet old Tegel again very soon. Even now he awaited Toussaint in the Dark Water, ready to enact a plan they'd agreed upon years ago.

Toussaint cast an eye over the empty space in the hold. There probably wasn't enough; but he could always throw some Satanists overboard, and make more.

Meetings of the Candlelight Society were convivial affairs, defined as much by the sharing of good whiskey and brotherhood as the sharing of Satanic devotions. There was not a member of the Society who could not claim to be a gentleman, so Martin Dunwood felt distinctly out of his element as he sat at the captain's table, surrounded by criminals and cannibals.

Walls had been taken down by the carpenters to make the room more spacious. The curtains were pulled back from the bay window, admitting a cooling, salty breeze. Twilight was falling over the waters; the sky was a smear of pastels. Two candelabras sat at either side of the table, filling the room with a warm light. Grimsley busied himself with taking away the plates from the meal, and replacing them with a sheaf of paper, a quill, and an inkpot.

Dinner had been intimate and quiet. Himself, Captain Toussaint, and the Cobbs. Their companions—Mr. Gully, Mr. Hu, and Mr. Major—dined in the mess with the rest of the crew. Conversation at the table had been muted; Martin detected a tension between Captain Toussaint and Mr. Cobb, though he was too preoccupied by Alice's presence to give it much thought. Alice was formal and polite with him, nothing more. He found it difficult to restrain himself from offering the occasional illicit smile, or to touch her foot with his own underneath the table. He did none of these things.

Once Grimsley had finished and retreated from the room, all eyes fell to Martin. He pulled in a steadying breath, and removed the cloth-wrapped candles from an interior pocket. He placed one into a silver candleholder as the others watched.

"It's ghastly," Alice said.

Now that his moment had come, Martin was nervous. But a breeze carried the scent of Alice's perfume to him, warming him with the memory of their secret nights in London. This, along with the slow rocking of the ship and the heave of the waves through the open window, conspired to produce a feeling of pleasant intoxication, steadying his hand and calming his nerves.

"Gentlemen—Miss Cobb—I'm prepared to light the hellward candle. It is customary for a member of the Candlelight Society to tell a story before applying the match, but—"

"For pity's sake," Abel muttered.

"—considering that we are pressed for time, I will forego it." With a flourish, Martin lit the match. The smell of burning phosphorous tickled his nose. Flickering orange light lit their faces; the skin appeared to crawl over the bones of their skulls. He glanced at Alice; he could not read her expression. "While this candle diminishes, its sister in the Black Iron Monastery, on the border of Hell, will rise in counterpoint. During that time I will be in communication with one of the monks in residence there. We will arrange a meeting place. It's crucial that I not be interrupted. Everyone must remain silent."

The match hissed in his hand. He paused, feeling his inexperience keenly. He'd been present at the lightings of hellward candles before, but had never performed the ritual himself. It occurred to him that if he botched it, the entire expedition would be undone. He would lose Alice as a certainty, and he would probably also lose his life.

Captain Toussaint leaned forward in his chair, sliding his hand across the table toward him. He did not touch Martin, but he breached the distance between them: it was a calming gesture. "We won't interrupt you. Light the candle, lad."

Martin touched the flame to the wick, and the candle flared to life. Martin sat. He aligned the parchment comfortably before him, and dabbed the quill into the inkpot, careful to let the excess drop back inside before positioning his hand over the paper. The hellward candle began to smoke, its acrid plume drifting out through the open window. Abel Cobb retreated a step, covering his nose with his sleeve. A trickle of melted wax began to drip down one side of the candle.

Martin closed his eyes—it was important to establish a sympathetic blindness with the monk—and spoke. "My name is Martin Dunwood, of the Candlelight Society. I request an exchange with the Order of the Black Iron, according to the protocols of the Coventry Accord."

The effect was immediate. A trapdoor opened in his mind and Martin seemed to drop out of his own head, plummeting down a dark tunnel with terrifying speed. Though he was bodiless, the terror of impact was quite real, and he found himself reaching with arms he no longer possessed to grab for purchase on a wall that did not exist.

Horror consumed him. He suddenly believed that his worship of Satan had been a terrible mistake; that every promise offered to the Society, to the Buried Church, to any of a thousand practitioners of obeisance, had been a lie. All had been fooled, all were destined to be swallowed into this endless black gullet. His little soul was nothing more than a crumb of the great human feast for the Burning Prince. Martin wanted to scream, but there was nothing left of him to do it.

⊸⊷

The Black Iron Monks take a vow of darkness upon entering the Order. Of all the people existing on Hell's borders, they alone cross into the final country. Upon taking the vow their heads are fitted with black iron boxes, which they wear until death. They experience no need for sustenance, no need for air. The boxes allow them to pass into Hell unaffected by its influence. Each passage into its territory is a pilgrimage; some monks go in solitude, though most go in a linked procession, guided by a native beast. The monks are the cartographers of Hell; all excursions are, in the end, illuminations.

Martin felt the closeness of the iron box around his head. He smelled the stink of flesh long unwashed, of a mouth filled with teeth left to rot. He existed as little more than a ghost in the monk's consciousness. Whatever epiphany he experienced moments ago was forgotten in the exultation of success. He was here, in the Black Iron Monastery. What he wouldn't give for the monk to remove his iron cage, so that Martin might see the interior: the maps and charts which he imagined must hang from the walls like illustrated curtains, the walls made of stone dug from Hell's earth, the quality of light which came not from the sun but from Satan's burning hide, unknown leagues away.

He felt a wordless pulse of thought: not so much a welcome as an acknowledgement of his presence. It was disorienting, and he was briefly overcome with nausea. The monk's mind recoiled, followed by another pulse, this one a mixture of surprise and curiosity.

Of course. He had been expecting Mr. Benson. Martin could not keep the memory of what he had done out of his mind, and it spilled across the Black Iron Monk's thoughts like flaming oil: the deception at the table, the poisoned brandy, the members of the Society expiring in puddles of their own blood.

Betrayed by his inexperience, Martin quailed. He had not meant to share that information. He feared that the monk would cast him out, dooming their expedition. But the ancient agreement between the Candlelight Society and the Black Iron Monastery superseded whatever crime he'd committed. He'd performed the ritual properly, and so the monk had no choice but to honor it.

Degrees of latitude and longitude seared into Martin's mind like hot iron pressed into flesh. It was the place they would retrieve the monk from the Dark Water. Martin's hand scrawled the coordinates onto the parchment, untethered from conscious thought.

And then another pulse: a demand. The price which would balance their equation. This time Martin received it as words, a sentence built by a being far removed from the use of language.

Tell me about sunlight.

The yearning in the monk's voice filled Martin with a kind of sadness he could understand: the wanting for warmth, the ache of skin waiting for the touch of a kind hand. The need to fill a hole which only grew deeper. Martin filled the monk's mind with a vision of sunrise over a field of barley, the air bright with drifting motes. It was summertime. Birds kept a quiet chatter. A girl was there, who smiled when she saw him. It hurt in the most beautiful way.

⊸

The hellward candle guttered out, plunging the room into darkness. Martin slumped onto the table, his fingers grasping weakly against the wood, tears gathered in his eyes. Abel Cobb took him by the shoulders and pushed him upright. "You're all right then, Mr. Dunwood, you're all right."

Martin stared at the coordinates he'd written on the parchment, and then lifted his gaze to Alice. "I did it," he said. "I did it."

Captain Toussaint opened the door and called down the hall. "Mr. Johns! It is time."

⊸

The sea grew increasingly restive. *The Butcher's Table* and *The Puritan* bobbed over the waves. Heavy clouds blotted out the moon and the stars, and the ships looked like floating chandeliers in all that darkness.

The crate had been brought onto the main deck. Mr. Johns and a contingent of deckhands positioned themselves around it, hooks and spikes held in defensive postures like medieval instruments, while Hu Chaoxiang and Randall Major watched from a modest distance. Mr. Hu and Mr. Johns had sailed with Captain Toussaint for years; they had served with him under Captain Tegel's command, and had previous experience with a lotushead.

To the rest, it was a new experience. Fear buzzed around them like a cloud of flies.

A tattooed, shirtless man pried off the lid and leapt back, swiping the air in front of him with a hook, as though an African jungle cat had launched for his throat. In fact nothing emerged from the crate, and the others laughed cautiously at his performance. Chastened, he approached again, wedging iron into a corner and leveraging it free. Twice more and two sides fell away. The lotushead slumped like a huge dead plant on the deck. Its trunk looked like an old man's flesh, gathered and bunched at its base. Its tapered neck sagged into itself, the glistening bundle of tongues which crowned it limp and gray. A light rain began to mist, dappling its flesh with beads that reflected gold in the lantern light.

"It's dead," the sailor said, looking back at Mr. Hu with something like hope.

"It ain't," said Mr. Johns. "Stop your ears, boys." He removed the wax plugs from his pocket and stuffed them into his ears, while around him the others did the same. The dull roar of the ocean became a distant hiss. The light patter of rain on the deck faded away, becoming only a cold sensation on his skin. Once this was done, he addressed the man who'd opened the crate. "You've got to coax it, lad. Give it a poke." He could not be heard, but he illustrated his meaning with a gesture toward the creature.

With a few shouts of encouragement, the sailor approached the lotushead again. He extended the hook slowly toward its bunched flesh; in the last moment, with a flash of courage, he lunged forward and pricked the beast's skin with the point of the hook. He leapt back into the fold of the other men, and this time no one laughed.

Muscle rippled along the length of the creature, and with a shiver of life it inflated to its full height, nearly six feet. Its body looked like an amalgamation of plant and animal, as though the stalk of some jungle growth was comprised of thick joints and rolled meat, with no thought to structure or function. Its cluster of tongues, only moments before hanging in a sagging wreath around its apex, began to writhe. The sailors stepped well back from it, apprehension plain on their faces.

Only Mr. Johns stayed his ground. He cast a glance at Mr. Hu, who nodded his assent. "Make it sing, Mr. Johns!" he cried, and the old man moved to obey. He extended his hand, and someone placed a meat cleaver into it. He stepped closer with a nervous twinge in his blood.

The squealing sound of wood being torn and splintered filled his senses; a moment afterward came the screams, and then the bucking of the deck beneath him as the ocean surged in a mighty wave. Mr. Johns fell to the deck, his senses disoriented. The cleaver slid away from him, toward silent lotushead.

"What the devil—"

He turned to see *The Puritan*—barely discernable in the rainy night though not a hundred yards distant—keeling to port, its masts forty-five degrees to the ocean's pitching surface. Something seemed caught in its rigging, as though it had flown there, and it took Mr. Johns a long moment to make sense of it in the light of swinging lanterns.

It was a squid, a deep-sea monstrosity with tentacles nearly as long as the ship itself, and it was inverted in the sky. Its arms pulled the sails from their masts, yanked yardarms free of their moorings. People slid from the deck and into the churning water. The squid hovered in the air, its skin split lengthwise, revealing the white flesh of its interior, as though something within itself did not fit. Ragged black feathers jutted from the wounds. Its tentacles splayed in the air around it, a corona of horrors. Its glaring eyes smoked in the beating rain.

"Holy mother of God," said Mr. Johns. It was a carrion angel. Mr. Johns pissed down his own leg.

"Mr. Johns! Now! Do it now!" It was Mr. Hu, holding onto the railing. His voice carried through the screaming din, through the wax plugs in his ears, and recalled the old sailor to his duty. He found the cleaver on the deck and crawled toward it. The carrion angel was here for the lotushead; it would tear through *The Puritan* like a flimsy box and then move on to *The Butcher's Table*, where it would devour the lotushead while every soul aboard sank to the cold bottom.

Mr. Johns grabbed the cleaver and staggered toward the creature. The deck lurched beneath him and he fought to keep his footing. A hand gripped his shoulder from behind, and Randall Major shouted into his ear. "No! Not yet! We have to save them!"

Mr. Major had come from *The Puritan*, and he knew its people. Sentimentality drove him to madness.

"They're dead already!" Mr. Johns shouted. He jerked his shoulder free and swung the cleaver with his full might into the lotushead's flesh. The creature bucked, knocking Mr. Johns backward. A sound emitted from somewhere beneath the mass of tongues, staining the air like blood seeping into cloth. The creature's tongues stirred, wriggled, flailed. In tandem they articulated the seventeen dialects of Hell, they intoned the Bleeding Harmonic, they recited the cant of the Angelic Brutalities.

Randall Major raged in protest. He threw Mr. Johns to the deck, knocking the wax plug from his right ear. Mr. Johns' fingers scrambled to find it. His hand shook, tears filled his one good eye. He'd turned his back to a man caught in the grip of madness; he cursed himself for his beginner's mistake. The voices filled the sky, occluding every other sound. Mr. Johns turned his face away from the milling tongues, but the language poured into his ear like boiling oil. Mr. Johns died in a paroxysm of joy, his eyes pouring out of his head in pale, heavy streams.

Around him, a quiet descended over the crew. The lotushead's speech stuttered into silence. The sea beneath them was black and calm, the sky cloudless and spangled with red stars. Whatever grave *The Puritan* had sunk to existed in a place unreachable to them now. *The Butcher's Table* had crossed into the Dark Water.

IV. The Darling of the Abattoir

Alice remembered the first time she'd taken Martin to the Buried Church beneath London. There were seven in the world, each a small series of chambers hacked from the raw earth, connected by tunnels and lit only with torches, if they were lit at all. Here they raised their human cattle—some stolen from cradles, some purchased in the smoky rooms of state power, some bred in the dark for their fates. These latter were the most desirable, with eyes and flesh unstained by sunlight. She had guided Martin through the pens, and he had been struck mute by the sight of them shivering in their cages. A few stared into the light with a terrible, manic look; but most turned away, as though from something holy.

The experience cowed him, as she'd known it would. Members of the Church had always been disdainful of the Candlelight Society, figuring them for little more than dandies playing at worship by swapping tales in front of polite fires in polite hearths. Alice always assumed they were something more than that—she was not susceptible to her father's prejudices—but no matter how serious they were in their devotions, the brute reality of the Church practice made everyone quail.

"How can you do it?" Martin asked, kneeling beside one of the cages and staring at the boy inside, no more than fifteen years old. The boy was one of those who stared back, though he did it from the far side of his cage. His mouth moved, as though he wanted to speak but couldn't remember how.

"Because we love them, and we love our Prince."

Martin shook his head. "They're people, Alice. They're people like you and me."

Alice knelt beside him. "Precisely so. We're slabs of meat for Satan's plate, waiting to be laid open by the stroke of His knife. We bleed onto His plate, ride gratefully upon the fork into His mouth. We are split between His teeth."

Martin stared at her, the torchlight turning his eyes incandescent.

"There is no greater expression of love for our Lord than to devour the human animal. To be the one devoured is to be the vessel of that most beautiful expression."

She could see him struggle with this. He wanted to align himself with her way of thinking. His love for her compelled him to.

"Let me tell you a secret," she said. She retrieved a key from a chain around her neck and slid it into the cage's lock. The boy inside watched this with rapt attention.

"What are you doing? He'll escape!"

"Not with you here to keep him subdued, surely."

The look of fear that passed over Martin's face almost made her break her composure. She touched his hand. "It was a joke. Forgive me." She opened the lock and swung the cage door wide. The boy hesitated, then approached, keeping low to the floor. Almost crawling. "The secret," Alice said, "is that my father can barely stomach the taste. He prefers to have his portion cooked."

Martin could not understand, of course, but that hardly mattered. What it meant was that her father's faith was weak. He had become drunk on his position in the church, and his ambitions were about power, not service. Sometimes she dreamed of informing the congregation that the Cannibal Priest himself was a fraud, a weakling who applied fire to the meat lest his delicate palate be overwhelmed by its potency. His blasphemy both shamed and disgusted her.

The boy reached them, and sat back on his haunches. He turned his eyes up to the cave's black ceiling and the firelight played over the angles of tendon and muscle in his neck. An artery pulsed there, bearing the heart's red tide.

A cleaver hung from a hook beside the cage, and Alice took it down. "It's always best when they're willing," she said, and then she went to work.

She'd fed Martin that day with her own hands, and though they'd eaten lightly, it was enough to confirm what she'd hoped: she could love him. He could bear the weight of it.

⟜

Martin slept. Since not all of Abel Cobb's retinue had survived the sinking of *The Puritan*, the old man had allowed him to move into one of the new rooms in the hold – an improvement from his previous berth. Mr. Gully stationed himself outside. At some point early in his fitful rest, Abel Cobb pounded on the door of his quarters, enjoining him to go topside. "How can you linger down here?" shouted Cobb through the door, "We've arrived in the Dark Water! Come up with me, Mr. Dunwood. Let us see this new place."

But Martin was exhausted by his ordeal. Furthermore, he was beset by a doldrum of the spirit; here, on the brink of his greatest achievement, he wished only to hide from his fellows, to bury his head beneath his pillow and slip into a dreamless abyss. Perhaps this was a common side effect of using a hellward candle. He instructed Mr. Gully to keep the Cannibal Priest away.

And so he passed some hours that way, bobbing along the surface of sleep like a cork at sea, until the door creaked open and Fat Gully's head intruded from the hallway. "Are you awake, Mr. Dunwood?" he whispered.

"I am ill. Send him away."

"Not this time," Gully said, and he opened the door for his visitor. Alice stood in the darkened door frame. She looked like a ghost, her white gown limned in lantern light from down the hall, her face obscured by shadow.

"Alice!" Martin sat up, collecting his bedclothes about him. "Come in! Hurry! What if you're seen?"

Alice stepped inside, and Gully closed the door behind her, remaining outside the room himself.

"Do you think I'm a fool?" she asked. With the door closed, he could barely tease out her shape in the darkness. He felt her sit beside him on his mattress. He leaned over and lit a candle beside the bed, providing them with a little island of light.

"Of course not."

"It's been hours," she said. "They've drunken themselves to collapse. They imagine they've done a great thing, and they're celebrating."

"Haven't they done a great thing? Haven't we all?" Martin was still tired, but he felt a twinge of apprehension at Alice's choice of words.

"We've only crossed the border. Others have done so before. Greatness, if we're going to find it, will be found in Lotus Cove."

That might be true, but it made him impatient to hear it. He was the first member of the Candlelight Society in generations to cross into the Dark Water. Surely some acknowledgement had been earned.

Perhaps he would just take it for himself. He took her by her shoulder and pulled her near, for a kiss. She allowed herself to be drawn closer, but resisted the final inch by buttressing her arm against the mattress. A few loose strands of her hair tickled his cheek. The smell of perfume filled his nostrils, and with it came the memory of the last time he had seen her—her body glazed with someone else's blood. He leaned toward her, but she stopped him with a finger to his chin.

"Not yet," she said.

"But why? Alice, it's been a year. Do not hurt me like this."

"You know why. If we're discovered, you'll be executed. Your part in this is done. It's only the strength of the contract that keeps you alive now."

"You forget. I have Mr. Gully to protect me."

She smiled at that. "Mr. Gully has his own purpose here, Martin. And it isn't protecting you."

Martin sat up, forgetting his desire. "What do you mean?" He recalled their secret conversation on the deck with apprehension. "What did you two talk about?"

"That is my business, and his."

"What? How can you say that to me? We're about to be married!"

"What does that have to do with it?"

"Well . . . you should obey your husband." He tried to present it as a joke, but he didn't really mean it as one, and they both knew it.

She sat upright on the bed. "You're making some dangerous assumptions, Martin."

He tried to sound conciliatory. "I'm not, really. Only I don't understand why you're being secretive. I have a right to know."

"It has nothing to do with you," Alice said. "I know you find that shocking." She leaned over him and graced him with a kiss. Just a small one; she withdrew before he could open his lips.

"Very well. I trust you, Alice."

"Do you now. We sail ever closer to Hell. It is not a place for generous inclinations."

Emboldened by this—as though she had issued a challenge—Martin fell back on the bed again, gripping her arm and yanking her down with him. His other hand snaked into her hair, pulling it loose from its stays so that it spilled in a bright tide from her shoulders. "Stay. I want you right now. I want them to think it is Satan Himself rutting in the hold, splitting the goats apart with His lust."

Alice pushed his head back, baring his throat. She took his chin between her teeth and bit gently. "I know what you want." She extracted herself from his grasp, and stood up. She took a moment to fix her hair as it had been. She turned to leave, paused, and gave him a small smile. "When we're finished, there will be no more rules." She leaned down and blew out the candle.

Martin wiped the sweat from his face, breathed deeply to slow the blood in his veins. She stood so close. A black pillar etched in the faint red light creeping in around the closed door, where Mr. Gully stood guard outside. They were surrounded by threat, by coiled violence, and by the possibility of extravagant fortune. He felt as though he rode on the crest of a towering wave. He felt like a usurper, like a new and terrible king.

"I think this is how the Burning Prince Himself must have felt," he said. "Before His grand rebellion."

Though he could not see her face in the darkness, he saw the shape of it change; he thought it must be a smile. Then she opened the door and disappeared down the corridor.

Mr. Gully watched her go, then leered in at him. "Everything all right then, Mr. Dunwood?"

"Shut the door," said Martin.

Mr. Gully did so with a chuckle. Martin consoled himself with images of the little man bleeding to death at his feet.

—◦—

Rufus Gully waited until he could hear the snores issuing from Martin Dunwood's room before he crept down the hallway. He felt a twinge of apprehension; he did not like leaving Mr. Dunwood unguarded. Now that his part had been completed, the rich fool was vulnerable to the murderous whims of the others. Civility may hold them in check—even the pirate seemed beholden to it—but Gully knew thieves. They did not like to share.

And yet. Miss Cobb had instructed him, and he was no stranger to his own heart. If Mr. Dunwood must be left unguarded in the wolves' den so that he could meet with her, then so be it.

Mr. Gully glanced into the main body of the hold. The light of a hanging lantern illuminated the stacked crates, the stores swinging in their netting, the mounds of burlap sacks. Goats and chickens were penned on the far side, and though he could not see them, their stink was overwhelming. He turned in the opposite direction and made his way down the corridor, between the new rooms built for the Cobbs. The ship pitched on a rough sea, and he lurched into a wall, barking his elbow. He cursed life on a ship, remembering fondly the London docks. If anything, life there was even more precarious, but at least the ground didn't leap under your feet.

"Mr. Gully." Miss Cobb's quiet voice, somewhere ahead. "You lumber like a gorilla. Come, you're almost here."

He pressed on into the dark and found her, waiting patiently by the locked door at the very back of the ship. He waited until his eyes acclimated enough that he could read her face, and then he whispered a quiet greeting.

Miss Cobb unlocked the door, ushering him in ahead of her. Not until she secured the door shut did she light a match, touching it to the wick of a small candle. The light flared and there in the corner cowered Thomas Thickett, naked now, shaved hairless as a salamander. He recoiled from the light, curling into a fetal position. He wrapped his arms around his head. Goosebumps peppered his skin.

"This is the Feast," said Miss Cobb.

Mr. Gully knelt beside the shivering man. He wanted to touch him but was afraid. He glanced up at the lady, the candlelight highlighting her pale skin and her red hair, and he felt the shudder of a complicated emotion. He became suddenly aware of his own ugliness: his squat, toad-like frame, the unappealing arrangement of his face. Alice Cobb was beautiful, as though she had just stepped out of a sonnet. Even Thickett was an expression of beauty: a vessel of Satanic love. The stink of his fear was gravy to the meat.

"Our presence here is a transgression," she said. "He is not meant to be seen again until he is brought to the table."

Gully did not understand. He felt he was in the presence of something holy, and his very proximity was spoiling it. "I've made a mistake. I'm sorry. I don't belong here."

Miss Cobb said, "You belong, Rufus."

Mr. Gully started at the sound of his Christian name. He had not heard it spoken aloud, especially by a woman, in a long time. It was always Fat Gully at the docks, Mr. Gully to his employers, or coarser names than those. He became freshly conscious of his position here, crouched in folded shadows with a beautiful woman and a beautiful man, the spare golden light of a candle giving them form, and he the lone wretch. The flaw in the art. "Why, Miss Cobb?" His voice cracked. "I'm ugly. I'm stupid. Why did you bring me here? Why did you listen to me?"

"Because all your miserable life, no one has ever loved you. Because yes, you *are* ugly, and you're mean, and you're lonely. I knew you for who you were the moment I saw you. Are you a Satanist, Rufus?"

"I've never given religion much thought, Miss."

"You should be. Love is Hell's breath. You crave it. Your whole soul shakes with it. *You* are suitable for the Prince, Rufus. Not this coward." She looked at Thickett, shivering naked on the floor. "He runs from the honor. He's perfectly suited to my father's weak palate. There's nothing left of him but fear." She prodded him with her toe. "I'm almost sorry for you, Mr. Thickett. You won't even get that, now. Your whole life was wasted."

"Please." It was Thickett, wrapping a hand around Mr. Gully's ankle. Blood ran from his nose and dribbled down his chin.

Gully extracted his foot and knelt beside him. "What is it you want then, ay?"

Thickett's hands continued to grasp for him, one on his knee, the other reaching for his hand. "Get me out."

"I'll just let you go then, shall I? And what of Miss Cobb?"

"Kill her. Kill her right now. Please."

"That's not very charitable."

"You don't know what she is."

"No? What is she?"

Thickett swallowed. His eyes fixed on Gully in a mad, hopeful stare. Did he sense some distant possibility here? He clutched Gully's sleeve. "She's a monster. They're all monsters."

"All of them!"

"Yes!" Thickett waited for some action. When it didn't come, he began to understand that Gully was toying with him. Watching his small hope crumble was a remarkable experience. "Don't kill her then. Don't kill anyone if you don't want to. Just open the door and I'll run. I'll swim for shore. I'll swim for it. I don't care if I drown. I just don't want this."

Gully slapped his hand away. He grabbed Thickett's lower jaw and squeezed, turning his head to the side. "Don't *want* it? You thankless shit. You don't *deserve* it."

He slipped his knife from its sheath and pressed it against the artery in Thickett's neck. Miss Cobb stopped him with a light hand on his shoulder. "Not yet, Rufus."

Gully withdrew the knife with some difficulty. The contempt he felt for this cowardly little man almost overwhelmed his better instincts. Thickett didn't even put up a fight. He just slumped back to the floor, curling into himself again. He shivered with cold or with fear.

Miss Cobb leaned closer to Gully from behind, her lips close enough to his ear that when she spoke it tickled his hair and stopped his breath. "Love must be earned, Rufus. With restraint, and with silence. Wait until the Feast. Do it when they have no choice but to turn to you instead. And then it will be your turn, Rufus. Your turn in the light, at last."

Gully wiped a tear from his cheek.

⊸

You're out there somewhere, Toussaint thought. He scanned the horizon, obscured by darkness and a pitching sea. The sky and its pinwheeling stars provided no light.

Captain Toussaint, Mr. Hu, and Mr. Johns had been to the Dark Water once before. Six years ago, when he was simply Beverly Toussaint, first mate to Captain Tegel, who commanded *The Butcher's Table* with vicious and bloody efficiency. They had found a lotushead on an English merchant vessel they'd captured off the Carolina coast. A member of the Church of England had custody, and he was quick to surrender his secrets when Captain Tegel displayed for him all his various instruments of persuasion, glinting in the hot sun. Upon learning what he wanted, Tegel had the man flayed anyway, as a rebuke against the God he represented. "Let us see how much of your blood I have to spill before He decides to make Himself known to me."

In fact he spilled all of it, and God remained absent.

Captain Tegel commanded Mr. Johns to hack into the lotushead's flesh, provoking the strange cries which opened the way from the Atlantic Ocean to the Dark Water. From there they sailed to Hell's coastline, and it was there that Beverly Toussaint first laid eyes on the galleons of the Black Law, enforcers of the infernal order. It was there that he learned of the secret commerce that transpired between Hell and his own world, right under the Black Law's nose.

Captain Tegel had found a place where he could unleash his cruelest aspect and be celebrated for it. He decided to stay behind, breaking Mr. Toussaint's heart. Toussaint feared he would never hear of him again, but over the years word began to trickle back to him: of the captain who commanded the brigantine *Angel's Teeth*, carving a cruel path through the dark sea; of the captain who left ships burning in his wake, whether pirates or vessels of the Black Law; of the captain who garlanded the rigging of his own vessel with the bones of his enemies, so that others told stories of hearing their clatter carried on the night wind, signaling his passage. Toussaint knew that his old lover was flourishing.

And unlike these men muttering stories under lamps of whale oil, he knew Tegel's true purpose, one they had agreed to share all those years ago: smuggling the Damned out of Hell and back into the world. Toussaint because he would spit in the eye of any god or devil which tolerated the enslavement of human beings; Tegel because he wished only to usurp the order of things. Any order at all.

And now Beverly Toussaint was a captain himself, and he stood at the prow of his ship to honor the contract he'd made with the man he loved.

He heard a familiar tread approaching from behind.

"I'm sorry, Mr. Hu," he said, without turning around. "I know you and Mr. Johns were close."

Mr. Hu leaned onto the railing beside him. He did not speak for a long moment, watching the dark horizon instead, where lightning bellied the clouds. "Well," he said. "It was the Virginian."

Captain Toussaint looked at him. "What do you mean?"

"The one called Major. He got in Johns' way, tripped him up. Wouldn't have happened otherwise."

Captain Toussaint took a moment to absorb the information. "What did you do about it?"

"Nothing. You know me better than that. We have a job to do."

He nodded. "I'm grateful for your restraint. You'll have your chance later."

"With respect, Captain, I don't need your permission for that."

"No. I understand." Mr. Hu and Mr. Johns had a long and complicated history, and the captain did not presume his own authority could outweigh it. Mr. Hu would handle the Virginian as he saw fit, and that was the end of it. "What about the lotushead?"

"Secured again, for the trip home." The return trip would likely kill the creature; they were notoriously fragile.

"And our friend Mr. Dunwood?"

"He's below, in the new accommodations. He and the priest are sleeping on soft beds tonight. Soft beds for soft men. I look forward to seeing the end of them."

"Soon, Mr. Hu. Very soon."

Mr. Hu shifted, and there was a hitch in his breath. Captain Toussaint observed him from the corner of his eye. "Say it," he said.

Mr. Hu deliberated for a moment. "Has it occurred to you that he will be different?"

He was talking about Tegel. Toussaint turned to face him. "Different," he said.

"Yes. He's been here *six years.* The whole atmosphere on this ship has turned sour just by the presence of that gang of Satanists we're carrying. What happens to a man who's chosen to live here?"

"You pick an interesting time to voice your concern, Mr. Hu."

Hu Chaoxiang put his hands on the railing and looked at them when he spoke. "I wouldn't have. But Johns was apprehensive too. He didn't want to do this. Now he's dead, so I have to say it."

His first mate was practical and efficient; in that way he reminded Captain Toussaint of Tegel. And he was a killer, too, but unlike their old captain he was always cool in the act. He possessed an admirable self-control, an ability to separate himself from the red moment with a thoroughness which had preserved his life many times. And so his nervousness now was almost charming.

Almost.

"Yes, Mr. Hu. It has occurred to me that he will be different."

Mr. Hu was still. After a moment, he nodded.

"Do you still have the stomach for this?"

"Yes, Captain. Yes, I do."

"Good." He slapped his old friend on the shoulder. "Put some fresh eyes in the crow's nest. We have to be sharp, now."

Mr. Hu turned and went about his task. Captain Toussaint returned his gaze to the strange sea, still looking for a glimpse of his heart's object, ringing with bone chimes and flying a black flag.

⊸⊷

At the coordinates provided by the Black Iron Monk, the rounded head of a giant protruded from the pitching sea, its skin as black as an inkpot, its pale white eyes irisless and blind. The lower half of its face remained beneath the waves. Martin stood beside Captain Toussaint at the prow of the ship, the questing tendrils of an oncoming storm whipping them with wind and rain. He stared at the vast creature through the captain's spyglass. The surge of waves made fixing the beast with the glass a difficult prospect, but it was large enough that at no time did it leave his vision. Martin's heart thrilled at the reality of the experience. Communicating with the monk through the hellward candle was one thing, but here was a creature of Hell in the flesh, in service to the Order of the Black Iron, which was in turn—for the moment—in service to him.

. . . I think this is how the Burning Prince Himself must have felt ...

Captain Toussaint said, "By God, is that him?"

Martin smiled. "No indeed. It is the vessel by which he arrives."

That seemed to be good enough for the captain. His voice boomed: "Drop the launch! Smartly now!"

The launch boat struggled through the waves toward the giant, six men heaving at the oars to the very limits of their strength, Mr. Hu perched at its prow, a coil of rope wound about his right arm. If any of them were afraid of the great beast, Martin could not tell.

The launch boat pulled up a dozen yards short of the giant. Mr. Hu stared at the monster, rocking with each pitch of the boat with all the ease of a man standing on solid English earth. After a moment, the head lifted out of the sea, runnels of water streaming like a heavy rain. The water churned around it in a vast radius, encompassing both the launch boat and even *The Butcher's Table* itself, its decks thronged with spectators.

Jet black tentacles rippled along the surface of the waters, propelling the head closer to the launch. It opened its mouth to reveal a red tongue, which it extruded toward the boat, and upon which stood the Black Iron Monk, standing as still as a pillar, his black robes fluttering about him. A black iron box encased his head: the physical manifestation of the Order's Vow of Darkness, and the device which protected them during their sojourns through Hell.

Mr. Hu had no need of his rope. The beast's tongue touched the tip of the launch with delicacy, and the monk stepped into Mr. Hu's grasp like a gentleman alighting from a carriage. The launch returned to the ship as the beast slipped beneath the waves again.

Once on deck, the Black Iron Monk was left to Martin's care. He reeked of Hell: char and smoke and, underneath it, something delicately sweet. Martin guided the figure below decks to the first mate's quarters, which he'd recently vacated. Since Mr. Johns had met his end, the room had been deemed unlucky, and no one had moved in to take his place.

It seemed a ridiculous set up. The monk was a figure of awe, even terror: someone who had actually passed across the border into Hell's radiant fields and recorded what he witnessed there, in whatever way the monks could witness a place. He was practically a figure of mythology to Satanists the world over, and now Martin had brought him to a small, cramped room, where he must sit on a box or swing on a hammock like any normal fool.

"Forgive me," Martin said, not even sure the monk could hear him from inside his iron box. "The accommodations are rough. We are ill-prepared for someone of your standing."

The monk gave no reaction. He simply stood in the center of the room, unconcerned with the furnishings. Martin had the unnerving thought that he was like a broom that had been tucked back into its closet, there to remain immobile until fetched to perform his function.

A step sounded behind him, and Martin turned to see Fat Gully standing there, his expression subdued for once, a hint of wonder in his eye.

"This is him, then, aye? The man from Hell."

"Not *from* Hell. The Order of the Black Iron resides along its border. They are cartographers."

"Does he talk?"

Martin felt a flush of shame at Gully's performance of ignorance. "The monks communicate differently. Please stand outside, Mr. Gully. But do not go far. I must speak with you."

"I'm never far, Mr. Dunwood." He gave the monk another lingering glance, and retreated from the room.

Martin retrieved parchment, quill, and inkpot from a drawer. He placed them atop a box and said, "If you'll be so kind as to produce the map. As specific as you can, please. Also, the routes of the Black Law's patrol. We must not be discovered. I know you understand."

When the monk neither moved nor spoke, Martin decided that he must leave him to it and simply trust that it would be done. He left the cramped room, securing the door behind him, and found Mr. Gully waiting for him there as promised.

Gully opened his mouth to speak, but Martin silenced him by grasping his bicep and ushering him further down the tight corridor. "When we arrive at the cove, upon my order, you will sever the monk's head from his neck. Regardless of whether the Priest endorses our wedding, Miss Cobb and I will not be returning with you. The head will serve as our atlas, and we will take it together into Hell. And you will be released from your contract."

"What, you and the lady are just going to wander off into Hell together? You've lost your senses."

"Well, it is love, after all. And what would you know of that?"

When Martin revisited the monk's quarters a short while later, the parchment he'd left behind was covered with instructions and a detailed map. Martin thanked him and carried the information to Captain Toussaint, who studied it carefully. Within the hour, he had plotted their course, wending carefully through the patrol lanes of the Black Law. He was convinced he could guide them through unnoticed.

The Butcher's Table filled its sails with wind, pushing through the rough waves and the whipping rain. Black clouds boiled overhead. Martin could no longer distinguish night from day. Alice stood by his side. She seemed happier than she was the previous night, even unconcerned that her father might notice their attachment to one another. He was curious, but he had learned long ago not to press her. She would tell him what she wanted to, when she wanted to. He was content with that.

Fat Gully hovered nearby, never out of eyesight. That his engagement with him was fast approaching its end gave Martin the will to bite back a curt dismissal. He was so tired of the little man's grotesque appearance, his sneers and his effronteries. Leaving him behind to fend for himself would be one of the greatest joys he'd ever known.

Behind them all the crew labored in eerie silence. The white sails had been taken down and black ones raised in their place. Captain Toussaint had issued an order that no man should speak aloud, all communication to be done through hand signals. Although the constant storm made it unlikely that the sound of their passage would reach the Black Law, he took nothing for granted.

Martin peered into the white foam below, conscious of the vast creature that had delivered the monk to them only hours before. He imagined whole civilizations beneath them, cities of such monsters with heads bent in contemplation of alien philosophies, engaging in wars, creating strange art. The thought both thrilled and appalled him.

Alice touched his arm, breaking his reverie, and pointed ahead. He squinted into the spitting rain, seeing nothing but the rolling waves, the spray of water, the shifting clouds. After a moment's patience, though, he saw it: land. A jagged coastline, like teeth from a jawbone, barely discernible in the turbulent air. Excited, he turned to alert the crew, only to discover that they all saw it. Men hung from the rigging, or paused on deck, and stared. Captain Toussaint, standing on the aft deck, held his spyglass to his eye. Mr. Hu stood at his side. Martin turned to look again, his heart leaping. Here was Hell's coast.

He felt a kind of fear he could only describe as ecstatic.

Alice whispered into his ear: "Soon, my love."

He took her by the waist and kissed her recklessly, heedless of the consequences for either of them. Inviting them, even. He felt that old surge of power, that kingly entitlement. This time, she did not resist him. Perhaps she was no longer afraid of her father. Perhaps she was unable to resist the magnetism he felt exuding from his bones like an elemental energy.

Let Abel Cobb come for him. Let Fat Gully, let Captain Toussaint, let them all descend upon them with knives drawn. He would christen Hell's ocean with their blood.

⟜

They sailed several leagues down the coastline. At no time did Martin see a place they might make landing; the land was jagged stone and tall cliff, the waves breaking themselves against great, toothy rocks well before the shoreline. If he did not place so much faith in the infallibility of the Order of Black Iron, he would have begun to despair already. He could already see the doubt kindling in the eyes of the crewmen who passed him as they performed their duties. He doubted them before he doubted the map; how long would Captain Toussaint's influence keep them on task?

Mr. Gully seemed to share his apprehension. Always close, he now seemed fastened to his side like a barnacle, the hilt of his knife prominently displayed where it protruded from his belt. Alice, for her part, seemed completely untroubled. Whether in the company of himself or of her father, she expressed nothing but delight at their imminent success.

What they were seeing was not the landscape of Hell itself. That existed further in, beyond a range of mountains which could not be crossed without protections and guidance. What they were seeing here was just borderland. Scrub. Martin understood there to be small settlements throughout, and somewhere in there, close to the mountains, was the Black Iron Monastery.

And yet, they caught glimpses of things on the shore that could have had no other provenance. A pinwheel of arms and hands, connecting in a knot of tissue bearing one staring blue eye, kept pace with them for hours, leaping in what appeared to be play, sometimes disappearing behind rocks for a mile or more, only be spotted again as the landscape evened out; a small shack at the base of the cliff, with three charred black figures, paused in their construction of a wooden pyre to fix them with a red glare as they sailed past, while something small and frightened bucked beneath the pile; a great centipede, twice the length of their ship, descended from the crags and slipped into the crashing sea, where it disappeared to join whatever horrors lived in that briny abyss.

After a time even these sights became mundane. Martin turned away from the wonders unfurling alongside him, his thoughts turning inward. He found himself thinking ahead to the crossing of the border into Hell, hand in hand with Alice, with the Atlas to guide them. They would take no protections from the environment, as the monks did; they would let the atmosphere work its effects on their flesh and on their minds, transfiguring them into whatever shape or condition pleased the Burning Prince. Alice assured him that the purity of the Feast would grant them favor.

A cry came down from the crow's nest: "The cove! Lotus Cove, Captain!"

Alice rushed to the port railing, Martin following. Mr. Gully approached as well, his flat little eyes alight with wonder. Behind them, the entire crew went silent.

The rocky shore stretched on, seemingly interminable, but for a break in the line which showed where an inlet lay hidden; Lotus Cove must be around that bend. But how, wondered Martin, could the lookout be sure? What did he see?

Alice saw his bewilderment and put her fingers on his chin, turning his head incrementally to the left. His gaze shifted, and the blood drained from his face.

Dangling over the edge of the near cliff-face, so large he mistook them for earthen formations, were the enormous upturned fingers of a left hand. Now that he saw them he could not fathom how he had missed them before: alabaster and smooth as stone, they might have been mistaken for a statue were it not for the damage they had taken: a pink wound, like an incision, along the meat of the thumb, from which some dark-rooted trees seemed to have sprung; and the snapped digits of the first and second fingers, the latter broken so thoroughly that splintered bone—a dingy yellow in comparison with the pale flesh—jutted into the air like cracked wood. The hand seemed luminescent against the dark flow of clouds overhead. Martin found himself short of breath. He lowered his head, closed his eyes, and concentrated on the work of his lungs.

"What is it?" said Gully, cowed with awe.

Alice said, "I daresay it is an angel's corpse, Mr. Gully."

Martin turned to look at the captain. Toussaint had trained his spyglass not at the cove, but back toward the sea, as if waiting for something to materialize behind them. Most likely he was only concerned about being discovered by the Black Law. Still, it seemed odd that his attention would be distracted at this moment.

Rounding the bend into Lotus Cove took the better part of an hour. Once the turn was made, though, they might as well have passed out of the Dark Sea and into the Caribbean again, or someplace stranger and more beautiful. The cove was large enough that it might have given shelter to a small fleet of ships the size of *The Butcher's Table,* and the water here was calm, clear, and bright blue. Schools of fish flitted beneath them, and large, eel-like shapes undulated just beyond the range of vision.

Dominating everything, though, was the angel's corpse. It lay on its back, a luminous wreckage. Its head—as large as one of London's great warehouses—lay shattered and half submerged in the water, a hole in its side gaping like a cavern, large enough to sail the ship into. The rest of its body stretched on a sharp incline of earth, spread out in a mangled heap on the barren plain above. Martin tried to make out some sense of order to its body, so that he might intuit what shape the creature would have had in full flight, but it was a hopeless task. It was a tangle of broken limbs, exposed meat, and a score of torn wings.

The water proved deep quite close to the shore, enabling Captain Toussaint to maneuver *The Butcher's Table* to within a few hundred feet of the angel's broken skull. He ordered launch boats dropped, and within minutes the ship was disgorging its crew and materials to the shoreline, where Abel Cobb's retinue worked quickly to assemble the banquet table. The angel's corpse was so large that there was little room to either side of it, so the site of the feast was to be the interior of the skull.

The skull's contents had long ago spilled into the cove, leaving dry planes of bone covered by curtains of seaweed. Clusters of rooted plants grew in bunches where remnants of the brain survived, bearing pink, bulbous growths which sagged like the heavy heads of kings. Chairs were ferried over, as well as a white tablecloth, and numerous sets of silver cutlery and dinnerware. Abel Cobb's own chef, one of the first to arrive on shore, presided over the whole business, barking orders with as terrible a mien as any Caribbean tyrant.

In the meantime, Captain Toussaint sent a contingent of sailors, led by Mr. Hu, on a steep climb up the side of the angel's ruined head. By means of ropes and grapples they would achieve the creature's upturned chin, from which point they would descend into its open mouth and down its throat. There they would dig out the lotusheads, which grew in profusion in the place where the angel formed its speech. The captain had no interest in joining the Feast; his business was the harvest. And, perhaps, something else; Martin noted that he still seemed more interested in what might be coming behind them than what lay before.

Beside him, Alice had no eyes for the preparations: she looked instead up the long slope to the vast, dry field which separated them from Hell's true country. It would be an arduous crossing—but the monk's guidance would make it possible.

V. THE FEAST

At last, the table was set.

Alice took her place at her father's right hand. Above them, the angel's curved skull blocked the sky. The bone was completely covered in hanging vines, moss, strange growths which pulsed with light, and suspended sacs gravid with ochre liquid. Animate life crawled through the foliage, hidden to the eye but emitting a low, constant susurrus. From this vantage point she could see the bright blue water of the cove, so unexpected in this setting, and *The Butcher's Table* anchored in the distance. Randall Major had taken a launch to fetch Thomas Thickett to the dinner plate, and should be returning any moment.

The table was laden with food. Cobb's chef had toiled mightily in Grimsley's kitchen, preparing a modest but worthy repast—better, in any case, than anything they'd eaten since leaving the colonies nearly a week ago. Roast pheasant, carrots and onions, and blood pudding crowded the table, along with boats of gravy and carafes of red wine, situated in such a way that a large oval of space was left free in the middle.

Martin sat across from her, to her father's left. Beside him, though of course he would not be dining, sat the Black Iron Monk, inscrutable in his stillness. On her right were the only two other members of the Buried Church to survive the sinking of *The Puritan*—typical church functionaries, as uninteresting to her as roaches haunting an alleyway. Mr. Gully sat on a rock some distance away; her father would not welcome a man like him to this table.

One seat remained empty, positioned directly opposite Abel Cobb. It was reserved for Satan Himself.

Alice watched the sea for the return of the launch. Soon enough, she saw it. Mr. Major worked the oars, bringing Thomas Thickett to the table.

Captain Toussaint watched Mr. Hu and the others descend into the angel's open mouth, the small team provisioned with rope and leather, knives tied to their waists or clenched in their teeth. They would return with half a dozen lotusheads, and no more. The rest of the hold was reserved for the Damned.

Once they were out of sight, he turned his spyglass back out over the cove, where it opened into the ocean. A chiming carried softly over the water—the hollow music of bones knocking into each other as *Angel's Teeth* heaved across the waves. Beverly Toussaint stared into the white mist beyond the cove's lip, waiting for the ship to materialize. He felt the working of his heart in his chest, could feel it too in the pulse in his fingers, each heartbeat a jostle against the spyglass, a shuddering of the world it contained. When the ship parted the fog, he exclaimed quietly to himself. It was as he had been told: skeletons hung from the rigging, separated bones suspended from ropes and masts, clacking into each other in the ship's steady motion. An ornate chair, fit for an island governor, had been affixed to the bowsprit, and the skeletal remains of some fallen regent reposed there. Antlers grew from its sagging head, and seaweed draped its body like a vestment. Standing at the bow was the outline of a man. He could not discern its features with any clarity but he knew the shape of Josiah Tegel as well as he knew his own.

He felt that old bruise in his heart.

When he barked his order, though, his voice carried all the usual power. "Prepare to receive them, boys!" he said. "Smartly! Smartly!"

Another voice came down from the crow's nest. "A ship, Captain!"

Toussaint stared up into the rigging, trying to catch sight of the idiot. "I can see it, you damn oaf! What's your name?"

"Not *Angel's Teeth,* Captain! To larboard! Look!"

A chill washed over him. Captain Toussaint did look, his spyglass pressed to his eye again.

Another ship pushed through the mists, about a mile out. Sails and hull so dark that the eye wanted to slide right off them, as though it were only the night coming. But it wasn't the night; it was the Black Law. They had been discovered.

Abel Cobb struck a fork against his wineglass, summoning the company's attention. Thomas Thickett lay on the table between them, breathing shallowly, his eyes unfocused and wandering. Blood trickled from his nose: an aesthetic blemish to the proceedings, which Martin fixated upon, to his lingering discomfort. It seemed a teasing glimpse of what would shortly fill their plates, like a bead of fat perched upon a boar's roasted carcass. Martin's stomach rolled over sluggishly, and he wrenched his gaze away from it, fixing it onto his folded hands instead.

"My friends," said Cobb, "whether you are members of the Buried Church or honored guests"—here he nodded once at Martin and once at the Black Iron Monk, standing a small distance away, like some terrible obelisk—"you have the privilege of sitting at the table of the most significant Feast in our history. Tonight, we dine at the lip of Hell. Tonight we honor the Burning Prince with living flesh, and invite Him to join us at the table."

He looked at the empty chair across from his own position: carved of black wood, a single staring eye painted red at the peak of the chair back. Before this chair a table setting, cutlery polished and ready for use. Thickett's head lay nearest this setting, in an inversion of the typical arrangement. The Cannibal Priest surrendered the honor of the skull's sweet morsel to the true head of the table, should He arrive. It was Cobb's hope that the Prince would be there to crack it open himself.

"At this table, we honor the rutting goat, the feasting worm, and the ache of unanswered yearning. We honor the bruise in the heart. To honor Satan is to honor love itself," said Cobb, and he gestured to Alice. "If you would, please, Daughter."

Martin watched the woman he loved rise from her chair and take a long, slender carving knife from the table. She placed its tip near Thomas Thickett's left shoulder. She pressed the blade down and drew an incision to the midpoint of his chest. Thickett shrieked, and blood spilled in a sheet. Martin fought the urge to put a hand over his eyes. Alice repeated the gesture from the right shoulder. Once the two incisions met, she carved a new line from their meeting point down to his groin. Blood ran in a heavy tide, flowing onto the table and running off the edges. Thickett's scream filled the hollow of the angel's skull.

A gunshot cut it short. Martin's ears rang with it. A warmth spread over his body and he looked down to see that Thickett's brains had splashed across the table and the guests, all his red fears sliding onto the soft earth.

Mr. Gully stood some distance away, a flintlock pistol smoking in his hand. He stared at the table with an expression of dismay or wonder, like a child might wear. He said something which made no sense to Martin—"I done it, Miss! I done it!"—but all his attention was focused on Thickett, who was still alive despite his fatal wound, writhing in mute agony between the dinner plates.

A wind blew in from across the plain, hot and sand-ridden. It slipped into a fissure in the angel's corpse and through its cavities until it funneled through the angel's throat, shivering its old vocal cords. Hu Chaoxiang and his small company, suspended on rope ladders and hacking lotusheads from their bases, froze in place as the sound of it carried over them. It passed through them like a razor, and each man wiped a trickle of blood from an ear or a nostril. The sound shaved little memories away, slivers of themselves they would never recover nor even miss.

And then the sound of a single cannon shot reached them. Captain Toussaint's signal: the Black Law was coming.

Mr. Hu shouted orders, but they were unnecessary. The men were already hoisting themselves to the angel's lip, leaving several lotusheads hanging by fibrous threads. They would take what they had. It would have to be enough.

A wooden plank dropped between the two ships, and the Damned began to cross from *Angel's Teeth* to *The Butcher's Table.* They did not look like men anymore. Rather they looked like gross imitations, clay roughly shaped. Their skin was gray and soft, and it hung from their faces like wet laundry. They shuffled slowly. Captain Toussaint resisted an impulse to hurry them; they were beyond any human directive. They were cattle now, and the captain just another human trafficker. The irony was not lost on him.

But he was no cannibal, and he was no slaver.

Once on board they were directed into the hold by the crewmen. They offered no resistance, nor even acknowledgement. Toussaint hoped that they would remember their lives once they returned to the world; but perhaps they would never be more than living corpses, staring into the sun with pale, hell-haunted eyes.

But he had more concerns than only the Damned.

Behind them stood Josiah Tegel. He still wore his old brown greatcoat, now frayed and scorched; his long beard had turned white as the moon. Whatever chaotic impulse had driven him near to madness in life served him well here. He seemed almost incandescent with power. He was a creature of the Dark Water now, and it made him magnificent.

Tegel spoke to him, and though they were separated by hundreds of feet and the clamor of the crews preparing for the Black Law's arrival, Toussaint heard him as clearly as if he had whispered in his ear. "Come with me, Beverly."

Perhaps he would. Perhaps, when this was finished, he would allow himself what he wanted.

Captain Toussaint turned his eye to the approaching ship. It seemed to move with an impossible speed. He swiveled his gaze to the angel, where his men were emerging from its mouth, securing what they were able to gather. They moved so slowly, and the Black Law was so fast.

"Ready the guns," he said.

⟜

The sound of Alice's laughter snapped Martin from his stupor. Thomas Thickett was staring at her. The bullet from Mr. Gully's shot had passed through his right eye and into his brain, and now he leaked jelly onto the table. He still lived. Martin rose from his seat, suddenly conscious of the red scramble on his shirt. He brushed at it, as though he might flick it away with a napkin.

"Alice, what's happening?" he said. She looked at him, and he saw pure delight. Whatever this was, she had orchestrated it. Why hadn't she told him?

Mr. Gully let the pistol fall from his hand. "I'm ready, Miss Cobb." He began to tug at the laces of his shirt.

Abel Cobb left his place at the table's head, dazed, and started toward Mr. Gully. His arms were extended, his hands prepared to accept Gully's throat into their possession. Alice interceded, the carving knife extending from her hand like a talon. She opened a seam beneath his great belly in a quick, confident motion. Cobb gasped, clutching her arms. "Alice," he said. The weight of his spilling guts pulled him to his knees.

Martin reeled. He grasped the edge of the table to steady himself. Behind him, Randall Major stood transfixed where he had been stationed, either as shocked as Martin himself, or—more likely, he realized—loyal to Alice, and already privy to her intentions.

"But the Feast," Cobb said weakly, gathering his innards into his arms as they slipped out of himself. He started to weep. "My Feast."

"There it is, in your hands," she said. "Eat it, or starve."

It dawned on Martin that the greatest obstacle to their plan had just been dispatched. He looked toward the shore. In the cove, *The Butcher's Table* was receiving human cargo from a second ship. Smoke curled from one of its starboard guns, aimed harmlessly over the dead angel. A signal shot had been fired. As if on cue, Mr. Hu and several crewmen hustled toward it further down the beach, hurriedly dragging a collection of bound lotusheads behind them. They made for the launch boats beached on the shore.

Randall Major, silent until this point, was goaded into action at the sight of this. "They're leaving us! The traitors!"

Martin said, "You'd better stop them, I think."

The Virginian needed no further incentive. He pulled his pistol from his belt and ran after them, shouting invectives. At the boats, Mr. Hu turned from his work and observed his approach. He waited patiently for his arrival, as behind him the first of the launch boats pushed out into the cove.

"Alice," called Martin. "Now is the time. Let's go." He was giddy with anticipation. Everything was so close.

"The monk," she said, climbing to her feet.

Of course. The Black Iron Monk stood by the table in terrible silence, indifferent to what transpired before it. Martin turned to Gully, who stood mutely transfixed by the proceedings.

"Mr. Gully! The monk! See to the monk!"

Gully was staring in bewilderment from Alice to Martin. He had managed to strip of his shirt – what the devil had he been thinking of? – but now he stood stunned, as if struck by a hammer. "No, you're not leaving. She promised me." He sounded like a little boy whose greatest hope had just been dashed.

"She promised you what?"

"It's me. I'm to be the Feast. I'm the one. It's supposed to be me."

On the table, Thomas Thickett tried to crawl away, but he could get no purchase—his hands kept sliding in his own blood. By this time most of the contents had leaked from his head; there was little of him left aside from a mute recognition of agony.

"Do what I tell you!" said Martin.

Mr. Gully recovered himself. He withdrew his little knife and pointed it like a finger at Martin. "I told you you would come to regret that tongue," he said. "Now I'll carve it out of you."

Martin took a step backward. "Do what I tell you, Mr. Gully."

Gully strode toward him, the knife thrust ahead like a guiding element. Martin retreated and stumbled to the ground. For a moment all he saw was the curved arch of the angel's skull above him, grown over with vines and hanging plants. Then Gully filled the world. He had time to scream Alice's name before Gully stuffed his fingers into his mouth with one hand and pushed the knife in with the other. Pain spiked him in place, and his throat filled with blood.

"Rufus, no." She said it quietly, almost casually. He could not hear her, of course, bent over his bloody work, his back to her. She approached him calmly, her knife dripping in her hand. Dimly, she heard the sound of skirmishing carrying across the water behind her, and coming from the shore where Randall Major engaged Mr. Hu and his cohort. But she focused on Gully now, working his knife into Martin's mouth. Only Gully remained to be dealt with.

A quick glance toward the Black Iron Monk stopped her. It no longer stood by the table, where Thickett still sluggishly moved. Her stomach dropped. Without the monk's head they would be lost. It would all be for nothing.

There it was: heading in the opposite direction of the launch boats, wading now in shallow water, meaning to leave the angel's skull and presumable walk back to its monastery.

Very well. She was the butcher of the Buried Church. She would do this work herself. Martin's garbled screams echoed through the skull. He would have to fend for himself. Her father grazed her leg with one bloody hand as she passed, letting his armful of viscera slide heavily to the earth. "Alice," he said. "Is He coming?"

She caught up to the monk in the shallows. He was short but difficult work. He did not attempt to flee, had no idea what was coming for him. He was like a lamb in that way. Alice swung the knife into the soft flesh just beneath the iron box. A sheet of blood sprayed her face. The monk staggered backwards, all sense of awe and mystery dissipating as it crashed into the water, hands pressed against its throat as it scrabbled for life. Alice set her foot on the box, holding it in place. She hacked at the neck, sending the monk's fingers rolling like little pegs. Blood greased her hands and forearms. The surf turned red.

A thin, reedy noise escaped the monk: air whistling through a torn throat. The sound of it was like a small razor sliding through her brain. Her eyes started to bleed. This was the language of Hell, the language of her Prince. Love's sweetest vocabulary. She worked furiously until the head was entirely separated. The hissing air stopped. A panel slid shut underneath the iron box, and whatever the monk said now was contained inside. She made her way back to shore, taking the box with her.

Several feet away, Gully rose from where Martin lay prone beneath him, his ghastly trophy oozing between his clenched fingers. He stepped over Martin and held it out to her, like a gift.

"Here's a liar's tongue," he said. "Now I'll take yours."

Martin spat blood from his mouth, but more came in torrents. He curled into himself, shuddering in pain. He was obscurely aware of the others around him, satellites to his own experience, but Alice occluded them all. It was Alice to whom he extended his bloody hand. He watched Fat Gully approach her: an avatar of death. He tried to push himself to his feet but collapsed each time. He could do nothing to save her. All of this, for nothing. All of it broken at the feet of some dockyard scum.

His tongue. His speech. His means of worship. No more stories told, ever again.

He rolled onto his back. Blood backed into his lungs and he watched arcs of it leap from his mouth as it choked the life from him. Beyond it was the curve of the angel's skull, and he found himself wondering at the brain that once resided here. What terrible dreams still haunted this place? Were they living one out now, like vessels possessed by ghosts? The thought gave him a strange comfort.

Martin closed his eyes and allowed himself to be consumed by this idea. He became separated from responsibility and consequence. He was only a figment of a dead dream, carried away by his own red current.

Gully closed on Miss Cobb, his volcanic anger already cooling. The monk's body rolled in the surf behind her, its limbs moving slowly. In her right hand she held loosely the carving knife with which she had performed all the work of her life. Gully moved toward her in a delirium of heartache. Thomas Thickett, Abel Cobb, and Martin Dunwood lay in a bloody tableau behind him. That Thickett and Cobb still lived was an undeniable miracle, whether due to their presence in the angel's hollow skull or their proximity to Hell's border he could not say, and did not care. What it meant was that if she had kept her promise to him, he would have lived as they feasted on his body. He would have experienced the translation of his solid flesh into an expression of love; to come so close to acceptance and to lose it was more than his mind could bear.

"Why?" he said, when he arrived beside her. The knife was ineffectual in his hand. He could not kill her. No one here could die. The gravity of his failures pulled him to his knees. "You said I could be loved."

"I lied," she said. She walked around him and headed toward Dunwood, carrying the head of the Black Iron Monk.

Let them have it, then. Let them love each other. That was never for him, and he accepted it now. He pulled himself to his feet and headed for the boats.

⊸

There was no time left. Captain Toussaint ordered the plank between ships to be withdrawn. They had taken about threescore of the Damned. Less than he'd hoped. Captain Tegel held his gaze from his own ship. Toussaint had always known they'd be hurried, had always known there would be no time for anything more. And yet he had allowed himself to hope. The sting of it hurt beyond all reason. He wanted to shout across to him that he would come back, that next time Tegel should return with him—or that next time he would accept Tegel's offer, and stay.

He turned his gaze one last time toward the beach, where the worst people he had ever known had gathered for their terrible feast. The people who came here to worship the very hook in Toussaint's heart. Slavers, conquerors, murderers, gluttons—they gorged themselves in celebration of everything that stank, everything that was rotten in the world. It would be a pleasure to leave them all beached on Hell's shores, but it was not enough to satisfy. He commanded the starboard guns to fire, and they did so, hurling enough iron at the feasting table and everyone around it to shatter a frigate's hull.

⊸

The cannonfire hit the beach without warning, and Gully found himself airborne. He landed hard, half submerged in water. Through garlands of smoke he saw severed limbs, splashes of blood, splayed viscera. The table had been smashed to flinders. Spread across and beside it were human remains, still quivering with life. One hand extended skyward from a bloody morass, fingers grasping for something or someone it would never find. Miss Cobb crawled across the beach. Her legs were gone just above her knees, yet she was undeterred. She wore a terrible grin. He heard Mr. Dunwood's wail somewhere beyond his sight; surely it was to him she crawled.

Gully surveyed his own body. Aside from superficial injuries, he seemed unharmed. A wave pushed in from the cove and submerged him, so he crawled further up the shore. Pain flashed through his body with each movement; he felt as though his joints had been fitted with knives.

A few feet away from him lay the severed head of the Black Iron Monk, still contained in its box. Gully fought his way to his feet, gasping at the effort, and pulled the box from the sand. If Dunwood and Miss Cobb would go into Hell, they would do it without their precious atlas. It was the only revenge available to him.

He staggered toward the last of the launch boats, some distance away. Mr. Hu was attempting to push it out into the water. The Virginian floated face up in the surf close by, a gunshot wound in his chest, his face battered and broken. His mouth opened and closed as he struggled to produce words. They were beyond him now. The tide pulled him further out with each wave.

Gully heaved the iron box into the launch boat and put his shoulder to it; between them, he and Hu succeeded in getting it past the breakers, and floating free. They climbed aboard, not a word exchanged, and put themselves to the oars. Further out, *The Butcher's Table* turned toward the cove's entrance as two other ships skirmished nearby. Gully had no idea what was going on; he only wanted back on board. He only wanted to be rid of these narcissists, these traitors, these grovellers. He wanted the familiar odor of the docks, its comprehensible confines, its knowable hierarchies. He wanted to go home.

-<o>-

The Black Law was almost upon them. Figures stood gathered at the rails, waiting to board. Their skin smoked, obscuring whatever features they had. They seemed composed of cinders. They wanted only to burn.

Captain Tegel maneuvered *Angel's Teeth* between them; he would buy him what time he could. The crewmen herded the Damned and all the lotusheads save one below decks. Captain Toussaint was prepared to give the order to slash the creature and provoke the crossing back into the Gulf of Mexico, when a cry from the crow's nest stayed his tongue.

"Captain! Mr. Hu is approaching!"

And indeed there he was, working the oars of a launch boat, Rufus Gully rowing beside him.

Behind him, *Angel's Teeth* was boarded by the Black Law: the air grew heavy with the sound of clashing blades and gunshots, with the smell of burning meat. The man he loved was risking everything to buy him time to escape.

"Captain, we have to go now."

"We'll wait for Mr. Hu," he said.

"But—"

"We'll wait."

In those short minutes, *Angel's Teeth* fell. Josiah Tegel went down beneath their weight; he would not die, but there were darker fates in store for those caught here. Toussaint turned away, tears stinging his eyes. Half a dozen of the Law threw grappling hooks toward *The Butcher's Table*, their iron spikes hooking over the rails and digging into the wood. They were living cinders; their very proximity caused the wood and canvas to smoke.

Mr. Hu and the little wretch beside him came alongside *The Butcher's Table*, and men were ready with a rope ladder. Mr. Hu climbed quickly; waiting hands grasped his shirt and hoisted him aboard. Fat Gully retrieved the iron box with one hand and made an awkward attempt to scale the ladder himself.

"Cut him loose," Toussaint said.

With a flash of knives the rope ladder was severed at the railing, and it fell in a loose tangle over Gully as he stumbled backward into the launch. "No! NO!" he screamed, but the captain had already turned his back.

"Do it now," he said.

A hatchet sank deep into a lotushead's trunk. Its tongues flailed to life. *The Butcher's Table*, once more, made the crossing, pulling Gully's launch in its wake.

⊸⊷

Martin opened his eyes. Alice was beside him. His chest had been cracked open like a walnut in the cannonfire. She dipped her hands into him, removed a glistening portion and fed it into her mouth. Her stare was unwavering. There was no intelligence behind it, no recognition. Nothing at all. Alice was gone. There was only brute impulse at work now. He tried to say her name and was rewarding with an overwhelming pulse of agony.

He did not want this. This was not love; it was an atrocity.

Please, he thought, *let me go mad. Let me go mad. Please let me go mad.*

The Black Law passed through the sinking ruin of *Angel's Teeth* and poured into the open chamber of the angel's skull, where the members of the Feast still twitched and struggled in the lowering light. Abel Cobb, Thomas Thickett, the drifting body of Randall Major, the surviving parishioners of the Buried Church, Martin and Alice: they shivered in the red mud, each sobbing plea or groan of pain a supplication to their Lord. Their bleeding bodies were His portrait, their wailing throats His opening eye.

The carrion angels waited for them in the Gulf. *The Butcher's Table* manifested at the precise point from which it had disappeared, Rufus Gully's launch pitching against its hull as the waves heaved beneath them. *The Retribution,* arriving at last while they'd been gone, immediately flew canvas to bring their guns into position. Captain Toussaint was unprepared. Still reeling from Josiah Tegel's loss, still disoriented by the crossing, he lost fatal seconds staring at the enemy ship, and at the misshapen thing which had once been Bonny Mungo perched in its rigging like a hellish vulture. *The Butcher's Table* received a full broadside from *The Retribution*; masts snapped in two, sails were torn and rigging fell like a net. A flying cannonball sheared the head from a sailor standing directly beside him.

Mr. Hu grabbed his captain and hauled him away from the side, but there was nowhere to turn. The carrion angels shed their human costumes in bloody sheets; the one still wearing the squid's body wrapped its great arms around the belly of the ship and tore it in half. The sea filled with the wreckage, with flailing crewmen, with harvested lotusheads, and with the rescued Damned, sinking into the blue fathoms like heavy stones. The carrion angels darted after them, the water boiling in their wake.

One of them detoured to Rufus Gully's launch, pitching and yawing in the frothing sea. It grasped the black iron box in a claw, tearing a rent in its side. A tumbling spar slammed into its body as it fell, driving it underwater. The box tumbled back into the boat. Panicked, Gully grabbed the oars and pulled away from the sinking vessel, his muscles screaming in protest.

Eventually he eased his rowing, and watched as *The Butcher's Table* sank beneath the waves. Scattered survivors clung to floating spars or planks of wood. Their calls floated across the water. He did not answer them.

The Retribution, divested of its occupying forces, drifted at the whim of the sea. What crewmen remained found themselves with no desire to exert their will upon the ship. Their brush with the divine had ruined them. There was nothing left inside but a mute passivity. Eventually a lantern slid from its place on a table and smashed into the hold. Within an hour, the whole ship was ablaze. Gully watched it burn for hours. When twilight fell, he had drifted leagues away, yet still he could see it shining like a torch against the early wash of stars.

Gully did not know how to read the constellations. There was no sail on the launch. He rowed weakly for a while, then surrendered himself to fate. He closed his eyes and listened to the lapping of the water against the hull, and it was not too difficult to pretend it was the sound of the Thames lapping the posts of the London dock. He dozed somewhere in the night, and dreamed of a whispering voice. The voice spoke in a language he couldn't understand, but it filled his brain with thoughts he recognized well enough. Red thoughts, murder thoughts. He dreamed of his mother, sitting quietly in the dark of their small flat, rocking incessantly in her chair. She told him a story of a witch who lived in the chimney, who crawled out at night, all covered in black, looking for a little boy to eat. His mother would not touch him or comfort him. He dreamed of his father, distant and harsh, driven by some nameless rage, dead of an exploded heart while still a young man.

Gully awoke to the glare of the sun. The voice whispered still. He peered into the bright air around him, his eyes gummy, the heat blistering the naked skin on his back. He called out for his parents. When he remembered himself, he went quiet. He kicked at the black iron box, rolling it over. He saw the gash the angel had rent in one side. The whisper leaked out of it. His skin had cracked and charred at the fingertips. He wiped at his eyes and saw that it was blood that made them sticky.

"What are you?" he said to the box.

Eventually he remembered what Martin had told him. The monk's severed head was an atlas of Hell. It recited its dreadful litany, listing all the landmarks of that burning country—the Breathing Mountains, the Love Mills, the Grieving Fields. It outlined the paths of the travelers there—the Crawling Eye and the Voyeurs, the pilgrims and the priests, and all the roaches of heaven. He understood none of the words but he saw these places clearly. Rufus Gully listened to the atlas speak for all the time it took for the sea to push him across hot open leagues of the gulf, to the swampy shores of New France, in a district called La Louisiane.

By the time the launch became entangled in the trees there, the voice had transformed Gully into something far different than what he used to be. Tumors and growths blossomed across his body—from inside of his mouth, from beneath his eyelids, from his ears, from under his arms and around his neck. His body was burnt, both inside and out. Smoke trailed from his nostrils in an unceasing plume. Only in his mind was there life, as he soared over the landscape of Hell, exulting in its bleeding vistas.

In time, the boat would decay, and the iron box sink deeply into the mud, where its voice would be silenced for generations. Before then, though, Rufus Gully lay prostrate in its bottom, his body a glorious feast for the swamp's vermin. They ate him while he lived, and he sighed with gratitude beneath a carpet of flies.

"I love you," he said. "I love you, I love you, I love you."

HONORABLE MENTIONS

Addison, Linda D. & Manzetti, Alessandro "The Place of Broken Things," (poem) *The Place*
Armfield, Julia "Stop Your Women's Ears With Wax," *Salt Slow.*
Barron, Laird "We Used Swords in the '70s," Weird Fiction Review Fall.
Bartlett, Matthew M. "A Strange Haze," *Wicked Weird.*
Baxter, Alan "The Ocean Hushed the Stones," *Served Cold.*
Begg, Charlotte "After I Devoured the Beast," (poem) Vastarien Fall.
Benedict, R.S. "All of Me," F&SF, March/April.
Bestwick, Simon *And Cannot Come Again*, (novella) *And Cannot Come Again.*
Bodard, Aliette de "A Burning Sword for Her Cradle," *Echoes.*
Breukelaar, J. S. "Fixed," *Collision.*
Bruce, Georgina "The Lady of Situations," *This House of Wounds.*
Bryski, KT "The Path of Pins, the Path of Needles," Lightspeed #115, December.
Cadigan, Pat "About the O'Dell's," *Echoes.*
Chronister, Kay "Thin Places," The Dark #50, July.
Cisco, Michael "Their Silent Faces" *Spirits Unwrapped.*
Cluley, Ray "6/6," Black Shuck Books.
Coffman, Frank "The Witches Rite at Beltane," (poem) Spectral Realms 10.
Connell, Brendan "All the Wild Animals," *A Miscellany of Death and Folly.*
Dean, David "The Squatter," EQMM Sept/October.
Ford, Jeffrey "The Jeweled Wren," Echoes.
Gardner, Cate "The Mute Swan," *Terror Tales of Northwest England.*
Grant, John Linwood "Records of the Dead," *The Twisted Book of Shadows.*

Hodge, Brian "One Last Year Without a Summer," *Skidding Into Oblivion.*
Holmes, Carly "A Shadow Flits," *Pareidolia.*
Jamneck, Lynne "Lies I Told Myself," *Nox Pareidolia.*
Johnstone, Tom "The Wakeman Recreation Ground," *Last Stop Wellsbourne.*
Kassel, Mel "The Coffin, The Ship," Black Warrior Review Fall/Winter.
Kiste, Gwendolyn "The Eight People Who Murdered Me . . ." Nightmare #86 November.
Langan, John *Natalya, Queen of the Hungry Dogs,* (novella) *Echoes.*
Larson, Rich "Painless," Tor.com April 10.
LaValle, Victor "Up From Slavery" Weird Tales #363.
Littlewood, Alison "The July Girls," *Echoes.*
Lombardi, Nicola "Striges," *The World of SF, Fantasy and Horror vol. IV.*
McCarthy, Cori "You Wake With Him Beside You," (poem) *Betty Bites Back.*
McHugh, Maura "Suspension," *The Boughs Withered When I Told You My Dreams.*
Meijer, Maryse "Pool," *Rag.*
Moore, Tegan "A Forest, or a Tree," Tor.com July 10.
Oates, Joyce Carol "The Surviving Child," *Echoes.*
Raye, J. C. "Eternal Roots of Lane County," *Nightscript V.*
Read, Sarah "Into the Wood," *Pareidolia.*
Rees, Matthew "The Lock," *Keyhole.*
Lee, Seulmi "When I Stopped Eating Earth," Black Warrior Review Fall/Winter.
Sharma, Priya *Ormeshadow,* (novella) Tor.com
Smith, Michael Marshall "The Burning Woods," *I Am the Abyss.*
Tantlinger, Sara *To be Devoured,* (novella)
Tem, Steve Rasnic "When You're Not Looking," *The Night Doctor and Other Tales.*
Thomas, Lee "Flowers For Bitsy," *Spirits Unwrapped.*
Volk, Stephen "Unchain the Beast," Black Static #68, March-April.
Warren, Kaaron *Into Bones Like Oil,* (novella) Meerkat Press.
Wilkinson, Charles "The Festival of Conformity," *Dark Lane 8.*

ABOUT THE AUTHORS

Nathan Ballingrud is the author of the collections *Wounds: Six Stories from the Border of Hell*, and *North American Lake Monsters*. He is a two-time winner of the Shirley Jackson Award, and has been shortlisted for the World Fantasy, British Fantasy, and Bram Stoker awards. His novella *The Visible Filth* was adapted into the movie *Wounds*, written and directed by Babak Anvari; and *North American Lake Monsters* is being filmed as *Monsterland*, an anthology series at Hulu. He lives in Asheville, North Carolina.

Simon Bestwick was born in Wolverhampton, bred in Manchester, and now lives on the Wirral while pining for Wales. He is the author of six novels, the novellas *Breakwater* and *Angels of the Silences*, four full-length short story collections and two miniature ones. His short fiction has appeared in *Black Static*, *The Devil and the Deep*, and *The London Reader* and has been reprinted in *Best Horror of the Year*, *Best of The Best Horror of the Year*, and *Best British Fantasy 2013*. Four times shortlisted for the British Fantasy Award, he is married to long-suffering fellow author Cate Gardner and strives to avoid reality in general and gainful employment in particular. His latest book is the collection *And Cannot Come Again*, recently reissued by Horrific Tales. He's usually to be found watching films, reading, or writing, which keeps him out of mischief. Most of the time.

Daniel Braum is the author of the short story collections *The Night Marchers and Other Strange Tales*, *The Wish Mechanics: Stories of the Strange and Fantastic*, and *Yeti Tiger Dragon*. *Underworld Dreams*, his third collection, will be released from Lethe Press in October 2020. *The Serpent's Shadow*, his first novella, was published as an eBook by Cemetery Dance. He is the editor of the 2019 anthology *Spirits Unwrapped*. His work has appeared in publications ranging from *Lady Churchill's Rosebud Wristlet* to the *Shivers 8* anthology. He can be found at https://bloodandstardust.wordpress.com, www.facebook.com/DanielBraumFiction, and on Twitter @danielbraum.

Ray Cluley is a British Fantasy Award winner with stories published in various magazines and anthologies. Some of these have been republished in 'best of' volumes, including Ellen Datlow's *The Best Horror of the Year* series and *Nightmares: A New Decade of Modern Horror*, as well as Steve Berman's *Wilde Stories: The Year's Best Gay Speculative Fiction*, and *Benoît Domis's Ténèbres*. He has been translated into French, Polish, Hungarian, and Chinese. His short fiction is collected in *Probably Monsters* while a second collection will soon be looking for a home. He is currently writing for Black Library's horror range, as well as working on his own novel. You can find out more at probablymonsters.wordpress.com.

Kristi DeMeester is the author of *Beneath*, a novel published by Word Horde, and *Everything That's Underneath*, a short fiction collection published by Apex Books. Her writing has been included in Ellen Datlow's *The Best Horror of the Year Volumes Nine and Eleven*, *Year's Best Weird Fiction* volumes 1, 3, and 5, in addition to publications such as *Black Static*, *Pseudopod*, *The Dark*, and several others. She is at work on her second novel. Find her online at www.kristidemeester.com.

Born in London, England and bred in Toronto, Canada, **Gemma Files** is the author of five novels—the Hexslinger Series (*A Book of Tongues*, *A Rope of Thorns*, and *A Tree of Bones*), *We Will All Go Down Together*, and the award-winning *Experimental Film*—and four collections of short stories, as well as three chapbooks of speculative poetry. Her work is currently available from Aqueduct Press, Trepidatio Publishing, and Open Road Media.

Stephen Graham Jones is the author of sixteen and a half novels, six story collections, a couple of novellas, and a couple of one-shot comic books. Most recent are *Mapping the Interior*, *My Hero*, *Night of the Mannequins*, and *The Only Good Indians*. Stephen lives and teaches in Boulder, Colorado.

Sam Hicks is a writer living in southeast London. Her work has appeared in or is forthcoming in *The Fiends in the Furrows, Nightscript V, Unfading Daydream 9,* and *Dark Lane 9.*

Sarah Langan is the award-winning author of the novels *The Keeper, The Missing,* and *Audrey's Door.* Her next novel, *Good Neighbors,* is due out from Simon and Schuster in spring, 2021. She and her family moved from Crown Heights, Brooklyn to Laurel Canyon, Los Angeles in 2016. These places are very different.

Joe R. Lansdale is the author of fifty novels, over four hundred short works, and has won numerous awards for his writing. The Edgar, ten Bram Stokers, The Spur, is a member of the Texas Literary Hall of Fame, Texas Institute of letters, and many more. His work has been made into films, TV shows, and comics. He lives in Nacogdoches, Texas with his wife, Karen, and their Pitbull, Nicky.

Tim Lees has been reading creepy fiction ever since the old *Pan Books of Horror* used to keep him awake at night. Born and bred in Manchester, England, he now lives in Chicago. He is the author of *Frankenstein's Prescription* (Tartarus Press/The Brooligan Press) and the Field Ops books for HarperVoyager: *The God Hunter, Devil in the Wires,* and *Steal the Lightning.*

Jack Lothian is a screenwriter for film and television and currently works as the showrunner on the HBO / Cinemax series *Strike Back.* His short fiction has appeared in a number of publications, including *Weirdbook, Hinnom Magazine,* the Necronomicon Memorial Book, and *The New Flesh: A Literary Tribute to David Cronenberg.* His graphic novel *Tomorrow,* illustrated by Garry Mac, was nominated for a 2018 British Fantasy Award.

S. Qiouyi Lu writes, translates, and edits between two coasts of the Pacific. Aer work has appeared in several award-winning venues. Ae edits the magazine *Arsenika* and runs *Microverses,* a hub for tiny narratives. You can find out more about S. at aer website qiouyi.lu or on Twitter @sqiouyilu.

Laura Mauro was born and raised in London and now lives in Essex under extreme duress. Her short story "Looking for Laika" won the British Fantasy award for Best Short Fiction in 2018, and "Sun Dogs" was shortlisted for the Shirley Jackson award in the Novelette category. Her debut collection, *Sing Your Sadness Deep* is out now from Undertow Books. She likes Japanese wrestling, Finnish folklore, and Russian space dogs. She blogs sporadically at lauramauro.com.

Diana Peterfreund is the author of thirteen books for adults, children, and teens, as well as many short stories. Her work has appeared in Amazon's Best Books of the Year; the Lonestar, Sunshine State, and Capital Choice Reading Lists; and the *Best Science Fiction and Fantasy of the Year*. She lives outside Washington, DC, with her family.

Sarah Read is a dark fiction writer in the frozen north of Wisconsin. Her short stories can be found in various places, including Ellen Datlow's *The Best Horror of the Year Volume Ten*. A collection of her short fiction called *Out of Water* is available now from Trepidatio Publishing, as is her debut novel *The Bone Weaver's Orchard*, both nominated for the Bram Stoker Awards. *The Bone Weaver's Orchard* won the Stoker for Superior Achievement in a First Novel. When she's not staring into the abyss, she knits. You can find her online on Instagram or Twitter @inkwellmonster or on her site at www.inkwellmonster.wordpress.com.

Sam Rebelein is a recent graduate of the MFA Creative Writing program at Goddard College. His work has previously appeared in *Shimmer Magazine*, *The Macabre Museum*, *Bourbon Penn*, *The Rappahannock Review*, and elsewhere. It's also forthcoming in *Planet Scumm*. He lives in Brooklyn and on Twitter @HillaryScruff.

Robert Shearman has written six short story collections, and between them they have won the World Fantasy Award, the Shirley Jackson Award, the Edge Hill Readers Prize, and four British Fantasy Awards. He was resident dramatist at the Northcott Theatre in Exeter, and regular writer for Alan Ayckbourn at the Stephen Joseph Theatre in Scarborough; his plays have won the Sunday Times Playwriting Award, the World Drama Trust Award, and the Guinness Award for Ingenuity in association with the Royal National Theatre. A regular writer for BBC Radio, his own interactive drama series *The Chain Gang* has won two Sony Awards. But he is probably best known for his work on *Doctor Who*, bringing back the Daleks for the BAFTA winning first series in an episode nominated for a Hugo Award. His latest books are *We All Hear Stories in the Dark* and a novelization of his Dalek episode for Target.

Paul Tremblay is the award-winning author of *Survivor Song*, *The Cabin at the End of the World*, *A Head Full of Ghosts*, and *Growing Things and Other Stories*. His essays and short fiction have appeared in the *Los Angeles Times*, EntertainmentWeekly.com, and numerous "year's best" anthologies. He has a master's degree in mathematics and lives outside Boston with his family.

Catriona Ward was born in Washington, DC and grew up in the United States, Kenya, Madagascar, Yemen, and Morocco. She read English at St Edmund Hall, Oxford, and is a graduate of the Creative Writing MA at the University of East Anglia. Her debut *Rawblood* won Best Horror Novel at the 2016 British Fantasy Awards, was shortlisted for the Author's Club Best First Novel Award, and a WHSmith Fresh Talent title. Ward's second novel, *Little Eve*, won the 2019 Shirley Jackson Award and the August Derleth Prize for Best Horror Novel at the 2019 British Fantasy Awards, making her the only woman to have won the prize twice, and was a Guardian best book of 2018. Her next gothic thriller, *The Last House on Needless Street*, will be published March 2021 by Viper (Serpents Tail). Her short stories have appeared in numerous anthologies. She lives in London and Devon.

Ren Warom is a writer of the weird and the speculative, variously published by Titan books, Apex Publications, and Fox Spirit Books. Currently Ren can be found questioning her sanity whilst juggling three spawn, eight cats, two books that won't shut the heck up, and one full time PhD. Life is invariably messy, but always interesting.

Gordon B. White has lived in North Carolina, New York, and the Pacific Northwest. He is the author of the collection *As Summer's Mask Slips and Other Disruptions* (Trepidatio Publishing 2020), and his stories have appeared in venues such as *Daily Science Fiction*, *Pseudopod*, and the Bram Stoker Award-winning anthology *Borderlands 6*. Gordon is a 2017 graduate of the Clarion West Writers Workshop, and also contributes reviews and interviews to outlets including *Nightmare*, *Lightspeed*, *Hellnotes*, and *The Outer Dark* podcast. You can find him online at www.gordonbwhite.com.

ACKNOWLEDGMENT OF COPYRIGHT

"~~Ice Cold Lemonade 25¢~~ House Tour: 1 Per Person" by Paul Tremblay. Copyright © 2019. First published in *Echoes: The Saga Anthology of Ghost Stories,* edited by Ellen Datlow, Saga Press. Reprinted by permission of the author.

"A Song For Wounded Mouths by Kristi DeMeester. Copyright © 2019. First published as episode 641 of *PseudoPod* on March 29, 2019. Reprinted by permission of the author.

"Birds of Passage" by Gordon B. White. Copyright © 2019. First published in *Twice Told: A Collection of Doubles* edited by C. M. Muller, Chthonic Matter. Reprinted by permission of the author.

"The Puppet Motel" by Gemma Files. Copyright © 2019. First published in *Echoes: The Saga Anthology of Ghost Stories* edited by Ellen Datlow, Saga Press. Reprinted by permission of the author.

"The Senior Girls Bayonet Drill Team" by Joe R. Lansdale. Copyright © 2019. First published in *At Home in the Dark* edited by Lawrence Block, Subterranean Press. Reprinted by permission of the author.

"The Night Nurse" by Sarah Langan. Copyright © 2019. First published in *Hex Life* edited by Christopher Golden and Rachel Autumn Deering, Titan Books. Reprinted by permission of the author.

"They Are Us (1964): An Oral History" by Jack Lothian. Copyright © 2019. First published in *Twice Told: A Collection of Doubles* edited by C. M. Muller, Chthonic Matter. Reprinted by permission of the author.

"As Dark As Hunger" by Qiouyi S. Lu. Copyright © 2019. First published in *Black Static* #72 Nov/Dec. Reprinted by permission of the author.

"I Say (I Say, I Say) by Robert Shearman. Copyright © 2019. First published in *The Shadow Booth: Vol. 3*, edited by Dan Coxon, (The Shadowbooth). Reprinted by permission of the author.

"The Pain-eater's Daughter" by Laura Mauro. Copyright © 2019. First published in *Sing Your Sadness Deep*, Undertow Press. Reprinted by permission of the author.

"The Hope Chest" by Sarah Read. Copyright © 2019. First published in *Black Static* #72 Nov/Dec. Reprinted by permission of the author.

"Nor Cease You Never Now" by Ren Warom. Copyright © 2019. First published in *Great British Horror 4:Dark & Stormy Nights* edited by Steve J. Shaw, Black Shuck Books. Reprinted by permission of the author.

"Playscape" by Diana Peterfreund. Copyright © 2019. First published in *The Magazine of Fantasy and Science Fiction*, March/April. Reprinted by permission of the author.

"Adrenaline Junkies" by Ray Cluley. Copyright © 2019. First published in *The Porcupine Boy and Other Anthological Oddities* edited by Christopher M. Jones, Macabre Ink. Reprinted by permission of the author.

"Watching" by Tim Lees. Copyright © 2019. First published in *Black Static* #72 Nov/Dec. Reprinted by permission of the author.

"Mr. and Mrs. Kett" by Sam Hicks. Copyright © 2019. First published in *Nightscript* edited by C.M. Muller, Chthonic Matter. Reprinted by permission of the author.

"Below" by Simon Bestwick. Copyright © 2019. First published in *Terror Tales of Northwest England* edited by Paul Finch, Telos. Reprinted by permission of the author.

"My Name is Ellie" by Sam Rebelein. Copyright © 2019. First published in Bourbon Penn #18. Reprinted by permission of the author.

"Slipper" by Catriona Ward. Copyright © 2019. First published in *Great British Horror 4: Dark & Stormy Nights* edited by Steve J. Shaw, Black Shuck Books. Reprinted by permission of the author.

"How To Stay Afloat When Drowning" by Daniel Braum. Copyright © 2019. First published in *Pareidolia* edited by James Everington and Dan Howarth, Black Shuck Books. Reprinted by permission of the author.

"This Was Always Going to Happen" by Stephen Graham Jones. Copyright © 2019. First published in *Terror at 5280* by The Denver Horror Collective. Reprinted by permission of the author.

"The Butcher's Table" by Nathan Ballingrud. Copyright © 2019. First published in *Wounds: Six Stories From the Border of Hell*, Saga Press. Reprinted by permission of the author.

ABOUT THE EDITOR

Ellen Datlow has been editing science fiction, fantasy, and horror short fiction for forty years as fiction editor of *Omni* magazine and editor of *Event Horizon* and SCIFICTION. She currently acquires short stories and novellas for Tor.com. In addition, she has edited about one hundred science fiction, fantasy, and horror anthologies, including the annual The Best Horror of the Year series, *The Doll Collection*, *Mad Hatters and March Hares*, *The Devil and the Deep: Horror Stories of the Sea*, *Echoes: The Saga Anthology of Ghost Stories*, *Edited By*, and *Final Cuts: New Tales of Hollywood Horror and Other Spectacles*. Forthcoming is *Body Shocks*, a reprint anthology of Body Horror.

She's won multiple World Fantasy Awards, Locus Awards, Hugo Awards, Bram Stoker Awards, International Horror Guild Awards, Shirley Jackson Awards, and the 2012 Il Posto Nero Black Spot Award for Excellence as Best Foreign Editor. Datlow was named recipient of the 2007 Karl Edward Wagner Award, given at the British Fantasy Convention for "outstanding contribution to the genre," was honored with the Life Achievement Award by the Horror Writers Association, in acknowledgment of superior achievement over an entire career, and honored with the World Fantasy Life Achievement Award at the 2014 World Fantasy Convention.

She lives in New York and co-hosts the monthly Fantastic Fiction Reading Series at KGB Bar. More information can be found at www.datlow.com, on Facebook, and on twitter as @EllenDatlow. She's owned by two cats.